VENCO

ALSO BY CHERIE DIMALINE

Empire of Wild
The Marrow Thieves

VENCO

A NOVEL

CHERIE DIMALINE

WILLIAM MORROW

An Imprint of HarperCollinsPublishers

HarperCollins books may be purchased for educational, business, or sales promotional use. For information, please email the Special Markets Department at SPsales@harpercollins.com.

FIRST EDITION

Designed by Nancy Singer

Library of Congress Cataloging-in-Publication Data

Names: Dimaline, Cherie, 1975- author.
Title: VenCo : a novel / Cherie Dimaline.
Description: First Edition. | New York : William Morrow, [2023]
Identifiers: LCCN 2022016713 | ISBN 9780063054899 (hardcover) | ISBN 9780063054912 (ebook)
Subjects: LCGFT: Novels.
Classification: LCC PR9199.4.D56 V46 2023 | DDC 813/.6—dc23
LC record available at https://lccn.loc.gov/2022016713

ISBN 978-0-06-305489-9

22 23 24 25 26 LBC 5 4 3 2 1

For Wenzdae Anaïs, my favourite witch

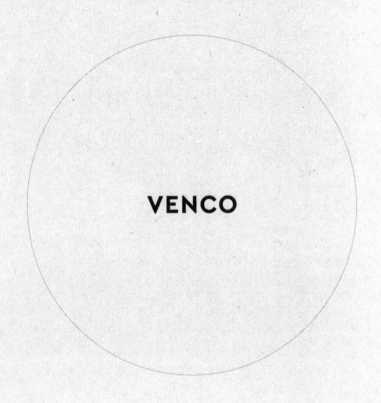

VENCO

THE ORACLE SPEAKS

The sky over Los Angeles was streaked with watery orange and soapy pink, as if the receding sun were a pulled plug. Three sleek vehicles drove up to a Bunker Hill building and stopped, waiting for the valet. When the first car's door opened, loud hip-hop poured out as the Maiden emerged. Tight braids, designer boots disguised as army issue, cargo pants, and full-sleeve tattoos—the Maiden flashed a quick smile, revealing a diamond embedded in her left canine.

The second car's driver—a bulky man in a pinstriped suit, with a leather cap and a well-oiled beard—tipped his hat to the Maiden before opening the passenger door for the Crone. Her slender cigarette holder appeared before a lace glove, fingers curled in anticipation of the driver's hand. The Crone was taller than one might expect, wearing head-to-toe Chanel circa 1958, with a Dior clutch to hold her smokes. Her pale face was half covered by exaggerated sunglasses tinted the same deep beige as her outfit.

A pit bull jumped from the third car, all ticking muscle bundled under grey velvet. She sat near the front bumper awaiting her mistress and was rewarded with a pat on her massive head. The Mother paused beside her dog, throwing a curtain of black hair over her shoulder and tapping her stiletto, the red bottom bright against the pavement, until the valet ran over to retrieve her key. Her makeup was all shades of plum to match the Yoruban beadwork at her throat and in her lobes. When the Mother moved, the dog followed, keeping an eye on the terrified valet, who was shaking so hard the keys jingled in his hand.

Together the three women entered the building, glided past the security desk and the first bank of elevators, stopping at the gold elevator doors set along the back wall. The Crone's driver pushed the button, the doors slid open, and they were carried to the top floor. He waited till each woman had exited before stepping out, then ran ahead to hold a heavy glass door open for them. Printed on the glass, in black letters, was a single word—VENCO.

The office could have been a fashion magazine, or a brokerage firm, or a front for arms dealers—there was no way to tell. In reality it was a massive enterprise to headhunt, recruit, and place exceptional femmes into exceptional roles—captains of industry, influencers of culture, makers of laws. For the chance to brush shoulders with feminine greatness, companies paid dearly, unknowingly shaking their own colonial foundations.

The reception area was art deco glam, jewel-tone greens with smoky glass and gold trim. The woman at the desk stood at their arrival, nervously pushing her heavy-rimmed glasses up her nose, patting her bun of twisted dreads.

"Ma'ams," she cooed, her eye dragging on the Maiden, who flashed that diamond once more.

"God, I love coming into the office," the Maiden remarked, and the receptionist grew shy, sitting down and answering a call on her headset.

"G . . . Good afternoon, you've reached VenCo, where the circle is the strongest shape."

Behind reception was a long hallway painted deep purple, with a Turkish runner in pinks and golds that muted their footsteps. Offices on either side held neat desks and dramatic artwork and women speaking in a dozen languages, each one pausing to bow her head as the trio passed.

At the end of the hall was a wide oak door with a gold plaque— CEO: COVEN ENGAGEMENT ORACLE. This was where they went now, taking off their gloves and sunglasses and piling them into the driver's arms. The Crone sat at the round table, the only furniture in the room save for the Indonesian woodwork bar against the back wall. She handed over her clutch and patted the driver on the front of his pants, over his zipper.

"Good boy, Israel. Now go," she instructed. He said nothing, but his eyes narrowed. He would sit quietly in the waiting room until she was ready to retrieve him. Perhaps they'd have time for a detour before he drove her home to her husband.

The Mother poured herself an absinthe, plopped in a sugar cube, and joined the Crone at the table. The Maiden checked her phone one last time, swiped right on the screen, then deposited it in one of her pockets before sitting. There was a small whirring as the blinds folded down over the expansive wall of windows and the city disappeared. In the darkness, someone snapped her fingers and a circle of candles emerged from a mechanism in the table, popping alight.

The Mother turned to the Crone. "How much time do we have for the final two?"

"Pas assez," she answered first in her native French. "Not enough."

"They have to make it." The Maiden put her elbows on the table, the snakes inked on her forearms slithering in the candlelight. "No room for error now."

"First of all, how long do they have to get the sixth?" the Mother asked.

"It's complicated, always changing. The first had seven years to find the second, but the second had half that to get to the third. Deadlines got shorter from there; the fourth, the fifth, they went down by years, then months . . ." She trailed off.

"How long?" the Mother asked again.

"Half a year—not time to panic." The Crone fidgeted with her cigarette holder. "Finding the sixth is not the issue." The Crone was a Booker, the keepers of the texts, the interpreters of words found on the page and in the sky. Her family had passed down this seat to her, and from a careful study of old stories, she knew there was enough time to gather the sixth.

"What is the issue, then?" The Maiden was no-nonsense. She wanted the facts so that she could strategize. Coming from a long line of Tenders, the women who manned the bars and collected the news, she understood the value of information.

"Once she is brought in, this sixth witch?" The Crone paused. She hated being the one to deliver hard news. But the stars were complicated, and having the right kind of eyes to read them? That was an inherited skill. "She will have seventeen days from the moment we find her."

"Seventeen days? Are you fucking kidding me?" The Maiden raised her voice. "That's not enough time to get a decent reservation, let alone find a whole-ass witch!"

The Crone sneered. "Perhaps you need better foresight. You are a member of the Oracle, n'es tu pas?"

The Mother sighed, then told the Crone, "Make sure you let the Salem leader know the time frame, please."

"You know what, fuck the rules." The Maiden was agitated. She liked to win, and the stakes had never been higher. Plagues, wars, the climate crisis—no, things had to change, and now, before it was too late. "The spell wears out soon, and they have seventeen days to complete the circle. We need to step in ourselves."

"That's not up to us, is it?" The Mother reached over and patted the Maiden's shoulder. As a Watcher, the Mother was their oversight, their protector, keeping them on track. "We keep the network engaged, place our women in the right positions, tend to the coffers, but we do not step in. We are not coven witches and don't have that power."

The women grew quiet, watching the flames, which flickered on their faces so that they looked very old and infinitely young at the same time. This could be a messy business, and being as powerful as they were, representatives of their kind, heading a massive enterprise but still being powerless where coven business was concerned? That was a delicate balance, if only for their egos.

"The spell is clear—one witch finds the next. There's nothing we can do," the Mother continued. "Whoever this sixth is, she had better be ready."

"Seventeen days? She'd better be a fucking mage," the Maiden added. "Have they located her yet?"

"Non." The Crone rubbed her temples. "But my headaches are back, so she's close."

The Maiden rolled her eyes. Enough with this headache bullshit already. "We're always a couple of Advil away from being helpless . . ."

"And how are you helping?" the Crone snapped.

"I'm working out the plan, getting my people ready," she shot back. Then she turned to the Mother. "And you? What's the update?"

"I am keeping an eye on our friend in the desert," she answered. "The whole reason we relocated here. And let me tell you, that asshole has a particularly disturbing appetite. I feel like I should be paying a subscription fee to watch him."

"Any creature who has believed itself into immortality is not to be taken lightly," the Crone said. "So step carefully. And don't get too close. Should we share news of him yet?"

"Not yet," the Mother replied. "He is quiet. We don't need to deal with the panic that knowledge of his existence would cause. Especially now." She turned to the Maiden, the most reactive of the three. "Is that clear?"

The Maiden gave her a quick salute. "Yes, sir. Since we placed a local Tender in his household as a maid, I feel better. We know his comings and goings."

The Mother and the Crone nodded their approval. Since they answered only to one another, it was important they all agreed.

The Maiden's legs bounced with nerves. The clock was ticking. "I'm serious—this sixth one? She better be ready to roll when she's found. She better be some kind of living-at-Hogwarts, spell-work-in-her-sleep legacy witch."

"Have faith," the Mother said. "She will be exceptional."

1

THE LEGACY OF
LUCKY ST. JAMES

Before she moved into the attic of her grandmother's apartment in the dilapidated East End of Toronto, Lucky slept in a queen-sized canopy bed scavenged from the trash.

It was what her mother called "a real score."

"Holy shit, Luck. Would you look at this?"

Hauled out of bed early on garbage day to help Arnya do her rounds, Lucky dragged her worn tennis shoes across the sidewalk, grumbling. At seven, she was old enough to feel embarrassed by her still-inebriated mother's "treasure hunts."

"Hurry up, come check this out."

Her mother was standing at the end of someone's lawn, staring at a carved mass of curlicued oak coated in glossy varnish—the headboard and footboard of an enormous bed, propped against a small tree.

"Wow," Lucky said. "Is that a bed?"

"Hells yes, that's a bed. That's a beautiful bed. A bed for a princess. No, a bed for a couple of queens. C'mon, Lucky, we have to grab this before some vulture does."

"And we're not vultures?" Lucky was genuinely curious.

"No, we're bargain hunters. There's a difference."

"What is the difference?" Lucky asked.

Arnya sighed, thinking. "Well, vultures grab up shit all frantic-like. We grab up shit with style." She snapped her fingers, then made them into guns and pointed at Lucky.

Even with two of them, it was hard to wrestle the weighty pieces to the sidewalk. Then they spent a good ten minutes trying to figure out how to load them onto their borrowed shopping cart.

"Shit. We gotta make it work, babe." Arnya St. James was no quitter, except at last call (one of her better jokes). Breathing hard, she extracted a bent book of matches from her jean shorts pocket, lit a cigarette, and scratched her forehead with a thumbnail. "Maybe we have to balance them across the top?"

Bigger pieces secured, they'd come back to get the four columns and frame for the canopy. Arnya carried them one by one to the dumpster beside the nearby elementary school, hefting them up and dropping them in, her ropey arms flexing with lean muscle.

"Gotta hide them. We'll come back for those fuckers on a second run. Hope the damn truck doesn't come. Should be okay, seeing's how school's out for summer." Then she broke into the Alice Cooper song of the same name and sang it with a bobbing head, with air guitar thrown in at red lights when the awkward cart was coaxed to a stop.

Lucky was mortified when they went back; garbage runs were usually in the wee hours, and it was now approaching noon. They also usually didn't involve her drunk mother hanging ass-end out of a dumpster screaming for Jesus, Mary, and Joseph, and some motherfucking help, while the St. Brigid's summer tennis league watched. But when the pieces were all home and the bed was assembled with the help of her mother's latest man friend, Lucky forgave Arnya everything. It was indeed a bed for a couple of queens, one of whom immediately passed out facedown with her boots still on, while the other lay with her thin arms folded under her head, wondering what they would do for curtains. A week later, they arrived in typical Arnya fashion.

Lucky woke to Arnya's blurry face in her face. Her mother gave her shoulders a shake. "C'mon, I need some help here!" She let go and disappeared.

Lucky heard uneven footsteps and something being dragged. More steps, then the sound of the front door closing. She drifted off.

"Goddamn it, girl, wake up!"

Lucky jerked so hard she rolled off her towel and onto hardwood. Must have fallen asleep on the front room floor watching TV. A little hard on the bones but better than being all alone in that big bed.

Her mother shouted from the bedroom, "In here. You're gonna love this!"

Anxiety spiked in Lucky's stomach. She never knew what was going to happen when Arnya got that excited.

She pulled herself up, scratching her bare bottom, exposed by the wide cut in the leg of her mother's Budweiser one-piece bathing suit. The neckline scooped low and the crotch hung between her thighs, but it was the perfect pj's for a sticky summer night.

She found her mother standing on top of the futon mattress they'd hauled up onto their new bed frame.

"Ma, you're wearing your shoes!" Lucky pointed at her mother's feet, still clad in her favourite pleather ankle boots, the uneven heels showing their plastic bones. "Those are the nice sheets! They take up a whole load at the laundromat."

Arnya took the last drag of her cigarette, plucked it out of her mouth, and expertly flicked it out the open window behind her. "Oh Christ, Lucky, quit menopausing and give me a hand."

Lucky finally noticed the voluminous bundle of red fabric spilling across the bed like a murder scene, its edges trimmed in every hue the rainbow could throw up. Arnya bent to lift a swath, throwing an arm out for balance, looking like a goddess statue in a fountain of cherry Kool-Aid.

"It's a parachute," she said. "Do you like it?" Arnya's smile was so wide Lucky could see the silver caps on her back molars. Standing on their bed at four in the morning, with a head full of whiskey and a desperate plea in her dark eyes, Arnya was at her softest.

"Yeah, Mom, it's great."

"It's the perfect canopy! Help me get it up over the bars."

Lucky hopped up on the bed, too, and they struggled with the slippery fabric until they managed to get enough of it over the two longer bars that they could yank it into place. Then the two of them flopped down underneath it to catch their breath, hair wild over their gritty pillows.

"Now we can go anywhere we like. Anywhere in the whole shit world—and we'll have a safe landing." Arnya curled into her daughter like a drying flower, the whiskey congealing into sleep.

Lucky lay awake in their shelter of red parachute silk, braiding pieces of her dark hair with her mother's rusty strands. She had no idea where Arnya had found it, and she didn't care: she took what was offered, when it was offered.

"It's perfect," she whispered.

It was one of the best memories Lucky had, the one moment in childhood when it seemed the whole world was in front of her, full of all the adventure she could handle. Soon after dragging that canopy home, Arnya was gone, and for a long while, it seemed like she had taken all the adventure with her, leaving Lucky behind with nothing.

"HOW DO I TELL STELLA they're selling the building and we have to move?" Twenty years after the parachute score, Lucky sat at the bar, peeling the label off her second bottle of beer.

"Want another before I call it?" Harley was already reaching for the handle on the beer fridge behind him.

"Nah, I've got a job this week."

Not a good job, just another gig the temp agency had set her up with. And tomorrow was only Thursday. That meant two more days in her shit cubicle, at her shit desk, before the weekend. And then Monday would come again, like a fresh hole in her life, one she could fall into and never get out of. *Is it still anticipation if all you are anticipating is nothing? No, it isn't, it's—*

"Dread."

"Huh?" Harley glanced her way as he leaned over the bar, using a damp cloth to wipe up the night's layer of sticky.

"It's *dread*, not anticipation," she said to him, or to herself, or to no one in particular.

"Preach," he replied. He was used to Lucky's general moping. "God's gotta listen sometime."

He tossed the rag into the small bar sink and put his hands on his hips, surveying the collection of functioning alcoholics and depressed divorcés. He checked his watch. "Time to end the dream, people," he announced. "Back to the nightmare."

He flicked on the overhead lights, and the bar revealed itself in all its Wednesday-night glory. A collective sigh replaced the hum and buzz of the neon lights, which had become audible in the sudden silence after the music clicked off.

Lucky stood, pulling on her hoodie and jean jacket. "Alright, then."

Harley came out from behind the bar to start the work of shaking a few people awake and politely pushing them towards the sidewalk. He left Darla, also known as Sweet D, for last. She'd come in after her drag show for her usual glass of milk and shot of bourbon, still in heels and padding. Darla was always welcome to stay until he was done mopping the linoleum.

"See you soon, Luck?" he said as she passed him.

"Probably." The bells above her chimed as she made her way out into the night.

She stopped by the front window to put in her earbuds and pull her hood over her head. It wasn't that cold, with spring starting to muscle its way into April. You never knew in Toronto. She could wake up to a blizzard. But right now it felt like walking weather. So with head covered and eyes down, she hit shuffle on her favourite playlist and started for home.

The East End of the city was like the aftermath of a love affair—broken and messy, shrieking at intersections, moaning in doorways. The parking lots were small and hard to get into. The shoe stores were run by grandfathers, and the bakeries featured meringues collecting dust in their yellowed front windows. A single block housed four different cell-phone repair stores. Sales posters were more often misspelled than not. The nail salons were suggestively named things like Finger Bang or Just the Tip. Lucky's neighbourhood was a place people moved on from rather than into—a spot reserved for the very old and the very young, or the renters who couldn't fork out a security deposit for a West End studio with underground parking.

The moon watched Lucky cut a small figure down the grey sidewalk, giving her a half wink from between the streetcar wires and eternity. Eyes on her Converse and the pavement, she missed the moon and she missed the tall woman in a salmon-pink tulle gown skipping into an alley ahead of her. When Lucky crossed the street to avoid two drunks fighting, she also missed the two foxes carrying a netted bag of oranges between them. She didn't see a half-dozen bats careening from an open apartment window, looping calligraphy onto the dark sky, then chasing one another into the parkette. Focused inward and down, she missed all the magic and chance.

Dread, Lucky kept thinking. *Nothing ever happens except more of the same.*

She turned up the volume on her phone to drown out the screech of an ambulance headed for the hospital where no one went if they had another option. She'd had to take her grandmother there last month after a bad fall. Thankfully Stella hadn't broken anything, but the attending physician suggested that she needed full-time care. Who the fuck could afford a nanny for an old person?

"Not many," the doctor had agreed. "There's always the province-run homes." Over her dead body, Lucky had thought, but now that they were facing eviction from their apartment, she had no idea what to do.

Her street was dark: half the streetlights were dulled to a muddy waver, and none of the porch lights were on. She stood still. She felt like if she turned onto her block, the quiet would swallow her.

I could just keep walking. I could walk to the bus station. Buy a ticket to Santa Fe. Sell jewelry on the side of the road. Live in a motel with my own key and thin towels. Be alone. Be happy.

The wind picked up, and soon she was shivering. Why was she stalling? It wasn't like she had to tell Stella tonight. It wasn't going to be easy. This was the place her grandma had lived in since the day after her wedding, the place she'd shared with the love of her life until his heart blew out. The only place that held happy memories of her son, from before he'd fallen in love with Arnya, moved out, and disappeared down an opioid drain hole.

She decided she'd look for a new apartment before she broke the news. Who knew? Maybe she'd live up to her name for once and find a rental in the neighbourhood, so Stella wouldn't get too confused— even one with two bedrooms, so she wouldn't have to sleep in an attic crawl space anymore. She'd probably have to take on another job to afford current rents, but she'd cross that bridge . . . Deep breath in. No, she wouldn't tell Stella tonight. Lucky pushed all the air out of her lungs and started walking again.

It was only yesterday she'd opened the letter saying they had ninety days, but already the street felt like *any* street, not *her* street, the one she had lived on for more than half her life. It made her feel adrift, without the anchor of belonging. She was surprised how quickly it was happening. She almost passed the little walkway that led to her front door, not recognizing it, but caught herself and turned in. She stopped again at the foot of the steps.

If you didn't look up, her building appeared normal, maybe even charming. Thin and tall, the Victorian had already been converted into apartments by the time her grandparents moved in. The glass in the windows was now wavy with age, and the shutters hung, lopsided, from the remaining hinges. The whole place had been painted bright violet, a hue that had scandalized the neighbours when this was a suburb set apart from the downtown core. Over the years, as the city thickened and poured into every available nook, the purple faded to a matronly mauve, the preferred shade of Easter bonnets and sweater sets, and then to a dull mushroom, darkened by the subway overpass that now swooped above the sharp roof like a concrete cloud. Now Lucky did look up, drawn by the sweep of lights as the train took the curve overhead. Since that bridge had been built, there was no sun for their windows. No moon to weep under. Just the train's headlights at night, and the shuddering of its passing on the way to somewhere else.

Behind her, a bright yellow bird landed on a branch, hopping carefully over the new buds to the tip, then turning its head as if to get a good look at the girl. Maybe an escaped pet, so confused by freedom it was roaming at night. Lucky didn't notice it, though, because her eyes had dropped from the bridge to the window at the top of the house, now glowing with light that flickered with movement. The window was propped open with a book, and a steady plume of smoke was streaming out.

"Oh, fuck me."

Lucky took off up the steps in a rush that sent the bird flying back into the dark.

Inside, the smoke alarm was blaring. "Grandma, Jesus!" she screamed as she burst through the door. "What the fuck is going on?"

Black smoke and a horrid stench emanated from the microwave in the kitchen, the timer set for another twenty-three minutes. She pressed stop and opened the door. A blackened bag of popcorn hissed inside, too hot to touch. She went to the window and pushed it open wider, then pulled off her jean jacket, using it like a matador's cloak to sweep the smoke away.

Jinxy, Stella's one-eyed cat, came to wind his way through Lucky's legs, meowing angrily.

"Fuck off, Jinx."

Lucky was allergic to him, and so, of course, he wanted nothing more than to be with her.

"Stella Sampson," she shouted, "what the hell were you thinking?"

Lucky found her in the living room, sitting in her floral easy chair in front of the TV, where an old vampire movie was playing. Stella looked up, one eye—in the lens of a heavy magnifying glass—as huge and wobbly as an uncooked egg. She turned her face back down towards the *Reader's Digest* splayed on her lap.

"Do you not hear that?" Lucky went to the smoke alarm and pulled it out of its socket, then flipped it over and took out the battery.

The alarm stuttered and stopped. That was when Lucky realized her grandmother also had the stereo on, at a seven.

Lucky snapped off the music and plopped down in the love seat opposite her grandmother, more tired than she'd been all day, all week. "Seriously, Stella? It's two in the morning."

Stella put the magazine and the magnifying glass on the floor by her feet, and Jinxy promptly sat on both.

"I told him he should have the foundation checked." Stella shook her head, the red pom-pom on top of her toque flopping back and forth.

"What are you talking about?"

"The landlord, Pinkerton. Old fool." Stella rocked herself in her chair, pom-pom bobbing steadily. "There were cops everywhere. The fire department showed up, but the firemen just stood there, leaning against their trucks, laughing, watching the nurses lead all the patients outside. It was cold, too, an early-spring night, but they didn't help. They thought it was funny to watch all the carrying-on from the inmates, some crying, some screaming, others laughing. Once in a while, they'd even whistle at one of the nurses, skirts all hitched up, bobby pins falling out." She reached up and touched her fingers to her own hair spilling out from under the wool hat. "We had big hair back then. I liked the French rolls. You know about French rolls?"

"Are you talking about the old hospital next door? Grandma, that place has been vacant for years now."

"Pinkerton, he went over to see if we needed to evacuate. Me and Oswald watched out the window. Oswald was dying to get out there too. Just like a man. But I wouldn't let him." Oswald, her late husband—Lucky's grandfather. He haunted Stella, and, in return, she facilitated his haunt with stories.

"So we see Pinkerton down there talking to one of the cops, the fattest one, which meant he musta been the most important. He talked for a long time, three smokes' worth. Then he comes up to our place to fill us in."

Stella got up and went to the kitchen window, where she stood looking out at the brick hospital wall. "One of the patients was locked up after he tried to carry off a mannequin from a department store, said it was his wife. He had tried to escape. He did, I suppose . . ."

She turned back to Lucky. "He'd quieted down after a few months inside, so they figured he was getting better. Ha. Fooled them, he did."

She nodded, a faint smile on her face. Stella loved an underdog.

"He'd been sneaking out of his bed at night, down to the basement, where he was trying to tunnel his way out. Trouble is, he started digging on the east side, heading under the entire length of the building and out the west end towards our house. Poor bugger, but I guess if you're deluded to begin with . . ."

She returned to her chair and sat. Jinx jumped up and draped himself over her lap like a luxurious fur stole. She paused while she stroked him. Then she picked up the story again.

"He cut through any of the studs that got in his way with whatever he could find to use. Who knows what he did with the dirt, mighta ate it, maybe. He did such a good job, nobody noticed, but when he got all the way across the basement, the whole damn building collapsed—still standing, but with no foundation, all crooked and messy. It was pure luck none of the other patients got hurt."

Lucky couldn't help herself. "What happened to him?"

Stella held up a finger, instructing her to wait. "Afterwards, they shipped everyone to a new asylum out there in Collingwood. The old place here got boarded up and forgotten. Since they built the overpass, no one bothers to look under it anyway."

She raised her voice, finally rounding the corner to her original point. "But I told Pinkerton, 'Henry, you don't know where that lunatic dug to. He could have made it all the way over into our basement. He could have escaped right through our back door while the cops were at the hospital shrugging their stupid shoulders.'"

Lucky also liked an underdog, and she liked a good story. She'd been parented by them both, after all. "So they didn't recover his remains?"

"Nope. And by the time they realized his corpse wasn't in the rubble, they figured he'd slipped away and was halfway to Mississippi. Me? I don't think they even bothered to look."

"Did you and Grandpa ever see him?"

"Nah." Stella shook her head. "But I swore I heard him a couple of times when I was down in the laundry room, banging and scraping on the other side of the wall.

"I complained to Pinkerton. He told me I was imagining things. So one night I went to his apartment—he lived on the main floor where that awful woman lives now—and dragged his lazy ass off the couch. There was all kinds of rumbling and banging going on behind that cabinet down there in the basement—you know, the big green metal one that takes up damn near the whole wall. Well, Pinkerton listened good. Then he said it was just animals messing around."

She clucked her tongue. "I wasn't taking no chances, though. I made Ozzy put a padlock on that cabinet. I wasn't having no maniac popping out at me while I was down there doing our laundry."

"Did you guys ever find out what it was?"

Stella got up again, and the cat dropped from her lap onto the floor and stretched. She went back to the window. In the murky light from the streetlamp, a pair of raccoons huddled inside a window grate across the way. No human escape artists to be seen.

"Huh? Oh, nothing. The noises stopped." She turned her head to look at her granddaughter. "You're down there all the time—do you hear anything?"

Lucky shook her head. "Is the cabinet still locked?"

"Most likely. But that key's around here somewhere. I'll look, Ozzy. I'll look . . ."

Lucky walked over to kiss her grandmother on the cheek. If Stella noticed, she didn't let on.

She left Stella still staring out the window at her past. In the hallway just in front of the bathroom, Lucky reached up and tugged on a cord, and a set of stairs slid down. She climbed them to the attic, pulling the staircase up behind her.

Before the hatch clicked closed, she shouted down, "No more cooking tonight, Stella."

There was no answer except from the TV: *"A creature dwells within these walls."*

In the dark, cramped space under the slanted roof, Lucky felt around for a plug and then slipped it into the socket near the base-board. The room jumped to life in the bright glow of a hundred white Christmas lights. Lucky stood in the one spot where she could stand up straight and pulled off her clothes. There wasn't much up here besides the mattress—neat piles of folded clothes and a stack of journals filled with her writing. She grabbed the book on top, a pen stuck in the middle pages; then, down to her tank top and boxers, she slid under the covers to write. Before she opened the cover, she looked up at the faded folds of her red parachute, brought from her mother's house and hung loosely over the rafters.

She opened the book and wrote one line before falling asleep.

What's the point of a safe landing when you never leave the ground?

2

THE KEY TO LIFE

For the next two days, Lucky woke to the pulse of a high-pitched alarm, already filled with dread. Each morning, she went downstairs to the bathroom to get ready. Brushing her teeth, she looked out the window facing east, where the sun was coming up for people who didn't live under a bridge. Next door hunched the old asylum, the windows boarded up with rotting wood and the backyard dotted with urban archaeology—shopping carts, milk crates, bags of old clothes, and broken toys that the city wouldn't pick up. Then she gazed up at the underbelly of the bridge, all steel girders and concrete fittings.

This week, Lucky was working on the seventeenth floor of a building with mirrored windows that refused a view into its bureaucratic guts. Her job, inevitably, involved moving papers around her desk, shuffling copies from red folders into blue ones, answering the phone, typing out schedules, and generally trying to ignore the futility of it all. All she ever wanted to do was write, but there was nothing marketable in what she produced. Plus, she'd never had a real cheerleader for it. In fact, she'd heard nothing but how impossible it would be to make a living.

"You know how many wannabe writers there are out there?" her grade-eleven English teacher told her after giving her another A. "I mean, you're good, but so am I. And if I can't get a book deal, you sure as hell won't." At the last minute, he added a minus beside the A, just to keep her expectations real.

With Stella's paltry pension cheque, Lucky didn't have the luxury of chasing dreams. Plus, the temp agency was pretty good at keeping her employment—and pay cheques—steady. Somewhere along the way, she learned to just accept it.

The first day at the new office was set aside for orientation—training videos and handshakes and names she wouldn't bother to learn. The second day there was nothing but a pile of folders waiting in her inbox to greet her. She threw her bag under her desk and plopped into her seat, swivelling to look out the window at the view of other buildings. She wondered if other temp workers were looking back at her through their own mirrored glass.

When the corporation opened an artery at five o'clock and the office bled out into the lobby, Lucky was a part of the flow. She rode the subway into the east each night. Ironically, she did not take the number 2 train, which made Stella's teeth clink against the drinking glass where they spent more time than in her mouth; the number 2 did not stop anywhere near their house. She took the number 5 and then had to walk three blocks.

In the winter the walk from the station was not bad. Snow covered all the imperfections: garbage, broken eavestroughs, empty buildings, spray paint designs, and shivering junkies. It rendered the streets Dickensian. But in the summer, it was horrid. Lucky would try to hold her breath for most of her walk, the heat cooking the garbage into a rancid street stew. The broken-down residents crawled out of their stuffy bachelor apartments and rented rooms to stand around on cracked feet, drinking cans of warm beer. Over the years she'd written some very bad poetry about those walks.

According to her grandma, in the days before the bridge, the neighbourhood had been hopeful. It had sprung up over spring and by mid-August had already filled out, with the western border having lawns and enough mowers pushed by husbands in sweater vests to cut them. A few corner stores supplied the pedestrians with bread and milk and bins of penny candies, and by that Halloween the ladies had started a book club and a Neighbourhood Watch.

Today was Friday, so Lucky walked two blocks in the opposite direction, head down against the strong wind, then stopped in front of a store on the corner and went inside. It smelled like somebody's basement.

The shop used to be a movie-rental place. Now it was more of a nostalgia shop. The mortgage was paid by the rental units above, and the owner kept the store as a passion project. Along with DVDs and the occasional VHS, it stocked books on film and filmmakers, souvenirs from both popular and obscure franchises, and magazines that the film students came in to purchase or shop-lift, depending on who was working the till.

A young man in a white T-shirt entered the room through a beaded-curtained doorway behind the cash register. Every time someone came through that door, Lucky had a vision of them being born to a large belly dancer.

"So, Lady Luck, what's new and traumatizing in your corner of the world?" Malcolm settled onto the stool behind the counter and nestled his chin in the apex of his bony hands, held open as if in interrupted prayer. Tattoos covered every available canvas from his fingers to his neck—mermaids and pirates and playing cards all co-habiting nicely. His dark hair was newly cut, edges shaved so that she saw the raw pink of freshly revealed skin at his neck. She held her own hands together to stop from reaching out.

"Nothing at all." She leaned on her elbow, propped against the counter on the opposite side, her face inches from her friend's face, pretending at nonchalance. Being this close to him made her aware of the weight of her thighs, the volume of her breath. God, why couldn't she just find the balls to tell him how she felt?

"Jesus, sounds interesting."

"I know." She sighed, looking out the front window, the words *You should be in THE MOVIES* stenciled across the surface, old-fashioned style. "Life is just a non-stop music festival. Great, now it's raining. I hate April."

They both paused, listening to the rain hit the street. They watched the night open up like theatre curtains, with all the hushed anticipation of an old couple at the ballet. Water slid slowly down the glass, like liquid-filled spiders spinning languid webs in the semi-darkness. From somewhere close by came the sound of a siren, and across the street an early raccoon knocked over a row of empty trash cans, chattering his disappointment at the garbage collectors' efficiency.

Malcolm stretched his arms out on the counter and whispered to her, or the night, or maybe even the raccoon lumbering down the sidewalk with his graceless girth: "What do you suppose comes next?"

In a moment of bravery, Lucky slipped a finger into the soft arch made by Malcolm's bent thumb curving in across the palm of his hand lying on the desk in front of him like a forgotten, broken thing. There was a bright flick of electricity, and she caught her breath. *Just tell him*, she screamed to herself. *Tell him*. She leaned across on both elbows and put her mouth very close to his ear, holding her breath so it wouldn't shake.

Then she paused, and it was too much delay not to deflate. "Everything," she whispered. Malcolm's eyes closed, made heavy by her warm breath. She popped up her hood and yanked it down to sit low on her forehead and left.

The front door jingled merrily as she pushed out onto the wide, wet street, moving like a pinecone down a rain-swollen ravine. *Everything?* That was what she came up with? *Everything* was too much. *Everything* was not nearly enough.

LUCKY LET HERSELF IN AND heated up a microwave dinner. Stella was downstairs at her pal Clermont's house. Clermont was what Stella referred to as "a bachelor," and what he referred to as "an old queer." They'd recently taken up knitting together and spent long nights getting drunk, pretending to make gifts for the children's hospital. Lucky fell asleep to the TV.

Like most nights, she dreamed of Arnya.

When Lucky was nine, her mother was diagnosed with colorectal cancer. She'd been sick for a while, but the day they took the bus to the hospital and sat in Dr. Sakamori's green office and heard those oddly shaped words, her mother became sick in a profound way. At first she thought Dr. Sakamori was speaking Japanese, as he was apt to do when Lucky pestered him enough. She loved the way the harsh consonants became like toffee when rolled against his back teeth. But her mother understood the words as soon as she heard them. Lucky saw that much in the way her eyes grew wide, then closed in like an explosion played in reverse.

After that, Arnya stopped dancing in their apartment, giving in to the aches and knots that made her double over. She stopped combing her hair and lacing her shoes. She started a slow metamorphosis from a tall woman who liked to sing old bluegrass tunes on the fire escape with a thermos of gin into a hollow-boned bird, slowly melting into the upholstery of the easy chair.

Then, a week after Lucky turned ten, Arnya was gone. She'd been in the hospital for what seemed like forever, hooked up to machines that pumped, gurgled, and whispered into her body. Lucky was staying with her grandmother, who had supervised the packing of everything she and her mother owned into reinforced boxes from the liquor store.

After their apartment was cleaned out, it was rented to a Russian family. Lucky saw them the day they moved in. She rode her hand-me-down ten speed out to her old building every day after school for those first few months. She'd park just underneath the third-floor window and watch the Russian parents dance together across the living room floor, unsmiling, as if they were being forced to hold each other close and swing across the threadbare carpet. As if a man with a gun were sitting where her mother's old easy chair had been, tapping his foot to the music and pointing the metal barrel at the swirling couple. The two blond boys would watch her without speaking, their stockinged feet dangling off the same fire escape where her mother had performed her bluegrass symphonies.

Each morning over the six months, from the time Dr. Sakamori spoke his strange words to the time her mother passed away, Lucky would wake up just after dawn and wait at the window, first at her own apartment and then at her grandmother's. She wasn't quite sure what she was waiting for, but she knew that something was on the way. She could smell it. It was like what glass would smell like if it had a scent, cold and hard. That was when she started writing, pages and pages of messy text, trying to pin it down, trying to understand.

When Stella brought her in to see her mother the day she died, there was only the stuttered coughing of the lung patients from down the hall and her grandmother's soft sobs. Lucky broke from her embrace, went to the bed, and pulled back the sheet from her mother's face. Before Stella grabbed her up, before the nurse pulled the pea-green sheet back up over the dead woman, Lucky heard what glass would sound like if it had a voice. It was pouring out of her mother's nose, rolling across her mother's lips—it was thick, deafening silence.

ON SATURDAY MORNING, LUCKY WOKE up on the couch with the TV still blaring. She hit the mute button and sat up, listening for her grandmother. Once she realized Stella's basket of wool was gone, she relaxed; that meant she was downstairs at Clermont's again, or maybe still.

Lucky got up to look out the window, sneezing twice on the way. "Fucking cat."

Great, the rain had turned to snow. She decided to spend her day cleaning—there was nothing else to do. But first she'd escape the cat dander in the humid safety of the shower.

Getting out, she wiped the steam off the mirror and examined her face. Large hazel eyes, apparently so similar to her father's she could have plucked them straight out of his head with her chubby baby fingers. Not that he'd been around to give her the chance.

Straight black eyelashes. Tiny freckles strewn across the bridge of her nose, a few slipping off onto the curves of her cheeks. Her mother had often lamented how few features they shared—Lucky looked nothing like her side of the family. Aryna would loudly proclaim, "Half-breeds, we may get forgotten, and we may argue too much with each other, but dammit, we look good, even standing still."

She would have loved to feel that confidence, to see Arnya's eyes looking back at her now, to see her mother's signature smile in her own face. But there was only Lucky, small and unremarkable. She swiped her palm across the wet mirror and finished toweling off.

She threw on old clothes and got to work. There was cat hair everywhere, along with abandoned Froot Loops, Stella's favourite cereal. Multicoloured hoops floated in the kitchen like tiny life preservers on a tile sea.

When she was done sweeping, she grabbed the wicker laundry basket from the bathroom and made her way through the apartment, picking up dirty clothes as she went. Then she grabbed the soap and dryer sheets and left the apartment.

In the ground-floor hall, she balanced the high basket on the tops of her feet, reached in through the dark basement doorway, and flipped the switch. The lights flickered and ticked and finally jumped into dim life.

"Cheery."

Hoisting the basket, she carefully navigated the narrow stairs. The basement had once stretched the entire length of the sizable house. Now it accommodated a spacious bachelor apartment where a very short bald man named Mr. Godet lived with his collection of *Star Wars* figurines. Passing his door on the way to the laundry room, Lucky wondered if Godet knew the story of the Great Escape. Would he even notice if the ghost of a lunatic appeared to him while he dusted Boba Fett with high-end makeup brushes? Then again, maybe all that was left of the escaped prisoner was the latticework of his skeleton crushed under the apartment floor.

The laundry "room" was an olive-green washer-dryer set installed between the old boiler and a shelving unit full of archaic-looking tools. Shivering a little in the damp, Lucky set the basket down and began sorting the whites from the colours. Head full of ghost stories, she couldn't stop glancing around her, the space having morphed into something sinister. Several corners of the basement were filled with brooms and mops, huddled like stooks of corn and throwing sharp shadows. But it was the long army-green metal cabinet along the east wall that kept stealing her attention.

Once she got a load into the washer, she squared her shoulders and walked over to the cabinet. She'd never really inspected it closely before, but sure enough, there it was—a dull silver lock, looped through the handles and clamped tight by her own grandfather.

She took the lock in her hand. It was heavy, dusted with coppery rust, with a keyhole in the bottom. She let it drop, and it banged against the metal doors, making her jump.

As the washing machine splashed and sloshed, Lucky leaned in cautiously and placed her ear against the smooth metal of the door. She closed her eyes and exhaled on the cool surface, and then, with the tip of her pinky finger, she quickly traced the word *escape* into the condensation.

She imagined a man in torn blue pyjamas. He would have a long beard and wild tangles from years without a comb, his eyes rimmed red from dust. At this very moment, she imagined him leaning on the opposite side of the thin metal door, hoping that she would open the lock that would release him.

She was so far gone in her fantasy that she damn near choked when the spin cycle unbalanced and the washer started banging and shaking.

"Dammit!"

She pushed in the dial and opened the lid to reposition the wet clothes. As she separated the sopping fabrics, she heard metal clatter to the bottom of the tub and went up on her tiptoes so she could reach in far enough to scoop up whatever it was. Three dollars in change, a bell off a cat toy, and a key. She really needed to remember to check Stella's pockets, since it was obvious the woman had given up doing it herself.

Wait . . . a key. Could this be *the* key? Stella had said she was going to look for it. Lucky held it up and studied it under the light of the bare bulb hanging from the ceiling. There was nothing unusual about it—she wasn't sure why she thought there would be. Maybe this wasn't it. There was only one way to know for sure.

She went back to the cabinet and hefted the lock. She lined up the key with the slot in the bottom and pushed. It fit.

"Holy shit, holy shit . . ."

Taking a deep breath, she turned the key and the lock snapped open in her palm. Before she could second-guess it, she pulled the lock from the latch and yanked on the stiff door. It screeched as it released, and she squinted, bracing for impact.

But there was nothing, just a little wash of cold air in her face.

She bent to peer in. There were shelves at the top, laden with rusted cans, a cloudy jar of nails, and a collection of screwdrivers and rope. But the bottom section had been kicked out, the broken metal back warped and pushed to curl against the locked door. The floor was littered with contents that had fallen—broken glass, stiff paintbrushes, and some rags. Behind the broken metal was a dark hole where the cold air whistled through.

Lucky got down on her hands and knees and shone her phone flashlight into the hole. It was a tunnel, an actual fucking tunnel.

She sat back on her haunches, taking a few seconds to psych herself up, and leaned in farther, past her shoulders.

"Hello?"

Nothing in return except silence, not even an echo.

"Anyone here?"

How can anyone be here? she asked herself, feeling a little embarrassed. Even if this was *the* old tunnel, no way was the patient still here. She had the sudden image of a grinning skull an inch from her face and pulled her neck in. What if there were rats in there? Or bugs? She snatched her hand to her chest and wiped it on her T-shirt.

She decided she was being ridiculous. "You're being ridiculous," she said out loud. But she'd come this far. It was all-or-nothing time. She already had nothing, so instead she chose all. Focusing her phone flashlight into the hole, she passed over the crunchy rags and fragile glass and crawled inside.

It was tight on all sides, bare dirt under her knees, rocks clotting the walls like hard warts. Twenty feet in, the tunnel dead-ended in a spill of rubble from the cave-in. Was that where he was buried? No, she was going to believe he had really escaped out through the cabinet into the bright world—decades ago, before her grandfather locked it up.

"I hope you made it, buddy," she whispered. "I really do."

She turned around and sat on her butt, sweeping her small light over the space, looking back at the rabbit hole she'd come down. She could hear the washer thumping through its last spin like a beating heart.

She realized this probably wasn't the safest place to sit. If the tunnel had collapsed once, what would stop it from collapsing again?

Sticking her phone in her teeth, she crawled back towards the opening. Halfway there her hand hit something hard poking out of the soil. Sitting back on her heels, she grabbed her phone and directed the flashlight down. It was a piece of tarnished metal, embedded in the ground. She used her fingernails to pry it up. After she brushed off the clotted dirt, she realized it was a small spoon. Maybe from the hospital cafeteria? Maybe this was what he'd used to dig, like an old movie cliché. She slid it into her pocket and kept going.

Once she'd carefully extracted herself, she closed the cabinet back up and locked it. Looking down at her mud-caked knees, she said, "Great. More laundry."

After tossing the first load into the dryer, she pulled off her pants and threw them in with the rest of the darks. Before she closed the lid, she fished them back out and checked the pockets—two quarters and the spoon from the tunnel. She set them on the dryer, threw her pants back in, and started the machine.

In her underwear, she climbed up to sit on the washer. It took a moment before she realized she was smiling, that she'd been smiling since she discovered that the tunnel was real. She picked up the spoon and rubbed more dirt out of the bowl and from the handle, revealing markings. No—letters, which spelled . . . *S* . . . *A* . . . *L* . . . *E* . . . *M*?

Salem. And there was more: the engraving of a figure of some kind, and a pointed line that could have been an arrow?

"You're coming with me," she whispered to the spoon, tucking it into the laundry basket so it didn't get left behind.

THE CRONE DROPPED HER FORK. It clattered against her plate, a startling sound in the quiet of the dining room. She clutched at the lace by her throat, eyes wide.

"Anything the matter, dear?" Her husband looked up from his

paperback on the other side of a very long table. "Shall I have Israel reheat your food?"

Israel stepped from the corner. Without his cap and shucked of his pinstriped blazer, every contour of muscle and hair pressed against his white dress shirt. There was a small white apron tied at his waist.

"No, no, my food is fine. Israel, could you bring me my phone instead, please?" He left without sound.

Her husband placed the book beside his plate, picking up a crystal wine goblet. "Is something troubling you?"

The Crone placed both hands flat on the table, straightening her already impeccable posture. The room contained floor-to-ceiling shelves stuffed full of books. She may have been dining in a library, except that her entire house was this way—books, scrolls, old pages held aloft in glass frames. Her eyes jumped around the walls, searching for something, though she wasn't sure what.

"No. Everything is fine." She took a sip of her own wine. She checked her gold wristwatch, holding it up to her ear to listen for the old-fashioned tick. "What time do you have, Maury?"

"Um." He checked his own wrist. "Five oh six. No, five oh seven. Plans this evening?"

The Crone sighed. "No. Just suddenly feeling a bit pressed for time."

3

MEENA GOOD

GETS LUCKY

In the dream, Meena walked through a forest of branchless trees with peeled trunks. If she leaned even slightly one way or the other, a hard buzzing erupted like a mason jar of bees. She moved slowly—at the cadence the dream demanded, like she was moving underwater, using her hands like oars to paddle ahead. She couldn't push the pace, or panic would jolt her awake or into a darker dreamscape.

Still, she asked the dream, *Where are we going?*

Home.

Home? She pictured her father standing on their porch, his collar starched and yellowed with sweat.

To the coven, the dream clarified.

The coven? She didn't have a coven, not yet.

She wanted a coven. More than wanted—she needed a coven. All she had were five—herself, Wendy, Morticia, Lettie, and Freya. The

Oracle had said there would be seven. Seven to close the circle and begin the next epoch.

She could see bright light ahead, and, forgetting herself, she tried to speed up. She stumbled and reached out to grab a tree. The buzzing sound dialed itself up to more of a crackle, as if the bees were now throwing themselves against the glass jar, and the wood under her hand grew hot. She turned her head just as the trunk burst into fire. Then, one by one, all the trees in the forest started to burn. *I'm sorry, I'm sorry.* She threw herself back on the path, but it was too late—the fires kept burning. They looked like stakes. She held her breath and walked slowly now, between the burning columns, towards that bright light ahead.

Pushing past the last of the flames, she found herself in a circle of tall trees, none of them burning. There were seven of them, unrolling slim branches and lush leaves like fists unclenching, fingers reaching, growing as she watched. There was no buzzing here. The light here wasn't coming from the sky, but from the ground. She looked down and saw a postcard at the centre of the circle. She picked it up. In orange bubble letters, over a faded image of a tall grey tower with a ridiculous glass hub near its top, was written *"Greetings from Toronto!"* She turned the postcard over, and on the back was a single handwritten line. *Luck has entered the game.* That was all. Not even a return address.

Meena turned in a slow circle. *I get it, I have to go to Toronto, but for who? What the hell?*

She was getting frustarted. In response, the trees pulled their arms back and coiled their fingers into fists and began to buzz. Before they burst into flames, she heard them exhale one word— *sixth*—before she was pushed backward by a great wind.

Meena opened her eyes, and the universe spun above her—the glittery, off-kilter mobile Wendy had made for her on their first wedding anniversary, with a card that read, *I would give you every star in the sky, if I could*.

The dream had been fire and light and panic, but three things stuck: luck, Toronto, and *sixth*. The sixth witch had been found.

She threw off the blanket and climbed out of their four-poster bed, a romantic throwback to an era neither she nor Wendy would be welcome in. She unwound the silk wrap from around her head and walked to the balcony doors, throwing them open. A cool spring breeze blew in. She perched on the edge of the clawfoot tub they'd refused to move into the adjoining bathroom after they bought the old house and ruminated on the dream before it fell away, stretching out her legs and back. She was only fifty this year, but already arthritis was threatening.

Their house was in an older part of Salem, a neighbourhood Meena had always loved but could never afford to live in before she joined VenCo. She and Wendy had bought it not long after Meena's father passed away while writing a sermon in his attic office. Ironically, or perhaps prophetically, the subject was "Our Eternal Paradise." She wondered if that paradise had been waiting for him, if he had willed it into being after all. If the manifestation of heaven could be achieved through sheer stubbornness, Josiah Frederick Good, the descendant of one of the original colonial witches, would be the one to do it. Because of his genealogy, Pastor Good had spent his entire life trying to make good with Jesus.

A yellow bird sang her down the stairs, like the opening trill of a musical. She walked past portraits of the women from her family lines—the British peasants, the West Indian healers, the revolutionaries and mothers—every eye following her.

MEENA LOVED HER HOUSE—A fresh start. It helped that VenCo had a realtor on the books who had guided her to it right away and had gotten her a great deal. It was wide where it should be wide and narrow in the places it should be narrow, like a gorgeous body, like a secret that revealed more of itself every day. There'd been so much cleanup over the past five years, it would have been easier to just renovate completely. But both she and Wendy agreed the house was a part of their family now, too, so they took the time and effort to reclaim instead of redo, adding to it when the mood struck and funds allowed. The crystal chandelier hanging over the main entrance alone had taken them a month to clean, unhooking and soaking each bead in soapy water. When they got it all done, it looked like a giant glittering birdcage made of light itself. In fact, there were two wild birds on it now. They couldn't keep them out. Every time someone lifted a window or opened a door, little birds shot in and perched.

Meena crossed the foyer into the bright, clean kitchen. Two full walls were covered in small shelves that held all manner of ingredients in carefully labelled jars. The wide island with its curved faucet and farmer's sink held bundles of herbs and a stack of books. Since this was also Wendy's home, there was no room without books. The glass doors to the back were thrown open, and the smell of coffee lingered.

Wendy Kiwenzie sat outside on their stone patio at a heavy oak table that was meant for a formal dining room but now lived here, with vines winding up its carved legs like stockings being knitted into place. Still in her nightshirt and silk dressing gown, she had a pair of small glasses perched on her nose and was reading the Arts section of the *New York Times*, her long hair in a loose braid over her shoulder.

"Ah, my love," she said, looking up. "How did you sleep?"

Meena poured herself a black coffee and drank half the cup in one gulp. "The sixth has been found."

Wendy put down the paper and wrapped her robe more tightly around her. "Where?"

"Your old stomping grounds . . . Toronto."

"Well, at least it's close. So you're not having to run off to Turkey, or someplace even farther."

"I told you, love, this doesn't go farther than Turtle Island." Meena finished her coffee and stretched her arms over her head, then tipped her neck from one side to the other. The dream had left her stiff and drained and yet also weirdly energized. "The Oracle said the spoons are New World only. Not that this place is new, just to borrow a troubled phrase . . ."

"How do they know for sure? What if there are more than seven spoons? What if this is bigger than here?" Wendy didn't add what she was really thinking. *Is this about to get dangerous?*

"The Oracle said . . ."

"How can we even be sure the Oracle is right? If they knew everything, wouldn't they gather the damn coven themselves?"

Meena could read the worry in her wife's tone, so she softened her own. "Wendy, you know that's not how it goes. They divine, and we act. They are the guidance, and we are the hands."

She was still trying to wring the meaning out of last night's dream. The clues for finding the other spoons had been more straightforward. She got a location and a name and sent the last witch off to get the next witch. That was how it was done.

She took a calming breath. "'Luck has entered the game.' That's the line from the dream. What do you think that means?"

Wendy scrunched her forehead in worry. "There's always been a name before," she said. "Even if it's only partial."

"Not this time. This one feels different. Heavy." Meena wasn't sure what she meant by *heavy*, but knew it was true as soon as she said it.

"What if that's the name?" Wendy said. "Luck."

"Luck? What kind of a name is that?"

"Maybe one for a witch from Toronto."

Meena ducked around the table to plant a kiss on Wendy's head. "You are brilliant. You know I married you for your brains."

"Don't kid yourself. You married me for my ass."

"That too." Meena grinned, then went straight to planning. "I hope this is the one that can do it, finish this hunt. Especially with the deadline."

A wave of anxiety sent a shudder up Wendy's spine. "Seventeen days from now. Yikes, that's a tough one. I'm sure she'll be ready to hit the ground running."

Meena was biting her lip. "I don't understand the celestial work plan of it all—that's the Crone's wheelhouse. I just know it's now or it's never."

Wendy reached for her wife's hands. "Listen to me, if there was ever a witch in the entirety of this doomed humanity who could pull this off, it would be you. You, Meena Amari Good, descendant of West Indian sorceresses and the witches the Puritans failed to burn. You got this. And I got you. I'll make sure Freya is prepared."

Meena smiled. As with most things, as soon as Wendy stepped in and put a thing into perspective, it seemed doable—exciting, even. She headed back to the kitchen. "I suppose I'll be off, then."

"Where are you going?" Wendy was gathering her belongings to follow.

"Book Club, of course. I need some heavy hitters to help me find out who this Luck might be."

Wendy arched an eyebrow. "Of course. Just don't spend all day smoking up with those potheads. Medical marijuana, my ass."

Meena laughed, and a small yellow bird flew from the house and landed on a tree by the gate, singing like crazy into the green corners of the garden.

THE BOOK CLUB NORMALLY MET once a month, but Meena called and asked them to move up the date by a week.

"I need you, all of you," she'd said on the phone. "It's about the sixth."

"Give us an hour. Then come to my house," the voice replied, thick with a Boston accent. Before hanging up, she added, "Bring cheese. And crackers. And some cold cuts wouldn't kill ya."

"So a charcuterie tray, then?" Meena replied.

"What are ya, deaf? I said cold cuts. And cheese—"

"And crackers," Meena interrupted. "Yes, will do."

An hour later she was ringing the doorbell of a suburban bungalow, carrying a charcuterie tray. The Bookers were assembled and ready to get to work. The Salem chapter was made up of older women, so the youngest, the one they called "the Kid," was well into her sixties. Meena gave them the appropriate time to get settled, make themselves small snack plates, complain about their small snack plates, and get settled again; then she told them about the dream.

They sat in a variety of chairs pulled into a loose circle in a very blue living room, chewing thoughtfully.

"No return address?" one asked.

"None," Meena confirmed.

"No small print, you know that fine shit you gotta get glasses for?" another asked.

"None," Meena replied.

"Write it out for us." The Kid pushed a piece of paper and a pencil across the coffee table, and Meena dutifully wrote out the words.

"Exactly that?" she asked. "I mean, *exactly?*"

Meena looked down at the page, then added an exclamation mark and quotation marks to the text across the front. They repeated the two lines at least a dozen times at different volumes, with different intonations.

"'Greetings from Toronto!' Luck has entered the game."

"Quotation marks around only the first part, like someone is saying it," the Kid observed, tapping the page. The women all nodded, muttering their encouragement for the youngest Booker. "So the witch is talking to you herself. Interesting. Powerful."

"What direction?" asked the woman who had answered her call earlier.

"How do you mean? It was the CN Tower in downtown Toronto, that's it." Meena was trying to trust the process but couldn't see where this was headed.

"That's it, then? Just a close-up of the tower with nothing around it?" It was asked sarcastically.

Meena sighed, rubbing her palms together. "Okay, no. It was, uh . . ."

"What? From the water? From the north end . . . What?"

"It was . . ." Meena closed her eyes to see better. "It was . . . There was a dome behind it. A white dome."

There was a flurry of movement as every member of the Salem Book Club pulled out a laptop or an iPad and starting typing and scrolling.

"Looking west, so the speaker is standing in the east," the Kid called out.

"Okay, then, let's start looking for anyone named Luck in Toronto who lives in the East End," another called out.

There was a steady clicking of keys and small chatter as the Bookers scoured lists, profiles, directories, and databases, searching for the missing witch.

4

PLAYER TWO ENTERS
THE GAME

Jay Christos lived in what some people would call a house and what other people would call a compound, depending on which end of the economic scale you inhabited. The main building was a twenty-thousand-square-foot bungalow that poured out onto the acreage like an oil spill. The grounds were coated with tamed Bermuda grass, buzz cut, then sprayed to ensure no dot of riotous colour, no foreign weed dare push through. Even the insects avoided the lawn.

The drive was sliced off from the road by steel gates, a full three feet above code, but no one had challenged him yet. Besides, he didn't have any real neighbours out here in the California desert, only dirt and scrub for hundreds of miles.

An indulgently long and narrow in-ground pool had been dug into the dust so that Jay could do his laps. A cedar platform surrounded it, scattered with several chaise lounges for sunbathing that no one had ever used. Different varieties of cacti stood like bristly thumbs at the far end of the deck, and beyond them was the tallest structure on the grounds: a metal pole that held the dishes necessary for a high-speed internet connection that allowed access to streaming channels in forty-seven languages, all of which he understood.

The house was furnished in a style that was minimal and masculine. Dark wood, black leather, steel accents. His main bathroom had a Japanese toilet with LED lights, overlooking the countryside through a glass wall. Most people would be uncomfortable with that kind of exposure, but Jay liked looking out over his kingdom while taking a shit. A huge aquarium acted as a dividing wall between the living room and the kitchen in an otherwise open floor plan. That there was so much water used for leisure in his desert home was itself a flex. The aquarium alone required a cleaning specialist to drive out once a month for maintenance. When the cleaner, wearing a scuba suit, was in the tank, Jay retreated to his study. He didn't like people in his home, and he certainly didn't like having to make small talk. He'd chosen his new weekly cleaning lady partly because she was mute.

Only one other creature besides the master, and the fish, lived in this house: a small, grey, hairless cat named Benedict, after the patron saint of holiness of mind. The lithe animal was delightfully independent and smug about it, and, like his master, he was a relentless hunter.

Jay had been around for a long time—a very long time. He didn't look anywhere near as old as he actually was, which made him feel good, valued, rare. He liked being valued. He loved being rare. He took intense care of his body, swimming for two hours every day, practicing yoga in the morning and evening, consuming nothing but lean meat and sweet fruits, with gallons of springwater he had flown in from Southern Italy monthly. His skincare regime was eccentric and involved bribing customs agents twice annually. Every night before bed he oiled and braided his long black hair to preserve the curls he'd developed in childhood, back when boys wore pantaloons. He was his own greatest achievement. Well, almost.

He was proud of other things he had accomplished in this world, even though, by and large, people had forgotten he was responsible. Jay Christos's name was not in the history books or in the economics texts. He had never been honored for displacing the old women and story holders from the land, paving the way for the rise of capitalism. He did not have a monument on Wall Street or a chair named after him at Harvard Business School. But *he* knew what he had done, and most of the time that was enough. He had amassed a fortune over the years. When one doesn't believe they will die, they make different decisions, play a longer game in the market.

THE WITCH'S DREAM CAME TO Jay when he was in the bath, listening to Monster Magnet on surround sound, his eyes closed and his wet hair hanging over the edge of the tub, so long it almost reached the heated floor.

It was an old trick, this ability to link to a target's dreaming, one he'd learned from a witch who had ripped into his chest and left him surrounded by fire, a witch who had taken his heart long before she almost pierced it. The only problem was that, try as hard as he liked, he couldn't link in real time, the visions coming to him late— sometimes by a few hours, sometimes a few days. All these years and all these resources and he still had to wait for the visions to appear, like a peasant without a satellite dish. Even worse, his reception was spotty, jumping in places and moving at irregular speeds—now slow motion, now comically sped up.

"Oh, come on," he moaned, eyes still closed. "Alexa—turn music off!"

In the silence he tried to focus. *Trees, fire.*

"Have you pulled together the coven, little bird?" he asked in the echo of his bathroom thousands of miles away, even though he knew it wasn't true. The tension in his shoulders told him she was one step closer, which was too close. He was kept alive and motivated by a singular purpose—to keep the witches from assembling, to keep the old guard safe and prosperous and male. But this witch—the bitch in Salem, of all obvious places—had gotten further than he'd expected, and he would not fail.

He focused harder, trying to adjust the sound and the contrast. Was that . . . bees? The film skipped to a postcard. He let the scene run, catching a glimpse of the front and back of the card.

"Greetings from Toronto!"

He breathed a sigh that ended in a rumbling groan. This was the one he *had* to stop. He felt it where he felt most serious matters—in his testicles.

The witch had a jump on him, and she was closer to the mark in Toronto, which was far away and cold and boring. He had to get moving. But first, he'd finish his bath.

He leaned back, luxuriating in the heat. The last thing that came to him before he closed the portal that had opened in his mind was the word *luck*. It was something he would need.

5

NEW COLOUR IN
THE WORLD

After Lucky hauled their laundry back upstairs, she realized she didn't want to tell Stella about the key, or the tunnel, or the spoon. She needed time to let it sink in, or maybe she just liked having something completely and utterly to herself for once.

Instead, she threw herself into a deep cleaning of the whole apartment. By the time her grandmother rolled back in after a long day with Clermont, it was dinnertime and the place was spotless for the first time in months. Lucky was tired, a good tired, the kind of tired that lived in your muscles. So she ordered in shawarma, and she and Stella watched sitcoms until midnight.

After Lucky went to bed, she lay sprawled out on top of the covers, examining her spoon. Using her fingernail, she dug more dirt out of the engravings on the handle and realized the figure was actually an old-timey witch. Odd and, somehow, also exciting. Sticking her earbuds in, she swiped to a meditation app on her phone and fell asleep clutching her small prize.

Her dream was a memory. Lucky was a little girl again, and there was Arnya walking in the front door of their old apartment with a bandana wrapped around her head so that it covered her right eye.

Lucky jumped off the couch and reached for her mother's swollen face. "What happened?"

"Ah, some asshole decided it would only be a fair fight if I had one eye tied behind my back." She went directly to the fridge, grabbed a two-liter of Pepsi, and drank directly from the bottle. "I still whipped him."

"You got into a fight? With a man?" Lucky was only seven, but she understood the rules: A man never hit a woman. No exceptions.

"More like we didn't see"—Arnya paused, then pointed to her face—"eye to eye. See what I did there?"

Lucky didn't laugh. She didn't smile. Instead, she padded on bare feet past her mother. She got up on tiptoes and retrieved a bag of frozen peas from the freezer.

Arnya accepted the bag and went to sit on the couch. "Thanks, Muffin Man." She tipped her head back and placed the peas over her bandana. She tried to be all nonchalant, but Lucky saw her wince at the sudden, slight weight.

"Did you *moydur* him?" Lucky asked, employing the old-timey gangster voice they sometimes used when discussing such things. Pushing aside her *Goonies* sleeping bag, she crawled up onto the couch close to her mother.

Arnya didn't answer. Her lip trembled a bit, and she covered it by taking another swig of pop.

"You can smoke in the apartment if you want," Lucky offered.

She got up to get her mother's at-home pack from the top drawer of the dresser under the TV, but Arnya grabbed her arm. "I have a better idea. Since I already have the patch, why don't we be pirates?"

"Now?" Arnya was prone to wild bouts of imagination, but pirates? In the middle of the night?

"Yeah. We need a box for our treasure chest. Look in the bedroom closet. Just dump out the shoes or whatever." Arnya sat up and plopped the peas on the table. "Make sure it has a lid."

Lucky brought back a Nike box, only a little battered. While she was gone, Arnya had found a glass and filled it with Pepsi, to which she added a bit of rye. She took a big swig, set down the glass, and rubbed her hands together. "Alrighty then, the first thing pirates need is treasure. I mean, we probably need a ship. But we be land pirates, so this'll have to do." She slapped the couch cushion beside her. "Off you go—find me some jewels!"

Lucky ran around the apartment scooping up trinkets and coins. She brought each find back to the "Captain," who squinted her one eye at the potential treasure and declared it be thrown back into the deep or added to their chest. A pile of discards quickly accumulated on the floor. Soon the box held coloured pencils, a plastic bubble from a gum machine that once held a ring, two nickels (Arnya pocketed the quarters), a stick of incense, a single beaded earring, and the worn copy of *Cujo* Arnya read to Lucky when she couldn't sleep.

Downing the rest of her drink, Arnya leaped to her feet, retrieved her cigarettes, and lit up, turning in a circle in the centre of the room.

"What else do we need?" Lucky couldn't stop yawning now, but her mother seemed energized.

"We need real treasure. The kind thieves would kill for." Her hair was wild, sticking up and out from the bandana. "Go get the wench's jewels!"

"What's a wench?"

"A badass like your mother, that's what. Now grab the jewels!" She raised her cigarette like a sabre and pointed to their bedroom.

From among the piles of odds and ends on top of their dresser—an Allen key, pantyhose, sample-size bottles of lotion and mouthwash, four different half-finished packets of gum, and a pile of old photos—Lucky grabbed two boxes. She flipped open one box that used to hold bobby pins and hair elastics, but they always forgot to put them back, so now it just held some safety pins and an empty can of mace. The other box was where Arnya kept her jewelry.

"I got the wench stuff," she called, carrying the jewelry box to her mother.

"Over here, ya scallywag." Arnya was back on the couch with the peas on her forehead. "Open her up! Actually, hold on a sec."

Arnya grabbed the box, a box Lucky had been forbidden to open before, and turned slightly, pulling out a small baggie and stuffing it into her bra. Then she handed the box back to Lucky, who had settled beside her on the couch. "There, now you can open her up."

Lucky unhooked the tiny brass latch and pulled up the lid. A miniature plastic ballerina sprang up and began twirling to an out-of-tune song, her pirouettes reflected in the mirror on the underside of the lid.

"Wow!"

"You like that?"

Lucky was mesmerized by the little dancer, spinning in her single-ply net tutu. It was so delicate. And how did the music work? How did she keep turning? "I love her."

"Then, in she goes," Arnya cried, and plucked the twirling girl off her brass pedestal, tossing her into the shoebox.

Lucky covered her mouth. What had Arnya done? Separated from her magic, the magnificent doll was just a cheap plastic toy with paint-work so sloppy her lipstick touched one side of her yellow hair. Her hands had no fingers. Her legs were uneven. Pulled from where she belonged, she was junk.

Arnya dug around in her jewels, stirring necklaces and strands of beads with a finger. "What else have we got in here good enough to be buried?"

"Buried? Like in a grave?" Lucky's breath caught. Her head felt light, and her eyes felt heavy.

"No—like treasure. You have to bury your treasure. That's how it stays safe from other pirates." Arnya pulled out two chains, one silver, one gold, twisted together. "What about these? I think the silver one is the genuine article."

Lucky felt the tears build and tried like hell to hold them back.

Arnya dropped the chains and the pirate accent. "What's wrong?"

"I don't want to bury her."

"Who?" She followed her daughter's gaze to the little dancer and chuckled. "That doll? It's not like the bitch has lungs."

When Lucky's face didn't change, Arnya sighed. "Okay, look. We'll poke breathing holes in the box."

She picked up a pencil crayon and stabbed the cardboard lid a few times. "There. All better. Now help me pick out the rest of the booty."

"I . . . I'm tired," Lucky said. She stood, keeping her head tipped back, hoping gravity would prevent the tears from spilling down her cheeks. "I'm going to bed. Night."

"Lucky!"

Her mother's call stopped her, but she didn't turn around.

Arnya said, "You can't keep everything safe all the time. You have to hide the important stuff you have, the things that make you *you*. Just put it all away. Keep it out of reach. If you hide the precious stuff, then no one can take it. No matter what they do."

One tear fell and slipped between Lucky's lips. Salt. Grandma Stella told her salt was good for protection. Without turning back towards her mother, she walked into their room, climbed into the big bed, and pulled the comforter up to her chin. Before she fell asleep, she heard her mom in the living room, sorting more treasure from junk, filling their pretend box. She knew it was no longer a game, and it wasn't about crappy chains or broken dolls at all.

THE NEXT DAY, WHEN LUCKY went out to run errands for Stella, she was greeted by another sudden change in the weather. The air was filled with the smell of spring, that good earthy smell of rain and roots and sun on concrete. It couldn't have snowed just days ago. There was no way the thin blue of this sky could have held such weight. A small yellow flicker in the green-studded branches of the front trees—a bird silently watching her.

An old man raked his small lawn behind a low fence. Two little girls squealed by on a single BMX with rusted wheels. Squirrels chased each other across the sagging telephone wires. Windows opened. Mowers revved up. People lingered on their front stoops, faces turned to catch the new heat. Lucky walked quickly, not from cold or hurry, only because it felt like she had somewhere to go.

She was one house from the corner when the fox appeared. It pulled itself out of the bush on silent paws, with more of a pour than a step. Lucky stopped abruptly, swinging her arms back and coming to a stop.

"Whoa, whoa." She was scared for a minute. Like most city people, Lucky believed that anything outside of a domestic pet was something to be feared. Rabies and mange crossed her mind. She stood very still. The fox turned his head slowly and looked at her, not sharing her fear.

Rabies, for sure, she thought. Fear was normal, a natural state of living. Anything else must be suspect. He held her gaze for long seconds, long enough for her to notice the flash and contraction of irises. Stranger than seeing a fox was being seen by a fox. She was seen. She felt uncovered. She felt singular. It was as if she had just begun to exist in the wider world and things were taking notice. And then the fox slid off along the hedges and back in through a small gap in the shrubs.

The corner store had put out fruits and vegetables in the front bins, bins that had spent all winter holding snow and wet leaves. The lemons were remarkable, thick skin pitted and shiny. The oranges were like small citrine beads strung by a passionate stock boy. Lucky ran a finger along the glossy red curves of firm peppers.

"Sexy," she said under her breath, then laughed. It was ridiculous, but she meant it.

Swinging her bags on the way home, she took her time, pausing to read the graffiti on the side of a mailbox (*LAND BACK*) and to watch the girls on the BMX take turns jumping off a small ramp.

She was fishing her keys out of her pocket when her phone buzzed—a text from Malcolm:

Backyard hang at Stacy's tonight.
Meet me at the store at 6?

She typed back a thumbs-up and went inside. Things were different today—somehow brighter, clearer. Maybe today was the day she told Malcolm how she felt.

THIS PARTY IS GREAT. STACY'S *a real peach*, Lucky thought, sitting on the floral-patterned couch someone had dragged outside. *A real fucking peach.* Lucky was a little drunk—not a lot, just the beginning part of drunk where you want to laugh and take up space.

"Hey, why are you all by yourself?" Malcolm plopped down beside her on the couch.

"Just watching this parade of humanity." Her stomach was filled with butterflies and Jägermeister. *Here he is, tell him!*

"I like a good parade," he said, throwing his long arm over the back of the couch. "Anyone interesting?"

She surveyed the crowd and pointed to a woman in heavy platform boots with a dozen metal buckles on each. "That girl's calf muscles must be jacked."

Malcolm nodded. "I do admire her stamina."

"I mean, plus she looks hot in those, so there's that."

"She does indeed." He moved on. "What about that guy, old-school flip-glasses guy?"

He used his chin to indicate a thin man with a mullet and a pair of round spectacles with a sunglasses attachment. He was demonstrating his double-jointed arms for two extremely perplexed women.

"That man is a champion of the pick-up game," she agreed. "I mean, no one's used that double-jointed trick since that movie . . ."

Malcolm sat forward, excited now that they were on films. "I loved that one! I mean, it was lowbrow and punching in the featherweight division, but it knew what it was and it did it well."

"Uh, yeah," Lucky drawled. Fucking film students. "I just thought it was fun . . . but sure, lowbrow and self-aware. Also cool."

He gave her a slight push, and she exaggerated the shove, tipping over. He yanked her upright and kept his arm over her shoulder. "Okay, who would you take home?"

She wanted to answer honestly. She had some drinks in her and was in a good mood. She thought about it, she really did. And then he ruined it.

"That guy right there, he's totally your type." He pointed with his beer bottle to a gangly weirdo hanging like a monkey from a low branch, scattering the Instagrammers from their photo area like little birds. "You should take him home. Come on, I'll be your wingman."

Suddenly the weight of his arm was suffocating. She shrugged it off and stood.

Anger or disappointment or the new balls she had grown since yesterday after crawling through a fucking hole in the wall made her do it. "I would take you."

She raised a hand to her mouth to stop the words. They came out anyway.

"I pick you." She was horrified but couldn't stop herself. "And maybe, just maybe, you should pick me back."

He looked at her with a confusion that morphed into pity. When he didn't answer right away, when he looked at her that way, she felt like she might throw up. Instead, she ran across the lawn and along the side of the house.

She hoped he would follow her. She even slowed down in the narrow space between town houses. Why wouldn't he follow her? Even as a friend?

"Fuck it," she said out loud. "And fuck you!" she shouted over her shoulder. She made her way to the front yard, sat on the stoop, and called herself an Uber.

Sliding through the city in the back seat of a Mazda with a mercifully silent driver and a headache behind her eyes, Lucky dozed off, her cheek, held by her forearm, propped up on the window.

"You're here. Lady . . . you have reached your destination."

Lucky jerked awake in the back seat of the Uber. The driver was looking at her in the rearview mirror, impatiently waiting for her to leave so he could catch his next fare.

"Shit, sorry." She grabbed her bag and opened the door. She paused before shutting it. "Uh, five stars. And I'll add a tip. Sorry about that. Long day." He gave her a thumbs-up, and she closed the door behind her.

She took a deep breath on the sidewalk and pulled her phone out of her pocket to give the promised rating. She had two missed messages.

I'm an asshole. Sorry for being a
bad friend.

She sighed. He just had to make sure he got the *f*-word in there. "Fucking Malcolm."

We need to talk.

She didn't answer him. Instead, she sat on the curb in front of her darkened house. The street was so still now. A small breeze scattered newly shorn grass across the pavement. A wind chime tinkled from a porch across the way, and a skinny black cat slid in and around the spikes of a fence as if he were showboating at an agility competition. All around her, life was happening behind so many windows. She watched an old man eating from a coffee mug. Two girls, maybe the ones on the BMX earlier, pored over a magazine in a window seat, stopping to dissect the images and laugh. A young woman wrapped in a kimono practiced flute in her bedroom, elbows raised so high, any music teacher would be proud. And after a few minutes, a kind of anticipation settled into Lucky's joints.

Even now, after the Malcolm humiliation, there was still that feeling that things were changing, that things were bright. Maybe there was more out there, waiting for her. She just wondered what that meant for Stella. Could Lucky live a new life knowing she'd sent her last family member away, stashing her in a nursing home where she couldn't drunk knit or watch horror movies at an impossible volume late into the night?

She looked over her shoulder just as a third-floor window lit up. Stella lifted the pane, stuck her head out, and began to clap.

"Great job! You're magnificent!"

It took a moment for Lucky to realize she was shouting at the black cat, not her. She sighed and stood up.

"Oh, hey, Lucky. Come on, dinner's getting cold. I mean, it's cereal so it's supposed to be cold but still . . . Did you see that cat? God, what style." She went back in and shut the window.

"You're also doing a great job," Lucky muttered to herself, dusting off the seat of her pants. "You are magnificent! Working every day and taking care of everyone. God, what style."

She made her way inside to her underwhelming dinner.

THE MAIDEN ANSWERED THE FACETIME call on the balcony of her condo, a curvy woman in a gold bikini sunbathing beside her.

"Is this a bad time?" the Mother asked, seeing that her colleague was not alone.

"Actually, this right here is a great time." The Maiden smiled. "Also, she's asleep." She gently slapped the sunbather's thigh, and the woman groaned and rolled over onto her side. Even still, the Maiden got up and walked inside to the kitchen island, pouring herself a glass of water. "I hear he's on the move."

"Yes, so is the fifth—Freya," the Mother answered.

"God, I love Freya," the Maiden replied. "And she has the exact location?"

"Yes, the Bookers helped." The Mother fed strips of bacon to her pit bull, cooing as she did. "There's a good girl, Hecate."

"So they have a jump on him. Should we let them know he's searching?"

The Mother paused before answering. "No. I don't want them rattled. They need to stay focused."

"Isn't that—I don't know—careless? Shouldn't we tell them there's a Good Walker on their tail? He's not being quiet anymore—he's activated." The Maiden sat on a stool and propped her phone against a bottle while she cleaned up the makings of lunch from the island counter.

"We'll keep a careful eye. If he gets too close, we'll inform them. But for now, we say nothing. We have to think of the entire group before any individual witch." The Mother was maternal, as her name suggested, but could also be the most cutthroat of the Oracle. After all, she had a large brood to care for.

"Alright," the Maiden drawled. "I just . . ."

Her phone beeped at her—the call had ended.

She passed a hand over her braids and finished her thought. "I just think we need to remember the entire group is made up of individual witches."

Then she went back out onto the balcony to bask in the golden heat waiting out there, hoping she could take her mind off the mission, even if just for another hour.

6

A COMPLETE FUCKING 180 OVER GENERAL TSO CHICKEN AND SHITTY RICE

On her lunch break on Monday, Lucky scrolled through the apartment-for-rent ads on her phone while the sauce on her plate of Chinese takeaway turned to jelly. She sighed a dozen times in as many minutes. The places that were decent either were out of her price range or so far away it would take her two hours to get to work.

Everything even remotely in their neighbourhood cost way more than they were paying now. She hadn't noticed much in the way of gentrification, but clearly it was sneaking up on them. The most affordable were the basement units. But there was no way she could rent a place where the landlord lived upstairs: Stella got so loud so late at night they'd be kicked out inside a month.

"Fuck this." She dumped her phone on the table and focused on eating the last remnants of her nasty noodles.

"Lucky St. James?"

She looked up to see what could only be described as an ethereal woman in a well-cut dark green suit approaching her table. Gold rings glimmered on every finger, and she was carrying nothing but a long, envelope-flap Fendi bag. Clearly, she did not shop in the places Lucky did. This couldn't be good. No one with this kind of presence ever talked to her, not for any reason that wasn't trouble.

"Are you Miss St. James?" Up close, the woman was young, younger than Lucky, even. Her hair was blond and flawless, her skin clear and unlined.

"Uh, yes, that's me."

Maybe she was a lawyer. Maybe Lucky was being served? But why? She didn't have enough time to get into trouble or enough money to make it worth anyone's while. And then it was like the woman could read her mind.

"Don't freak out," she said. "I'm here about a job." She slid into the chair attached to the other side of the table and placed her purse in front of her.

"A job?"

"Yes. You work for McManus Personnel, right?"

Lucky glanced anxiously at the very expensive bag sitting so close to the sticky food tray. Then a thought occurred to her, and she dropped her fork. "Are you from McManus? Oh shit, am I being fired? Listen, I'm on my lunch break. I know its two o'clock, but I only got to take it now—I'm not late or skipping out. I—"

"No, I'm not from McManus. God, I would never . . ." The woman sure didn't seem very corporate.

So who *was* this woman? Lucky thought she was too well-dressed to be a Bible thumper, out to save a stranger's soul, but you never knew. Whatever she was selling, especially if it was salvation, Lucky wasn't having it. She said, "I'm not interested."

The woman sat back in her seat, squinting. "But I haven't even told you what I am offering."

Lucky also sat back and folded her arms across her chest. "Listen, I don't know how you know my name—that's a little creepy—but I do not need Jesus. What I need is an affordable apartment, and unless Jesus has a two-bedroom for under fifteen hundred dollars, he can't help me, and neither can you."

They looked at each other in silence for a long moment. And then the woman tipped her head back and laughed. Uproariously. When she was finally able to stop, she took a tissue out of her bag and wiped her eyes. "Oh shit," she said. "I've never been mistaken for a Mormon before. That's a good one."

Lucky was not amused. "Seriously, how do you know my name?"

The woman wiped her eyes again, examining the tissue to make sure her mascara was intact. "I know a lot about you, because that's my job. I research employee prospects for a company based in LA—out of the Massachusetts office. We only recruit the most exceptional people and bring them in to do meaningful work. Work that can pay them the kind of money they need to rent decent apartments."

Now she had Lucky's attention.

She opened the flap on her bag and pulled out a slim silver case, clicked the clasp, and extracted a business card.

The card stock was heavy, the print saturated. Lucky read it aloud:

THE CIRCLE IS THE STRONGEST SHAPE

Freya Monahan,
Recruitment Officer

VenCo. She repeated it under her breath as she flipped the card over to see the woman's contact info.

"We pursue social equality and balance for our employees and are dedicated to giving them the kind of support they need, especially those who are caretakers of children, dependents, elders . . ." Freya leaned towards her, elbows on the table.

"Okay, I don't mean to be an asshole here, but you're making me very nervous. First, you put a purse that I'm pretty sure costs more than my rent on this table, and now you have your jacket touching it." Lucky moved her tray onto the empty table beside theirs, then used a Wet-Nap to wipe the surface as best she could.

Freya watched her check to make sure the purse was clean. "This is exactly why you need to come work for us, Miss St. James."

"You're looking for a janitor?"

Freya smirked. "You're hilarious. No, we're looking for women who say what they think and who care. Why should you give a shit whether my bag gets sticky when I interrupted the only break you get from a job you hate?"

Lucky felt a bit sheepish. She wasn't used to compliments. It had been years since anyone even paid attention to her. So she deflected. "I just don't want to have to pay for your dry cleaning."

Freya snapped her fingers in response. "You're fun."

Lucky was still confused. "I just don't understand. Why?"

"Why what?"

"Why me?"

Freya stood up. "Why not you?"

"It's just—Massachussetts? It seems like a long way to come for a new admin person."

"Admin?" Freya looked confused for a minute. "Oh! You think this is for the same job you have now?"

Lucky nodded, not knowing what to say.

"Oh Christ, that *would* be stupid. No, no. We don't need a secretary. We are looking for a writer to join a boutique female-led publishing house."

Freya gathered up her purse, and Lucky sat there in silence, too shocked to respond, even though it was all she could think of: A writer? A publishing house?

"Wait . . . how did you know that I write?"

"Well, we read some of your early blog posts. Plus, there was that letter to the editor you penned in the paper, the one calling the book reviewer an amoeba with single-celled taste? Classic."

"You . . . you found my work? And you read it?"

Freya's face softened. "I know sometimes you look around and think, 'I deserve something better, something more.' Lucky, this is better. This is more. Come to Salem and see what we have to offer you. We'll put you up while you decide and, of course, pay your expenses. Call me."

She walked away, leaving Lucky reeling.

WHEN SHE GOT HOME THAT night, she found Stella sitting on the floor in the living room surrounded by boxes, their contents spilling out onto the hardwood.

"Look what I found at the back of the closet. A whole museum's worth!" She held up handfuls of random items—lengths of ribbon, bracelets, a small wooden carving of a giraffe.

Lucky sighed. It wasn't that finding old stuff wasn't fun, or that it was so much work to clean up after her. It was just that Stella had "found" these old boxes just last month. Her memory was getting progressively worse.

"That's great, Gram." She checked the stove and counter for signs of meal prep, found none, and grabbed a frozen lasagna out of the fridge. "What'd you eat today?"

"Cereal. Look at this!" She held up an orange-and-brown flower-patterned muumuu. "I really went for the Mrs. Roper look back then." She dropped it in a pool of garish fabric, and the cat curled up on top. "Jinx likes it."

Lucky turned on the oven, then went back to the fridge. "Do you want salad?"

"No. Hey, look at this." She removed a small shoebox from a larger Tupperware container and held it up. "I don't remember this." She read the side. "Size nine. Who the hell wears nines?"

"My mom did," Lucky replied, digging through the crisper. She'd make salad anyway. Drowned in enough dressing that she could probably get Stella to eat some. "Do we have cheese some-where? We really need to organize the fridge better. It's a shit show in here."

"Was this little doll yours?"

Lucky looked up. Stella held a plastic ballerina by the scrap of netting that made her skirt.

"Holy shit! I remember that." She closed the fridge door and went into the living room, sitting down beside Stella in the rubble of their past lives. "It was from Arnya's jewelry box. When you opened the lid, she danced." She took the doll from Stella and slowly turned it, imitating its childhood magic.

Stella was already on to the next thing, an old Superman comic book where someone, probably Lucky's dad, had circled all the boobs. "Christ, this is pervy."

Lucky kept digging through the shoebox, then remembered the night of her mother's black eye. The night Arnya told her to put anything valuable she held out of sight, safely buried. An old brooch with fake gems in an abstract pattern caught her eye. She picked it up and slipped it into her pocket, where it clinked against the spoon.

7

DIG

Freya had called to report back on the meeting. She told Meena it had got off to a bumpy start: that girl was spicy. But she'd set the hook. And she'd also managed to slip a little sachet of herbs, meant to open the mind, into the girl's messenger bag so that Meena could do some extra convincing while she slept. It felt like the girl was already on the brink of change. Sometimes the spoon did that to a person. More often than not, life did it. But they didn't have the luxury of time; they needed to reel her in, and fast.

After dinner with Wendy, Meena slipped off on her own and ran herself a bath, as hot as she could stand. Before she got in, she poured in the oils that would scent the steam and fill her head. By the time she was finished soaking, she was ready to sleep and feeling very sensitive. Then she crawled between the high-thread-count sheets, under the weighted duvet, and said, "See you soon, Lucky."

MEENA WAS IN A GARDEN. It wasn't full of evergreens and vines like her own backyard but sliced through with bright birch and crowded with white trilliums. The air was heavy with leaves and the smell of soil. She wore a long pink dress with tight sheer sleeves that ended in the middle of her palms, and a high lace collar. She was a stroke of oil paint on a watercolour canvas. She closed her eyes and listened.

Crickets, gathered in a symphony.

Frogs chirping through the hiccupping of a nearby creek.

A low hum of movement like pressure against the landscape. That was the sound she followed.

She tried not to crush the flowers, but there were too many of them. They felt like velvet under her bare feet. Here and there a cluster of mushrooms bloomed like fat fingers, reminding her of how her wife found her spoon. She smiled. She liked the way memories followed her into dreams, especially when they were ones of Wendy.

She had to push her arms ahead to carve a path through the birch. She was amused by this. You never knew what the dream would demand. Apparently, in Lucky's dreams, she had slowed time so that movement had to be forced.

Through the trees was a clearing carpeted with violets like small eyes that squinted at her approach. There was Lucky, with her back to Meena, engaged in a conversation with someone mostly hidden by the billows of Lucky's massive gown, deep oxblood red and layered like a delicate pastry.

Meena paused to eavesdrop.

"I feel like I'm drowning," Lucky said, "like the world is so much heavier than me."

Meena couldn't make out the response, but something about the purring lilt of the other person's voice told her it was feminine.

"Which way am I supposed to go?" Lucky lifted her arms and pointed in opposite directions. "I'm stuck." She dropped her arms and lifted the hem of her gown, and, sure enough, she was rooted in the ground—a couture tree in a haunted forest.

She flexed her knees and pushed up, but her feet stayed fast.
More purring.

"I *am* trying!" Lucky squatted and tried to jump, but the soil would not let go.

She screamed, "I do want it! I know I have to go."

A murder of crows, the biggest grouping Meena had ever seen, swirled into the sky. And whoever had been counseling Lucky was gone.

"No, wait! I'm sorry! Come back! Mom!" Lucky was yanking at her feet, trying to tear them free, the kind of violent movement that meant she was tossing around in her bed. Meena had to move now, before the girl woke herself up.

She took a step onto the flower carpet. Somehow the violets were sharp and stuck into the soles of her bare feet. Nice! Such protection was a witch move if she'd ever seen one. She reminded herself that her feet weren't really being cut, that the pain was only an illusion. But it was a good one—the next step hurt just as much.

This girl was powerful.

"Lucky," she called.

The girl twisted as best she could to look Meena's way, shocked to see a stranger in her dream.

The violets were growing, tangling in Meena's toes and cutting the thin webs of skin between them. "Dig! You need to dig."

Meena could feel herself fading. She was actually being kicked out of Lucky's dream.

"How? With what?" Lucky shouted back, frantic.

"You have it with you. It's always with you now." Meena reached into her sleeve and pulled out her own spoon, holding it up in a hand that was almost transparent now. She could feel the soft give of her pillow under her head.

Lucky reached into her voluminous skirts and pulled out her spoon.

"Just dig. And then come home," Meena said out loud, into the dark of her own bedroom. She sat up, sucking air between her teeth. She had pins and needles up to her waist. Gently rubbing her legs, willing the blood to move, she breathed out. "Holy fuck, who is this girl?"

LUCKY WOKE UP, SWEATY AND tangled in her sheets. In her right hand, she was clutching her little silver spoon.

8

A DARK ARRIVAL

Hello, Mr. Christos. I'm Vivian, and I'll be your host for this flight. Is there anything I can do to get you settled in?" She was cheerful, as her job required, and pretty in a milk-fed kind of way, a little too pale for his liking. But it had been a long time since he'd been out and about, and he would take what he could get.

Jay Christos handed her his blazer and settled into his first-class pod. "Not unless you can divert coach passengers to a different aisle, so they don't bump into me as they board." He didn't make eye contact. He wasn't joking and didn't care if she thought he was.

She gave a short, flustered laugh. "I'm afraid I can't manage that, sir."

"Then I guess, Vivian, the answer is no. There is nothing you can do to get me settled in."

There are two ways to make an impression on someone: be exceedingly kind or be a total dick. Jay preferred the dick move; it made the target feel grateful when you ceased to be one.

So when Vivian brought him a bowl of warmed cashews on a silver tray, he smiled up at her, a slow smile that seemed to grow the longer he took her in. No words, not even a thank-you, just that smile. It made her blush.

Later, he ordered the best red wine off her shitty cart and asked her if she had ever been to the South of France. She had. And so they bantered about their shared travels, until the woman seated behind him grew tired of waiting and loudly demanded a whiskey, neat.

"Well, I guess you'd better get her that drink," he said, leaning in as if he and Vivian had a secret, making sure she caught his quick glance down her blouse.

The next time she came by, ready for more play, he refused her. Instead, he snapped that the cashews were stale and asked her to take them back and open a new tin. He couldn't have hurt her more if he had told her she was too fat for her uniform. That was the beauty of the game. Once he got it rolling, it took so little effort to maintain the momentum, pushed by the woman's self-doubt.

For the next four hours that was how it went. Sometimes she'd catch him eyeing her appreciatively and other times she would catch him laughing. Both brought her blood to her skin. Was he laughing at her? Did he notice her lingering too long? As soon as she retreated to a stance of professional courtesy, he'd touch a finger to the inside of her wrist as she delivered his wine or comment on her jewelry. Push-pull, push-pull.

In the quiet stretch before cabin cleanup, about forty-five minutes before landing, Jay slipped through the curtain and into the semi-dark galley where Vivian was checking her phone.

He'd been so quiet she jumped when she noticed him. "Oh, Mr. Christos! Can I help you with something?"

"I'm hoping you can," he said, and put a hand on her lower back and pulled her against his length.

"Oh god."

"Almost."

And because of all that push-pull, instead of asking him to return to his seat, she allowed him to guide her into the first-class lavatory and yank up her skirt. She actually was too thick for her uniform, and her ass gave a satisfying bounce when it was released. He took it in both hands and growled in her ear, pressing her against the sink and lowering his face into the shallow of her collarbone and biting at her. Then he spun her around so that all that good flesh was heavy against his front and peeled her lace panties down her thighs.

He wasn't unreasonably cruel, so when she came by twenty minutes later to collect garbage and remind people to fasten their seatbelts and to put their chairs and tray tables in the upright position, he smiled at her conspiratorially and complied with her instructions. He accepted his jacket back from her with gratitude, and as he passed her as he disembarked, he said, "I had a lovely flight, Vivian. Thank you for everything."

AS SHE WATCHED HIM WALK up the ramp and away from her, Vivian was pissed. That was it? No "Here's my card," no "I have a hotel room for the night if you'd like to join me"? But as he turned the corner and disappeared into the main terminal, the oddest thing happened. She couldn't figure out why she was staring up the walkway. Her head felt fuzzy. She must be jet-lagged. Too many long-distance flights this week. She decided she would check into the airport Sheraton and order room service. No drinks with the crew tonight. Clearly, she needed to rest.

Just then the other stewardess whispered to her, "Girl, your skirt," pointing at the small tear up the side split where the fabric had been ripped. "What happened?"

Vivian fingered the tear. "I don't know. Must have caught it on something." Then she went about her business, checking the seats for left items and then collecting her own things. She hummed to herself as she rolled her wheelie bag into the terminal. She was tired, but at least it had been an uneventful flight. It was almost as if it hadn't happened at all.

WHEN JAY CHECKED IN TO his suite at the Royal York, the desk clerk handed him a manila envelope with his name written across it in florid calligraphy. His assistant, Laurent, was very efficient but fond of his flourishes.

"It was delivered an hour ago," the clerk said.

Jay gathered his things and walked across the lobby to the elevator. He liked these older hotels with their thirty-dollar room service smoothies and dimly lit restaurants with velvet banquettes. He enjoyed the fresh linens and patterned carpet covering every inch of floor so that footsteps were muffled. This hotel even had the Library Bar, staffed by ancient male bartenders. He might indulge, given that it was guaranteed he wouldn't run into a member of the witches' Tender network there, posing as a regular bartender.

He disembarked on the executive floor and let himself into his suite. The air smelled like clean dust, the way he imagined a silk-lined coffin would smell from the inside. Once, in Russia, he had dug himself a grave to lie in, just to see what it felt like to be so close to your own mortality. Then he'd filled it with the bodies of three young witches he'd slaughtered in the cold-to-creaking woods.

He threw his coat and bag onto the end of the bed and picked up the phone to call room service. After ordering a rare porterhouse, a bottle of Chianti, and a large bowl of fresh grapes, he sank into a low chair by the fireplace to open the envelope. Inside was a single sheet of creamy paper with four handwritten entries, each one followed by an address and directions.

> Luck Nguon
> Freshly New Salon, nail tech
> Lucky Simpson-O'Reilly
> Mother St. Theresa's Catholic Secondary School,
> grade 10 student
> Luck-Ann Manchester
> Homemaker
> Lucky St. James
> McManus Personnel, temp worker

That Laurent had found only four women in the Greater Toronto Area with first names that were a variation of *luck* was, well, lucky. This wouldn't take too long. He placed the page on the glass table in front of him and leaned over it, concentrating.

"Who are you? Who . . . are . . . you?"

A knock at the door.

He got up, tipped his head to either shoulder, and smoothed his dark hair, then went to answer the door.

"Good evening, Mr. Christos. I have your room service order."

He stepped to the side and waved the server in.

The boy was beautiful—fine-boned with long lashes and strong legs under his stiff uniform pants. He pushed the cart inside, laden with silver domes, the bottle of wine, a crystal wineglass, and a slim vase holding a single white carnation. It was an odd choice, such a cheap flower with such an expensive spread.

Jay followed him and watched him remove the domes. The boy

looked up, smiling a polite room service smile that revealed crooked teeth, a glimpse of the real under the uniform.

Jay waited for it, the small sign that would let him know if a new game was beginning. And then the boy's eyes dropped, moving across Jay's torso. Ah, here it was. He really must travel more often, even if it was commercial.

"Excellent," he said. "I'm famished."

9

THE FIRST LEG OF
THE JOURNEY

W ell, well, if it isn't Miss Lucky St. James and her wicked old grandmother." Clermont had opened his door holding a martini adorned with a toothpick spearing a sweet pickle. "Just in time for afternoon cocktails." He was dressed in the muumuu Stella had unearthed the other day and then gifted to him. It was too long, trailing behind him like the world's ugliest wedding gown.

Lucky had been seriously considering the VenCo offer but too scared to make the leap, until she woke up from a particularly vivid dream. Then she'd emailed Freya and told her she was in. At the last minute, she realized there was no way she could leave Stella behind, so she spent a few hours convincing the woman to leave her cat and come on a quick road trip. She'd just leave her at the motel when she actually went to her meeting. It was better than leaving her a whole country away.

Freya had replied with an address, assuring her they would take care of all the arrangements while she was on the road. So here they were, dropping off instructions for Jinxy's care with Clermont, who had agreed to look in on the cat—two pages, single-spaced, with numerous bullet points.

"Jesus Christ, is this a cat, or a bomb I'm supposed to defuse?" he asked, scanning the pages as Stella and Lucky stood at the door.

"Oh, and don't open the window too much. He's liable to jump," Stella said. "Maybe you should write that down too. Lucky, do you have a pen?"

"I don't need to write it down." Clermont rubbed his forehead. "What the hell, Stelly, you think he's stupid enough to leap from a third-story window? Is he missing an eye or a brain?"

Stella said, "He is not a moron. But we're very close. With me gone, he might try to leap to his death."

Lucky elbowed her in the ribs.

"Oww! What? The cat doesn't know how long I'll be gone for!" Stella rubbed her side. "He might think I abandoned him with this nut."

"A fruit, honey. Not a nut." Clermont was not only used to Stella; he loved her, and wasn't insulted. "And unless you're not telling me something, you'll only be gone for two days. He'll be fine. We'll bond over your absence."

After he'd given Stella a big hug, and a sip of his martini for good luck, they carried their stuff down the stairs to Stella's old green Pathfinder and tossed it into the back seat.

As Lucky climbed in on the driver's side, she heard her grandmother muttering, "Ozzy'll have my head for not taking it through the car wash before we head out." It was always a bad sign when Stella started talking about Grandpa Oswald in the present tense, and Lucky hoped this trip wouldn't send her over the edge. More than that, she hoped that whatever this job offer was about, it would mean she wouldn't have to put Stella into some publicly funded home.

"Alright, we're off!" Lucky tried to sound cheerful as she turned the key.

"Jesus, why are you making such a big deal about this?" Stella said. "We go get groceries every week."

"Grandma, we're going to the States, remember? We brought our passports." Lucky backed out onto the street.

"Right, right," Stella replied. "I *know*. Massachusetts. So you can see someone about a job. I know where we're going." She sounded testy now.

"Right. Sorry." Lucky turned onto the main road that would lead them to the highway they would take south and east.

"Did Jinx seem sad to you when we left?" Stella was biting the thin skin around her nails.

"He looked fine. He's probably pissing in my shoes as we speak."

"That's because you hate him and he knows it," Stella responded. "You don't hide your shit all that well."

Lucky concentrated on the road and tried not to read too much into things. She wanted this trip to be fun for Stella, especially if their little family had to be broken up after it was over. She used her cheerful voice: "I heard the world's smallest church is just outside of Syracuse. We can stop there on the way."

"Do I have time for a nap?"

"Yeah. I'll wake you up when we get to the border crossing at Niagara Falls."

Stella leaned against the window. "I hate Niagara Falls. Makes me have to pee."

CROSSING THE BORDER WENT ABOUT as well as could be expected with a senile senior who made inappropriate jokes about being kidnapped and couldn't remember if she had ever been to the States before, let alone when. The agent took Stella in stride, though, and they had passports and vaccination certificates, no priors, and nothing weird in the car except for themselves. Once they were onto the interstate, Stella fell asleep again, waking with a start about an hour into New York State. "Let's stop for the night—I wanna watch TV."

"Can't you just listen to the radio for a bit?" Lucky wanted to make a little more distance. "I don't want to be late for the meeting tomorrow."

"What is this, 1952? I don't want the radio, I want to watch TV. We have options now, you know." She crossed her arms over her chest. She got surly at night, more confused than in daylight hours.

Lucky sighed. "Okay, look, we're close to Rochester. We'll find a place there. Does that work?"

"I guess. You know, Ozzy's not gonna like that we left him behind. He likes road trips. We used to take them all the time when we were younger." She giggled a bit. "They used to make him all romantic."

"I don't need details," Lucky cut in. She definitely did not want details. Sometimes she got them anyway, like when Stella explained that after her grandfather passed on, she stopped cleaning the floor, because that was one of their games, him "walking in" on her down on her hands and knees, scrubbing away. Lucky never pushed her to help with the floors again. Maybe that had been Stella's plan all along.

Her grandmother kept on talking. "We would drive to some small place and hole up in a motel for a few days, checking out the local sights even if there were none. Shopping in another town's Walmart makes you feel like Indiana Jones. God, I love Indiana Jones. You ever watch those movies, Luck, the old ones, with the hat and the whip?"

Lucky turned on the radio to drown her out. Twenty minutes later they pulled into a Red Roof Inn on the outskirts of the city. Stella complained that there were no parking spots right by the rooms—"I like to see my car from the window." But once she kicked off her tennis shoes, pulled off her pantyhose, and settled on the bed with the TV remote, she seemed just fine.

"I'm going to go get us some snacks from the 7-Eleven across the way," Lucky told her. She paused at the door, raising her voice and enunciating so she wouldn't be ignored. "Do not go anywhere."

"Yeah, yeah, where am I gonna go? I don't even have shoes on!"

"Well, where'd you go last week in your socks, eh? Down to the corner store for smokes."

"So?"

"You don't smoke!" Lucky shook her head, closing the door with a bang. Out in the hallway, she immediately felt bad. This was maybe their last adventure together, and it was turning into *The Odd Couple* on the road.

"Dammit." She stuffed both hands into her jacket pockets and found a skinny joint. She must have put it there months ago and forgotten about it. Thank god she hadn't been searched at the border.

She held it up and gave it a quick kiss. This was exactly what she needed right now. She went to the end of the hallway and opened the heavy glass door to the parking lot.

She breathed deep, appreciating the moment of solitude. Silence in an outdoor space had a presence instead of an absence. She blew out and watched her breath condense in the cool night air. She looked around the half-filled parking lot, picked a spot on a concrete curb lit by the orange glow of a pole light, and sat.

She lit the joint and took a pull. "Oh, gross!"

It was stale and half tobacco. Still, after a moment, it started to do its job. She felt her shoulders relax and settled into a long lean, watching the navy night.

She was actually doing this. *Was* she actually doing this? True, so far they had only made it, like, three hours into their nine-hour journey to Salem, and, yes, she was still refusing to consider the concrete steps that would take Stella from her lifelong apartment into some other kind of care, but she was definitely at the beginning of doing this. She had an appointment at VenCo tomorrow.

Never had something felt so good and so horrible at the same time. And yet she couldn't help but think there was something deeply romantic about this. She was finally focused: not like Stella, always off on the next weird tangent, not like Arnya, always rushing after the next man or the next gig. This time, for once, Lucky was going for herself. She was going to take the leap. She was already mid-air.

When she went back to the room, she was lighter from the weed and heavy with snacks. She hadn't been able to decide on salt or sugar, so she'd grabbed a good cross section of both: chips, pretzels, chocolate, chocolate with peanut butter, chocolate with almonds, gummy bears . . .

"Ready to eat?" she called as she unlocked the door and pushed it open.

The lights were off. The TV was still on, but the beds were empty.

"Grandma?"

She stepped inside and let the door close behind her. No one by the window.

"Stella?"

She dropped the crinkly snacks onto the first bed, the comforter wrinkled from where her grandmother had sat.

She checked the bathroom. The soap and plastic cups had all been unwrapped, and the towels had been unfolded and rolled into the little sausage shapes her grandmother preferred. No Stella.

"Shit." Lucky went back out into the hall and headed for the lobby.

As she passed the closed doors, she could hear TV news, very loud porn, kids jumping on a bed, someone crying, a man's loud snoring, what sounded like someone practicing karate, and a quiet argument in the tone reserved for breakups. An audio tour of motel life.

The lobby smelled of industrial cleaner. There was no one at the front desk, no one in the little area reserved for guests to gather in front of a TV mounted above an electric fireplace. She took the hallway to the left of the desk to the breakfast area. It was closed with the lights off. Coming back up the hallway, she saw that the clerk had returned.

"Has an elderly woman come this way? I'm looking for my grandmother." Her voice sounded a bit panicked.

The clerk, a woman of about twenty-five with her long hair in two tight French braids, asked, "Do you mean Stella?"

"Yes, that's her!"

"I just opened the pool for her." She smiled and leaned in conspiratorially, her beaded earrings swinging. "It closes at five, but Stella convinced me to give her an hour to swim."

Lucky had never seen her grandmother swim. She didn't know she could swim. God, what if she couldn't swim? "Which way is the pool?"

"Past the breakfast room and through the metal door at the end."

Lucky took off running.

She pushed the door open and entered a quiet, chlorine-filled space. The high ceiling was lit by reflections of the water that wavered like knockoff northern lights. Hands on knees, she caught her breath, looking up just as Stella dove into the pool, curving her body so that she slid along the turquoise-painted bottom and broke the surface with barely a ripple at the halfway mark.

Stella sliced pointed hands through the water in a graceful breaststroke, then treaded water, her limbs moving like pale, wide fish.

"Gram?"

"Hey, Luck. I feel great." She said it as if she had been asked how she was. "I'm good. You should come in."

What the hell was going on? She really shouldn't have smoked up. It was way too much watching her senile granny move with all the grace of a silver-haired mermaid in a motel pool on the side of a lonely American highway.

Stella made her way back towards the deep end, waving the girl on. "Come in."

"No, no, that's okay. I don't have a bathing suit."

"Neither do I," Stella answered, dunking her head back under.

Lucky looked to the side of the pool then and saw a pile of clothes—her grandmother's clothes, big wired brassiere and all.

"Oh no." She shook her head, watching the pale, naked shine of skin as Stella began climbing the ladder. "Oh god, no."

BACK IN THEIR ROOM, ONE of them exhausted from exercise, the other from weed and trauma, they relaxed in front of the TV, sharing small bags of chips. They watched a sitcom about a family living with a robot and then a crime show about detectives working in a Florida city with way too many murders for anyone to think it was normal. By the time the late-night news started, Lucky was passed out, a bag of M&M'S in her hand.

Stella turned the TV off. She got up and removed the M&M'S, then tucked Lucky under the thin blanket. She placed a hand on the girl's chest to feel the rise and fall of her breathing. It was something she'd done when Lucky was smaller, just to be sure. She carried too much stress, this one, even in her sleep.

"I know we have to move," she whispered. And she did. Clermont had told her about the eviction after he got his letter. She forgot about it right away, but every now and then, it came back, the knowledge that she would have to leave her home. She knew that Lucky was trying to protect her, to find a way to make sure they were safe and housed, hopefully together. And that Lucky couldn't bring her into those decisions, because, well, Stella didn't hold information that well anymore. She didn't know when it had started, but she knew it was the truth. Like tonight—she'd been watching TV, trimming her toenails, and the next thing she knew, she was naked, at the edge of a pool.

She watched her granddaughter sleep. She looked so much like her father when she slept. It brought back the good memories of Jerry, before she lost him, before he started breaking into their apartment to steal things to pawn for the drugs that hollowed him out.

She walked to the window and looked out over the parking lot to the headlights passing by on the highway. She felt something gnawing at the blurry edges of her thoughts. Something was changing. She wrapped her arms around herself and squeezed tight, hoping that it would hold her together long enough to make it to whatever end was coming.

THE MOTHER SAT AT THE boardroom table by herself. She hadn't bothered to call in the others. She needed time to think and the freedom to be worried. With the Oracle together, she very often had to be the calming balm in the mix. But today, with the sixth on her way to Salem, she needed to consider everything carefully, and that meant she needed to be worried.

The truth was, the asshole in the desert was more dangerous than anyone could imagine. She wanted to ignore the rumours, to chalk up the texts as old-fashioned hysteria, to boil him down to machismo gone awry. But Jay Christos was Benandanti—the men who hunted at night and sometimes in the dream space—and an immortal one, at that.

Several of the Crone's ancient volumes were splayed on the table in front of her, open to faded line drawings. Illustrations of men in long cloaks gliding over the crops of sleeping farmers; men in seventeenth-century pomp on horseback, chasing hags through the woods; men setting fire to woodpiles with struggling women crying out on top. These were from the before time, before the Inquisition decided anyone who had the power to travel outside of their body—even men who claimed to use it to fight evil for God—were themselves witches. The Benandanti were soon hunted like the women they pursued. Historians said they were hunted to extinction. Actual history saw it differently.

The men went underground and now had both God and

vengeance fueling their mission. Their persecution was because of the witches, and, salt in their holy wounds, they were being called by the same name. Burrowed as they were, hiding in plain sight, they wormed their way through the years, killing anyone who could be a witch—rumour was Jack the Ripper himself was Benandanti, hunting the dark streets of London for powerful women.

After 1913, there were no more sightings, no more talk. It seemed they had well and truly been bred out of existence. The witch community waited to make sure the coast was really clear before forming their own group—VenCo—and starting work on the right to vote. This would be a new era for women and witch-kind. Once again, witches started popping up in proper society, séances became fashionable, and the occult was dinner conservation. But slowly, quietly, the killings continued.

The first Oracle was pulled together with the Mother's own grandmother sitting in the position she now held. She was the one to write down the whispered story of the spoons, to demand a Booker who could read the stars be brought in to help, who turned out to be the mother of the current Crone. It was this grandmother who went missing, only to turn up murdered at the hands of the last remaining Benandanti, one who played by the old rules because he was, in fact, very fucking old—Jay Christos.

The Mother had to make tough decisions—that was part of being a Mother. She had to think of the entire family at all times, before herself, before any one person or cause. The Crone and the Maiden knew about Christos, but they didn't know how he stole sleep from the Mother. How he featured in her nightmares when she did manage to nod off. Just how big a shadow he threw over her life.

And now, knowing that Christos was on the move? Knowing that he was sharp and angry, trained and—most dangerous of all—

having the time of his life hunting? Some days she envied the general public. Today she would have given anything to be a barista or a soccer mom with two mediocre kids. Today it was a very bad day to be a witch. Especially one who alone understood the danger that was slinking around the new coven like a wolf.

10

JAY FINDS THE
WEAK LINK

There were no lights on in the top-floor apartment, hadn't been all night. No movement in the windows. No one came in or walked out. The bitch wasn't home. It was starting to feel like no one in the entire building was home. He considered giving up, but then a woman in a housecoat opened the front door carrying two very full bags of garbage.

Jay sprang from the back seat of the sedan and bounded up the steps.

"Here, let me help you with that," he called out, both gloved hands held up to show that they were empty.

Therese looked up, frowning, to see Jay Christos in all his charismatic glory. Long, sleek hair, black as a raven; smooth skin shadowed around the hard jawline with soft stubble, the kind you wanted to feel on your skin, preferably the inside of your thigh. Eyes, dark and flashing. A starched collar, white shirt, buttons working hard to lay flat against a muscled chest, tailored coat, the flash of a gold watch between a leather glove and a buckled sleeve. Tall enough to need a stepladder, hot enough to get on your knees, and she had one thought.

Money.

And then one more: *Yum.*

She set both bags down, letting her robe fall open. Thank god she was wearing her good nightie, the one that made her feel like Dolly Parton in *9 to 5*, all spit and tit. "What are you? A gentleman or something?"

"Well, we do happen along once in a while." Jay gave a little bow, then picked up her garbage. "Where am I taking these?"

Therese fluffed her short curls. Dammit, why hadn't she gotten Harry to redo her roots yesterday? "Uh, just in the bin at the side there."

Jay hefted the bags into the bin, then came back to her, brushing his hands together. "Okay then, Miss . . ."

"You can call me Therese." She was leaning on the railing now, freckled cleavage held aloft and together by her crossed arms.

"Therese," Jay purred. "You are a tenant here?"

"Main floor. Biggest apartment in the building," she boasted.

"Therese, I was wondering if you could do me a favour?"

"Sure, just give me a minute to send my old man to the store," she said, and cackled. It was a grating sound, like a series of small coughs.

"Oh, you *are* bad, aren't you?" Jay smiled at her so warmly that Therese actually blushed. "I was thinking more that you could help me find someone I'm looking for."

"And here I was hoping you were looking for me."

"Well, this is more of a business matter. I need to deliver some papers to someone whom I think lives in your building, but I'm not sure."

"Legal papers?" Therese loved drama, and in terms of juiciness, legal drama ranked right behind love drama.

"I'm afraid I can't say," he demurred, managing to imply that she was completely on the mark.

"Okay, Mr. You've Been Served, who is it you're tracking down? The fruit on the second floor? He seems like the type who would be getting sued, probably over his big mouth." She glared up at the window above them, where velvet drapes were pulled tight.

"I am looking for a St. James, actually."

"Miss or Mrs.?"

There were two of them? Well, one was sure to lead to the other. "Lucky. But either will do, actually."

"They live on the third floor, but I haven't seen them lately. Still, why don't you come in and try knocking? Top of the stairs. I'll take you."

This one was going to be hard to shake. "That's very kind of you. Please, lead the way."

Therese did her best shake and shimmy up the first flight but was breathing hard by the second landing. Jay followed close behind, sniffing the air as they went. There was no indication of a witch nearby. He needed this ridiculous woman to get out of his way, and soon, but he maintained his composure.

At the top of the stairs was a single door. Breathing hard, Therese staggered over and knocked. "Stella, hun? You in? Lucky?"

In a stage whisper, Therese said to him, "Ridiculous name, right? Her mother was quite the character. Dead now, but she was a honky-tonk bar on legs, let me tell you." She knocked again, calling, "Stella?"

Still no answer.

She turned back to Jay, a hand on her hip, looking him up and down. "Maybe you wanna leave a message for them?"

He was on her before she could draw breath, pushing her up against the door, his palms flat against the wood on either side of her head. "What I want, Therese, is for you to go back to your apartment and . . . What is the name of your *old man?*"

"H . . . Harry," she gasped.

"Harry, right. So I want you to go down to your apartment and find Harry and pull up that nightie." He moved a hand down her body to her hem and lifted it an inch or two with one finger. "And I want you to sit on him."

Her nipples were suddenly at full attention, tenting the fabric at alarmingly different angles.

"Do you understand, Therese?" he cooed, his breath warm on her skin. "I want you to sit your pretty ass right on his face."

"Mmm-hmmm." She nodded.

"You'll do that for me?"

She nodded more emphatically. "Uh-huh."

"Good girl." He stepped back, turned her around, and gave her ass a sharp slap. She moaned in response, then shivered violently.

"Fine, then, thank you for your help today." His voice was formal, his smile polite. "I appreciate it."

"Sure, sure thing, you're welcome." She smiled back, her eyes hectic. "You okay to show yourself out? I need to go . . ."

She wasn't sure why, but she was frantic. If she didn't see Harry right this minute, she was going to stop breathing. Embarrassed, she clutched the sides of her robe and belted it closed. What was she even doing on the third floor?

"You have a great day," Jay called after her as she ran down the stairs. He waited until he heard her door slam shut behind her. Then he pulled a pick out of his coat pocket and fiddled with it until the lock popped open.

He took off his shoes just inside the door. After all, he didn't want to be rude. He was a contemporary man but with very old manners. "Little witch, little witch, let's see where I might find you."

AFTER GOING THROUGH LUCKY'S SOCIAL media on her unlocked laptop, Jay Christos stood outside You Ought to Be in the Movies. He'd followed a likes-and-comments spiral to a boy. There was always a boy. And thank god for that. Boys could be moved easily around the board.

Jay opened the door, and the bells hanging from the spring stayed silent. He wrinkled his nose at the smell of mold, the warp of the wood. He preferred new buildings and for all things to have exact angles. Too many years in the melt and creak of old Europe had given him very specific preferences. This entire store was upsetting to him at a cellular level.

There was a wide man in the far corner with his back to him, wearing a puffy set of headphones, humming under his breath while he stocked the magazine rack. Jay inhaled long and thoughtfully. This wasn't him.

The boy he was looking for was an illustrated man—tattooed across his hands—Jay had gotten that much from his Instagram page. Which was either passionate expression or poor judgement. Either way, Jay would find an angle. He liked exact angles. They made sense.

Then the right boy walked through the backroom door and stood behind the counter. When he passed his hand through his hair, there were letters below his knuckles. Jay inhaled, picking up the distinct scent of frustration, the kind borne of jealousy and selfishness. He smiled. This was going to be fun.

"Good day, sir," Jay began, bowing a bit from the waist. "I was wondering if I could trouble you for a bit of guidance?"

Malcolm jumped. He hadn't heard anyone come in. He hadn't seen anyone when he came out. Even now it was like there was no one else there.

"Shit, sorry, dude." He put a hand on his chest. "You scared me."

Jay smiled. "I'm known for my stealth, which isn't always a good thing."

"What can I help you with today?" Malcolm was nervous. The kind of nerves he usually got around beauty or authority. This man was something entirely different, or else an uncanny combination of both.

"I'm looking for the work of Kenneth Anger," Jay said. "Is that something I could find here?" He knew it was.

"Yeah, we have the *Magick Lantern Cycle*, for sure."

"Can you show me, please? I'm afraid of getting lost in this maze." The store was small; you could see the entire width and breadth of it from the counter.

"This way." Malcolm walked quickly to the front of the store, with the man close behind. He grabbed *Magick Lantern Cycle* off the shelf like a relay baton, thrusting it between them.

Jay took it, one finger at a time tapping the cover, his pinky overlapping the boy's thumb. "Ah, yes, perfect. I have an interest in the cross section Anger works in."

"Esoteric and surreal?" Malcolm asked, hesitating before pulling his hand back.

"Occultism and the homoerotic."

Malcolm flushed deep red, and Jay went in for the kill. "What time do you get off work?"

AT ONE O'CLOCK IN THE morning, Malcolm sat on his couch, watching his hands clench and unclench. His hands seemed to know what had happened, even though he himself did not.

They'd gone to Kensington Market, an old neighbourhood tucked in behind Chinatown. The bar they went to was narrow and crowded. He thought maybe he'd been there with Lucky before, or maybe he was just thinking that because that was where their conversation had gone—to Lucky.

He was drinking shots, which he never did, not until he'd had enough beer to make him forget he didn't drink shots. Wait . . . how had they gotten there? In a car, a black car. He also wasn't sure how he'd gotten home. Which was odd, because he really wasn't that drunk.

The man—Jay—talked to everyone in the bar, and they, in response, fawned all over him. And for some reason, Malcolm hadn't liked that.

They'd stayed for longer than he wanted. But his feet were heavy when he tried to lift them. The opposite was happening with his arms, which lifted easily to carry alcohol to his mouth. He remembered the man's breath smelled of black licorice.

He put his hands over his face and rubbed his skin vigorously. "Come on, Malcolm. What the fuck happened?" He fished around in his pockets for his phone. It was dead.

He had a sudden urge to text Lucky. But to say what? They hadn't parted on great terms. In fact, their last interaction had been a short text exchange.

> Lucky, I really want to talk. Can we meet up?

Headed to Salem. Might not be back.

> Why?

Why not?

He had the feeling that he'd betrayed her tonight, but he couldn't quite remember.

He stalked off to his bedroom, but he couldn't lie down. He stripped off his clothes, smelling each piece, searching for the scent of black licorice. *What was the man's name again?* He needed a clue to this fear and loathing that was wreaking havoc on his guts. He rubbed his flat stomach. That felt better, soothing, comforting. Nice easy circles with a light touch of skin on skin. The curtains were open, and the streetlight shone into the room.

Naked now, at the foot of his bed, his tattoos livid against his pale skin, he was suddenly overcome with lust. It was the kind of lust that shot blood and want into every part of a body; the kind of lust that came with a warning sign—THIS IS A BAD IDEA—so you only needed it more. He grabbed his cock, already stiff, and the heat of his hand brought him fully to attention. His head lolled back so that he was staring at the yellow streetlight streaking across his cracked ceiling.

"Oh godddd . . ."

It didn't take long. He was soft and slow with himself and then hard and fast. And when he was done, his stomach unclenched. His head emptied of anxiety and instead filled with the slow slur of alcohol. Suddenly he was drunk. Suddenly he was ready for bed.

Lying spread-eagle in his queen-sized bed, under a single sheet, with a pleasant throb in his groin, he tried but couldn't really remember the night. There was a man, he thought, maybe someone he just met? Maybe someone he knew once? But then he thought, no, there was only a series of strangers and a steady line of shots. He could really use some company tonight. He should plug in his phone and call the redhead he met last week. Lulled by booze and orgasm, he fell asleep.

11

FEAST DAY

The house was clapboard painted matte black with shiny black trim, from the shutters to the gingerbread over the covered porch. Maybe it was the layers of black, or the depth of the porch, but the front door didn't seem to get any closer as Lucky climbed the stairs.

She hesitated on the fourth step and turned around. "C'mon, Stella," she called.

Her grandmother was still at the car, straightening her kerchief, using the tinted window as a mirror. They'd come straight here, not having had time to check in to the motel. "I said I didn't want to be late!"

"Keep your shirt on, I'm coming." Stella straightened and stared at her granddaughter. "But I don't know why you want me in there."

"Actually, that's a good point." Lucky tossed the keys, and they landed in the grass at Stella's feet. "Why don't you wait in the car." At least she wouldn't have to explain why she had an elderly chaperone at a job interview.

"I'm a senior citizen, for fuck's sakes!" Stella said, making a big show of the effort it took to bend over to retrieve them. "But I'm listening to the radio. You can't stop me."

"Why would I stop you?" Lucky swept the street with her eyes in case anyone was witnessing this elder abuse ruse.

Keys in hand, Stella straightened up smoothly and went around to the driver's side, got in, and slammed the door shut behind her. Soon she had the radio cranking.

With her grandmother safe in the car, Lucky climbed the last step and crossed the porch to the door. Beside it was a small brass plaque engraved with a single word, *VenCo*, over a doorbell embedded in a black curlicue frame. She took a deep breath. "Here we go." She pushed the button but heard nothing. Maybe it was broken? She was about to try it again when the door was opened by the woman from the food court, wearing a chic black suit.

"Lucky. Come through." The woman turned, smooth as a dancer in street shoes.

"Freya, how nice to . . ." But Freya was already walking away. "Alrighty, I'll just get the door, then."

She followed, taking in the grey flocked wallpaper, the feminine curve of the staircase, lined with portraits of women who seemed to watch her pass, the ceiling that soared two storeys. Above her, small birds hopped from stem to swag of a massive crystal chandelier, singing freely.

"Ummm, your birds have gotten loose."

"They're not my birds." Freya shrugged, still walking.

Lucky quickened her pace. When she caught up, she whipped out her professional office voice and tried to make a good impression. "So how long have you worked here?"

Freya's stare stitched Lucky to the high-gloss hardwood beneath her boots. "We don't need to talk," she said. "I'm not the one who decides if you're in. I was just the recruiter. Meena Good is the head of this . . . office. You'll be meeting with her."

Head down now, Lucky trailed her into a wide hallway inset with alcoves holding shelves of books and jars and statues. The runner carpet that muted their steps was deep green and patterned with striped snakes slithering in all directions.

"Whoa, wouldn't want to walk over this thing high," Lucky blurted. *Nice. Bring up weed at the first meeting. Good move, St. James.*

"Wait till you see the garden." Freya smiled.

They stopped in front of a rounded door at the end of the hall. Freya rapped lightly before entering. "Meena, your guest is here." Then she sashayed away without another word.

Meena Good sat behind a massive desk in a tall chair upholstered in blood-red leather. She was backlit by a triptych of curved windows that matched the rounded door. "Hello, Miss St. James. A pleasure to have you join us. How was your journey here?"

"Since I was travelling with a seventy-seven-year-old, it was like mapping a route from one restroom to the next." *And now I'm talking about pee breaks. Awesome.*

Meena laughed. "Yes, near the end, my father was a difficult passenger. He could barely make it to church on Sunday, and he was the minister." She stood, and Lucky saw how tall she was—statuesque, in a cream silk blouse and oatmeal wool slacks, a wide silver clasp bracelet on each wrist to match the rings on her long, elegant fingers. "I am glad you brought your Elder with you." She closed a book on her desk and added it to a small stack of hardcover notebooks.

"Oh, you saw her?" How the hell had she seen Stella? Maybe she'd heard her? "I had care issues."

Meena smiled. "Elders are invaluable, and she is most welcome."

Lucky didn't know what to say next. As the silence stretched, she felt more and more awkward. Here she was, at what was beginning to feel like Hogwarts, Massachusetts, standing in front of a beautiful woman who was paying eerily close attention to her, and wilting under the scrutiny. Fuck it, she decided, just ask.

"So how does this work exactly? Is the publisher in town here or . . . ?"

Meena came around to sit on the edge of her desk but didn't offer Lucky a chair. "We can worry about all that later. Why don't you get settled? I'll tell you more about the position after you've both rested and we've had dinner."

"Right, I should have checked in to the motel and changed." She was suddenly self-conscious. "We ran out of time."

"Motel? No, you misunderstood. We're putting you up here. We have a suite all ready for you and your grandmother." Meena smiled.

"Here?" Lucky looked around, her eyes caught by a mounted deer head draped in a cascading crystal necklace, dangly earrings looped through what appeared to be pierced ears. Underneath it was a glass curio cabinet laden with old manuscripts. "In this house?"

"This is my office, but it's also our home, my wife, Wendy, and me. Often others stay. Right now, there are five of us here—seven with you and Stella."

How did she know her grandmother's name? Had she mentioned it? *God, this could be a nightmare.* She imagined Stella wandering around in her pajamas looking for where they kept the cereal. "Are you sure? I don't want to put you out."

"Freya's gone to retrieve your grandmother from the car and will get her settled. Why don't you go relax for a bit? We'll all meet for dinner at, let's say, seven o'clock?" Meena stood, and Lucky understood the meeting had concluded.

"Okay, then. Thank you. Um, is she . . . ? Are you . . . ? I'm not sure where our room is."

"Go down the hall, turn right, up the stairs, and you'll find it." Meena was already back in her chair, head down, opening a heavy book.

"Okay, then, thank you."

Outside once more on the snake carpet, Lucky was quite sure she would not find her room. She wasn't even sure she could find her way back to the front door. There was something arterial about the hallways; they felt shifting and alive. She turned at the only right she saw, which opened into another hallway. There were no windows here. Instead, the light came from sconces shaped like ship figureheads, each holding a tapered bulb of yellow light, set at equal distance above dark wainscoting. This wasn't Wayfair shit. They felt bespoke and very old.

All the doors along the corridor were closed, except for one that opened onto a solarium, draped green with hanging plants and climbing vines and striped with late-afternoon sun. At last she heard birds singing and stepped into front foyer. It wasn't until she took a deep breath that Lucky realized she'd been holding it.

"Well," she said to the birds, quiet now and watching her, their bright heads tilted. "Nowhere to go but up, I suppose."

The steps were wide and plush. As she climbed, she had the feeling she was under surveillance, and sure enough, a canary had fluttered over to follow her up the stairs, peeping at her disturbance. "Judgy asshole," she whispered. "At least I'm not shitting on the hardwood."

With a series of small hops, the bird turned its back to her and twitched its hind feathers, dropping a white turd.

Startled, she laughed. "Well played!"

The top of the stairs opened onto a mezzanine that wrapped all the way around the second floor, overlooking the foyer. A dozen doors led to a dozen rooms. Stairs led up from opposite corners. Was there a third floor? She hadn't noticed from the outside. The interior was like origami—neat folds and creases hiding the actual size.

How was she supposed to figure out which room was hers? She pictured accidently walking in on Freya, who would likely hiss at her like an angry blond cat. She eyed each door, looking for a hint. And then she got it.

"*Oooooh, baaa-by, you—you got what I neee-eeed.*" Stella Luna, singing at the top of her lungs, the sound pouring from under the door right in front of her.

She found her grandmother, using a hairbrush as a microphone, sliding across the floor in her white socks, barely missing the twin bed and the turquoise bachelor's chest topped with a frameless etched mirror.

"Grandma." No response. "Grandma!"

Stella spun around, took a deep breath, and wailed: "*But you say he's just a friend. Ooooh, baaaa-by . . .*"

Lucky snatched the brush as if it were an actual mike. "Listen, can you be normal for a minute? Jesus. I'm trying to get a job here."

She tossed the brush onto the bed beside Stella's suitcase, open and spilling out pantyhose and colourful sweaters.

The window was open, too, and the breeze, carrying the smell of green, billowed the gauzy white drapes. The walls were painted a light sand, and the bedspread was a quilt made of muted multi-coloured patches.

"Hey, Ma used to have one of these." Lucky ran a hand over

the bed's bumpy surface. "She got it from her mom. God, I can't remember. Did we bring it with me after . . . ?"

"It's a starblanket," a voice interjected, causing both Stella and Lucky to jump. They hadn't heard anyone approach. "That one was made by my great-auntie Flora."

A woman wearing a friendly smile leaned in the doorway. Her long hair was streaked with grey and looped up in a messy bun. She wore black jeans rolled up to her calves and a sage-green peasant blouse with the ties hanging loose.

"I'm Wendy," she said, hand outstretched. Lucky shook it first, then Stella, who threw in an extra pump in honour of the way the Three Stooges closed business deals. "I didn't mean to startle you, but you must be Lucky and Stella."

"Yes, that's us. Sorry, my grandmother, sometimes she's a bit loud."

"What, you're supposed to whisper songs?" Stella was indignant.

"You should always give'r when you sing," Wendy said, smiling at the old lady. "I just came to make sure you found your room okay. And, Lucky, here's yours." She crossed the space to a door they hadn't noticed, because it looked just like the wall, complete with a watercolour sketch of ships at sea hanging on it. "Here you are." She pushed on the top corner, and the door popped open.

Lucky walked through and into the next room. Her space was a little bigger than her grandmother's, but it too had a twin bed and a chest of drawers. It also held a small round table and a lion-footed chair embroidered with purple violets. The walls were deep blue like the waves in the ship sketch.

"Perfect, this is perfect," Lucky said. "I appreciate you making room for my grandmother and me with no notice."

"Nonsense." Wendy waved her off, opening the long grey panel curtains to let in the sun. "I had your rooms made up yesterday. It was no trouble at all. Meena told you about dinner?"

Lucky was confused. How had they known Stella was coming? Had she told them and forgotten? She just nodded. "Dinner . . . seven o'clock, right?"

"Great. I'll see you both then."

After she left, Stella came to check out Lucky's view of the back-yard, which was full of flowering trees strung up with round bulb lights. "Well, she was great. Of course, lesbians usually are."

"Jesus, Stella, you can't say things like that." If Stella heard, she didn't let on.

"Well, I'm gonna get some sleep. You should too—you look like shit," the old woman shot over her shoulder as she sauntered back to her own room.

"Thanks, man." Lucky closed the door behind her grandma and wished there was a lock to keep her out.

"Fuck me," she said with a sigh, throwing herself onto the bed. "What am I doing?"

HER PHONE WOKE HER UP at six-thirty. That left just enough time to wash up and get dressed for dinner. She was about to go make sure Stella was awake and help her pick out something not-insane to wear. Then it occurred to her, maybe it was better if she just let her sleep so that she didn't have to deal with elder care while she was also trying to impress potential new employers. Quietly, she slipped into the small bathroom and flicked on the light.

The room was tiny—a stand-up shower just big enough to turn around in, a toilet, and an old sink. There were no cabinets, so she balanced her face wash, toothbrush, and toothpaste on a narrow glass shelf above the sink. Then she stared at her face in the round mirror, at the dark circles under her eyes, her chapped lips and bed-head.

When she'd done her best to make herself clean and presentable, she got dressed in a thin black sweater, black jeans, and ballet slip-ons. Good enough, unless these women dressed for dinner. Oh god, they seemed like the kind of people who got dressed for dinner. She hadn't brought anything fancier, though, so pulling her hair back in a sleek low ponytail and applying red lipstick would have to do. She dumped the contents of her pencil case, where she kept her meagre jewelry collection, onto the bed.

Some silver rings, a pair of beaded earrings, a pearl barrette she had never worn and would never wear but couldn't throw out, a couple of silver bangles, the spoon she couldn't seem to be without, and the worthless brooch made of coloured stones set in brass that Arnya used to wear when she wanted to be "all extra." Probably swiped it from a thrift store. Or straight off the jacket of an old lady who'd passed out at the bar—Lucky wouldn't put it past her. Still, it reminded her of Arnya, and memories of Arnya made her feel strong. She wrenched open the stiff pin and stuck it into the elastic that held her hair back and clipped it shut.

Just as she was about to leave, she grabbed her phone and the spoon and slipped them into her back pockets. She leaned to put an ear to Stella's door. Loud, even snores carried through the wood. Perfect. She was free from obligation and looking as fly as she could after six hours on the road.

Freya was waiting at the bottom of the stairs, still dressed in her impeccable suit. Lucky was relieved—at least it wasn't a fucking cocktail dress.

"Hey." Lucky smiled at her.

Once again, Freya just turned and walked away, and once again Lucky assumed she was to follow.

"So, Freya's a pretty name. Does it run in your family?"

"No, I got it from a book on pagan goddesses."

Lucky had to jog to keep up. "You named yourself? What was it before?"

"Matthew." She stopped then and turned to Lucky, wrinkling her forehead. "Do you think I should have just gone with Susan or Mary or something old-school? I considered Esther for a while."

"I like Freya. Goddess of beauty and rebirth. It's as old-school as it gets."

Lucky had earned an actual meeting of the eyes. "Agreed." Freya extended a red-tipped nail, pointing to Lucky's chest. "You can sit beside me."

Lucky smiled. The thaw had begun.

They turned left down a narrow hall that opened into a huge room with vaulted ceilings. Now it was Lucky who stopped walking.

One wall was covered by a muted mural. A woman, naked and pale, rose from the treetops of a night forest as if she were being drawn towards the moon, which was spread in all its phases across the sky. The opposite wall was all glass, framed by huge swags of black curtain held back by gold tasseled ropes, and looked out on an overgrown garden riotous with twisted greenery.

Meena sat at the head of a huge wooden table that groaned with tiered serving platters of fruit and grilled vegetables and platters of chicken and a ham and what appeared to be a rabbit. Mismatched crystal goblets reflected the light from a massive chandelier in the shape of a tall ship, sailing between the rafters and the feast. Wendy sat at the other end of the table, and two more women, striking strangers, were already in their chairs and looking expectantly her way.

"Jesus Christ." It slipped out before Lucky could stop it.

"Oh, he has nothing to do with this," Freya said, leading her to her place.

"Welcome, Lucky," Meena said, looking regal in a lush green turban, gold earrings hitting her shoulders. "We are so happy you could join us."

"Stella isn't coming?" Wendy turned towards the door, looking for the old woman. She actually seemed disappointed.

"Uh, no," Lucky said. "She's still sleeping. The trip really took it out of her."

Freya slid into her seat and pulled out the chair beside her.

Lucky sat, then struggled to shift the heavy chair closer to the table, its wooden legs screeching on the stone floor. "This is really amazing, this place," she offered nervously.

"Yes, we think so too," Meena answered. She cast a glance around the table. "Let me introduce you to the two people you haven't had a chance to meet yet." She started with the person nearest to her, a woman with an angular black haircut and intricate eyeliner.

"Morticia is from New York City. She is a rare-book collector and has a fine arts background.

"Next to her is Lettie."

Lettie nodded to Lucky, her smile sweet and slow.

"She hails from Abita Springs, Louisiana, and has a young son who is already in bed. You'll meet him tomorrow—he really is the most remarkable child. Lettie carries these beautiful old Creole stories from her family."

"You've already met Wendy, my wife. She is a historian and an excellent researcher. Freya, beside you, is our most recent addition. She's from small-town Ohio, and we're trying to convince her to go on to university now. She has quite the knack for languages."

As Lucky was wondering, once again, what she was doing here among all these talented people, Meena put her on the spot. "And you, Lucky? Tell us about you."

She wished she could slide out of her chair onto the floor, but cleared her thoat. "Lucky St. James. Uh, from Toronto . . . Canada. I live with my grandma, also a remarkable child who is in bed right now."

This got a few laughs, and she relaxed a bit.

"She's, ah, well, her name is Stella and she's seventy-seven. She's my dad's mom. I'm hardworking and always show up. I don't think I've ever taken a sick day. Mostly because I've never been sick."

Wendy patted the back of her hand. "Relax, dear—this is dinner, not an interview. I'm from Canada as well, though I'm not Canadian exactly. I'm Anishinaabe, so more pre-Canada and post-Canada. I gather your mother was also Indigenous?"

Lucky gave a quick nod, thinking about how Arnya used to say, *I'm Ab-original and an original, in every fuckin' sense of the word.*

Wendy smiled. "So you're with friends, and family, in a way. Now tell us, what are you passionate about?"

There was a pause that verged on awkward. Then she blurted out, "Writing." It felt like a lie. "I'm a . . . writer."

"Scribes are important. We need one of those," Meena boomed. "All hail the Scribe!" She raised her glass of red wine, and everyone did the same. Lucky fumbled about for her own and laughed as she toasted a dream she hadn't yet realized. The sudden potential of it was intoxicating.

As they began to pass the platters around, Meena talked about growing up in Salem, the daughter of a pastor. Morticia talked about New York City, where she said the hipsters had washed out all the grit so that there was nothing left but photo backdrops. Lettie explained a little about her degree in computer science with the kind of passion an artist reserved for their work.

The only uncomfortable note was when Wendy leaned in to ask Lucky about her mother's community. "It's near the Bay, right? Those old Métis communities have some amazing musicians." Lucky didn't want to admit that her mother had never taken her out of the city. She was ashamed of the disconnect.

After the crème brûlée had been cracked and the tea had been poured, Meena stood. "Gratitude to the cook," she said, nodding towards Wendy, and everyone cheered. "And now I think we need to truly welcome Lucky—to our home, to this table, and to the circle."

The room fell quiet, threads of conversation wrapped back around a spool of singular attention, the clatter of cups and forks carefully muffled. All eyes were on Meena, who reached into the pocket of her pants and pulled out a small silver spoon, which she placed on the table in front of her. Morticia stood next, opening her fist to reveal a similar silver spoon, which she also placed in front of her. Lettie lowered her spoon by the tips of her slender fingers onto her placemat, followed by Wendy. Finally, with a scrape of her wooden chair, Freya got to her feet and put her spoon on the empty plate in front of her.

Lucky's eyes went from one spoon to the next—all the same size, all with the letters spelling out *SALEM* down the handle. The women, still standing, waited quietly as she tried to take in what she was seeing. At last, like an automaton conducted by shock, Lucky got to her feet, leaning on the table to keep herself steady. Then she straightened, pushing her shoulders back to stand tall, reached into her own back pocket, and took out her spoon, the one she had found in the basement tunnel, the one she had been carrying ever since. She placed it in front of her, the small clink of silver against the porcelain edge of her saucer ringing like a bell.

Later, that tolling, as if of a bell, would sound in her memory, marking the separate halves of her life being stitched together: the time before she knew and the time after. The click and pull of metal through velvet time; the slip and stretch of material moments around that ecclesiastical clang. When it echoed to a conclusion, Lucky was, for the first time, both completely pulled together and completely torn apart.

Then, one by one, the women sat. Freya had to guide Lucky back into her chair.

"Could someone please tell me what the fuck is going on?" Lucky asked.

Meena leaned in so that her gaze took in the entirety of the table. "Let's begin with a story."

12

THE FIRST SPOON

M eena wasn't surprised to learn she had been chosen to play the lead in *The Witch Women of Salem Town*. She was a natural— an actual descendant of one of the original Salem witches. She was also an experienced singer and actor to boot: summer theatre camp, a chorus role in *Annie*, and an ongoing position in the First Baptist Church of the Savior choir. Never mind the naysayers and the try-hards who complained that her box braids weren't period appropriate. She'd suggested that perhaps their mediocrity wasn't appropriate.

As she walked home from the community theatre, the sun pushed out from behind the clouds and filled the street with light. The heat and the rush she felt from her successful audition cleared the stress she'd been carrying lately—that something was wrong at home, that she was forgetting something important, that maybe a tumor was growing in her left lung. There was just the sun and the sidewalk and the fact that she had come out on top.

"This is good. This is right. I am exactly where I should be, doing exactly what I should be doing," she repeated over and over under her breath.

Meena was going to be an actress and not just in *The Witch Women of Salem Town*. She was going to Broadway. Or LA. Or wherever the best opportunities were waiting for her. And she was finally old enough to make a move without asking her father for permission. The Reverend Josiah Good couldn't stop her this time. He would have a lot of say, for sure, but now she wasn't legally obligated to listen.

She'd done her time. After her mother died, she'd helped with her little brother, cleaned the house, and typed up her father's sermons for almost a decade. Now it was her turn. And she was ready. Once the play was through its run, she was hitting the road.

She didn't want to go straight home, where this shine might wear off under the pressure of chores and regular life. Instead, she detoured into the old part of town and just wandered.

The historic district had become Tourist Town, but unlike some of the locals, Meena didn't mind. Tourists were good for the economy. And they were good for her self-esteem. Her father may not want to shout from his pulpit about their connections with the accused witches, but these people drove for hours and lined up outside the House of Seven Gables just to get a glimpse of her history. She was proud of it. At sixteen, she'd even gotten a summer job at the Witch House, eager to make some extra cash, but her father found out and forced her to resign.

"You don't need to be seen working at that place. What would my parishioners think?" he had blustered.

"That your daughter is hardworking and involved in her community?" She refused to eat the dinner she had cooked and set out on the table.

"Let them see that in the church, then—you can take charge of this year's fall food drive."

"I've been in charge of the food drive since I was nine. Maybe I want something different."

"Tradition is good," he said, turning his full attention to the food on his plate. He always ended arguments with silence instead of shouts. It was just as effective. You couldn't argue with silence.

"Exactly," she said, "tradition is good." She got up to scrape her plate into the garbage.

She headed over to the Derby Street area, a series of small stone squares filled with witchy stores and cheesy tourist attractions. It made her happy to see the wooden ship busts fixed to the lampposts and the crowds of people browsing the five-dollar spell bags. Maybe she'd buy herself something—a small token to remember today. But first, she grabbed a lemonade from a street cart and sat on a bench to people-watch, something she'd read that every great actor should spend her time doing.

A shadow fell on her, blocking out the sun.

"Twenty-five years, that's when you have to start."

A woman in a long green dress stood over her, her silver hair catching the breeze so that it looked like dark fire against the sun.

"Excuse me?"

"Go to the Burying Point in twenty-five years, and you will begin," the woman said.

Meena looked around, but it was clear the woman was talking to her and no one else. "Do I know you?"

"You will," she replied, with such assurance that Meena started to think she was dealing with someone unhinged. You never could tell around here. Maybe she was a street performer hamming it up, thinking Meena was a tourist.

"Look, my dad is the pastor at First Baptist. I'm not new. I'm not even close to new, so if that—"

"The Burying Point," the woman interrupted. "That's when the first one will be found." She turned and walked quickly away, disappearing into a crowd of camera carriers gathered around the front of the museum.

Meena called after her. "Hey!"

A small child with red hair turned at her voice and stuck out her tongue. Meena returned the gesture.

"Nut job," she muttered.

By suppertime that night, she'd forgotten about the woman and her strange words.

And just as she planned, when her critically acclaimed run in *The Witch Women of Salem Town* was over, she got on a bus headed for California. And she didn't come home to Salem until her father was dying, twenty-four years later.

2015

The funeral was just as Josiah Good would have wanted—a quiet, humble affair devoid of pageantry but full of Jesus. The pews were packed. Every lady wore an Easter-worthy hat over sprayed curls and laid edges. The men wore dark ties and hummed through the sermon. Neither Meena nor her brother, Paul, spoke at the service. Instead, they accepted handshakes and well-wishes and, at the reception, nodded along to stories about the Reverend Good's abundance and grace, his patience, the ways in which he'd enriched the speakers' lives. Rejoice, her father's people said—the Good Lord would have him in His arms by now.

But no one stayed long, maybe not knowing how to reconcile the Meena they remembered—the dutiful teenager or the little girl in pink sundresses—with this tall woman with the shaved head and gold hoop through her septum. No one knew how to carry on a conversation with a woman who ran the Black American Arts Gallery or who had founded the San Francisco chapter of the Lesbian Literary Society. They couldn't deal with the degree to which she occupied space, the fullness of her presence—to them, being too much of anything was too close to being prideful. And the reverend himself had spoken against pride. So they rocked themselves through the service, fanned themselves at the graveside, handed over casseroles at the house, and quickly left.

After Paul and his wife packed up their kids and headed home, Meena was alone in her father's house with the cleaned plates and Saran-wrapped leftovers. That was when she knew he was gone, that there was no one left to be disappointed in her. No more disapproving phone calls. No one left to shock with her "life choices."

She moved through the sparse rooms, with their minimal furnishings and framed religious prints, like a ghost haunting her own past. No room slowed her down. Not one chair tempted repose. The kitchen smelled like dish soap and strangers. She decided that if Paul didn't want the house, she would put it on the market. She didn't want to spend another minute here alone, so she walked right out the back door and through the yard. She slipped through the back gate and into the alley, scaring a cat into dropping the rat it had just caught, which made a clumsy escape, shocked by sudden freedom.

The moon was full, and the streetlamps threw small puddles of light she glided through like a seasoned swimmer. Cars passed like strange fish. She walked until the weight of being weightless began to lift, until the space around her returned to familiar shapes and structures. Past the wax museum, she turned in to a crumbling graveyard, not like the orderly one where her father lay on his first night underground. Presumaby, he was already in the arms of God, just like the people told her, and not in a pine coffin in the cheap suit he had insisted was his best. But all Meena could think of was bones—his bones, her own bones, the way their bones were whittled from the same molecular chalk.

The wind picked up, bringing Meena back to herself. She stopped and looked up at the moon, then around her at the burial grounds bathed in its watery light. She reached for her phone, but her smart black shift didn't have pockets and she'd left her purse at the house—the house she'd left unlocked.

"Oh, for the love of God."

She needed to head back, grab her stuff, lock the doors, and go back to her hotel. There was no way she was staying in her father's house. Paul had offered up a couch, but that wasn't exactly inviting. He had a two-year-old and a new baby, and children were great and all, but also sticky and loud. She'd go back to her room and order room service, then watch something dumb until she fell asleep. And tomorrow she'd wake up when her body wanted her to, not when a toddler decided to put its sticky fingers on her cheeks.

She turned herself around and headed for the entrance, careful not to step on the graves, pulling her heels out when they started to sink into softer ground. Only when something hit her in the side of the face did it occur to her that there could be other dangers here in this old cemetery than a twisted ankle.

"What the hell!" She stopped dead, putting a hand to her cheek.

Now a light blow landed on the back of her head. She swung around, fists raised.

Nothing.

But then she noticed something—it was glinting in the moonlight, dangling from a silvery string looped up in a bent tree. She ducked out of the way as it swung past her. On its return swing, she grabbed it, yanking it free from its tether, which was only a spider web after all. And in her hand was a small silver spoon.

It went from cool to warm in her palm, sucking the heat from her body, leaving her shivering. She turned it over. There were letters and markings. She held it at an angle towards the moonlight and was able to read the single word: *SALEM*.

Carrying the spoon, she hurried through the front gate. Back on the sidewalk she turned to read the white wooden sign—THE BURYING POINT.

She shivered again, and the shiver shifted into a constant tremble. She walked as fast as she could back to the safety of her father's home. Vivid in her mind was the strange woman who'd once told her she was supposed to go to the Burying Point. It had been twenty-five years to the day. And she, according to the woman, had begun.

When she got back to her father's house, she found a woman sitting on the porch swing, her feet dangling. She wore a chic black suit with tailored edges and was smoking a cigarette stuffed into a slim holder. Her hair was silver, and her jewelry was gold.

"Who are you?" Meena asked.

"Sit, chère. I'm here to make sure you know what's coming now that you have found the first Salem Witch Spoon."

Meena squeezed the small souvenir spoon in her hand. How had she known about it? "Listen, I need to know who you are and just what in the hell you're doing on my daddy's porch."

"I am the Crone. The Oracle has sent me."

"The Oracle? What the hell is the Oracle?" But a part of her already knew. Hearing the name felt like déjà vu. "Wait. Is that who came to me twenty-five years ago?"

"That was the previous Crone, my predecessor—one-third of the Oracle." The Crone took a long haul from her cigarette and blew the smoke out with great relish. "Come, asseoir—please." She patted the seat beside her, and Meena sat.

The Crone took a last drag, pulled the butt out of the holder, and tossed it onto the lawn. "We should start. There's so much for you to learn."

"About this spoon from the tree? And how someone knew where and when I'd find it?"

"That one was not so difficult. The date came to Sarah's sister and was recorded in the old stories. And their mother is buried in that cemetery. It was a place that was important to her. So it was just putting two and two together." The Crone rotated her wrist, indicating the ease of the prediction, waving it off as if it were nothing at all.

"Are you a ghost?" Meena asked.

The Crone laughed. "I have been called old, but never so old that I am a ghost."

She fitted a new cigarette into her holder. "But now, down to business. You among the witches have been chosen to reassemble the missing coven."

"Witches? Coven?" Meena was taken aback, but if she were being honest, there was excitement in her surprise. She had that feeling again—*This is good. This is right. I am exactly where I should be, doing exactly what I should be doing.*

"I don't understand . . ."

"We have waited so long, and now it has begun. And you, my love, will see it through. You must find the others now."

"What others?" Meena felt a coolness against her palm and looked down to see she was still holding on to the spoon. "What do I do now?"

The swing started to move. From up and down the street came the barking of dogs and the sound of car alarms going off. A thick rumble was building, thunder low in the sky, vibrating the porch.

"Meena Good of Salem, you have to allow for change, because it is coming. Everything changes. That's how it begins."

The Crone got up and started down the steps. From in front of the house, a car engine turned over. Meena hadn't noticed the vehicle parked there when she arrived. A large man in a leather cap came around the side and opened the back door.

"Wait, that's not an answer. What do I do?" Meena was starting to get scared. Trees shook and leaves fell onto the front lawn. She got to her feet too.

"The Oracle will be in touch. For now, you need to learn, chère. Seek out the Bookers, the Tenders, the Watchers. They will help." She was climbing into the car. "We will send names."

"Wait!" Meena yelled. "How do I find you?"

"The spoons will lead the way to the witches. We are only here to guide, but you have to bring the coven together." The door closed, and the driver got back in, and they drove away.

"I . . . I am exactly where I should be," Meena said to herself, trying to hold on to clarity. "Doing exactly what I should be doing."

She stood alone on the porch while wind shook the street to fury.

13

THE CIRCLE IS THE
STRONGEST SHAPE

What exactly is this?" Lucky picked up her spoon and examined it for the thousandth time. Below the Halloween witch with her straw broom was a single straight pin, pointing towards the bowl. She threw the spoon back down onto the table, and it bounced before settling on the placemat. "Honestly, just tell me what the hell this is all about."

There was a moment of silence. Someone cleared her throat. A glass was lifted and lowered. The women looked at each other and then down at their own spoons. Meena was the one to answer.

"This," she said, drawing the word out as she gestured to the women around the table with her wineglass. "This is a coven."

Lucky laughed. She didn't know that was what she was going to do before the sound jumped up her throat and out her open mouth. "A coven? Like, an actual coven."

"Yes, Lucky St. James. Like an actual coven." Meena smiled wide and knocked back the last of the wine in her glass. She pushed back her chair and stood. "I'll grab us another bottle. This is going to be a long night."

"Where do you think the name VenCo came from? *Ven-co. Coven,*" Freya sneered. "Hiding in plain sight, babe. Just like us."

"My turn, I guess," Morticia interjected, stirring sugar into her tea. "I have a story."

"So, wait, are we going in order of where we're sitting?" Freya cut in. "Or should we go based on when we got our spoons?"

"Freya . . ." Wendy started.

"No, no, Mama W, I don't care. I'm last either way." She slung her legs over one arm of her chair and settled her teacup and saucer on her lap. "I'm just figuring out the formula we're following here."

Wendy smiled at her indulgently, then turned to Morticia. "Tish, love, please, go ahead."

NEW YORK CITY, 2016

Morticia knew that soon she would be Patricia again. More likely, even, Pat.

Her thirtieth birthday was two weeks away, and nobody over thirty was allowed to have hair dyed blue-black and wear six-inch platform boots and still be taken seriously. And since she had never developed an aptitude for computers like other goths, she would also likely find herself unemployed, especially with the bookstore's precarious lease.

"Fucking Pat. How am I going to live as a Pat?" She pulled on her Marlboro. Yet another thing she'd have to give up. "Soon I'll have to get a vape. I'll be fucking Pat who smokes vanilla juice out of a fucking vape." She flicked the butt into a puddle in the alleyway and turned to Bo, who was chewing black polish off his nails. "Just kick my ass now. I would if I could."

"Why are you being so existential?" Bo narrowed his eyes at her and shook his head. "Thirty isn't the end. It's not like it's thirty-five or anything. Christ."

"Easy for you to say." She stomped a boot and anxiously fiddled with the skinny tie knotting the collar of her extra-small uniform shirt, a leftover from her Catholic school days. "You have the Yang family dynasty to fall back on. You're allowed to be morbid and interesting until they bury you in a black marble coffin."

Bo looked down the alleyway, a tunnel to the lights and cars and too many people on the street. "Ooo, you think they'll drop roses over the city as I descend? Like, thorns and all . . . extra thorns. From a helicopter. No, no, from a blimp playing Smiths ballads."

"Roses, really?"

"Yeah, you're right. The Yangs can deal with either the goth thing or the gay thing, but not both at the same time."

"I'm serious here! I'm about to become a suburban housewife named Pat right in front of you. The least you can do is commiserate." She walked over and leaned hard against the brick wall beside him.

"I'm here, I'm commiserating." He slapped her arm lightly, his hand mostly covered by the stretched-out sleeve of his black hoodie. "But wasn't Patricia the name you were born with? You must be used to it on some level."

She growled at him. "Maybe I should just move."

"To where? We live in New York City, Brooklyn even, which is, like, the coolest place on earth. If you can get away with the aged goth spinster thing anywhere, it's here."

Morticia picked at the holes in her fishnets, held together by strategically placed safety pins. "So that's it, then. Game over."

Bo pulled his phone out of his pocket and checked the time. "We got to get back. Just suck it up, at least for the next two and a half hours. You can finish your breakdown when we close. Then we'll pour whiskey on it."

He held out a hand, and after a few seconds, she took it and allowed herself to be guided through the back door and into the familiar dust and shuffle of the store.

Late-summer sun was muscling its way in through the wide front window, filtered by a layer of yellow grime. Gabriel stood behind the antique front desk, his bald head gleaming. "Hey, we got an unpaid drop-off to sort. *Not it!*"

"*Not it!*" Bo echoed. He turned on a delicate heel towards Morticia and scrunched up his face. "Sorry, babe."

She sighed. "Yeah, sure, guys, let me be the one to sort through the trash someone couldn't fit in their recycling bin. Why not?"

And it was sure to be crap. The people who brought in good books didn't donate and dash. They hung around for the assessment and took their cut from the cash register, usually after haggling or whining, neither of which got them anywhere. When faced with a haggler, Morticia would remind them that the Salvation Army on Bushwick was accepting donations, and that usually ended it.

She sighed again. It was turning out to be a breathy kind of day. "You take a look yet?"

"Nope. All yours, M," Gabriel said, head buried in his comic.

"Whatever. Someone help me carry it to the back."

PERCHED ON A HIGH METAL stool with a cup of milky tea, Morticia was almost glad she'd drawn the short straw. She'd put the radio on NPR and closed the door, and the room, crowded with wavering floor-to-ceiling stacks of old paper, was almost cozy.

The banker's box sat on the wooden table in front of her. Good signs—the corners were dry and the loopy cursive writing on the side wasn't smudged or spotted. "'Mrs. L. Shipton,'" she read. "Okay, Mrs. L. Shipton, let's hope you aren't dropping off earwigs with your romance novels."

She took the lid off and lowered it onto the floor beside her. No pungent reek of damp. And more than the absence of decay was the presence of something else, something she couldn't really define but that brought up a childhood memory of sitting in front of the small fiber-optic Christmas tree her mother kept on the dining room table.

Morticia pulled the box closer and lifted out the first two hardcovers. They were volumes on plants and herbology, old, but not old enough to have that elusive antique value.

"Not bad," she muttered. After a quick flip-through for rips and dog-ears, she used a red pencil to write *$8.99* on the first page of each. Next, she pulled out a dictionary with a crumbling spine and tossed it in the recycle pile. A second hardcover in better shape: *Malleus Maleficarum*, or *The Hammer of Witches*.

"Oh snap, no way!"

Morticia collected *Hammer*s. She had six of them on the shelf in her studio apartment. But hers were all paperback, one in French, one in German, the other four in English. This one was leather-bound, with gold lettering. She opened it to the copyright page—it was the 1928 edition.

"Almost ninety years old, not bad."

She flipped through the pages, which were thick and textured, the best kind. "At least two fifty. Let's say . . . two sixty-five."

She readied her red pencil but paused, her hand hovering above the open front cover. No one else knew about this. Which meant no one would miss it. She closed the cover and checked the spine. Not even one crack.

"Prepayment of the inevitable severance," she told herself, and got up to slip the volume into her tote bag, which she'd left by the back door. With the new condo development grabbing up half the street, by the end of the year the store was probably going to be closed, and there sure as fuck wouldn't be any golden parachute for a retail clerk.

Back on the stool and feeling a little less morose, she continued digging through the box. *The Egyptian Book of the Dead*, *The Alchemist's Kitchen*, an early copy of *A Vindication of the Rights of Woman* . . . all good. "Damn, L. Shipton, you were alright."

She tipped the box onto its side to get at the layer of newspaper pages jammed in the bottom. They were crunchy with age, yellowed and seemingly random, some torn at the edges, others whole sections of the *New York Times*. They dated from the 1930s to 2002. Morticia laid them out on the desk like they were puzzle pieces.

1974: "Apartment Fire Claims Four Women"
1962: "Fatal Automobile Accident—Town Mourns
    Beloved Mother and Volunteer"
1959: "Homosexual Perverts Arrested at Local
    'Women's Bar'"

Every article was a death notice or an obituary or some kind of arrest involving women, from all over the country.

"You had some morbid interests there, Mrs. S," Morticia mumbled, shuffling the newspaper into a pile beside the discarded dictionary. She picked up the empty box to drop it on the floor, and something shifted. She looked inside and saw a small rectangular box, navy blue and faded around the edges, the kind good jewelry came in. In the centre was a company stamp. She reached in and pulled it out: LOW & COMPANY, SALEM, MA.

She placed it on the table in front of her. "Let's see what we have here . . ."

The case was stiff to open. When it creaked back enough for the springs to snap, she lost her grip, and it skidded away from her. She grabbed it back. Something important was in this box, something precious and rare, even. Something that was going to mean something in her life . . . She just knew it. Her heart was beating fast and hard. She took a deep breath and wrenched the case open.

Nestled inside was a small souvenir spoon, the kind a grandmother would hang in a decorative rack beside dozens more just like it. There was some tarnishing of the bowl, nothing a polish wouldn't fix. The silver was dark around the markings, too, but they were clear enough. She slid it out from the molded silk lining and turned it over. God, her fingers were shaking. But it was just a spoon. There was nothing on the back. Nothing else in the box. Just this spoon with an engraving of a little witch hovering over two straight pins crossed like a pirate's skull and bones, and up the handle the word *SALEM*.

Later, sitting at the bar with Bo, with the spoon tucked into her bag, Morticia felt better. Bo attributed it to the drinks and music, and congratulated himself on being such a supportive friend. But she knew it was because, somehow, things had shifted. She knew, somehow, she was going to be okay. Better than okay, because she would never be Pat ever again.

14

HEX THE PATRIARCHY

"Oh, Tish, you went next?" Meena said, carrying a dusty bottle of merlot to the table. "Wasn't it Wendy's turn? She got her spoon after me."

Freya leaned over and made a face at Morticia, who rolled her black-lidded eyes.

"We went clockwise, not chronological, dear," Wendy said to Meena, who was circling the table filling wineglasses.

"Hold on a minute," Lucky said. So far, the stories weren't making things any clearer. "I don't get it. Did someone *give* us the spoons?"

"Well, yes, in a manner of speaking," Meena said.

"But I *found* mine. You both *found* yours."

"In a secret tunnel off your basement?" Lettie replied. "Really? Hanging from a spider web in a graveyard on a specific day? At the bottom of a box of donated books? Statistically improbable."

"Never mind probability, what about the laws of nature? The world *cannot* be just a series of randoms," Freya chimed in. "Might as well believe in some beardo in the sky."

"I so do enjoy these intellectual dinners, dear," Wendy whispered to Meena as she filled her glass.

Meena leaned down and kissed her on the forehead. "Me too. We should do this more often."

Lucky couldn't wrap her head around it. And everyone was being so casual. "So who is responsible, then? Some old woman calling herself 'the Crone'? What is she, some kind of culinary Easter bunny, dropping little silver spoons?"

"Ooo," Freya said, wiggling her fingers at Lucky. "New girl, already throwing shade at the Crone."

Wendy stood. "I think it's time to reconvene in the garden. Grab your drinks."

Everybody but Lucky got up and followed Wendy into the kitchen. Freya paused by the doorway. "Come on, kid. You're gonna be fine."

Lucky remained seated, eyeing the not-so-special-looking spoon in front of her. "I just don't get it."

"Yeah, but you *did* get it, and that's the point. The rest we can explain. You need to be open to hearing it, though. Because it gets weird."

Lucky turned around and looked up at her. "Weirder than this? I came here for a fucking job interview and now I'm having dinner with witches?"

Freya smiled. "First it gets weird. Then it gets absolutely amazing. Come on."

The glass kitchen doors opened onto a small cobblestone patio where a wood table held a stack of books and a collection of clear lanterns with pillar candles burning like little hearts inside them. Mismatched chairs were pulled in around the table, but no one sat. Instead, each woman picked up a lantern and followed Meena down a narrow path through the trees. Lucky picked up the last lantern, a metal cylinder laced with holes in the shape of stars to let the light seep out, and followed. She felt an odd flutter under her ribs and realized it was nerves. Arnya thought nerves were for pussies, so Lucky had done her best over the years not to let herself feel them. But here they were, like tiny feet running along the perimeter of her lungs. She glanced back at the warm glow of the house, eyes travelling up the black clapboard to the upstairs windows. Behind one of those, her grandmother was sleeping. Lucky wasn't alone, not really.

Deep breath. She took the first step into the trees.

Sound was different in here. The hum of insects was amplified and the noise of the city around them rubbed smooth. Certain spaces held the light of the passing candles in cupped leaves, and others absorbed every glimmer. The path seemed overly long for an urban backyard and mysteriously twisty. Lucky, feeling the wine she'd drunk, wished she had brought bread from the table to leave a trail of crumbs.

She stumbled over a root, and Freya looked back. "Hey, listen, you're fine, I swear," she said, as if she knew exactly what Lucky was thinking.

"Freya, there wasn't anything in the wine, was there?"

"Just grapes and booze, I suppose." She was gentle in a moment when she could have been offended or snarky. "It's always disorienting stepping inside. Don't worry. I'm right here." She held her hand behind her so Lucky could see it, but neither made the final movement to link together. It was enough—the potential of connection. She followed it.

Up ahead, the lights and the women holding them disappeared one by one as they stepped through a hedge. Lucky held her breath as she pushed through the brush.

On the other side was a circular clearing lit by the lanterns, now hanging from hooks on the trees. Freya took Lucky's from her and hung the two from the remaining hooks.

The sound of waves was suddenly loud. Meena pushed aside some branches. Behind them was an iron filigree fence, and beyond that, a bruised expanse of water past an open jawline of rock.

"When Wendy and I bought this house, we also purchased a slice of land from the neighbours—a right-of-way to the shore. No beach, of course," she said, waving at the violent jut of stone, "but who needs a tame thing like a beach?" Meena released the greenery and the women were enclosed again. Cut off. Held in, together.

"Before we carry on with how each of us found our spoons, it's time to tell the larger story. Not all of it—that would take several lifetimes—but enough to give you some context."

Meena sat on the ground, and the rest of the witches followed suit, arranging themselves in a circle. The ground was mossy here but not wet, and round white stones, laid out in the pattern of a star, stretched across the entire space. Freya pulled on Lucky's hand, and she landed unceremoniously on her ass. Morticia stifled a laugh.

"Are we having a formal circle?" Lettie asked. Back straight, legs crossed in lotus position, her beautiful face tipped up towards the moon.

"No, Lettie," said Meena, taking a sip, then setting her wineglass down in front of her. "Not just yet." She met Lucky's eyes, and asked, "Why don't you write?"

The question caught Lucky by surprise. "I . . . I am, I mean, I do." She had asked herself this very question many, many times. "I need to make money, to have medical benefits. It's just me and my grandma. I can't afford to just write."

"But why do you need a job you hate to be able to take care of your Elder?" Meena was gentle but straightforward.

"Because that's the way it is." That was the best Lucky could do.

"There, that right there." Meena pointed at her as if the answer had become clear. "'*That's the way it is.*' But why is it that way? Why are our Elders, especially women, pushed aside? Why are talented people—artists and thinkers—forced to work shitty jobs? Why are we a part of a broken system that leaves both struggling to keep their head above water?"

Lucky didn't know what to say. It felt like familiar ranting—she'd heard it before. So she shrugged. "What can you really do about it, though?"

"Tell me what you know about witches." Meena said it with an indulgent smile, rounding to a favoured topic.

"Well, I know there are Wiccans, right? Like a religion?" No one gave her any indication she was on the right path, so she kept talking. "And there are Halloween witches—like vampires and demons and all that. And I know about the bullshit witch trials. Thousands of women burned at the stake for being smart or queer or loud. I guess that's about it."

Meena nodded. "Each holds a small piece of a larger truth, in a way. But the larger truth is this—what we really are is a fire that can burn down the system that holds us, that holds you and Stella, that keeps you small and struggling."

Lucky could see flames reflected in Meena's dark eyes now.

"We have been told that people are above mere nature but also vulnerable. That we have no connection to the ground. At the same time, we're told we alone cannot talk directly to God. That we need others—men—to speak for us, so we have no connection to the sky. Where does that leave us? No ground and no sky. Floating without roots or voice, in need of protection. Say, the protection of a larger system, of the church."

Listening to Meena, Lucky couldn't help but feel angry—every hour she'd spent working, every minute being anxious, so much effort to collect a small pay cheque. She imagined Stella whittling away in a depressing nursing-home living room, ignored by overworked nurses.

"Witches were never capitalists. We were the thing that stood in the way of capitalism, which is just the engine of the patriarchy, after all. Witches were not all killed by fire. We *are* the fire."

Meena poured herself more wine and paused to listen to the water, crashing both wild and controlled on the other side of the fence, giving Lucky a chance to catch up before continuing.

"The men who took power, they took away access to healing and control over one's own circumstances—they denounced anyone capable of magic or medicine. Because, if the people believed in magic, something that cannot—by its very nature—be commoditized, they couldn't get people to buy in to their system.

"They started shutting down the communal lands, the places where people worked and harvested together and made sure everyone ate. Once those lands were all private, people became vulnerable, especially women. Especially people who didn't have husbands—widows, queer women, nonbinary folks . . . They were ostracized, and many were reduced to begging for the charity of others, which is probably where the image of the old hag began."

"So this all comes back to finances?" Lucky thought it might be too simple an answer, but Meena nodded.

Lettie piped up. "Baby, what doesn't?"

Meena continued. "The women are largely the ones who carried stories. And stories are the collective remembering of the people. In a time when the state wanted people to change and leave behind their old ways, stories were poison. Every witch burned at the stake meant hundreds of stories in the smoke.

"During the Reformation, when the Catholic Church was challenged by new powers, witchcraft hysteria grew. They needed to prove themselves. Ironically, it was the very same Church that could provide the remedy, keep you safe, and have your back against the ultimate evil. It was the perfect PR stunt. It was the beginning of something truly horrible."

"But I still don't understand. What do the spoons have to do with all this?" Lucky interjected.

Meena smiled. "These spoons were imbedded with a kind of siren call, to bring us together. They were enchanted by a Salem witch named Sarah Mansford, who knew there would be a moment when a powerful coven could be brought together that could finally light the match after so many years of slumber. She saw us coming. And she found a way to reach out to us."

"With spoons?" Lucky couldn't keep the doubt out of her voice.

"With the very spoons made to celebrate our demise, created on the anniversary of the Salem witch trials."

Just then, a faraway yell broke through the night.

"Lucky!"

It was Stella, and she sounded scared.

"Shit, it's my grandma." Lucky got to her feet and started running, pulling herself through the hedge so quickly, the branches grabbed at her hair and clothes.

"Wait." Meena got up and grabbed her lantern. "We'll come with you." But Lucky was already rushing up the path.

Meena paused by the hedge, bending down to pick up something shining in her lantern light. It was the brooch from Lucky's hair.

"What is it?" Wendy looked over Meena's shoulder.

"I'm not sure. It's Lucky's. But I can tell you this, I've seen it before . . ." She was distracted by the plastic glass, the muted colours.

"Well, take it up to the house and we'll give it back to her."

Meena muttered an answer and slipped it into a pocket. Where had she seen it before?

LUCKY EMERGED FROM THE TREES, her heart sinking when she saw her grandmother standing there in the weak light, looking like a Dickensian ghost in her long white nightgown. The fact that she was also wearing men's long johns underneath did not help. She seemed too small, fragile, even.

"Oh, Grammy, I'm sorry." Lucky ran to her and took her in her arms. Stella needed a minute before she returned the embrace, remembered Lucky and then where they were.

"Come on, let's go inside," Lucky said. "We'll head to bed."

"Screw that, I wanna watch some TV." Stella slapped Lucky's forearm but still held on to her granddaughter's hand. She was shaken, and this was her way of coming back.

Meena and Wendy went to bed right away. Meena had been a little off since they returned and needed some time away from the group. Something was tugging at her thoughts, and she wanted to lie in the dark and see what was there.

Lettie, who had been carrying her baby monitor the whole time, clipped to her belt like a walkie-talkie, went up to check on her son and never came back down. She had fallen victim to the ruse of "just lying down for a minute" with a sweet, clingy toddler, a game no parent ever won.

Morticia wandered off to "make some offerings" in the garden. Lucky saw her take nothing else but her ever-present phone, so she guessed her offerings were probably just some dark tweets.

Freya got changed and then hung around, grabbing a plate of desserts that had been left on the dining room table and carrying it into the entertainment room to share with Stella. It was she who offered to sit with Stella when Lucky started to fall asleep on the couch.

"Just go, I stay up at night anyway. Sleep is for mornings." She waved her off.

"Thanks, Freya, I appreciate it."

"Jesus, don't act like it's a chore," she responded, indignant in her dinosaur pyjamas and fluffy slippers.

Lucky did a shit job of taking off her makeup and changing out of her clothes. Her hands were shaking, and she was exhausted in a way she couldn't remember ever being before. It was too much, it was all too much. She thought she'd never be able to rest after that dinner. How could anyone do anything normal after learning they were part of some spoon-collecting witch club, let alone sleep? But as soon as her head hit the pillow, she started to fade. For the second time that night, she wondered if someone had slipped something into her drink.

The dream came right away, as if the witch had been waiting on the insides of her eyelids.

15

LUCKY'S DREAM

The witch named Sarah, otherwise known as Daniel Low's maid, stood stock-still in the hallway under a dim sconce, hidden in the shadow of an armoire. From here she could see only a part of the parlor, the fireplace and the flames throwing the men's limbs in a shadow dance on the wall. It was too far into spring for a fire, but wealth has no common sense. She could hear every word.

She actually didn't want to see them, this father and son, so well-fed, in their fine linen and wool, their hair oiled and their cheeks round. But she needed to know what they were up to. Men were always up to something, and Seth, Daniel's oldest son, was just back in Salem after a long trip to Germany, supposedly in service of the family silversmithing and jewelry business.

"They brought me up to the site of the original dark Sabbath, to the Brocken summit of the Harz Mountains," Seth told his father. "It was littered with their evil markings up there."

"To this day?" Daniel sounded shocked.

"Yes. The women stopped for almost two hundred years after the trials and the burnings, but they're gathering again." Seth's shadow paced, flickering on the plaster ceiling. "All manner of ungodly goings-on."

"What is it the Church men asked of you?" Daniel was quickly business-minded. That these men picked his son could be no accident. The Low name must be well-gilded even in the old country. This pleased him. He deserved renown outside of this small haunted town.

"They're truly frightened, I think. They spoke to me of a renewal of sorts, of these hags returning to their pre-Inquisition days of revelry and power."

What was it with this hag business? Sarah thought. Men, fearful of being able to hold up in a debate, always tried to debase and dehumanize their opponents. Bullies!

She could hear Daniel tamping fresh tobacco into the bowl of his pipe. He said, "Women should never be allowed to gather and think independently, it's beyond them. Those idle hours only create a space for evil to thrive." A match was struck.

"Keep them busy," Seth agreed. "It's why I try to have Margaret constantly with child."

Sarah barely restrained a snort. It was infuriating to hear men talk when they thought no woman was around to hear them.

"Son, you haven't yet told me what they want from us," Daniel said.

"They've requested a show of allegiance."

"To Europe?" Daniel sounded outraged.

"No, to the Lord and the Lord's cause," Seth answered. "They want us to be the voice in the Americas that lets the fiends know we are onto them, that we are standing guard and will not allow another wave of witches to crash upon our good shores."

Sarah rolled her eyes. As if witches had ever gone away.

"And what will they have us do?"

Sarah heard the sound of paper being unfolded, then Seth's voice. "This kind of spoon is the latest trend on the Continent and could be a new venture for us, something to put us on the map."

"A spoon?" Daniel blustered. "We already have spoons in the catalogue!"

"A souvenir spoon," Seth said. "One that can be sold as a token of the city of Salem but will have a dual purpose, reminding the harpies we are onto them, while also reminding people of their hideous nature."

"That image is grotesque. So much so that I cannot imagine them selling."

"Remember, Father, people are titillated by fear. And, like it or not, Salem is known for witches. Our customers will love it."

"ANNIE HAWTHORNE," SARAH CALLED OUT, approaching the bar of the pub nearest the Low household. "I am in need of a drink."

The bartender turned, slowly drying a thick glass with a thin cloth. She had a pleasant face, bright green eyes, and a wide, white streak in her dark hair, and she was easily a foot taller than most women. When she smiled, a gold tooth shone in the corner of her mouth.

"Well, well, well. If it isn't Sarah Mansford. One drink, coming right up."

"Thanks, Annie," she said in a low voice as the woman poured her a glass of ale. "I'm actually most in need of a Tender. I have news."

The witch and the Tender leaned in close and spoke at length. They discussed the Low trip, the mission to produce the Salem Witch Spoons, and how magic people were once again under attack, or would be soon.

"It is said that the coven that will bring us back to our rightful place is still far off," Annie lamented. "Will this renewed interest from the Lows and their ilk change the trajectory?"

Sarah tapped the wooden bartop. "That is why we need to act. We have to ensure the coven can come together, that they can find one another no matter what. This message must get through the years, even if our mouths are silenced. Even if the Benandanti catch wind and use the latest campaign to hunt on a larger scale. We need to attach the message to something, an object of sorts, so that it can be found no matter what is to come."

"An object?" Annie repeated, pouring a tray of ale for the rowdy tables around them. "What object are you thinking of, then?"

Sarah smiled with good mischief. "I think the Lows are about to create one that could be of use. Repurposing a thing of one intent to the exact opposite intent is in itself a powerful spell. It's perfect."

They made plans to meet when necessary and began the work of both procuring the object and developing the spell. When Sarah could get away to the pub in the following weeks, the Tender passed on information as she got it—warehouse shift schedules, cargo routes, when the shipments might be alone and vulnerable. As a Tender, her job was to gather, to provide, to make the connections a witch might need to carry out her work. Each time they met, they talked until the candles sputtered and the bar emptied. And they ended their meeting with small sips of whiskey from glasses they clinked together with the merriment of people plotting a damn good conspiracy.

SOME MONTHS LATER, SARAH MOVED quietly through the wet snow, the moon shining blue on the frozen ground. She slipped into a wooden warehouse near the docks and blew on her hands before lighting the lantern she found hanging inside the door.

She wended her way through the pillars of wooden crates, each stamped with the logo for Low & Co. Jewelers. When she found the stack she was searching for, she set her lantern down and produced a crowbar from under her cloak, which she used to pry open the nailed lid. From the crate, she carefully extracted seven shiny souvenir spoons, each embossed with the name of the city and a hideous old hag carrying a broomstick. She unhooked her cloak and laid it on the floor to use as a surface for her work.

From a pouch tied about her waist, she brought out shards of bone—the chalk and DNA of women who'd walked before her on this land, some who died for their beliefs, others who evaded scrutiny and lived to old age. She placed these at the corners of the cloak. The pouch held other offerings: herbs, a vial of viscous liquid that seemed lit from within, the tail of a rabbit, and other items unidentifiable to the untrained eye. When she had it all arranged, she knelt and went to work.

It took most of the night, but just as the sun was sliding through the warehouse windows, throwing stripes across the floor, she walked among the Low & Co. stacks, using her crowbar to pry open random crates, then inserting one of her seven spoons. She barely had time to gather up her things and hide in the shadows before the morning crew arrived.

She slipped out the door and into the bright snow when the workers began to load the crates onto the docked cargo ship. There would come a day when the right bloodlines and teachings would come together in seven descendants, bringing the exact right seven witches into the world. These witches could form a coven to bring down that which sought to destroy them again and again. The spoons, now safely sailing away to shops and homes across the country, would act as the calling card to bring them together—the right witches at the right moment.

SPRING WAS ON THE WAY, the air full of moisture and the promise of warmth. Sarah was humming, nodding her hellos and holding up her skirts on the way to the pub after a workday. The trees scattered around Salem were starting to bud, and soon the rains would end. She was thinking, as she pulled open the front door and stepped inside, that she could live with the muck for a few more weeks if spring was the reward. She paused to shake the water from her umbrella. Then it clattered to the ground.

Inside the pub stood a small circle of men, Daniel Low, Seth Low, and three of the workers from the warehouse. In the centre of their gathering in the otherwise empty room was Annie Hawthorne, swinging from a rope thrown over a low rafter.

"Good evening, Sarah," Seth greeted her. "We should like a word with you."

Lucky sat up in bed, gasping for breath, then reached for her spoon.

16

MEENA'S DREAM

The Atlantic is only blue where it's shallow or where the land underneath is pale. Across its depths, it is darker than blue and deeper than green; it is black, true black, the kind of black that moves and absorbs. In the dream, she knew it was the Atlantic, even without the sting of salt on her tongue or in her open eyes. The blue was almost black here where she was submerged, the shade of a shadow in the gloaming. And she was moving up, up towards the light.

And then the skin of the sea pulled back from her face and shoulders like a silk sleeve, and cold air hit her pores, making her gasp. And she was lifting up and into the sky.

Ahead of her was the crust of shoreline, craggy and abrupt, green scoops of shaggy hill and grey ribbons of road. She looked up, but there was only opaque light, no specificity in the sky even as she cut through it. She wasn't flying and she wasn't floating—she was just readjusting her perspective. She glanced down, and then watched more carefully as the scene began to shift.

There was an island to the west, a jagged oval surrounded by rocky beaches. The sea curled into a bay that was almost the shape of a uterus. She knew this place: Buzzards Bay, south of Salem.

Rising higher still, she saw the colours grow matte and flatten out. The land and sea assumed smaller shapes that rested against each other like dull beads in an abstract design, surrounded by crystals butting up against the dark of night.

I know this, too, she thought.

Now the clouds, misty and wet against her skin, swirled around her, obscuring her vision. Through a sudden gap, she saw the abstract pattern shift. The dark became a swathe of hair against a pale cheek. It took a moment to recognize the face, but then she saw that it was Lucky. Lucky and the odd brooch she had pinned to her ponytail.

She woke up saying her name.

Carefully, she sat up and slid out of bed, crossed the floor, and climbed into the empty tub. Outside, the moon was elusive, popping in and out between slow-moving clouds. Meena watched anyway, hoping for more direction from the sky. She fell asleep that way, legs over the rim, head at an odd angle, searching for clues in her dream. She got nothing more, but in the clear light of morning, she realized she had been given the next step, even if it was a small and uncertain one. Lucky's brooch was a map, and it was directing them to Buzzards Bay.

17

THE GIFT OF SILVER

Lucky woke up with her hand protectively holding her own neck. She could still hear the creak of the wood under the weight of Annie Hawthorne's swinging body. She got out of bed and opened the small door connecting her room to Stella's. Her grandmother was sprawled out on top of the covers wearing Freya's fluffy slippers, snoring away. Lucky got dressed, slipped out, and went downstairs to the kitchen.

The day outside the kitchen windows was grey and heavy, calling for rain. The light in the room came from a fixture above the island shaped like a group of iridescent jellyfish. Wendy was at the stovetop making small crispy pancakes in a cast-iron pan. Lettie already sat at the table with a cherubic boy, who was carefully stacking Cheerios on his placemat with chubby fingers.

"Good morning, Lucky. Sleep well?" Wendy asked.

"Not really."

"Ah." Wendy turned, a spatula in hand. "Sarah came to visit?"

"Um, I think, maybe?" *Is that what happened?*

Lettie raised her eyebrows at her. She knew the answer but didn't push. "Lucky, this is my boy." She leaned over and brushed wild corkscrew curls back from his forehead. "Everett, can you say hi to Lucky?"

The boy looked up, fixing Lucky with his huge, dark eyes, and she was hypnotized. Delicate eyebrows and eyelashes so long they brushed his cheeks. He smiled, showing amazingly white, sweetly crooked milk teeth. "Hi, Miss Lucky." The words ran together and made a pleasing kind of song.

"Holy shit, that kid is pretty." Oh god, Lettie was going to hate her. She flat-out swore at her toddler, for chrissakes. "Hello, Mr. Everett. I, uh, like your cereal tower."

Lettie laughed. "He is pretty, right? Takes after his grandpa, on my side, of course."

"Sooooo," Wendy said, placing a plate with a fresh stack of pancakes in the centre of the island. "How are you feeling this morning?"

Something about Wendy made Lucky want to open up. "Confused, I guess. I came here for a job interview, and now I'm dreaming about murdered witches."

Wendy chuckled. "Yes, you are as in this as you can be at this point."

"But why me? Also, is there seriously a job here? I have Stella, and I'm all that's standing between her and the Abandoned Grandma Shelter."

"As to why you, maybe you need to readjust your idea of what makes someone worthy of having something like this happen to them. As to the job, we take care of our own. And yes, there is a position waiting for you." Wendy piled a couple pancakes onto a plate and slid it over to Lucky, followed by a bottle of syrup and a fork. "Eat."

"Thanks. No, I just mean, there's no way this is right."

"You think maybe someone deserves this opportunity, this community, more than you?" Lettie asked.

"Exactly."

"I used to think just like that. I thought the small life I had, with its big problems, was just the world showing me what I was worth. That the better things were for someone else."

"How'd you change that?"

"I left the asshole who made me feel that way." She put her hands up, indicating the big, bright kitchen and the sweet boy beside her. "Suddenly things are a whole lot better."

"Lucky, you and I have a lot more in common than you might think," Wendy said, sliding into the seat opposite. "So I'm going to tell you how I got here."

CAPE CROKER FIRST NATION, ONTARIO, 2015

There was a party on Saturday night, and Wendy was trying to persuade her weed dealer, who also happened to be her cousin, to spot her. Ever since the divorce, she had been taking it easy, or rather trying not to think too much about anything. Meaning, she didn't have any kids and both her parents had passed by the time she turned forty, so why not have some fun?

Her cousin wasn't having it, though.

"Don't give me that 'we're relatives' shit, Wen. 'Cause the guys who supply me sure as shit ain't my cousins and I have to pay in full."

Cheapskate.

Her job in the reserve school office didn't pay much. And after she'd made Junior move out, she still had to cover the mortgage and bills on a house they'd bought in anticipation of the children who never appeared. She knew what people said. "Oh, there's Wendy Kiwenzie, thinks she's so big. Couldn't hack it in that city school, so she had to come home."

She had come back a decade ago, sure, but only to take care of her father. Then her mother followed him into the ground as fast as she could. After burying them both, she realized she'd lost more than her parents, which was enough to lose all at once—she'd also lost herself. She wanted to stay home, but the whispers were probably the reason she agreed to marry Junior. The whispers of a girlfriend back in the city. Now all she had was a three-bedroom ranch by the water that she couldn't afford to heat.

So, with no extra cash, she'd asked Auntie Ethel if she wanted company picking morels. It was hard work, wandering the bush that hemmed in three sides of the reserve from the highway, scouring the base of dead trees. A morel looked like a little brain left to dry on the forest floor. Wendy hated them. But the white people in town? They loved them. And they paid on delivery.

Which was how she now found herself dragging a mesh bag a quarter full of fungal brains through the woods early on a grey Saturday morning. She had one earbud in, the other left out so she could listen to Ethel telling her who was shacked up with whom and how third cousins were still cousins so people should be more careful. Gossip was usually a welcome distraction, but Wendy had spent her Friday night playing euchre and had already got all the rez news from her auntie Maureen on her father's side.

She rolled her head around on her neck. Already sore and bored and they hadn't been out for more than a few hours. The air was heavy with held rain, and her hair was frizzing out of its bun.

"I'm going to check by the creek," she called, slipping into the more tangled brush that Auntie Ethel, with her arthritic knees, avoided.

"Try the birch, they like birch," Ethel yelled back, settling on a flat-topped boulder. "I'mma take a little breather, me." She pulled up her long skirt to her knees, revealing tie-dye yoga pants tucked into woolen socks. "Don't fall in."

Wendy waved and put the other earbud in, and the music spread evenly over the crunch of her boots. Right away she found a small patch of mushrooms under a birch. Ethel knew her shit. One by one, she twisted their pulpy stems, releasing the little brain while leaving the root—an investment for future hunts, and a band harvesting rule. The band also dictated the mesh bag, which allowed spores to fall out, ensuring there were enough morels for every member, even reformed lesbians too old to be collecting mushrooms for weed money, but who were, in fact, collecting mushrooms for weed money.

She dumped the new finds into her bag and wiped her fingers on her jeans. "Gross."

As she headed back towards her aunt, the wind picked up. Spring was unpredictable around here. Dressing in layers was essential. Wendy untied the flannel shirt knotted around her waist and slipped it on. Debris blew dizzily on the ground: dead leaves, shed bark, broken twigs. She watched them flex and coil. For all her angst and lack of direction, there was still something out here for her, something that soothed her. Something . . .

And that was when she saw it, there at the base of a papery birch. It was pale and impossibly tall—the biggest morel she had ever seen. How could she have missed it on the way to the creek?

"What the Jesus . . . ?"

She dropped to her knees. There was only the one, no cluster, no pairs. It was almost the size of her forearm from wrist to elbow, and just as thick. The head was honeycombed in tan and brown, with an underlying iridescence that reminded her of oil slicks on asphalt.

She laughed out loud and rubbed her hands together. It was almost too perfect to harvest . . . almost.

She leaned in to study it from all sides. She'd definitely need her knife. She straightened a leg and fished around in her pocket for the switchblade her cousin Gary had gifted her. She pushed the button, and the blade popped out.

"Alright, come to mama." She grasped the fat stem in her fist and circled it with her blade, scoring a path to guide the knife deeper. She needed a nice, clean cut—splitting the stem would cause it to spoil faster. Circling back to where she started, she applied pressure, tongue between her teeth. The knife bit deep, and the top started to sway like a tiny tree being felled. But then the knife stopped.

Her brow furrowed. Morels didn't have bones to hold them straight. She pushed harder.

"Christ."

She pulled her knife out and dropped it. Grabbing the stem below the cut, she took hold of the brain in her other hand and yanked. She overestimated how much force she needed, and when the stem popped, she was thrown back onto her ass. But at least she hung on to the morel, giant, squishy, and intact.

Collapsing on her back, she held it up above her face. The clouds shifted overhead and sudden sun filtered through the birch boughs. "Yes! King of the shrooms!" She laughed. Then the light caught something shiny sticking out the bottom.

"What the hell?" She struggled to sit up and turned the mushroom in both palms. Silver protruded from the cut edge, a smooth, rounded piece of metal. She pushed two fingers into the soft meat and pinched the metal between them, pulling down. It gave a little, but only a little. Without considering the loss, she picked up her dropped blade and sliced, then used both hands to pull back the spongy edges.

A spoon. A small silver spoon with a blackened bowl and tarnished handle. She extracted it, letting the morel fall to the ground, worthless now. The back of the utensil was smooth, but the front was covered in raised designs. Much of it was unreadable, but she could make out some letters—*S, A, L, E* . . . maybe an *N* or an *M*.

What was a spoon doing inside a mushroom in the middle of the bush? Wendy came from a family who hid the cards on top of the cupboard at night in case the devil came by to play, but she had always been practical. She considered the possibilities. Maybe someone dropped it and the mushroom grew around it? Maybe there was an old dump here and it got buried and then pushed up by a spring thaw? Maybe someone was a joker playing the long game and had put it there, anticipating just this kind of bewildered reaction?

There had to be a reasonable explanation. Even so, she placed the spoon in her jeans pocket with her knife and did not mention her find to Auntie Ethel. When she got home, she pushed the spoon into the bottom of a shoebox where she kept letters from her ex-girlfriend and her divorce papers, and slid the box back under her bed.

She made some good money that day, not the beaucoup dough she would have made if the giant had remained intact, but enough to buy some weed. But she didn't go see her cousin, and forgot all about the party. Instead, she noticed the moon was full and an odd shade of orange, like it was coated in brick dust kicked up from the toppling of a wall. Like something had fallen the fuck down and there was suddenly more to see.

And as soon as she could find a buyer for the house, she was on a Greyhound heading back to university in Toronto. She was going to finish her degree, the silver spoon wrapped in her best pair of underwear tucked into the bottom of her backpack. Even then, she knew it was the most valuable thing she owned.

"HOW LONG DID IT TAKE you to figure out the whole spoon thing?" Lucky asked when Wendy came to the end.

"Oh, things got weird right away, but I didn't really understand until I found Meena." She stopped to watch Everett carefully drop strips of pancake into his mouth, stopping in between each one to wipe his lips with the edge of the napkin his mom had tucked into his striped shirt. "Such a gentleman."

"Did she come to Toronto for you?"

"Well, we kinda met halfway. In Buffalo, actually." She smiled at the memory. "Back then she wasn't so good at reading the dreams, so I guess I had to be closer for her to find me. We circled each other for a whole weekend at an education conference. I was starting to think she was stalking me, but I was okay with that, because she was so hot."

Lettie laughed. "Morticia came to get me. Came right to my door. I thought she was child welfare or something. I tried to fight her off, got real mouthy about it."

"How did she know where you were?"

Lettie got quiet for a moment, watching Everett chew his last bite. Then she said, "Everett, honey, why don't you go grab your crayons and paper from the bedroom? Go on now, you can do it. You're a big boy."

He gave his lips one more wipe with the napkin, then smiled at his mother and climbed down from his chair. As soon as he was out of earshot, Lettie folded her hands on the table and examined them for a moment, then began her story.

COVINGTON, LOUISIANA, 2021

Lettie was sitting on the settee when the first roll of thunder hit.

"Shooting dice, I guess," she said to the sleeping boy in the laundry basket. He was too big to be in there, but he liked to sleep all curled up like a fiddlehead. Her grandma was the one who told her thunder was God throwing dice. She liked that image. Made him seem less smite-y.

She watched her son's eyes flutter as he dreamed. She wanted nothing more than to join him in slumber, but these boxes were not going to unpack themselves. And since she was the only parent now, it fell to her to get it done. There weren't all that many; after all, she had only what she could fit into her '96 Bronco. Clothes mostly, some linens, keepsakes that hadn't been smashed, a photo album, and the baby's things—diapers, blankies, his books, a plush fox.

Flash of lightning.

"Or maybe he's just welcoming us home." She smiled at her reflection in the front window, hair in a messy braid, eyes bagged and dark. "Throwing us a party."

Then her smile faltered. Parties were part of why they left. Parties and Smith. After-parties and Smith. Mornings after and Smith. Emergency rooms and Smith. Then the sickness hit, and the world shut down, and the parties stopped. Trapped at home, he got meaner, and with more frequency, having full access and nothing to distract him.

The lightning clicked off, and the sky returned to black, and more thunder rumbled. Her reflection, having flashed on the windowpane with the sudden light, disappeared. She had to touch her hands to her own elbows to make sure she was still there. Edges made the best checkpoints.

"Okay then, little man, time for your mama to run a bath upstairs," she whispered, picking up the laundry basket. "Uh, Christ, you're getting too big for this." She carried the bundle to the wooden stairs and ascended, slow and careful, watching his face as she went. "Should have called you Moses, little basket boy."

Smith was the one who had named him Everett, after his own father, the only gift he bestowed, the only thing that mattered to him—a name, a mark, a declaration of ownership. He'd been furious when she showed him the plus sign on the wet stick, but also confused. "How the fuck did this happen? You're old as dirt."

She was thirty-three.

She promised him she'd keep working, keep up the house, wouldn't let the pregnancy interfere with them, convinced him it made him more of a man and so even more desirable to her, and she acted on that notion, even when her back ached and her stomach turned over into her spine.

So he'd allowed the swell and push of a new life between them. It was a big leap, really, since he hadn't let her keep her cat when she moved in. He'd already made her quit grad school and refused to allow her to take a job at the tech company that wanted to hire her even without the PhD, convinced those "jack-off nerds" only wanted to look at her tits all day. She stepped carefully around him, trying to carry the clumsy sway of her new weight, but not too much weight; she still watched what she ate, substituting prenatal vitamins for lunch in case he complained about extra padding on her thighs.

"You're not carrying the kid in your hips, are you?" He pinched her side so hard she teared up. "Maybe hold back on the baked goods."

"I'll do better," she promised. She had to be quiet in her humiliation. Crying angered him, but no response also angered him. She was always picking her way through thorny patches. Any direction she went, she was bound to get hurt; it was all about which way hurt the least.

She couldn't have her dream job, but she still had to work, so she worked at a car rental place. She worked until the day her water broke, right there at her counter while she was explaining to a man from New Jersey that the insurance fee was an additional charge. "I'm sorry, sir, if I could just leave you for a moment to grab my manager to finish up here . . ." The fear in that man's eyes when he realized she had gone into labor was the first time she thought maybe Smith was more scared than angry—scared of her and all the possibilities of her, especially now. Motherhood was the beginning of immortality, and that meant she was becoming more, not less, no matter how he worked to contain her, to make her small enough to fit in his pocket.

When she left Smith, she headed south. South was the direction of home, even if her mother wouldn't be there waiting.

"Don't marry a white man," her mother warned before she passed. "Come home and find a nice Creole to sing you the right songs, the ones that make your muscles all long with pull."

Her mother would have loved Baby Everett, white daddy or not; would have sung about his loose curls and dark brown eyes. She would have loved him even more for bringing Lettie home, or almost home. At least they were out of Atlanta and back in Louisiana, even if the town wasn't Abita Springs. She needed some time on her own before she went *all* the way back home.

At the top of the stairs in her new rented house, Lettie flicked on the hall light because she could. Because no one could tell her not to. "Boxes can wait," she told that same no one, and carried her son to the bathroom.

This was the room that sold her on the house. She'd first seen it on her work computer, a slideshow of images taken with a shaky hand. Two weeks later she signed the lease through email and transferred the first and last months' rent, crossing her fingers it would work out. And now here she was, under the wrought-iron chandelier that held real candles, barefoot on the cold black-and-white checkered tiles.

The bathtub was a bit small, but it had claw feet and was deep enough to drown in. She let the water run, clearing the pipes out before pushing the stopper into the drain, thinking about what that would feel like, drowning in a ceramic tub on the edge of a small town on a Thursday night. She figured she'd felt worse things this past year.

She flicked on the lights over the sink, then flicked them back off. "Let's do this right," she whispered, dragging a short wooden stool from in front of the pedestal sink, then standing on it to light the candles.

Over the window in front of the tub, a length of blue ribbon hung from the curtain rod. In the corner by the door was a massive spider web with the dusty remains of a trapped yellow butterfly. And the mirror looked as if someone had painted a full portrait on its surface before trying to wipe it clean. She'd asked the landlord to leave the old furniture. He was more than happy to oblige, not wanting to have to pay to clear the place out. As a result, there were beautiful couches and chairs from the twenties, but also dusty credenzas from the fifties and a massive block tube TV from the eighties.

Earlier that day, she'd found old sheets eaten to lace by moths in a wardrobe and hung them outside on the line, loving the way the sun poked through onto her skin, making patterns like so many leaves. She found rosemary tied up in bunches and hanging on a thin strip of rope across the back wall of the pantry, too old to be of use but still beautiful. Sweeping the living room, she found a packet of letters from a man named Bilford tucked under the radiator. Bilford loved Augustine, who had lived in this house with Ernest, who wasn't a cruel man but an uninterested one. At one point, Lettie would have said indifference was worse than cruelty, because cruelty is at least full of passion. Now she knew different.

Sweet Augustine, she of the warmest month, the hottest night, I would give anything to catch you for just a moment, be free to run straight to you . . .

There were pages of love and abandon and, in the end, disappointment. After she'd finished reading them, Lettie wondered what Smith was doing right now, if he was crying in his car the way Bilford had watching Augustine walk with Ernest in town. If he was in his shirtsleeves, drinking brandy straight out of the bottle and writing poetry to his missing wife. The fleeting thought of him made her muscles tense and her back curl in protectively. He was no poet. She organized the letters, folded them into their envelopes, and put them back behind the radiator.

It was like moving into a museum. And with the future uncertain and the present precarious, Lettie found the past comforting. It was at least something to lean on while she caught her breath.

"And it's all ours," she said to the boy, who had pulled himself even smaller in the basket in his sleep. That right there, that was why she left—because her boy was making a habit of trying to be small, as small as he could be, invisible, especially when his daddy was around.

She stripped off her tracksuit and rubbed the stretch marks along her hips. She liked the way they were indented, like wheel marks in fresh earth, softer than any other part of her. She could fit a finger into each one, but only her own fingers, no one else's. They were the exact width. Running her fingertips across them like strings, she felt as if she were at the beginning of a song. That made her laugh. "I sing the song of myself," she quoted to no one.

Pulling the basket close to the tub so she could reach him if he woke up, she slid into the water like a dish into a sink: quiet, fully. The rolled edge of the tub was the perfect height to rest the back of her head on, and that was what she did. "Oh god, that's good."

The wind howled around the house, whistled through the cracks, and settled in the blocked chimney like a gasp. Lettie closed her eyes. She was here. She was alone. She was okay.

And then, suddenly, she was not. A loud crash sounded from down the hall. She sat up so fast water splashed over the side of the tub. She looked to the boy first, who grunted softly and rubbed at his face with one fist but remained asleep.

She was about to call out, then thought better of it. Instead, she rose in silence, wrapped herself in a towel and grabbed the lighter she'd used on the candles and a can of hairspray from the small box containing her toiletries. She wasn't fucking around. Not in her house.

"Not in my house," she whispered. Then she crept down the hall, her homemade blowtorch at the ready.

The hallway seemed twice as long now, and too full of shadows. She kept her eyes trained on the open door at the end that led to the dark bedroom. Her mouth had gone dry, and her mind was spinning around one figure—Smith.

How had he found her? Would he hurt her? Take the baby? Kill them?

She flicked the lighter to make sure it was working, and the flame jumped. Then she pressed the hairspray nozzle, and a hiss of liquid came out, wet with droplets at first and then changing to a fine mist. When it hit the flame, a whoosh erupted, lighting up the hall and throwing her shadow onto the striped wall. She watched it waver and then disappear as the flame went out.

"Come on, then, cocksucker," she whispered, shit-talking to make herself feel brave.

The floor was creaky, and she winced with every wooden moan, keeping her eyes fixed ahead. When she got to the door, she stopped to take a big breath and then reached around the frame, goose bumps up her arms. Her fingers found the light switch, and she flipped it as she jumped into the room.

"Get out!" she screamed, louder than she'd imagined she could. She'd spent so long being quiet, the volume startled even her. Down the hall Everett woke and started crying.

Movement on the other side of the bed. She flicked the lighter and pressed the nozzle and shot a long plume of fire in that direction.

It was an open window, with the curtains blowing in the hard wind. She took a few steps closer, and there it was: an old glass lamp had blown off the side table and smashed on the hardwood floor. Nothing else out of place, no intruder, no ex-boyfriend.

"Oh, thank the Lord." She took a huge gulp of air and almost choked on the acrid residue of the burnt hairspray. She slipped on some flip-flops by her unpacked suitcase and carefully walked around the shards of glass to the window.

The wind was wild, carrying the smell of rain on it. She pushed down on the window to close it, but it wouldn't budge. Using both hands, she pushed harder, and it moved a little, then stuck fast.

"Great." She leaned in to examine the frame, hitting it with the heel of her palm to try to unstick it. But there was something jammed in at the side, something small and metal. She muscled the window up an inch and reached for the object, but it was in there good. Must have been there for a while. Since the bottom of the curtains were stained from weather, she imagined this window had been stuck open for at least the better part of the season.

She started digging at the edge of the metal with her nails, and at last it popped out and clattered onto the floor. She dropped the window, and, after a quick look around the front yard just in case someone was lurking, she shut the curtains.

Lettie retied her towel, feeling all her muscles tic and clench from the surge of adrenaline. What if it had been Smith? What would she have done, what could she have done?

Everett was wailing louder now. She didn't want him to climb out of the basket and wander around in the dark. What if he fell down the stairs? She would clean up the glass on the floor later, but first she had to go get him. There would be no bath for her tonight.

SHE TUCKED THE BOY INTO the big bed and sat down beside him, singing silly songs and rubbing his ears until he fell back asleep. It took a while, long enough that Lettie herself nodded off, jerking awake so hard her head bounced off the headboard behind her.

"I'm up," she mumbled, wiping drool from the corner of her mouth. The boy was sleeping, curled up into a small snail shape. She shifted him gently to the centre of the bed and put pillows around him as a buffer. Even though he was almost two, she was still anxious about crushing him in her sleep. It was hard for her to trust herself after years of being called out and called down.

She got out of bed and opened her suitcase on the floor. She found and pulled on some pyjamas and went to the bathroom to drain the tub and brush her teeth. When she came back into the room, she remembered the broken lamp. She moved the shade to an old chair in the corner and grabbed a broom and dustpan from the hall and swept up the smaller shards, careful to go in wide circles to catch the littlest pieces that had exploded outward. She swept the mess into the dustpan, the glass tinkling against itself, and then there was a louder noise. She crouched in the half-light to take a look.

In her dustpan was a silver spoon, smaller than a soup spoon, hell, smaller than a teaspoon—the piece of metal that had been propping the window open. She picked it out and placed it on the edge of the chair and finished her sweeping. When she was done, and the shards were in a garbage bag in the closet where her boy wouldn't come across them, she carried the spoon back to her side of the bed and studied it in the light of the remaining lamp.

The top of the handle was embossed with a witch—sharp hat, sharp nose, broom, the whole ugly getup—and it looked like she was pointing directly at Lettie.

"I see you. Feels like you see me too."

The wind, now safely outside the closed window, whistled a response.

THE THREE WOMEN SAT AT the table together, each thinking of a small spoon and the first time they held it.

"Ah, I see you are all up and ready for the day."

Meena swept into the room in a long yellow kimono. A bird, chirping like a solo violinist, followed her in and flew past the women and out the back door. Wendy got up and handed Meena a mug of coffee and the *New York Times.*

"We're telling stories," she said.

"I'm glad to hear it." Meena leaned in to speak softly in Wendy's ear. Wendy nodded and left the kitchen; then Meena walked outside without another word.

"Hey, what's with the birds?" Lucky had to know.

"Yellow birds are witch birds," Wendy explained. "No one knows why, they've just always been that way. There was a time when we chased them away, after the Inquisitors figured out that a woman with yellow birds in her wake was very likely a witch. But now they're back."

"What do they do?" It seemed to Lucky that she was in a state of constant confusion. "Are they magical?"

"In a way." Wendy smiled. "It's kind of like crucifixes for Christians, I suppose. They are a physical reminder outside of our own bodies that we exist, that we are here. Sometimes you need to remember. There's magic in that."

Lucky looked at Lettie, who was nodding. "Sorry, I have to go grab Meena. I have some questions."

"I'd imagine you do, and more than just a few," Lettie said.

Outside, Meena sat at the table. She wore Wendy's glasses and was reading the front page.

Lucky threw her body into the chair opposite Meena, who continued perusing the headlines. She was frustrated, pissed off even. It made her grind her back teeth.

"Don't do that, you'll crack a molar," Meena said without looking up.

"Okay, what the hell is with the spoons? How did you know I found one? And what are we supposed to do with them?"

"One at a time, please. I have answers, mostly, but you need to let me finish my coffee before we start." Meena took a long, slow sip from her mug and went back to the paper. Lucky watched her read through two whole sections, until she had finally emptied her cup. She folded the paper and took off the little bent glasses.

"Did Sarah visit you last night?"

Lucky was annoyed at her question being answered with a question. "Maybe."

"Right." She leaned in. "Lucky, we'll need to be honest with each other, and we don't have much time to bond first. So, once again, while you were sleeping, did you dream about a witch who lived here almost one hundred and thirty years ago?"

The image of a woman hanging from the rafters of a pub filled her mind.

"I did."

"Good, so now you know the origin story. Sarah was a powerful conjurer who got herself a job in the Low household so she could keep an eye on those men. The Lows' silversmithing and jewelry store was in a former Unitarian church, which used to be a meeting-house back in Puritan days. You know what happened at meeting-houses in old Salem Town, right?"

Lucky shook her head.

"Trials. Witch trials," Meena told her. "Sarah knew as soon as the son got back from Germany that he had been brought into an inner circle of sorts. Seth Low was recruited to the same cause that started the Inquisition. He created the Salem Witch Spoons to give some juice to the old stories about witches being devil-fucking hags, but also to let the women know they were being watched, in an attempt to stop them coming together.

"So Sarah bewitched seven spoons, each one marked by a manipulation of the image of the pins on the spoon. You have yours on you?" Meena held out her hand. Of course Lucky had her spoon on her. She dug it out of her pocket and handed it over.

Meena pointed to the object Lucky had thought was a straight pin. "This is a witch pin. It's what they used to torture confessions out of women. The original mass-produced spoon has three crossed witch pins on the stem. Yours has only one."

Lucky asked, "How many does yours have?"

"Three, like the real one, but my pins are longer and stacked differently." She produced hers from somewhere in the billows of her robe and placed it in her palm beside Lucky's. "Morticia has two, Wendy has four, Lettie five, and Freya six."

"Who has seven?"

"It hasn't come home yet." Meena put both spoons down on the table. "And when they do, when we are all together—that's when I think we can help stop the end."

"The end of what?" Lucky asked.

Meena picked up the front section of the paper and unfolded it between them. The headlines screamed about bombings, war in Eastern Europe, civil unrest, racially motivated attacks. "This. This is the end. The men in charge are running us off the cliff like lemmings. They are running us as fast as they can to the end. But we can stop it."

"Seven women in some kind of self-love support group, that's who's going to change the world?" Lucky tapped the newspaper. "The seven of us?"

"This is not fiction, Lucky. These are facts. Someone needs to step in. And if not us, then who?"

Meena could see Lucky bouncing between doubt and discovery. "Okay," she said, "how do you explain the dreams I have every time a spoon is recovered that tell me by whom and where, or Sarah visiting each woman after she's found her spoon to show them the origin story? All that is just, what . . . coincidence?"

Meena had long ago reached the point where she shouldn't have to explain herself to anyone anymore. But she had a feeling this particular girl, this potential witch, was worth taking some time to lay it out for.

Lucky stayed silent, considering Meena's words. She had grown up with enough uncertainty from Arnya and now lived with enough uneven reality from Stella that she preferred facts—science, medicine, architecture, numbers—things with boundaries and rules. She didn't always follow the rules, but knowing they were there gave her comfort. So being here in this very old place, which was so new to her, and with all these strange people, was a test. Part of her found it exciting and felt like she was once again waiting to rob Santa on the fire escape with her mother.

"Listen, Lucky," Meena said. "I was hoping I could ask *you* a question."

"Sure."

"Your mother . . ."

"Arnya St. James."

"Yes, Arnya, where is she from, exactly?"

"Why do you want to know?"

"That brooch you were wearing last night in your hair. I dreamt it. I was hoping . . ."

Just then Wendy came outside.

"She can see us this afternoon. Two o'clock, and no later. She was pretty pissy about it."

Meena pushed back her chair and stood. "Well, that's it, then. I guess this will have to wait. We'd better get a move on."

"Wait, where are you going?" Lucky wasn't done. So many of her questions were still unanswered.

"Oh, don't worry, you're coming along for the ride. This is what you would call a witch family road trip." She smiled, and all her even white teeth showed. For some reason, the gesture made Lucky shiver.

THE MAIDEN READ THE TEXT out loud.

The witches are going to see the
Hawthorne Tender at Buzzards
Bay, 2 pm EST

"All six of them?" the Mother asked.

"Doesn't say."

"Then ask." The Mother was being short. She had spent the morning pacing in the boardroom, waiting to hear how recruitment was going.

The Maiden sighed and typed on her phone. There was a pause before a small ding.

All six are en route

"Excellent." The Mother slid into her seat. "Okay, so they are together and on the move. It's good that they are together."

"Because of the Benandanti?" The Maiden wouldn't let it drop.

The Mother made a kissing noise, and her dog lumbered over and put her head in her lap. She scratched behind her ears. "I am fully aware of your stance on this, but I cannot allow anything to slow them down. We don't have time to deal with anybody's feelings right now."

"How about their safety?" the Maiden responded.

The Mother dropped a fist onto the table. Hecate whined and retreated to the corner, and the Maiden took her feet off the table and sat up. "We do not have time! I will tell them if he gets close. Hell, you can tell them. Just . . . not now. Am I clear?"

Just then the Crone walked in, smiling as she straightened out her blouse. She had come from the ladies' room, where Israel was helping her with a "loose button."

"Dieu. What is going on in here?"

"Nothing," the women answered in unison.

18

THE TENDER OF
BUZZARDS BAY

Buzzards Bay wasn't far. They slid out of Salem just after lunch and down the wet New England roads, taillights flashing red around the sharp curves between rock and salt water. No one had argued when Lettie said she would stay behind with Everett. As good as he was, he would still be a toddler confined to a car seat, and the work they had to go do was not exactly kid-friendly.

Freya was in the front seat of Stella's Pathfinder, with Lucky at the wheel. Stella had climbed in back and drifted off before they hit the end of Meena and Wendy's leafy street and was now softly snoring.

Freya watched her in the rearview mirror. "She's awesome."

"I guess." Lucky readjusted the mirror. "If you don't have to deal with her full time."

"Some of us don't have grandmas, so, you know, count your blessings and all."

Lucky pulled her eyes from the road for a second. Freya was staring out her window, her feet propped up against the dashboard. She looked so young Lucky felt like she could be driving her to school.

"Aren't your parents weird about you living here in Salem? Shouldn't you be in class or something?"

"My parents are weird about me in general." Freya picked at her nails, a nervous habit Lucky had noticed was aggravated when the subject of family came up. "Also, I graduated early. I was in a hurry to get the fuck outta anywhere they were."

Lucky didn't respond for a moment, focused on following Meena's black Audi as it made the turns out of the suburbs and onto the freeway.

"Fuck." Freya cursed under her breath. "You got a file or something?"

Lucky motioned with her chin. "In the glove box."

Freya rummaged around and pulled out a hot pink nail file and began smoothing a broken nail. "If you're a girl like me, it's easier to finish high school online."

"When did Meena's crew come get you?"

"Not yet. I don't want to tell that story—not yet." Freya overly concentrated on her nail, grinding it down so hard Lucky could smell the burn.

The rest of the trip was comfortably silent, punctuated by Stella's snores from the back seat.

Their destination turned out not to be some secret headquarters, but the Trout Tavern, a seafood-themed pub that had seen better days, perched near the water but not directly on it. The first two letters on the neon sign were blinking from a faulty wire so that it read OUT TAVERN more often than not.

"Be pretty cool if it was a gay bar," Lucky remarked.

"Ha!" Freya laughed. "I wish. Nothing but old fishermen and young Republicans in these parts."

They pulled into the mostly deserted lot and parked beside Meena's car. Stella woke up on her own once the engine stopped. She was like a little kid that way.

"We home?" she asked a little too loudly, stretching her arms in all directions.

"Not even close," Freya said. "But at least you can get a decent Bloody Mary here."

"Deal. Order me two, Luck. I have to hit the little boy's room."

"I'll go with you," Freya said.

Lucky wasn't sure why Freya was so good with Stella. Freya didn't do nice, or even polite, but she seemed to have a soft spot for the old woman.

As if she had overheard her thoughts, Freya said, "I like authentic. Bitch is authentic." Then she climbed out of the passenger seat and opened the back door for Stella, who was putting her shoes back on. "Let's go, Don Wrinkles. I gotta pee too. Fuck the shoes. Who needs shoes anyway?"

Lucky sighed. Great. Stella would hold on to that one the next time Lucky tried to stop her from going barefoot. She leaned over the seat. "Hey, come on, you guys, it's wet outside."

Freya rolled her eyes. "Stella, your mom says you have to put your shoes on." She squatted to help her tie the long laces in extravagant bows; then they headed for the bar, laughing conspiratorially.

Opening the door, Freya yelled inside, "Buzz Bay!"

"Buzz Bay, wooo!" The response echoed back before the door slammed shut behind them.

Lucky sat for a moment in the new quiet of the old car and looked around. The tavern was covered in dark wood siding that was stained white with salt and warped at the edges. The windows were thick and dim, and the door was scratched red metal with silver showing through. Behind the building was an expanse of scrubby sand and a strip of ugly trees that couldn't find the right kind of purchase to get tall. Above them, screeching seagulls circled on strong winds over grey and roiling water she couldn't see.

Tap. Tap.

She jumped. Morticia was at her window, her pale face made more stark by her choice of black lipstick.

Lucky climbed out. "Jesus, you're a ghoul sometimes, you know that?"

Morticia just shrugged. Lucky followed her.

They entered a wide room with a bar on the far wall, a row of stools spaced along it. The rest of the place was filled with a dozen wood tables and chairs, the seats red pleather padding patched with duct tape. The theme was obvious: taxidermied fish and plastic replicas were nailed up haphazardly on the panelled walls, and the low beams were draped with dusty nets holding more fish and multicoloured pairs of panties thrown up there by randy last-callers. The place looked greasy and old, like every bar in daylight. The tables hadn't been set yet, and bottles of ketchup and vinegar sat at the end of the bar, ready to be wiped down and placed, still sticky, on tabletops. They were the only ones here.

Meena and Wendy were perched on stools. Morticia slid onto a seat at the end of the bar and pulled out her phone. The bartender was a woman who could have been thirty or seventy—it was impossible to tell. The only thing for certain was that she was very tall and very intimidating. Meena waved to Lucky impatiently, patting the stool beside her.

"Lucky, this is Lucille. Lucille, this is our newest member, Lucky—the holder of the spoon with the single pin."

As she approached, Lucille smiled, slow and even. By the time she slid onto her seat, Lucille had both hands resting on the bar, two gold incisors catching the dim light.

"Let me see her."

Meena put a hand out. It took Lucky a moment to realize she was asking for her spoon.

"Oh, sorry." She dug into her jacket and pulled it out, placing it on the bar between them. Lucille bowed her head so low her nose almost touched the metal, her mass of black curls pinned with strategic knots under a rust-coloured bandana. She began to hum, a low throaty sound like an animal about to eat—a hungry, wild animal.

"Lucille is a Tender. Descended from a long line of Tenders," Wendy said in a loud whisper. "We need them. They tell us what we need to know, put us on the right path. Plus, a good Tender gets you just as drunk as you need to be to follow it."

The women laughed, except for Lucille. Lucky wasn't sure she could even hear them right now. Then her head snapped up, and her face was only an inch or two away, her eyes vivid green and narrowed, peering directly into Lucky's.

"Jesus!" Lucky jumped but tried not to give an inch. In her experience, people who showed fear got made fun of. So she held the strange woman's gaze, but not before noticing a thick scar across her neck, disappearing into the curls at her nape.

"Vodka," Lucille announced, showing those gold teeth once more. "Vodka, then we talk."

She lifted her hands off the bar, then paused, tapping her long, stiletto-shaped nails together. "But I also think gin. For some reason gin is involved. We'll have both." She spun on her heel and started gathering bottles and glasses from the cloudy mirrored shelves behind her, like a mad scientist struck with a theory.

Lucky preemptively shivered, swivelling to face Meena, and whispered, "My mother drank gin. I can't stand the smell of it, even now."

Meena leaned in. "I'll have the gin, then. I like a cold gin on a rainy day."

Outside, the rain fell, plinking on the tin roof above them like piano notes from another room.

Lucille slapped down fourteen heavy-bottomed shot glasses, ran a vodka bottle over half of them, then a gin bottle over the others.

"Whoa, whoa, Lucille. We need to drive outta here at some point today," Meena said.

The Tender raised her head, her eyes jumping from spot to spot. She tipped her head to the side like a broken doll, listening to something that wasn't speaking to anyone else. "No, no. Tonight we have to get incredibly inebriated. Tomorrow you leave." She lifted her hands, crisscrossed them, and pointed. "In two different directions."

Meena sighed and started pulling off her jacket. "Fuck. Okay, then." She raised her eyebrows at Wendy, who mimicked the movement. Then she leaned over and called down to Morticia, "Can you grab us some rooms at the Sailor's Inn? We're here for the night."

Without looking up, Morticia flashed her a thumbs-up and started typing on her phone.

Meena draped her jacket over the back of her stool and rolled up the sleeves of her silk blouse. She took a deep breath in and sighed it out, then shrugged. "Alright. Time to get fucked up, I guess. Who am I to argue with the universe?"

"No one," Lucille replied, as if it had been a real question. "None of us are capable of arguing with the universe."

Stella and Freya came out of the bathroom just then and sidled up to the bar. Lucille grabbed one of the full shot glasses and each woman did the same. She lifted hers high and called out, "Drink up, witches!"

And the witches drank.

THERE WAS A JUKEBOX THAT Lucille had set up to play without quarters, so inevitably a sing-along happened. Johnny Cash and Diana Ross demanded it. The shots kept coming. Nothing else was served, not even when Wendy begged for a plain old beer. "Come on, it's not like you have to make it. Just twist the damn top. Hell, I'll twist it myself—I won't even dirty a glass."

"Vodka and gin. The end." Lucille was conducting this ritual, and it was getting sloppy.

Stella loved it. She drank half as much as everyone else, except maybe Freya, who winced every time she took a sip. But the two of them sang the loudest and were the ones who instigated the dancing, swinging each other wildly across the uneven floor.

"Careful, you'll call down a storm with those moves," Wendy yelled to them from the bar.

"Really?" Lucky was, by this point, wide-eyed and awed. "Can we do that?"

"No, we sure as hell cannot." Wendy laughed so hard she had to rush to the bathroom to avoid pissing her pants.

Meena watched her waddle-run across the bar and smiled. "God, I love that woman."

"I'm leaking!" Wendy screamed, pushing open the door to the toilet.

"Yup." Lucky nodded. "She's a real keeper."

Lucille leaned over and put two full shot glasses in front of them. They groaned in response. Before Lucky could grab hers, Meena picked them both up and indicated with her chin that Lucky was to follow her. She headed to the table that was the farthest from the group.

"I wanted to get back to our earlier conversation."

"What the hell were we talking about earlier?" Lucky had had enough vodka to reset her memory. For a moment, she wondered if this was what it was like to be Stella—off guard, forever catching up, and a bit euphoric.

"About your mother, Arnya."

"Oh man, she would love this." Lucky laughed. "All of this— witches, adventure, this bar. Especially this bar."

"She is a bit of a free spirit, I gather." Meena slid the shot glass over, and they clinked them together and took the shot.

"Yeah, I guess you could call her that. She was, anyway."

"She's settled down, has she? Happens to some of us when we age."

"Oh, she settled down, alright. Right the fuck down. She died."

Meena was taken aback. "I'm so sorry."

"It's okay. It was a long time ago."

"How long?"

"Uh, let's see. I was like nine, ten. So about eighteen years. I've been without her for almost twice as long as I had her." She looked around the bar, sudden and unexpected tears threatening. Fucking vodka, she thought. She never cried about her mother, hardly then and certainly not now. But it was true, Arnya would have dug this.

If it had been her, she would have left from the food court on Freya's arm and gotten on the first flight to Salem, provided someone else was paying, of course. Lucky kind of felt guilty, like she was stealing an adventure not meant for her.

"That brooch, the one you wore to dinner, that was hers?"

"Yeah. It's nothing special, really. She never had anything valuable." Lucky leaned her elbows on the table. "If you really like it, I mean . . ."

"It's just—I think it's connected somehow."

"Connected to what?"

"To this, I suppose. To us—the coven, certainly to tonight."

Freya suddenly appeared beside them. "Come on, come dance with us. Quit being all serious over here."

"No, no. I don't want to. I'm tired." Lucky laid her head on her forearms. Freya started tugging at her.

"Oh, come on. It's not even late."

"I'm so old, just leave me here . . ."

"Shut the hell up!" Freya commanded, and Lucky allowed herself to be pulled to her feet and onto the dance floor they'd cleared in the centre of the room. Freya spun her to Patsy Cline. Stella clapped and laughed, and Lucky forgot about everything except the music and her happy grandmother.

WENDY HAD RETURNED TO THE bar and was sneaking a glass of water from the tap when Meena came up behind her. "We need to talk."

She jumped. "Oh Jesus, babe, you scared me. I thought you were Lucille come to tell me I was messing with her ceremony because I don't want to die from alcohol poisoning." She chugged the water, keeping an eye on Meena, who was chewing her lip, eyes far away.

When she'd downed the entire thing, she placed the empty glass in the sink. "You look worried."

"I think I may have found the seventh witch."

Wendy grabbed her by the elbows. "What? That's great! So soon?"

Meena didn't return the smile. "Yeah, but it's not good news."

19

A BUSTED WIZARD

After a few more songs, Lucky was sweaty and a little too drunk to be hanging out with her grandmother. She needed air, so she headed outside. The door slammed shut behind her, muffling the music and laughter. At least the rain had stopped. Everything was wet and shiny under a half-moon, yellow and low, like a hammock strung between clouds. In this light, the bar didn't look so ordinary. It looked instead like it had grown from the rocks, built out of layers of salt and grit like a pearl, a hollow pearl lit by Miller High Life neon signs. She breathed deep, and the taste of the ocean filled her throat, so that was the direction she went, down to the shore.

The trees weren't thick. She had no sooner gone into them than was out the other side, with only a low, half-crumbled wall between her and a rocky beach. She sat on that wall, facing the Atlantic.

She was here, she had actually come. She'd followed the pull she'd felt, and she had met odd, wonderful women who were offering her the chance to be a part of something meaningful. She wasn't sure yet just what that was, or of the person she could become, but maybe it meant she wasn't stuck anymore.

"Lettie found me at the mall. Last summer."

Lucky was startled. She hadn't heard Freya approach, but then the water was loud here, like a constant exhalation. "I'm sorry, what?"

"My grandmother kicked the bucket while we were on family vacay last year. When we got back, we found out she'd left a small chunk of her savings to each of her grandchildren. And guess who was one of the lucky recipients?" She smirked and pointed at herself with both thumbs. "This guy."

"Wait . . ."

"Keep up, St. James." Freya joined Lucky on the wall. "Shit, this is rough." She stood and brushed the seat of her skinny jeans with the back of a hand. She loosened a stone with the toe of her army boot, picked it up, and chucked it at the water. It made a small plop. "Fuck. I never could figure out how to skip stones.

"Anyway, we got back from that disastrous trip, where I outed myself to my Christian parents, and within a week, like a miracle, a cheque was couriered into my hot little hands. Enough to get an apartment in Cincinnati, to make some changes, and to start actually living and not just waiting for each miserable day to end."

"What were you doing at the mall?"

Freya tossed a second stone. This one didn't even reach the waves, but it did slide nicely across the wet shore. "Working. I mean, the cheque wasn't that big. And Hot Topic was more than happy to add me to the team. Fit right in with the furry who worked the register and the Korean-boy-band-obsessed customers.

"One day I was folding oversized Rob Zombie T-shirts when in walks this angelic woman who comes right over to me and tells me it's time to go home—to Salem, to the coven. She said I needed to get my ass in motion, because they'd had to wait for me."

"Wait for what?"

"Until I could call myself by my real name. In order for them to find me, I had to find me first."

Lucky stood up, scanned the ground, found a flat, oval stone, and loosened it from the gravel. She handed it to Freya. "She had to wait until you started living."

"You got it, kid." She tossed the rock, and it skipped, just once, across the bruise-coloured water. Just once, just enough. She clapped her hands and jumped up and down, and Lucky saw that she was still so young. She pumped her fist, then clasped her hands together and turned to Lucky. "You come to the coven when you are ready, not when you want, not when it's easy. You come when you're really ready."

The wind lifted the edges of her bangs, making her squint, and Lucky saw on her face something so calm and steady that she was envious. She wanted it, whatever this was—this certainty, this trust. They walked back to the low stone wall and sat. Then Freya turned to her and said, "My spoon was waiting for me in the land of a busted-ass wizard."

SANDUSKY, OHIO, 2021

"Matthew, are you even listening to me?" Her mother's pitch was reaching the top register, like a kettle at boil.

That's not my name, Freya thought, closing her eyes against the bright sun, feeling the heat on her face, and trying to remain calm. "Yes, Mom," she answered out loud.

"Then get out of the damn car." Sarah-Beth Monahan sighed

heavily, slapping the wrinkles out of her beige culottes, the official pants of summer vacation. She wore them every second day, alternating with a pair of light blue slacks with an elastic waistband.

"I'm hungry," Freya whined, unbuckling the seatbelt and slouching out of the back seat.

"We'll get sandwiches after the first round," her father said. He hitched up his cargo shorts, clapped his hands, and headed towards the entrance. "Merlin's Mini Putt! A Monahan family tradition!"

"Come on, Matty-Matty Fee-Fi-Fatty," her little brother sang. She cuffed the back of his head.

"Oww!"

"Boys!" their mother hissed. "Cut that out. And stop teasing your brother, Casey. If anything, Matthew could stand to put on a few pounds. He's been wasting away. In fact, here . . ." She rummaged around in her oversized purse and tossed a chocolate-covered granola bar at her elder one. "Eat this. Now."

"Right, a slab of preservatives with a side of additives." Freya rolled her eyes.

"Good lord, Matty, just eat the damn bar." Her mom rolled her eyes back and scurried after her husband.

"Yeah, Matt-teee, eat the damn bar," Casey squealed, swivelling his hips and dangling a hand daintily. "Eat the pwin-cess bar."

She chased him past their mother, who tried to grab both of them and missed. Casey threw himself into their father, who was standing at the ticket booth, stuck out his tongue, and buried his face in his paunch. She drew a finger across her throat to let Casey know he was in for it, sooner or later.

This was it, August 2—conversation day. She'd marked it in her calendar months ago. But that was before her parents announced that it coincided with the timing of their annual family vacation to Sandusky. Still, she wasn't going to chicken out. It had been too long. She wanted to scream every time one of them called her Matthew.

"Matthew, let's go, buddy!" Her dad waved four Play All Day bracelets above his head.

"That's not my name," she said into her chest, shoving the granola bar into her back pocket.

Merlin's had seen better days. If it wasn't for the go-kart track with questionable safety standards, it would have shut down years ago. That was about when the owners stopped repairs on the mini putt course, anyway. There were slits worn into the Astroturf greens and divots where clubs had clipped the carpet. On the fourth hole, the wand that was supposed to swing like a pendulum, back and forth over the doorway to Merlin's castle, had a broken mechanism, so it had to be hand-operated.

"All part of the charm," Mr. Monahan said cheerfully, taking on the job of swinger even though Casey begged to be allowed.

On the fifth hole, Mrs. Monahan grabbed Freya's blond hair, which had grown four inches since the end of grade eleven. "Time to snip this, I think. You're turning into a hippie."

"Or a girl," Casey yelled from where he was climbing a plastic rabbit emerging from a scuffed top hat.

"Casey, enough! Leave your brother alone!"

"It's fine," she answered. How did Casey see it and no one else did? "He doesn't bother me."

"Yes, I do!" Casey retorted.

Distracted by her mother's prying fingers, she took the shot. It caught a worn patch and ran straight into the hole.

"Woo-hoo! Hole in one!" Mr. Monahan yelled, jumping up and down so that his eyeglasses slid down his nose. He held on to his bucket hat with one hand and raised his own putter in the other. "Attaboy!"

"Stop," she whispered, slouching to disguise her considerable new height. She wanted to be small. She needed to be small. As long as she was Matthew, she couldn't exist outside of small. "Just please . . . stop."

Merlin's course had nineteen holes, each one more convoluted than the last, ending in a "magical forest" that consisted of pine trees shedding needles on a litter-trampled path that separated the highway from the park. Among the trees, it was loud and quiet at the same time. The course wound around the wide trunks, so no one could finish it in fewer than five strokes. By the time the Monahan family got to it, they had been out in the sun for almost two hours. Between chasing Casey away from the Canada geese he insisted on "hunting" and helping him get through his turns, it was a real marathon game.

"Jesus, Marty, let's just get this done. I need a tinkle." Mrs. Monahan danced from one foot to the other in her cork espadrilles.

"We'll be through the last hole soon enough, Sarah-Beth. Then you can find the ladies' and I can grab a light beer." Mr. Monahan was still in good spirits. He looked forward to this trip all year. Leaving his desk at the DMV for a whole week, driving out to Sandusky, hitting Merlin's and Doug's Dig Your Own Fossils, staying in a Best Western, and waking up before his family to swim laps in the chilly pool and watch the young moms in their optimistic two-piece suits pull toddlers with water wings around. This year he'd saved up enough loyalty points to upgrade them to a suite. This was only day two, and nothing could bring him down, not his morose teenager or his hyperactive seven-year-old, not even his plain wife in her fucking culottes.

Casey had spun himself in a web of pink cotton candy and dirt, streaked through with tear trails, after he skinned his knee on the eleventh hole, which was what got him the cotton candy in the first place.

"I don't want to play anymore," he whined. "Don't make me!" He sat down hard on the needle-strewn ground and chewed his melting sugar. "Matty can do my shot."

His father wasn't about to tolerate a quitter in the family. "No, he cannot, that's not how this is done. Every man has to play through for himself. You are a man, aren't you? C'mon, Casey, show me those guns. C'mon." He flexed his biceps and grunted, trying to psych up his younger son.

"Matty, show him how it's done. Grrr!" He nudged his elder son, then snarled under his bushy mustache and lowered himself into a squat, puny arms bent and hands in fists.

"That's not my name." She said it louder now.

"Let's just call it. I really need the ladies'." Sarah-Beth was leaning against a tree trunk, wondering whether it was big enough to hide her from the road if worse came to worst and she had to go right there. She probably had some Wet-Naps in her purse . . .

"Ah, come on, now. We're men! We act like men. We're almost to the end! Matthew, show Casey how it's done. Grrrrrr." His face was turning red from his body builder posing.

"That is not my name," she said, articulating every syllable. She felt her voice in her muscles.

Casey stopped squirming to watch her.

"Okay, that's it, I can't wait any longer." Sarah-Beth shouldered her purse. "C'mon now, Matthew, grab—"

"THAT IS NOT MY NAME!" She screamed it.

Her parents stopped dead. Casey hiccupped in the silence.

"I am not Matthew! I'm not your *man*, I'm not anyone's *man*.

I'm Freya." She picked up her little purple golf ball, too light to be regulation, and tossed it into the woods. "I'm not a man. I'm not a boy. I'm a girl, and I always have been. Always. Why can't you see it? Why can't you see me?"

The sound of her own breathing was loud in her ears, like she was listening through a seashell.

This was it. The "conversation" she'd meant to have over tea on a patio after dinner or in an office with a therapist wearing a sweater vest—now screamed on hole nineteen at Merlin's Mini Putt while her mother's culottes grew wet down the leg and pee ran into her espadrilles.

Freya was seen, and she was no longer small. She was fucking huge.

Casey broke the silence of her father's shock and her mother's humiliation with a long, single wail, like a siren.

"Fuck this, I'm going to get a beer." Mr. Monahan tossed his putter. It spun in the air, then landed with a bounce where the false green met the real green. He threw both hands up and stomped off without a glance back.

"Now look what you've done, with your . . . ridiculousness," Sarah-Beth hissed at Freya, picking up Casey and holding him in front of her body like a shield. She wobbled off towards the parking lot, carrying a distraught Casey by his armpits, the soft pink of his belly exposed. She shook her head—no, no, no, no—with every step. And Freya was alone. But she had her name. She had said it. It was hers.

She straightened her shoulders and smiled, just a little, to test out the motion. She carefully gathered the putters left like aluminum feathers in the wake of her family's flight and stacked them by the final hole. Then she walked into the woods after her ball. Under the canopy of the trees, the light was different, every colour highlighted and every bough backlit. She saw the purple ball right away.

"What the hell?"

It had landed in a small clearing dotted with bright buttercups, discarded chip bags, and crushed pop cans, balanced like an Easter egg in the bowl of a small silver spoon.

Freya—Freya now for real, because she had spoken it out loud, no matter how uncomfortable the rest of the week would be, no matter how many beers her father went for or the silent drive back to their suburb two days ahead of schedule—*Freya* bent to pick up the spoon, holding it steady so the ball didn't tip.

Then she carried both out of the trees and headed back to their car, where they would wait almost an hour for Mr. Monahan to return, with one talisman in each pocket—the golf ball that she launched with her name and the spoon that would launch her into her new life.

FREYA'S FACE SHONE IN THE moonlight with booze and absolute glee. "Believe me," she said. "Once you understand that this has been you all along, well, that's when the real adventure can begin."

She raised both arms to the sky, closed her eyes, and spun down the rocky beach in wide circles, laughing. She looked so free. She *was* so free.

"Oh!" Freya stumbled to a stop, wavering a bit, and pointed at Lucky. "You just gotta watch out for the Benandanti. 'Cause those fuckers'll kill you."

"Wait, what?"

MEENA SAT WITH WENDY IN the front seat of their car, grabbing a moment of privacy from the bacchanal in the Trout pub. "Are you sure?"

"No." Meena rubbed her temples with two fingers. "I'm not sure of anything, none of it." She dropped her hand and looked out the windshield, as if searching the overcast sky for a god. "Can't I get a little fucking certainty?"

"Alright, alright." Wendy reached over the armrest and rubbed her leg. "We'll figure this out. So, okay . . . if you're right, if the seventh witch is Lucky's mother and she died years ago, what does that mean for the last spoon? For us?"

"Goddammit, I don't know," Meena snapped. She closed her eyes and took a deep breath. "I'm sorry. I shouldn't be taking this out on you. But what do I even say to the others? Do I say anything? Is this over?"

"I don't know, but I don't think the Oracle would have led you this far just to have it all collapse. Lucky's mom died before you even got your spoon. Why would the universe begin something it couldn't possibly finish?"

"Yeah, yeah, you're right. It's just—Arnya's brooch is a map. It brought us to Buzzards Bay, so that has to mean something."

"Maybe it has to do with Lucky. The brooch is hers, so she's a part of the next step. It could have nothing to do with her mother at all." Wendy's voice was soothing Meena's nerves. "Maybe it means that Lucky has seer skills. Maybe she divined the next step to Lucille, but it took a seer with more skill to read the step, hence your dream. She is just a baby witch, after all."

Meena leaned back against the headrest and looked at Wendy, beautiful in the soft light from the parking lot.

"You know what else this means?"

Meena sighed. "What else?"

"That it's time to bring in the others, about the deadline. You can't keep trying to puzzle this out by yourself when we're running out of time."

Meena sighed again. "It's just—I want to inspire belief, you know? I'm asking these people to believe in something unbelievable. How can I do that when I'm not completely confident, completely in control?"

Wendy grabbed her hand. "But six of us are here now. You did it, you gathered us, and now you need to trust that we believe in the spoons, in the coven, in you. Maybe that's how we find the seventh—together."

Meena squeezed her hand and leaned in, like she was about to say something profound. "You think we have time for a quickie?"

Wendy laughed and was just about to kiss her wife when the pub door swung open. Lucille stood in the entrance, a scowl on her face.

"Shit, we've been found out." Wendy reached for her door handle. "We should talk to the others, anyway."

Lucky and Freya were just coming through the trees from the water, hand in hand. Lucille gave them a scowl, too, holding the door wide for all the loose witches to get back inside.

"Hey, Meena!" Lucky yelled as Meena pressed the fob to lock the car. She wavered a bit on her feet. "Who the fuck are these Bellinis?"

Freya laughed so hard she had to hang onto her sides. It was a good thing they were staying the night, Meena thought. "Yeah, tell us all about the Bellinis!" she added.

Meena smirked at Wendy over the top of the Audi. "You're right. It's time to finish the story. I'm not sure these drunk assholes will remember, but I'll tell them anyway."

INSIDE, THE MUSIC WAS STILL loud, Stella was still dancing, and Morticia was still online. Freya plucked the phone out of her hands and threw it on the bar, guiding Morticia to the dance floor and picking up where she had left off—all chaos and wide spins. Lucky was pouring a shot down her throat at the bar, and Lucille was counting the empty glasses she'd been stacking beside the register.

"We almost there, or what?" Meena asked the Tender.

"Three-quarters of the way. Drink up." Lucille put two more gins on the bar and watched as Wendy and Meena polished them off, both grimacing. "Almost there."

Meena didn't understand the math Tenders used, the ways they read the signs, but she knew enough not to question Lucille. Tenders were, after all, the alchemists of the community, as well as being master strategists. In the early days, Lucille had helped her decipher the dreams. On her first visit to the Trout, Lucille told her, "You need to get yourself one of those antique atlases. Dreams tend to be a little old-fashioned. Oh, and ask for an upgrade, for chrissakes."

"An upgrade?" Meena was confused.

"Yeah, like how you upgrade your software. Ask for a new program. Get a later version, one that you can read better."

"It's not like there's a customer service hotline. How in the hell do I do that?"

Lucille had rolled her eyes and got up from the wooden table to grab them another round. "Be a better witch, for starters."

So she had done just that, making a trip to VenCo headquarters in LA to seek help. Now her dreams were like postcards mailed to her from the location of the spoons by the women who carried them. Turns out, it was about how she filtered the messages as they arrived in sleep that influenced how they were shown. She trusted Tenders, especially Lucille. Tenders and witches went together like macaroni and cheese. They needed each other and had an uncanny sense when it came to sniffing each other out.

Lucille poured another round. Meena took a deep breath and slammed it back. Then she clapped her hands to get everyone's attention. All it did was set the other women off, clapping along to the Hank Williams Jr. tune pouring into the pub. She looked back at Lucille, who nodded and pulled the plug on the jukebox. Before the women could start whining, Meena raised her voice.

"Alright, everyone, can we all sit together for a minute? I want to update everyone on where we're at."

"We're at Trout's," Freya yelled, pumping her arms. "Best bar in Buzz Bay, baby!" She whooped, and Lucky whooped too. The others, more experienced with when to take it down a notch, did not join in.

"Fine," Freya said, and ambled over to the bar's largest table.

Meena stood while they sat, Lucille watching from the bar as she stacked the empty shot glasses into an intricate pyramid, stopping to count off on her fingers now and then.

"I need to tell you more, and I need to tell you now," Meena began. Christ, how was she going to do this? She had to keep one eye closed just to stop their faces from blurring.

"We're on a clock here. There is a finite amount of time to assemble the coven once it begins. Years."

"That's a pretty generous timeline," Lucky called out. "We're on six already. How many years left?"

"Not years, Lucky."

"Okay then, how many months? Months are still good."

"Nine."

"Alright, nine months, I mean, a whole-ass kid can be made and born in nine months."

"Days," Meena said.

"Nine months is like forever, guys."

Stella leaned over and put a hand on Lucky's shoulder. For once, she was doing the reeling in. "No, no, Lucky. She said days."

"Nine days?" Freya dropped her head onto her forearms on the table.

"We have nine days left now to find the seventh spoon, that is correct." Meena said it more to herself than to the group. It was the first time she'd properly acknowledged how fucked they were at this point. Hearing it from the Crone was one thing. Saying it to the group was entirely another.

"But we don't know where the next one is!" Even Morticia was animated now. "I mean, it could be anywhere—Alaska. Regina, even."

Meena held her hands up, palms out, and motioned for them to quiet down. "Lucille?"

The Tender paused in her work of separating the empty glasses by some distinction known only to her into two pyramids. "Yup?"

"I think it's time for another round."

"Coming."

Meena waited until the drinks were in front of them before continuing. "Yes, we only have nine days. But we are all together, and safe. Lucille is getting us to the next step. And I feel something I haven't felt before."

"What's that?" Freya was slurring a bit.

Meena lifted her glass, and the others mimicked the motion. She took a deep breath and lied. She had to lie, because right now what they needed was to be inspired. "I feel hopeful. Because of you, all of you. With this group of crafty-ass witches, we're sure to succeed. To hope!"

They raised their glasses to one another. "To hope!" And then tipped the clear liquid down their throats.

Lucille plugged the jukebox back in and started bringing around large glasses of clear liquid with ice chips and greasy lemon wedges.

"What's this, more gin?" Stella asked.

"Water. Ritual's done, the work is over. Now we celebrate." Lucille smiled at the older woman indulgently, flashing her gold teeth, which Stella loved. "Lucky," she hollered, "next time we're at the dentist, I need to get my dentures souped-up." And she drank deep. They all did.

ON THE WEAVING WALK TO the Sailor's Inn, Freya and Stella hung on to each other, while Wendy was trying to skip, which just looked like she was almost falling, over and over. Meena caught up to Lucky.

"Hey, I have a question for you. What's up with your dreams?"

Lucky screwed up her face. "What do you mean? Like, what I want to do with my life?"

Meena found that exceptionally funny, and it took her a moment to compose herself. "No, no, no. I mean your actual dreams. They're all slow. They are . . ." She searched for the words. "They're set with booby traps."

"How do you know about my dreams?"

"I visited you, before you came. Don't you remember?" Lucky shook her head. "Well, we'll work on your recall later, as you grow into your power. So how do you do it? The traps? Stopping people from moving?"

"Oh, that's an Arnya special. My mom taught me how to protect myself when I slept. I used to get bad nightmares and she wasn't always home to deal with them, so she showed me how to make sure the boogeyman or whatever-the-fuck couldn't get me."

Lucky stopped for a moment, narrowing her eyes, deepening her voice, and pointing at Meena in an approximation of her mother, uneven sway and all. *Make it impossible for the monsters to move. Just like real life, you can't get caught if the fuckers can't catch up.*

Meena nodded. "Damn, she had some power. Not sure she'd ever get hired to teach kindergarten, but still."

"Yeah, she was powerful, alright," Lucky answered. Then she remembered: "Hey, Freya said I need to watch out for some Bennys or something? Who the hell is that?"

Meena looked up the road, all curved and eerily empty. Ahead of them was a tourist information centre, a corner store, the required fish-and-chips stand, and the inn. The other women were staggering along at their own pace, no one within earshot.

"It's the Benandanti. They're an old group. The name is Italian and translates to 'Good Walkers.' They're men who said they were born with a caul on their pointy little heads, so they could see visions and leave their bodies at night and other stuff that was totally not witchy at all," Meena said, her words dripping with sarcasm. "So stupid. They really thought their penises and a story about being godly would keep the Inquisition off their asses."

Wendy had come up behind them while Meena was talking. "Sorghum," she blurted loudly, her volume control thrown off by the vodka. She hiccupped.

"What?" Lucky asked.

"They used sorghum, grain grass, to fight. Pretty shitty weapon, if you ask me, unless those old witches had bad allergies." Then she broke out in a peal of laughter.

"I have to get this lady to bed," Meena said, hauling Wendy back from where she'd veered into the centre of the road.

"So why do we have to watch out for them now? If they're from back then? If they were Inquisited, or whatever?"

Meena let Lucky's question hang for a minute, the quiet punctuated by their footsteps on the gravel shoulder and Wendy's boozy hiccups.

"There are stories that some of the Good Walkers survived. As far as I know, it's only stories, though. Kind of like boogeymen for witches, I guess."

"Beware the boogeyman," Wendy said, once again almost shouting.

"There you are. Finally," Morticia called out from the curb in front of the inn. It was weird to hear her talk, let alone shout. There was a pile of room keys at her feet.

"Tisha, baby!" Wendy ran to her and hung off her neck. "You're the best."

"No, you're the best!" Morticia was tearing up. "The best, Wendy. And I just love you."

"Oh my god," Wendy gasped. "I love you too!"

Smiling, Meena untangled her wife from Morticia. "Alright, Wendy, let's find our room."

"Meena Good, am I flirting with you?" Wendy sang, mixing up her words, eyes blinking independently of each other. "Yes, yes, I am flirting with you."

Lucky managed to bend down and retrieve one of her keys, then took her grandmother, who was practically asleep standing up, off to bed, her head full of men with faces hidden behind cauls.

THINKING BACK ON IT LATER, Lucky couldn't be sure what woke her. It wasn't Stella getting out of bed or even the door opening, since she was gone by the time Lucky roused. The alarm clock had said it was 5:55, all those fives like angular S's, a glowing red shush.

She'd staggered to the bathroom, holding her head. The light was on, and the toilet seat had been left up after her bedtime puking. Towels were strewn on the floor from a clumsy attempt to shower afterwards. She was thirsty as hell. She unwrapped a plastic drinking cup from the bathroom counter and ran it under the tap, downing the lukewarm water before it had reached the top and then refilling it. She'd carried it back into the bedroom.

This room was exactly the kind Stella preferred, with a door that opened onto the parking lot so you could be at your car in a minute. Except their SUV was back at Trout's, because no one had been in any kind of shape to drive. Lucky pulled aside the front curtain and squinted across the lot and up the street. Yup, there was the Pathfinder, sitting under a lamppost in front of the dark bar. She opened the front door and stood in the frame, breathing in the cool predawn air. Wondering if she was being too loud, she glanced back at the second bed, and instead of there being a sleeping lump or a tossing Stella, the bed was empty.

"Oh fuck."

Lucky threw on her sneakers and wrapped a blanket over her sleep shorts and tank top. Before she closed the door, she remembered to grab the room key, attached to a blue plastic tag. She paused on the small walkway that connected all the rooms—which way? She listened for a minute and heard the ocean. That sound would have drawn Stella, so she headed down to the water.

The sky was still dark enough to demand she walk carefully, though it had started peeling back in places to the east. Birds sang from the high branches as she entered the trees. "Yeah, yeah," Lucky answered. "Anyone see an old coot come this way?"

A sudden silence.

"Thanks a lot." Clearly, this witch thing did not include interspecies communication. She wasn't sure it included any powers at all. Not even a wand, just an old decorative spoon. What a rip-off.

The roar and rush of waves filled every space between the trees, a violent gathering and retreating that fed her anxiety. The bay was all business. God, what if Stella had fallen in? Lucky picked up her pace and tripped, the blanket slipping off her shoulders.

"If you're okay, I'll murder you myself," she said aloud. The crashing of salt water on rock grew even louder as she came to the edge of the trees. She would have given anything to be arguing with her grandmother in person right now, instead of imagining her body floating like geriatric seaweed.

"Please be okay. Please be okay . . ."

Emerging on the rocky shore, she scanned the tide and the rocky canines of cliffs where they broke and bit the water. She looked out to sea. "Come on, where are you, where are you . . . ?"

She picked her way over the jagged stones, imagining Stella trying to manage this in the deeper dark. Christ, why had Lucky drunk so much last night? Why had she let Stella drink so much? How had she let her guard down so fully that here she was standing on the shore of Buzzards Bay looking for her rattled grandmother?

"Stella!" she shouted. "Stella Sampson!" Nothing greeted her but the audible movement of the kind of water that swallows you whole after the rocks chew you up.

"Oh fuck, oh fuck." Lucky turned in a circle, the blanket falling to her feet. She had to call someone, but her phone was back in the room. Not stopping to pick up the blanket, she ran back to the path and into the trees. Meena could help. No, fuck all this witch shit, she had to call the police. Maybe Stella had wandered in the other direction? Maybe she hadn't come to the water at all. Lucky stumbled over a root and fell hard against a tree. She sucked in air, got up, and kept running, bursting onto the back lawn. She knocked one of the lawn chairs over as she flew past, already fishing for the key in the pocket of her shorts.

"Come on, come on." She willed her fingers to steady and her mind to slow as she tried to get the key into the lock. She dropped it. "Fuck!" When she bent over to grab the key, gravity pushed the first tears to the front of her skull. Her sight went blurry. What had made her think she could have an adventure and keep her grandmother safe at the same time?

"Impossible. And you knew it was impossible!"

"What's impossible?"

Lucky spun around so quickly she fell back against the door. "Grandma!"

There was Stella, in long johns and a new souvenir T-shirt that read, *Trout's Tavern! Come in and catch something*. She was holding an orange Popsicle that got tangled in Lucky's hair when she threw her arms around the old woman.

"Jeez, watch out. I walked all the way to the gas station for this!" Stella pushed her away. "Cripes, you're a mess, you know that?"

The door to the neighbouring room opened, and a very sleepy, very barefaced Morticia looked out. "What the hell is going on?" She looked almost sweet with her skin flushed pink instead of bone white.

"Stella decided to go for a walk in the middle of the night," Lucky answered.

"It was an emergency!" Stella was outraged at the implication in her granddaughter's tone.

"Getting a fucking Popsicle is an emergency?"

"It is when you're hungover." Stella picked a long piece of dark hair off her treat and flung it on the ground. "And now you've cocked it up."

Morticia shook her head, flashed them the peace sign, and closed her door.

"I should go get another one," Stella mumbled, turning to leave.

"No, you most certainly should not. Get in this room right now!" Lucky jammed the key in the lock, opened the door, and walked in, but Stella didn't follow.

"Come on, let's go."

Stella stood, her Popsicle hanging by her side, a faraway look in her eyes. "I just had a terrible thought."

"I don't care about that. You scared the shit out of me, you know? And that you were out on the road, at god knows what time, all alone? What were you thinking?" She backed up and pulled the key out of the knob, then tossed it onto the desk beside their small TV.

"Lucky, I think your mother is gone," Stella said.

"What?"

"She's gone, Lucky. She's really gone, and I don't think she's coming back this time."

Lucky sighed, sitting hard on the edge of the bed, the door still open, Stella still standing outside. Arnya leaving Lucky and Stella alone was common enough. It hadn't occurred to Lucky before now that Stella might, every now and then, think she was still coming back. Now she thought about what leaving Stella at a home might do. Would she feel like she was being abandoned over and over, always anew, the hurt always fresh? Jesus Christ. She had to make this work. She had to find that fucking spoon.

"I know, Grandma. I know."

"You know?" She dropped her Popsicle and brought her hand to her mouth. "Oh, Lucky, I'm so sorry." She came inside and sank to her knees in front of her granddaughter. "Oh, sweetheart, I'm so sorry."

"It's fine, Grandma." Lucky lifted her to sit beside her on the bed. "It happened a long time ago—years ago."

"It did?" She sounded so small and so concerned that Lucky's anger began to fade.

"Yeah, years ago." She took Stella's hand. It felt like clumsily folded paper—an origami bird without sharp edges. "It's just been us, you and me, for a while now. And we're okay. We're good."

"We're all alone?" Stella looked at her, eyes big and wet, and Lucky's throat closed. She patted her hand and rocked slowly, a motion of comfort for both of them.

She swallowed hard. "No, Grandma. We're not alone. We have people."

"And each other." Stella grabbed both Lucky's shoulders. "We'll always have each other, right?"

"Yeah," Lucky agreed, guilt filling her limbs. She thought she might throw up again. "Yeah, we'll always have that."

Stella turned to put both arms around her and held on tight. Over her head, through the doorway, Lucky watched the Popsicle melting in the first rays of morning light, and that was the thing that finally sent her tears, held and hoarded, streaming down her cheeks. That was how morning found them, door open, hungover and embracing on a motel bed, on the ragged Massachusetts coast— the last morning before the adventure truly began. They were on their own, the two of them, because they would always have that, right?

20

EVERYTHING IN THREES

Meena had found the note tacked to the motel room door. It took her a long minute to decipher Lucille's terrible handwriting.

> Coven heads back to Salem by 9 a.m. to start looking for the witch in the bowl.
> Send the new girl to Pennsylvania—she needs to see Rattler Ricky and seek the spoon while you concentrate on the witch. Also, the Maiden stopped by the bar late last night. She says, "Hurry the fuck up." —L

"Christ," Meena said. "She wants us to use divination bowls to try to find the last member and thinks maybe she hasn't even gotten to the spoon yet. And Rattler Ricky? Half the time you end up waiting on her for a week. She comes and goes at her own pace, and you never know when that'll be."

"Who in the hell is Rattler Ricky?" Wendy sat up in the messy bed, one eye glued shut with sleep. She reached for the aspirin and water she'd left herself on the nightstand.

"A powwow woman."

"Powwow? As in, jingle dresses and big drums? Ooh, can we go?" She was suddenly animated. Even the thought of steady pounding that matched the throb in her head didn't put a damper on her excitement.

"No." Meena crawled back into bed beside her naked wife. "I wish. It's not that at all. Pennsylvanian powwow has nothing to do with Native powwows, or even Native people at all. They're German originally, very old thoughts and ways—prayers and charms together."

The women held each other under the wrinkled sheet, pulling against each other, skin to skin, with sore limbs and goose pimple flesh, bruised from the inside out by gin and revelry. This was the state Lucille sought for them—this brokenness, this vulnerability. She needed them unarmed to get to her answers. But that brokenness also made lovers ache for each other. Lucille clucked her tongue at one-night stands, not for any moral reason, but because she thought that such a delicious state was wasted on strangers too new to each other to get to the power of it all.

"We have to get up soon and hit the road," Meena whispered into Wendy's hair.

"I know, I know—just five more minutes."

"C'mon, we still have to break it to Lucky that she's been called forward." But Wendy bit the side of her breast, rubbed her cheek over the small indents, and laid a kiss on top of it, and Meena forgot what she was worried about, what she had to do, what she would ever have to do outside of this bed. She rolled over, pinning Wendy with her weight, and holding her arms above her head with one hand. She moved the other over her stomach. "Maybe just five more minutes."

"OKAY, WE'RE GOOD TO GO? Everyone got all their shit?" Their pathetic regiment was lined up on the walkway, reflected in the black lenses of Meena's oversized sunglasses. She was answered with groans and a few feeble yeses.

"Alright then, Lucky? You got the directions?"

Lucky held up a piece of paper with the motel name across the top.

"Where's your grandmother?"

"We don't have to check out for another two hours. She had an adventure last night, so I'm letting her sleep in."

"And you're sure we can't just take her back with us? We'd take good care of her while you're gone," Wendy asked from the passenger seat of the Audi. She'd had to sit down with a plastic bag on her lap, just in case.

"Thanks, Wendy, but I need to keep her with me. I don't want her taking any more midnight trips on anyone else's watch. She gets confused, and it's just better if I'm there." She felt this weight like a noose, the excitement of chasing the final spoon dampened by the knowledge that she had to bring Stella. She was starting to think she should have just left her with Clermont. At least their apartment would be close by, and the cat . . . Fucking cat.

"Okay, but call if you can't find Ricky," Meena said. "Lucille didn't say anything about you having a passenger on this trip, and any deviation from her instructions could mean you won't find what you're looking for."

"Should I ask Lucille?" Lucky offered.

The group laughed, quietly, so as to not shake their sore heads.

"You think Lucille exists in the daylight?" Morticia said. "In the sun that bitch would melt like she came from Oz."

"It'll be fine, I'm sure." Meena reached out and touched Lucky's shoulder. "You just take good care of each other." She turned and climbed into her car. "But call if anything goes wrong. And after you see Ricky too. Remember, tell her Lucille from Trout's sent you, in case she doesn't already know. She'll be able to take it from there."

The others mumbled their goodbyes and piled into the back seat, Freya briefly fighting with Morticia before stomping around to the far door and throwing herself in. Meena sighed, then climbed into the driver's seat. "Should be a fun trip home . . . Remember, call me."

Lucky waved as they pulled out of the lot. She was sad to see them go, partly because of her trepidation about the trip ahead, but also because she would actually miss them. Already they felt to her like some kind of fucked-up family. Lucky was good with that, being used to families of the fucked-up variety.

Behind her, the door opened. "Hey, some kid dropped a Popsicle in front of our room," Stella said, stepping outside. "It's all sticky out here. Little asshole."

She came to stand beside Lucky, who was watching Meena's car sliding up the road. Lucky put an arm around her grandmother's shoulders. "You're up already? We should go get breakfast, then."

Stella brightened. "Ooo, can we get Popsicles?"

THEY FOUND A SMALL DINER half an hour outside of Buzzards Bay and ate a quick, greasy meal, leaving with to-go cups of oily coffee. Stella passed out with a full belly in the front seat, and Lucky drank both cups herself. They had another seven hours in this first part of the journey. Stella dozed on and off. When she wasn't napping, she tried to get Lucky to play driving games, like I Spy and Place Names.

"I can't spy with my fucking eye unless you want us to crash into the ditch. Then all we'll be spying is the hospital."

"Jesus, you're grouchy. Just like your dad. He was a real grouch on road trips." Stella folded her arms over her chest and fiddled with the radio again.

"Did you guys go on lots of trips?" Lucky was immediately softer. Any information about her father was welcome.

"When he was little. Me and Oswald would go just about any-where we could get to in the car, all over. He'd be back there just sliding around the back seat of the Fairmont like the last bean on a plate." She laughed.

"Wait, you didn't strap him in?"

Stella shrugged. "Times were different. He made it through, safe enough. The hurts he suffered were self-inflicted. Me and Ozzy, we gave him everything, and he decided to go a different way."

They stopped for shitty hot dogs and shitty ice cream and lots of shitty canned drinks along the way. They filled up at an old-school gas station that didn't accept credit cards and had an ancient guy in denim coveralls manning the pump. Stella went to the bathroom each time they got off the road. Eventually it grew dark, and Lucky was so tired that holding the wheel required concerted effort.

In her exhaustion, a wave of anxiety about the whole future rolled over her. She had to make this work. There were no other good options. Soon enough, they would lose their apartment. Really, the only decision was about where Stella ended up. If they went back to Canada, either Lucky put her in a home so she could work full time—which might kill Stella—or she found a really cheap apartment and they both lived off government cheques—which would for sure kill Lucky. Driving into Pennsylvania, Lucky imagined feeding french fries to a catatonic Stella at a downtown McDonald's, both of them staring vacantly into space.

Guilt has a way of showing up when it is least useful and settling in so that it's hard to breathe. By the time they arrived in Schuykill County, all Lucky wanted was a drink to obliterate the shame that made it difficult to even look at her grandmother. Accordingly, she turned into a motel next door to a bar. She didn't have to search for Rattler Ricky until the morning, anyway.

"This one looks good," she said, pulling up to the office and parking.

"If you're a serial killer," Stella mumbled, wrapping her sweater tight around herself, eyeing the almost-empty parking lot, the neon sign with half the letters fluttering like moth wings.

"We're not exactly flush," Lucky said. "Meena gave us a budget, and we're sticking to it."

"Who's Meena? Is that a friend of your mother's? You know I don't like those people she hangs around with."

"No, Grandma. Meena is the woman who sent us on this trip, remember?" She had parked and was already getting out of the vehicle. She was not expecting a response.

"Oh, Wendy's wife. I like her. A bit of a snob, but she's a decent enough egg."

Lucky leaned back in. "You know who Meena is?"

"Sure, she's Wendy's wife . . . and Wendy is . . . my cousin?"

Lucky closed the car door and walked to the office.

FOR OVER AN HOUR, SHE paced inside their musty room, then back and forth outside the door. What if Stella got up again and wandered away while she was at the bar? Wasn't keeping an eye on her the whole reason she'd brought Stella with her?

The bar wasn't exactly banging. A few people had walked in from the road while she'd been watching. One pick-up had parked with the engine running while the driver stormed inside and then came out, ten minutes later, dragging a very drunk man behind her. She stuffed him in the passenger side and slammed the door, yelling, "If you aren't up for your shift tomorrow, expect to find your Xbox on the lawn."

Other than that, it was pretty quiet.

"So what exactly is Rattler Ricky?" she'd asked Meena that morning. God, had it been that same morning?

"She is a Booker, of sorts."

"Which is . . . ?"

"Someone who keeps and passes on knowledge, usually written stuff, but also oral. Ricky's more of an oral Booker."

"So would you say she's an oral expert?" Freya asked, stifling a smirk.

"No, I wouldn't. Not to her face, anyway," Meena said. "Bookers archive anything that could be useful, anything that can create maps—where we've been, where we need to go. Sometimes they gather, like in book clubs."

"Wait, like *book club* book clubs? Like Oprah?"

Meena looked thoughtful. "I've sometimes wondered about Oprah. Wouldn't it be amazing if she were one of us? Imagine the reach!"

"Maybe she has the seventh spoon." Morticia was uncharacteristically excited.

"I don't care at this point who has the seventh spoon, just that we find them, and soon."

"FUCK IT, I'LL JUST SIT by the window," Lucky said aloud. She jogged across the lot and pulled open the wooden door.

She had been in a lot of dive bars in her limited day, lots of tiny Greek pubs with two choices on draft, a few white-trash joints she left after one drink, and plenty of hipster bars set up to emulate both. But this one? It made the Trout Tavern look like the lobby bar at the Ritz-Carlton.

Except for the neon BAR in the window, it didn't even have a sign. The whole thing was more of a shack than a building. Exhaust from the road and the scent of cow shit from the field behind it filled the low-ceilinged room, mixing with the sour smells of old beer and unwashed skin. There were maybe a dozen people spread throughout, half at the bar, closest to the alcohol. Two played a slow game of pool on a duct-taped table in the back corner, and the rest sat as singles at different tables, the international sign of a real drinker. Alone. Focused.

She ordered a Miller Genuine Draft from the mute bartender, who seemed to resent having to heft his weight off his stool to get her a bottle from the fridge.

"Two dollars."

"Two bucks?"

"Two bucks."

She gave him three, and he looked confused. "I said two, lady. *Two.*"

"One's for you. You know, a tip."

They stared at each other for a moment. Then he grabbed up the ones in his giant hand and sauntered back to his stool.

"Alrighty then," Lucky said under her breath. Lucky walked carefully in the dim light, avoiding broken glass that hadn't been swept up and a round table with a particularly nasty-looking man who leered as she passed. She took her bottle towards the table closest to the front window so she could keep an eye on the red door with the backward *3* hanging loose on its single screw. As long as that door stayed closed, Stella was safe inside and, she hoped, still sleeping.

Music was coming from somewhere, but the speaker had obviously burst, and the strains of guitar and whine that together made country music were filtered through what sounded like a tin cup.

"Shit." She hadn't noticed that the table by the window was already taken. A small man sat in one of the wooden chairs. Inexplicably, there was a bottle of merlot on the table being drunk out of a cloudy pint glass.

Without looking up, they spoke as if Lucky had mused aloud. "I rent the glass. Chuck keeps my bottles behind the bar for me. That way I get what I want, and he gets some cash."

"Oh." Lucky was genuinely shocked. This was no small man; it was a small woman, who looked up at Lucky from under a wide-brimmed hat, a kind of outback-looking fedora with a wide leather band, a blue jay feather tucked in the side. "There's two seats here if you're ready to sit after all that exercise." She tipped her head in the direction of the window and the motel beyond.

"Oh shit." Lucky was embarrassed that someone had witnessed her frantic pacing.

"It's okay. We've all been there. Movement helps you think, most times."

"And sometimes it just makes you look like a maniac."

"Well, it helped you get over here. I've been waiting"—she lifted the bottle and looked at the contents in the light from outside—"almost half a bottle. I was starting to worry."

Lucky looked at her more closely. She was wearing what her mom used to call a "court outfit," a man's suit that didn't quite fit right, baggy around the shoulders, held to her thin body with suspenders and a belt. And there, dangling from a silver watch chain across her midsection, was a preserved snake's rattle. "Are you Rattler Ricky?"

"I am." She took a small sip of her wine and pointed with the glass across the table. "You gonna sit or did you maybe want to do laps around the lot to talk? I'm pretty sure Chuck wouldn't give a fuck if I took this alcohol off the premises, but I would. I'm out of shape and would just end up wearing it."

Lucky sat, and the two women clinked their drinks and sipped, taking each other in.

Ricky had a pleasant face, from what Lucky could see under the shadow of her hat brim. Fair-skinned with vivid freckles sprinkled across the bridge of her nose that made her seem younger than her hands revealed her to be. She wore a dress shirt under her wrinkled blazer, the collar stiff and yellowed, the top buttons undone to reveal old tattoo lines, blown out and blurry. She wore several bracelets on each wrist, each of them thin and delicate, with charms dangling. Her nails were short and clean, but her fingers were long and dirt-stained.

"I have a small farm up the road," she said, catching Lucky's eyes on her hands. "Some mud just never makes it all the way off."

"Sorry, sorry." Lucky shook her head. "I don't mean to be rude. I spent the day on the road. Guess I forgot my manners somewhere around hour six."

"It's okay. I had plenty of time to scope you out already. It's only fair."

"And what did you decide?"

Ricky sighed and sat back in her chair. "I decided you don't have parents. You move like a person with no net. I decided you are on the fence about this whole mission. A low fence, but, still, a fence. You are confused. It takes longer than a day or two to come to terms with a whole other layer to life, and you've only had a day or two, I'm guessing. You're skittish like that. Like someone who checks for the exits before they get fully into the room. Though I suspect you've had powerful women around you, because you hold that influence well."

"I do?"

Ricky finished her glass and nodded with her mouth full. "Mm-hmmm. In your shoulders, top of your spine." She pointed at those areas on Lucky. "Good places to hold power. Like a rifle sling."

Lucky sat up a little straighter.

"How did you know who I was?"

Ricky chuckled, pouring herself more wine. "Lucille told me to expect a young woman and an old lady, and I saw you guys go into your room. Not exactly magic. Also, I knew whoever they were sending on this damned journey would be in need of a drink." She opened her hand. "And here you are."

"So what exactly are we supposed to do?"

"Well, this, I suppose. We spend some hours together, and we piece together what it is you need to do to get to the final spoon. Hopefully, it'll become clear. If not, at least we get you to the next step."

"You don't know?" Why in the hell was she even here, then?

"What did you think would happen?"

"I thought I would find you, or maybe you would find me, and then you would tell me where I had to go." Lucky was frustrated and getting loud.

Ricky slammed her glass down on the table and leaned in a bit. "You really want me to tell you where to go right now?"

Lucky didn't answer.

The older woman picked up her glass and drank. "You ever fish?"

"Me? No. I live in the city. I mean, I have, once or twice. With my mom."

"When you fish you need one thing. You know what that is?"

"Let me guess . . . patience." Lucky rolled her eyes.

"No, dumbass. You can sit around as long as you want, but if you ain't got bait, you're not gonna catch anything but cold. You need bait." Ricky rolled her own eyes in direct mockery. "Lord, no wonder you got sent to me first."

Lucky had no idea what to say to that, so she chugged some beer, then checked the window for any sign of a wandering old lady.

"I think you're bait. In a way, anyway."

Lucky felt a chill start at the backs of her knees, that place you feel pain the hardest, the place where heartache manifests first as a physical sensation.

"But also . . . something else." Her voice had grown quiet. For some reason, this made it easier for Lucky to hear her, even through the echoey music and an argument that had started at the bar about what happened to the auto industry.

"Let's head out." Ricky downed the contents of her glass, pulled a cork out of her front pocket, and slammed it into the top of the bottle. She picked up her wine and stood.

"Wait, go? Where are we going?"

"Outside. We need some privacy."

"I can't leave. I have to watch—"

"We'll stay within eyeshot of your room, but we need to take this outside." She indicated the two angry men by the bar, who were now standing, hands balled into fists, one stool tipped over on its side. "It's about to get typical in here, and we have work to do."

Lucky stuck her beer bottle under her jacket and followed Ricky out the door and around the side of the bar, checking that their room was still in sight.

The grass underfoot was hard, crunchy with gravel and glass. They stood between the splintery wooden wall of the bar and the shell of a semi up on cinder blocks. Ricky put down her bottle and raised her arms. Her eyes closed, she began to whisper a prayer.

"What are you doing?"

"Ninety-first Psalm. The one that begins everything we do. If you know it, speak up."

"What if I don't?"

"Then shut up." She continued, speaking the words so fast they hung together like a song, the lines worn into the grooves of a mind that had focused on them for so many years. Coming from this tiny woman, as they stood between a wonky bar and the ghost of a rig, it didn't even seem strange to hear a Christian prayer. Out here it became something else entirely.

"A thousand may fall at your side, ten thousand at your right hand, but it will not come near you."

Lucky waited until Ricky had finished, put her arms down, and opened her eyes. "Are you a minister or something?"

"Not on your life. I'm, ah, I guess what some might call a cunning person. Others might say a powwow man. Or a German magi. Artist, even. Doesn't matter what the title is. I am connected, is all." She pulled scraps of paper from her oversized jacket pockets and shuffled through them.

"Connected to what exactly?"

"Well, that's a larger conversation, and I'm not sure we have that kind of time. Maybe after this is done, we can meet up at this same janky bar and share one of these bottles of mine." She was dropping paper like snowflakes onto the ground. "Right now, we'll just say God. That usually makes everyone feel okay."

Lucky felt a bit embarrassed, though she couldn't say why.

"It's weird for you. I can see that. But don't worry so much about what others might think. As long as *you* can still think, that's all that matters."

"I'm not doing that very clearly these days." Lucky kicked at the rocks by her feet.

"Hey, listen. I'm sure as fuck no counselor, but here's what I've got to say about it. You always felt something was missing, yeah?"

Lucky nodded.

"And then one day you found a spoon, and then a woman found you, and then you were in Salem at a creepy old house, right?"

She nodded again.

"And this woman, this one who came and snatched you from your regular old life where something was missing—but, dammit, it was still a regular life—she tells you there are witches, and powwow people, and secret keepers, and that she dreamt of you. And that you are, in fact, one of those witches. Next thing you know, you're meeting some weirdo at a shitty bar, so that weirdo sends you barreling across state lines to meet another weirdo in another shitty bar." She gestured with her hands, still full of random pages. "How would anyone be able to think clearly?"

Lucky took it all in. "Thanks, Ricky. You're right—I should give myself a break."

"Oh, now, I didn't say that. There's no time for breaks. Now is the time for full speed ahead."

Ricky held up one torn paper above her head. "Okay, found it! Let's do this. First, I'm going to need to revise it a bit. It's for bringing back stolen goods, and since the spoons were technically stolen from Low and Company in 1892, it might work. But we don't need the spoons to come back to us—that will take too long. We just want to know where to go and get the last one. Sort of a pickup-not-delivery kind of situation."

Ricky started taking off her jacket.

"So, do I need to, like, prepare somehow? Like, take stuff off too . . ."

"Yeah, your pants need to come off," Ricky responded, folding her blazer and placing it on the ground.

Lucky stared at her a moment, but then thought, fuck it, and started to unbutton her black jeans.

"Jeez, I'm only kidding." Ricky laughed real big. "No, no, I just need to get to my kit. You relax for a minute." She got down on her knees on top of the folded jacket. "Just keep your pants on." Then she laughed at her own joke while Lucky pulled her zipper back up.

"A comedian, eh? If this . . . thing . . . doesn't work out for you, you should get in touch with Comedy Central."

Ricky took off her hat, revealing short hair streaked silver and black, almost skunk-like. She slipped out of her suspenders and unbuttoned her dress shirt, whispering prayers the whole time, glancing at the sky now and then. Lucky felt like she was intruding on something deeply personal and shifted her gaze to the skeletal truck, noticing small reflective eyes watching her from the fire-damaged chassis, a raccoon wary of their noise. Ricky reached behind her back and pulled a long roll of red fabric from her waistband. She placed it in front of her on the jacket and gave it a push, and it unrolled like a sleeping bag.

"Alright, I know I have it here . . ." She pulled out scissors and a whittling knife and tightly wound scrolls, branches, and test tubes with cork stoppers, each held in narrow pockets sewn into the fabric. She pulled a smooth black rock from one pouch and dug around in the space behind it, her fingers reaching to the bottom of the pocket.

"Ah! Here it is."

She'd found a swatch of pink velvet, folded over like an envelope. She put it in the centre of one palm and picked the flaps open with her other hand. Lucky leaned in. There was nothing . . . almost nothing. Just some old slivers of wood. "What's that?"

"Wood from the old Low jewelry store. It used to be a church and a meetinghouse, did you know that?"

"Yeah, but how did you get them?" Lucky didn't realize they'd been whispering until Ricky spoke at a regular volume again.

"Prepared, is all. Knew it was coming. Where's your car?" Ricky was back in her jacket and hat like a proper gentleman, with three small slivers cradled in her right hand. Lucky imagined Stella waking and coming outside at this exact moment. No one would blame her for feeling confused, walking in on this odd scene. She herself was confused.

"Since the spell is to bring back stolen goods—if we focus, both of us, now, on the theft of the spoons, the original gathering of the implements from their owner, then this will work."

"But aren't the spoons ours? Or at least Sarah's? She was the one who hexed them."

Ricky laughed. "Hexed. God, you are a newbie. Yes. The intent of the spoons belongs to Sarah. But the spoons themselves, as physical objects, were designed, crafted, and paid for by the Low company. We need to really understand that. Think on it." She paused, watching Lucky in profile. "Come, girl, think on it!"

Lucky snapped her eyes shut and breathed out slowly. Okay, Seth Low came back from Germany. He had an idea, a directive, to make these spoons. So he drafted them up . . .

She could see him, sitting at a desk lit by an oil lamp. The office had electricity, but Seth didn't want to waste it. People said it was abundant, electricity, this new thing. But he didn't believe them. Everything but the Lord was finite . . .

Lucky opened her eyes. "I saw him. I mean . . . I heard him too. His thoughts."

"Who?"

"The man who made the spoons." Lucky was a little shocked. She had seen him as if watching a movie, clear, in colour. She understood his motives and methods.

"Good, good. You have a bit of a seer about you, then. Keep thinking on him. Go back."

Lucky closed her eyes.

That is why only the Lord could be trusted. Lamplight would suffice. It was just a spoon, and he already had the basic design. He just needed to refine the lines of the witch and the broom and the pins, keeping it simple for the smithies' sakes and for his own—the image had to project a warning.

Symbols of evil—the hag. Symbols of God's ire—the pins. The tie-in to the historical events of his hometown and the way he would sell them—letters spelling SALEM *down the handle. Yes, good. Perfect. He felt pride, ownership, a sense of purpose.*

"Do you have it? His claim over them?" Ricky's voice came from far away, somewhere outside of the simple office room where Lucky watched Seth work.

"Yes. He is proud. He thinks this will keep his name alive and make him important to important men."

"Good, good, now come back, but bring that feeling with you."

Lucky retreated from the desk, from the room, until the circle of light from Seth's oil lamp was just a flickering speck in a larger constellation. For a moment she wondered what those other pinpoints of light were . . . Other rooms, perhaps? Maybe she could see other people, if she just moved around . . .

"No, Lucky, come back to me. Bring his pride with you," Ricky called. Lucky followed her voice to the parking lot.

"Okay, take these." Ricky grabbed her wrist and dumped the slivers from her cupped palm into Lucky's. "Place them in three different places around the front right tire of your car."

Lucky was a bit unsteady. That unsteadiness stopped the questions that were starting to bubble up. She crouched and did as she was told, shoving some into the crevices in the rubber, jamming one into a crack in the old hubcap. "Now what?"

"Now get in." Ricky yanked the driver's door open with a loud creak. Both women looked over at the motel room, waiting for an interruption. But the door stayed closed, the window dark.

Lucky got in and turned the car on, keeping the lights off. Ricky stayed outside, standing by the open window.

"Put it in reverse and, when I tell you, very slowly, as slowly as you can manage, inch backward. When I say, okay?" Ricky pulled out the scrap of paper she'd dug up earlier.

"Got it." Lucky put both hands on the wheel. She felt the weight of Seth Low and his schemes in her ribs, balanced in the curves of bone, like a marble in a ladle. She had to focus to keep it centred, to keep it held—so focused she could barely hear Ricky reciting from the page.

"O Sophia, Wisdom herself, come forth." She repeated this three times. "Thief, allow us passage to gather the stolen goods. Thief.

Thief. Thief. Guide us to the property taken against the command-ments. Thou art not above consequences. This consequence is us." She paused and nodded to Lucky, who very gently stepped off the brake. The SUV began a slow roll. Louder now, Ricky continued.

"By the wood taken from the building you stole from, we shall find your path. We will come. We will recover. God the Father. God the Son. God the Spirit. Sophia and her daughters, all the gods of heaven will see. Lead us to the stolen goods. Thief. Thief. Thief. Guide us to the goods."

The Pathfinder had barely cleared the white lines of the room's parking spot when Ricky lowered both her voice and her hands and pocketed the worn page she had read from.

"Okay. Now go to bed." She turned to leave.

"What?" Lucky put the SUV in park and jumped out. "What do you mean?"

Ricky turned. "What I mean is, go to bed." She continued on her way, which seemed to be towards the main road.

"Aren't you forgetting something?" Lucky yelled after her.

Ricky stopped. "Oh shit, you're right." She switched directions. "My wine."

Lucky chased after her. "No, I mean, where the hell am I going?"

"I told you." She slung her bottle under her arm. "To bed. Hope-fully straight to sleep." She headed back towards the road.

"But where do I go after that? Christ, why are you all so secre-tive?" She threw her hands up and asked this question of the sky itself.

"We're not," Ricky called over her shoulder, pointing up to that same sky. "She is. We just need to have what you need for fishing."

"Bait?"

She was at the road now, standing under a yellow lamp thick with frantic moths. "Patience." Then she moved into the dark.

Lucky sighed, alone now in the parking lot. She headed back to the car to re-park it.

"I'll be back when the sun rises," Ricky said. Lucky was sure the voice had come from inside her own head.

She went into the room. The first thing that greeted her was a steady snore from the second queen-sized bed.

"Oh, Grandma," she whispered. "It sucks doing this alone." She stripped down, drank a glass of water, and crawled into the scratchy sheets. She fell asleep thinking about points of light constellating the night sky.

STELLA WAS SHAKING HER AWAKE. "Lucky! Lucky, get up!"

"Jesus, what? What is it?"

A quick glance at the clock told her it was not yet six.

"Someone's at the door. Get up!"

"Who is it?" She sat up quickly, throwing off the tangled sheets.

"A small man." Stella was squeezing her fingers, pulling her wedding band up to her swollen knuckle and back down again.

"A small man?"

"Yes. What if it's about the spoons?" Her eyes darted to the door and back, then to the window, the curtains pulled tight.

Lucky got up, went to the window, and peeked out.

"Oh, Grandma, that's just Rattler Ricky."

Stella's fear had woken her up, but Stella remembering the existence of the spoons made her pause.

"Grandma, do you know where we are?"

"What the hell kind of question is that? Go see him. Meena said we had to. I'm going to clean up." And she walked into the bathroom, closing the door behind her.

Lucky took the chain off and opened the front door. "Good morning. You weren't kidding about being here early."

"Come out." Guess she wasn't one for pleasantries.

Lucky grabbed a long cardigan from the chair, wrapping it around herself. She slipped into Stella's Birkenstocks and walked outside. It wasn't cold as much as that sense of sharpness—*brisk*, the word came to her. Ricky was crouched behind the Pathfinder.

"Wood says you need to head to the mountains next." She held up her fingers and rubbed them together as if testing oil. Ashes fell to the pavement.

"The wood says?"

"The wood wants mountains. So that's where you go."

"Is that where the last spoon is? And the witch that comes with it?" Lucky was exasperated. It was too early for this. She wasn't sure what the right time of day would be for this, but six A.M. was not it.

"Fuck if I know. I just know that's where it wants you to head. It's bound to get you closer, at least." She got up with a groan. "I need a helper. Getting too old for this."

She was wearing the same outfit as the night before. And in the early light, Lucky noticed lines around her mouth and eyes, like someone who'd expressed a lot over many years. "You ever think about coming back, I could use your hands." She tapped her forehead. "And your sight."

"Did the wood have an address I can put into the GPS or . . . ?"

"Oh, you're a funny one. It did not. But I have one. I know who you need to see. I could smell her damn cooking as soon as I got here." She pulled out another piece of paper from her never-empty pockets. This time it was a receipt. She reached down and got the stub of a carpenter's pencil out of her sock, licked the tip, and started writing against the rear windshield.

"May Moon Montgomery. She doesn't have an address, not really. Not even sure she lives on a legitimate street. But she has a place, and these are the directions. Get to the town of Blowsy Creek, Missouri, and then follow these." She handed over the receipt.

"May Moon . . ."

". . . Montgomery, yeah," Ricky finished for her. "It's her real name. Not like you're one to judge, Lucky."

"I have a question, Ricky. If all it took was some pieces of wood and a prayer, why in the hell didn't Meena just get you to find all the spoons?"

Ricky smiled, slow and wide. "It's cute you think that's all it took. There are consequences to everything—to every inquiry, every ask, every push. Each witch finds the next, and all things in their own time, according to the good Lord."

"Fair enough. So when do I leave? Is there, like, a time frame?"

"Well, considering you're running down the clock standing here, I'd get going now, or as soon to now as you can." She grabbed Lucky's hand, which was a shock. They hadn't touched before now. Ricky's skin felt like suede, a lot softer than it looked, a lot softer than any human's probably should be.

"Now repeat after me, and don't go interrupting the prayer." She closed her eyes and after a moment squeezed Lucky's fingers until she followed suit.

"I, Lucky St. James . . ."

"I, Lucky St. James . . ."

"Will go on a journey today. And by the Virgin Mary with her seven rings and her true things . . ."

The prayer was half familiar—old Catholic terms and words—

and half absolute weirdness to Lucky's ears and mouth. Ricky made her slow down at one point and paused so long in other places that Lucky peeked to check if she was finished. After an "Amen," Lucky started to pull her hand away, but the older woman held fast.

"Now you have to say three Hail Marys."

"The whole thing?"

"Jesus, girl, it's like the shortest prayer."

"Three times, though?"

"Everything in threes."

When they were done, Ricky tipped her hat, made the sign of the cross with her fingers in the air, and wandered back to the road without another word. She whistled as she walked, a cheerful tune that didn't fit with her dark court suit and her sombre office. Lucky watched her as she turned right onto the road and sauntered back towards where she had come.

"A legend, truly," she whispered.

"What's that?" Stella was at the door with her suitcase in one hand and stolen motel towels in the other.

"Oh, nothing. Just thinking about what I want to be when I grow up," she said. "And turn around, Stella. I need a quick shower before we go. I hope you left me a towel."

Stella gave her a furtive glance and handed one over. "Where are we headed to now?"

Lucky tossed her sweater on the chair. "Today we are going to the Moon."

She whistled on her way to the bathroom, a cheerful tune that didn't fit the road they were about to take.

21

A WOLF AT THE DOOR

The drive back to Salem was uneventful. Except for a quick stop so Wendy could throw up in the ditch, which then triggered Freya to vomit out the window, it was a straight shot home.

"Amateurs," Meena had scoffed.

Wendy spoke in a whisper. "Why does every visit to Lucille have to end like this?"

"Because that's how she does it. I don't question her methods."

"Maybe you should," Wendy groaned.

"Almost home, love. Then you can have a shower and a nap."

"I'm just going to get into the bath and drink it dry," Freya said from the back seat.

"Well, I don't approve of you drinking to begin with. You're much too young."

"I am a member of the coven, though. I didn't want to throw off the ritual."

Meena looked at the girl in the rearview mirror. "What a good witch you are, Freya."

"I am, aren't I."

"One of the best," Morticia responded. She'd been mostly asleep for the whole trip. Now that they were nearly back to the house, she lowered her window to let in some fresh air. At first, the breeze hitting her skin felt so refreshing, she pushed her face out the opening, letting her hair blow wild. She filled her lungs—

"Oh god, what is that smell?"

"It isn't me," Freya said. "I made sure I leaned out pretty far to clear the side of the car."

"It's not that." She shot Freya a quick look. "I mean, I smell you, and you're gross, like sour milk and garbage. But this is something else entirely."

She pushed her face back out the window. The scent was thick, deep. It was the smell of choral music and heavy books about the industrial revolution. It was unbuttered bread and rain in the winter. It was tall, dark grass and rocky, hard soil. Inside this smell, Morticia was Patricia again—no, she was Pat. There were no mirrors that weren't cloudy, no rugs that didn't reek of cat piss. In this smell there was barely air for Pat to breathe.

"Morticia, what's wrong?" The concern in Meena's voice snapped her back to the car. "Roll up the window now!"

She was crying, fat tears sliding down her pale cheeks and onto her blouse. Why was she crying? She couldn't remember how it started. She had only two images in her head. She spoke them out loud after sealing the window tight.

"It's like polished wood and clean fur."

Meena and Wendy exchanged a glance. A smell that could make you that sad and be that specific was not good. A literal ill wind.

"What the hell is it?" Freya asked, leaning over to rub Morticia's back.

"Something truly evil," Meena answered. Thinking out loud, she asked, "You don't think it could be . . . ?"

"No." Wendy felt queasy again. "No way. They're just stories."

"What?" Freya asked, growing anxious.

"Benandanti." Wendy said it quietly, as if the word itself might call it to them.

"I knew it!" Freya shouted. "I knew they were real. I was just talking about them last night, remember?"

"But why now? They've had plenty of time to try to interfere," Wendy said.

"If that's what it is, then, maybe they're scared we're closing in on the seventh witch," Meena answered.

"There's more than one? Are you sure?" Freya's voice was getting high.

"I have no idea! No one has any idea anymore." Meena took some deep breaths. *Say something to calm them down. Say anything!* "I guess that's a sign: we must be close enough for them to send out a wolf."

"Wait." Freya pulled herself up to lean into the space between the women. "Like, an actual wolf is here?"

"No, no. But also maybe yes. Who knows?" Meena's foot got heavy on the gas. "Lettie and Everett are alone at the house. Freya, put your seatbelt back on, please." Freya slid back and did as she was told.

Ten minutes later, they screeched into the driveway and sat there for a moment, gathering themselves inside the car as it ticked angrily from being driven so hard.

"What's the plan?" Freya whispered.

All eyes were on Meena. "Why the hell are you all looking at me? I don't know!" She twisted the leather steering wheel so that her hands wouldn't shake. They couldn't come up with any sort of plan until they knew what might be waiting for them. Plus she'd never had any experience with an actual Benandanti, not that she knew of. They could have been watching for years, could have been skulking around. Hell, they might be working at their grocery store or delivering their mail.

Finally she snapped out of it and said, "We need to go inside and make sure Lettie and Everett are okay. If they are, we batten down the hatches and then start locking up with protection spells." She cracked open the car door and sniffed, using her nose before her eyes to try to gauge the danger. She smelled buds in trees, some near to bursting with tightly packed green. Nothing else. She listened hard and heard the skitter and creak of the bugs that lived in those trees. A dog barked from up the road.

"I think we're okay," she said, and got out. The others followed, Morticia still shaking. Freya ran for the front door, pulling her keys out of her backpack as she did. She unlocked the door and rushed in, leaving it open behind her. "Lettie!" she yelled. "Everett!"

Meena, Wendy, and Morticia had made it to the front porch when she poked her head back outside. "Found them! They're okay. They're alright."

"Oh thank god!" Meena put her hand on her chest to slow her heart, and the three of them hurried inside. "That means we have time. Let's go!"

They locked the doors and windows. Wendy stuck a metal bar in the sliding door off the kitchen for extra security, and Freya ran outside with a knife tucked in between her teeth to close all the shutters, fitting each latch with a small brass lock. She held up a handful of tiny keys. "I don't know which one fits which lock. We'll have to figure that out when this is over."

Wendy closed all the fireplace flues and made sure their bedroom balcony door was locked and the drapes pulled tight. After Lettie put Everett down for a nap, she joined in the preparations. "What's really going on?" she asked. "What happened to you all at Buzz Bay? And where are Lucky and Stella?"

Freya explained as best she could while the two of them pushed an armoire full of gardening supplies and old jackets in front of the back door. "Lucille got us hammered. And she told us we had to split up, so Lucky took Stella and went to see a cunning person in Pennsylvania somewhere. And we are supposed to use a bowl to try and see the next witch, so we can let Lucky know. She's focusing on the spoon. Then Morticia smelled a hunter on the way home, like, literally smelled the fucker. Oh, and we only have nine days to complete the coven, or I guess it's eight now."

"Eight days?" Lettie stopped pushing, and Freya straightened to stretch out her back.

"Yup. Eight."

"And then what? What happens after eight days if we don't have the spoon?"

Freya shrugged. "I guess it's just over. We go back to where we came from. We go back to our shitty lives and our shitty mall job and try to forget this ever happened." For once, she sounded incredibly young.

"Holy shit, Freya." Lettie grabbed her arm. "How could we ever go back?"

"Well, it sounds like we're only a real coven when we're complete. Maybe we could try to stay in touch, or be roommates or something, but . . . that's it."

Lettie leaned against the heavy cabinet. It squeaked slowly across the floor. "Meena keeps saying 'find the seven, wait for the rest,' keeps talking about changing the world and shit, like she's starting a charity. I mean, what could one small coven do, anyway? Do you think she even knows?"

Freya added her weight, and with a final heave, the door was blocked. There was now only one way in or out, the front door, and that was locked three different ways. "I don't think anyone can really know."

They found the others in the dining room. On the way down the hall, Freya said, "Wait—you don't think we'll actually die if Lucky can't find her? That can't be what they mean by it being over, right?"

Lettie didn't answer. She wasn't sure what she thought, and she sure as hell didn't want to waste time getting scared, not now. Fear was paralyzing, and she needed to move.

The others were standing over the table, arranging items around a large glass bowl—crystals, a clutch of dried herbs held together by thread, candles, a big jug of water.

"What are we doing?" Freya asked.

"Hydromancy," Wendy answered, carrying an oversized book to the table. "Divination with water, also called scrying." She dropped the book with a thud, and Meena had to clutch the jug so it didn't tip. "Sorry." She began flipping pages.

"We need to focus, more than anything," Meena said. "At least two of us, but preferably all." She pulled her braids back over her shoulders, closed her eyes, and started breathing deeply.

Freya went to stand beside Wendy, who was running her finger down the yellowed pages. "Are we looking for the witch or the witch hunter?"

"The witch. I mean, both if we can manage it, but most importantly, the seventh witch," Wendy answered. Her finger stopped.

"Here it is—we need to pull attention to them, which will be hard since we don't know who they are yet."

"Can we do it without that?" Lettie was eyeing the back window nervously. She was having trouble thinking of anything but the hunter. She, more than any of them, knew what it was to be the object of a man's loathing, to have hands laid on her.

Meena opened her eyes. "Lettie, you are so anxious right now."

"Sorry, sorry, I just . . ."

"No, no, it's good—useful." She stepped away from the table without pouring the water into the bowl. "Let's save the scrying for later. Right now, Lettie, why don't you lead us in casting some protection spells. You have the focus we need to make them strong."

"Okay." She ran a shaking hand through her loose curls. "My intention—it's to keep the walls secure?"

"No, love." Meena slid an arm around her trembling shoulders. "It's to make us invisible. I don't want him to even be able to find our walls."

AFTER HE LANDED FROM TORONTO, Jay had to rent himself a car at the airport. How pedestrian. He stood in line, haggled for the best vehicle on the lot, which happened to be a matte black Range Rover, and then had to deal with the money aspect, which made him cross. His assistant usually handled these things, but he was travelling solo and had left in too much of a rush to plan ahead. He filled out the papers, was handed the keys by a beautiful Korean woman with plump cheeks and bleached hair—the one bright spot in the experience, but no time to dally—and tossed his Louis Vuitton duffel bag in the back seat.

Salem was too small for his liking. He spent so much of his time alone that when he went to a city, he preferred it be ostentatious, cocky even, like New York. Or London—London was so full of it-self it barely allowed traffic to flow. Salem was both too hokey and too aware of the limitations of being up against the brutal ocean. Even worse, Salem was satisfied with itself, felt no drive to become a better version.

But this was where the boy Malcolm had said the new witch would be. Jay hadn't thought the one in charge would be com-fortable enough to bring coven business to her own home. He'd underestimated her, imagined her flighty, like a rabbit. As it turned out, she might just be the cockiest thing about Salem. She was, after all, a descendant of two powerful lines of witches that went all the way back to two continents, both Europe and Africa. This was why she had been so hard to find, so impossible to render vulnerable so that he could pounce. He'd spent many years hunting witches, more than he cared to count. Her old blood had saved her from sudden apartment fires or brutal car accidents, the fates that had befallen others who had tried to build the coven on his watch.

He pushed start and drove the car onto the highway, then turned towards the centre of town. Once there, he just needed to find a spot and listen. Sooner or later, they'd be loud against the established landscape. And then he would be on them.

HE WAS ON FOOT NOW, near the Salem Witch House. He thought the irony befitting—seeking witches near a house made to appear occult for the tourists who also came looking for witches. Piggybacking on intention was always a good way to get a boost. He planted his feet carefully, making sure he felt the pressure of the sidewalk through his Italian brogues. He shook out his arms, twisting his hands at the wrists, working out the tension in his muscles. He folded his hands together in front of him and took a breath so deep his shirt strained, then blew it all out. He closed his eyes, stopped smelling the air, refusing to acknowledge the breeze over his skin, and just listened.

This was how Prudence had taught him, so many years ago.

"Listen, James. Lean into it. Don't use your ears."

He'd laughed and said, "How am I to listen without my ears?" He found her especially beautiful when she tried to teach him her ways, before his family line was revealed, when he was still human, still mortal. She was fetching all the time, but in these moments she was painfully beautiful.

"Scoundrel!" She slapped his arm, and he felt it in his thighs. "Ears are only the beginning of listening. Most people are so lazy they stop there, but you can listen with your body and soul attuned to all the real sound in the world. That's how the gods built us."

This talk of multiple gods was heresy, as was this work they were practicing. Even out here, alone in the woods, he caught his breath at the risks they were taking. That he was deeply in love with this witch was even more troubling.

"For you, Prudence, I shall try."

Every time he did let himself think about that afternoon on that English hillside with Prudence, even centuries later, he became weak with want. Even now, after the bliss of their affair had long ended, with the sting of her betrayal still lingering, standing alone and ancient in new Salem, Jay felt each rib in his chest vibrate with the pounding of his sick heart. At least he had this, if not the only woman he'd ever loved in his long life—he had the spells and ways of being she had taught him before the night she tried to take his life.

"Go away, old ghosts," he hissed, trying to clear away the thoughts that clouded his hearing.

Birds. Cars. Dogs. Even cats purring. He heard low conversations in living rooms. The sound of one hundred and sixty-two toilets flushing. People typing on laptops, sneezing, scratching dry skin, pushing greasy hair behind downy ears. He tuned some in and pushed others out, moving the range of his hearing like he was rotating sensitive dials. He listened for expansion and contraction, the music of magic.

And then he heard it: a low thrum pushing back against the skin of life, altering the assigned boundaries. Fixed on that sound, he opened his eyes, went back to his car, and started driving. He had found a powerful woman, and he was on his way to her now.

IT HAD TAKEN A WHILE to narrow in on a single point on the map, but he was here. The front door was closed, the windows covered with shutters, the walls solid. But what were walls to Jay Christos? He paused in the driveway, turned on *La Bohème*, and took a moment to remove his jacket, check his hair in the mirror, apply lip balm, and open up all his senses again. He didn't know what kind of power he'd be encountering, and he needed to be ready to dominate it.

Then he opened the car door, unfolded to his full height, and walked towards the building, past the one other car parked in the lot. The girl, Lucky St. James, had been here. And the woman who helped her on her journey was inside—he was sure of it.

"Is this you, Meena?" he whispered. "Clever witch, leaving your home for the outskirts. But not clever enough to know how to muffle your melody."

He pulled the handle, and the door opened. Inside, it was dim, and there was music, a soft undertone of cheerful rock—dreadful stuff. And there, behind the bar of the Trout Tavern, was a real, live

Tender. Lucille saw him right away, really saw him, all the way inside him. She couldn't hide the recognition, which overwhelmed her like a bad smell. And then he saw her, too—really saw her—all the way down the strands of DNA to her ancestors. He saw her mother at a bar in Boston, her grandmother pouring drinks in long skirts, and on, until he came to the Tender who, in 1892, led the witch Sarah to the Low & Co. warehouse, where she altered the spoons that were causing all this trouble now.

"Hello, great-great-granddaughter of Annie," he cooed, sliding onto a stool. How lovely to run into the descendant of such a troublesome Tender. He was genuinely pleased. "I would recognize that scar anywhere." He ran the tip of his index finger across his own throat, indicating the mark passed down to Annie's female descendants, the mark of a woman who had carried power and swung from the rafters for it.

Suddenly, Lucille found it hard to breathe, as if her own feet were dancing on open air.

THE MOTHER FINALLY CONCEDED. IT was time to call the Good witch. It was time to warn her about the desert-dwelling wolf. He was too close not to.

The Maiden was inconsolable. She'd smashed the absinthe bottle against the wall, pushed over a chair, and was now sobbing, head down, at the table. Lucille had been a great Tender, but she had been an even greater friend, and now she was gone.

The Crone stood at the window, smoking, watching the busy streets below illuminate into ribbons of moving light as the sun set.

"It never ends, does it?" She spoke softly in the presence of the Maiden's sorrow.

"It will end," the Mother answered. She walked over to the Crone, plucked the cigarette from her lips, and took a drag. "First, we need to contact the Salem witches."

Just then the office line rang. It was an unusual sound, even startling the Maiden into lifting her head.

The three women of the Oracle stood still, watching the red light blink with each shrill ring on the rotary phone. Finally, the Mother hurried to the bar and lifted the receiver.

"Hello."

She listened for several minutes.

"Yes, we understand."

She glanced over at her colleagues, listening some more.

"We will be in touch shortly."

Then she hung up, lowering her shoulders as she lowered the receiver back into the cradle. She sighed, then turned to face the other two, who waited.

"That was Meena Good. He has found them. He's in Salem."

"No shit he's in Salem! Who else would string Lucille up like a deer?" The Maiden jumped to her feet, hands balled into fists.

"Well, no. He came to Salem, but they hid themselves. That's probably when he sussed out poor Lucille." The Mother tried to speak slowly and calmly, to keep the anxiety in the room from boiling over.

"They have a powerful protector among them." The Crone smiled with satisfaction. "Must be the Creole mother. Motherhood can do wonderful things to a witch's power."

"I'm getting on a plane." The Maiden was already scrolling on her phone, looking for flights.

The Mother approached her with that same calm cadence, placed a hand on her forearm, and pushed the phone down. "I think it's time we . . . take steps."

"Mais non, we cannot," the Crone interrupted. "What can we do? We are not coven witches."

"Fuck it," the Mother said, with a raised voice. "There are ways we can use our influence. We are, after all, the best of our kind—a Tender, a Booker, and a Watcher together? There have to be ways."

The Maiden relaxed for the first time since they'd received word about the gruesome discovery at the Trout Tavern. "Influence?"

"Indeed." The Mother was already scheming. "We won't be able to directly play the game, but perhaps we can do some better sideline coaching. At least until the seven are united. Once they are together, we can focus on other things."

"Like gutting that Christos fucker." The Maiden smiled.

"I should like a good hunt," the Mother said, thoughtful.

The Crone walked over and closed the boardroom door. From the hallway, there was the sound of fingers snapping as the candles were lit and the circle was called.

22

DEATH RATTLE

Lucky and Stella left Schuykill County at a leisurely pace. Their destination was eighteen hours away, according to Google, a trip that would take them two days, so Lucky saw no need to push it too hard, not right away. They stayed that first night in an Airbnb she'd booked on her phone when they stopped for chicken and waffles at a diner. The place she found was a small cabin near Wayne National Forest.

"What the hell kind of name is Wayne for a forest? We really must be in hick country," Stella said, a little too loudly.

"Grandma! Don't be calling people hicks when—"

"When we're in hick country? Okay."

The text from the owners had said the key to the cabin would be under a pink painted stone in the front garden. Sure enough, she found a bunch of different-coloured stones, one of which was faded pink, and underneath it was the key.

"Odd security system," Stella remarked while she waited by the door with her bag.

"I don't think they have to worry about people breaking in

around here." They'd driven for twenty minutes on the first side road and not seen another house, and then had almost missed the driveway, it was so narrow and hidden.

"Oswald used to leave the apartment unlocked. Said it was on the third floor, no one would bother climbing that many stairs to steal our fruit bowl or his pyjamas anyway. But, sure enough, one day we came home, and the TV was gone." She shrugged.

"Well, here they'd have to find the key first," Lucky said, holding it up. "So I think we're okay." Still, she opened the door slowly, flicking the lights on and sweeping her eyes over the main room before letting the older woman in. Stella was exhausted, and so was she. Her grandmother had stayed awake for most of today's seven-hour drive.

The cabin was small and cute, just a main room with an orange couch and two green easy chairs pushed close to a large fireplace. There was a galley kitchen off to one side and, in the back, one tiny bedroom, which would be Stella's, with an adjoining bathroom. Lucky was used to sleeping on couches. While Stella ran a bath, Lucky sat on the couch, a long wood-framed antique covered in heavy brocade, and enjoyed the musical that had started up in the bathroom. Stella always sang in the bath. Tonight, it was a song about gambling and knowing when to just walk away. Before Lucky could call to check in with the others, she dozed off, right where she sat, still in her shoes, before Stella had even reached the end of the song. Like most times when she tipped over into sleep from exhaustion, Lucky dreamed of her mother.

THE FIRST TIME LUCKY LOST a tooth, the tooth fairy left her a bowling trophy. It was confusing, because when she asked Stella to read the little plaque to her, it said TO FRED, BEST GUTTER BALL IN THE STATE.

The second time she lost a tooth, she got nothing at all. She thought maybe it was a one-shot deal and she was left with a mouth-ful of duds. But a week later a ziplock bag of pennies showed up under her pillow with a handwritten note on the back of an Export label that read, *Sorry, I'm shitty with deadlines.* She quickly sent the delinquent fairy a thank-you prayer, since she wasn't sure how to reach her.

"Fuck 'em all, and let Jesus sort it out," Arnya would say. So Lucky got in the habit of relaying all her important messages through heaven, since Jesus was such a good organizer.

Arnya was a magician. She could make groceries appear over-night even though the stores were closed. She found ways to evade the landlady, where others would be stuck paying rent. With just one sentence, she could make Lucky feel both panic and relief.

Lucky grew used to her mother's mercurial nature, the comings and goings that meant she often stayed over at Stella's apartment. Once she could read, she collected magazines, which was easy to do, since magazines were transient in nature, the hobos of the written word, hopping on trains, sleeping in alleyway piles, abandoned on chairs in office lobbies where people came to wait. By the time she was eight, she had a wall of sloping, slippery magazines like pulpy pillars stacked beneath her window in her attic room at Grandma's.

"What do you need all these for?" Arnya was sitting on Lucky's mattress smoking a cigarette and painting the peeled heel of her black boots with a small bottle of black nail polish. "How much can you even read in grade one?"

Lucky was organizing the travel issues by continent. She coughed. "I'm in grade three, Arnya. And you shouldn't smoke in here." She pointed to the circular window over her shoulder with a thumb. "It doesn't open."

"Well, excuse me, braniac." Arnya ground out the cigarette on an empty plate on the nightstand after taking one last haul that burned the paper down to the butt.

Lucky felt the silence as a reprimand and hurried to fill the space. "I like the pictures. And I collect the words."

Her mother exhaled through her nostrils. She reminded Lucky of the dragons in Grandma Stella's stories, if a dragon wore purple eyeshadow and swore a lot.

"Collect words? Why don't you collect something normal, like dolls or some shit? Or cards. I used to have a collection of cards from casinos all over the Midwest. Until I left Richard. They stayed behind." She stabbed at the exposed white plastic with the nail polish brush until the fibers splayed and bent.

Lucky didn't really remember Richard. He was one of the boyfriends who lived "somewhere else," one of the ones her mother went to go visit for weeks at a time.

Lucky had a box under her bed filled with cut-out words. Things like:

can't understand
cosmic reckoning
Jilted
Separate
underestimated

She also had words like:

glamour by night
adventure
untold riches
listen to your gut

The last phrase was cut from a health magazine article about IBS and originally read *listen to your guts*—Lucky had to be extra careful to scissor away the *s*. They were the words she held in her hands, let slip through her fingers when Arnya was off chasing a job, or a gig, or a man, or outrunning a debt.

"Well." Arnya was shaking a cigarette from the pack, bouncing her thigh on the bed so that her wet boot dried quicker. "I'll be off, then."

Lucky felt a pinch in her stomach and that familiar feeling of guilt. "It's okay, you can smoke in here if you want to."

Arnya was already up and pulling on her denim jacket. She popped the unlit cigarette between her crimson lips and leaned over to place a heavy hand on her daughter's upturned face. "Nah, it's okay, kid. I gotta see a man about a horse."

She turned to leave, pausing at the door. "Be good and listen to your crazy old grandma. See ya later, alligator."

The girl listened to her mother's steps on the stairs, the crack of the exposed heel louder than the other. Then the front door shutting behind her.

Lucky dug through the second pile from the left, the one that held all the old *National Geographics*. She found a promising issue on animals of the southern United States, picked up her red-handled scissors, and hunted for the word. "Alligator . . . alligator . . ."

SHE WOKE HERSELF UP TALKING in her sleep.

"What's that?" Stella stood in front of her, wrapped in a beach towel, dripping bathwater onto the wood floor.

"What?"

"You were saying something." The towel slipped enough that one soft boob fell out. Stella regarded it but did not bother covering up.

"Probably just telling you to put some damn clothes on." Lucky was disoriented and grouchy. She pulled off her boots and tossed them towards the door.

"Okay, okay. Don't get all constipated." Stella went to the bedroom and put on her flannel pyjamas, the ones with the little cartoon penguins telling each other to "fuck off" that she loved so much. Ironically, she'd gotten them at a church garage sale.

Lucky sent off a quick text to Freya, then peeled off her black jeans and tossed them on the easy chair. She pulled a scratchy afghan off the back of the couch and unfolded it over her legs, up to her waist. "Good night."

"What, that's it? You're going to sleep?" Stella came back into the living room with an armful of magazines she'd brought from home. "I thought we could make pancakes or play a game."

"You go ahead. I'm too tired." Lucky turned to face the back of the couch. It was musty, but she needed to close herself off for a bit, to see nothing, to feel nothing. The key to the front door, which she'd locked from the inside, was safely in her shirt pocket. Stella wasn't doing any wandering tonight, so she was all clear to fall back asleep, and after a few minutes, she did just that.

THE REST OF THE COVEN was hunkered down in Salem, sticking close together and taking turns wandering the many halls and hidden rooms for any sign of a break-in. So far, it had been quiet.

Lettie's spells seemed to be holding, even getting stronger. By ten o'clock the next night, she was making entire wings of the house hard to see, even for the women.

"The snake woman sent them to the Ozarks," Freya reported, checking her text messages. "They're supposed to go see a Yard witch."

"*Yarb*, not *yard*," Wendy corrected.

Freya stared at the text. "Must have been an autocorrect. But what in the hell is a Yarb? Sounds made-up."

"A Yarb witch is no joke, that's what she is." Meena carried a tray of snacks into the entertainment room, where they sat on the couches and floor in front of a small fire with a muted movie on the screen.

"They're Ozarks people, mountain people, with generations of medicine and sight. Anytime magic is practiced on the regular, it gets stronger, like a muscle or a language."

"Are those the people that use the Doctrine of Signatures and shit like that?" Freya asked.

"What's that?" Lettie was on a break from casting, wolfing down stuffed olives and cubes of ripe cheese.

"It's when you think God made the earth like an apothecary, and every plant and herb exists just for you, like a giant green medicine cabinet," Freya filled her in. "Each one has a kind of signature, so that you know what it's for. So like, a walnut looks like the human brain so it must cure headaches. And ginseng looks like a dick, so it must be good for dick stuff."

Wendy laughed. "That is probably the most succinct and amusing explanation of the doctrine I've heard. You're right, that egotistic belief of humans as the beginning and end of the story is a problem. It also led to a lot of deaths over the years, because it's too narrow. You have to think differently to see the real signature—humans as a part, not as central."

"Yarb witches are more complex than that. They use methods handed down through generations of trial and error. They also recognize the spirit in things, not just the science, which isn't really all that different," Meena explained. "If Ricky sent them to the Ozarks, maybe the spoon is there too."

"Maybe," Freya said, looking at her phone. "But Lucky thinks it's another pit stop. She wants to know if we made any headway on our end. I'll let her know we were a bit distracted being hunted . . ."

Meena held up her hand. "No, no, there's no need to freak her out. If the Benandanti are in Massachusetts, they're not on Lucky's trail, so let's just leave her in peace so she can focus on her own mission."

"What if there's more than one?" Freya insisted.

"There isn't," Meena said quickly.

"But what if we each have a tail?"

"I said, there isn't." Meena was irritated. She was still waiting for the Oracle to call her back and was more scared than she preferred to show. Wendy gave her a quick look, trying to catch her eye.

Seeing the others waiting and not wanting to get into the now of it all, Meena gave them some more history. "In the old days, the Benandanti would string us up themselves. Of course, the official story is that they brought those under suspicion to the 'proper authorities' for interrogation, but they were always overzealous. And bloodthirsty. More than half of the women they detained never met an Inquisitor."

"So as long as we're under attack, Lucky and Stella are safe?" Freya clarified.

"Yes. So we just keep doing what we're doing and hope they find the spoon, and soon."

They finished their snacks in silence, and Lettie went back to the front door to throw her spells without anyone reminding her it was time to get back to work.

CLEANING UP IN THE KITCHEN, Meena jumped when Wendy slipped up behind her at the sink.

"Jesus, you scared me." She blew out her caught breath and finished rinsing off the plates.

"What's up with you?" Wendy asked, moving to lean against the counter, picking up a tea towel to dry the wet dishes.

"Uh, there's a lot going on. You're going to have to be more specific." Meena was being evasive.

"Meena Amari Good, don't take that tone with me," Wendy shot back.

After a moment, Meena muttered an apology. "Sorry, babe."

"Now please tell me why in the hell we are not telling Lucky about the hunter. Did the Oracle call back?"

Meena finished washing the last plate, handed it to Wendy, and turned off the tap. "No, they did not." She wiped her hands off on a corner of Wendy's towel and leaned her back against the counter, beside her wife. "It looks like I have to make the tough decisions for now."

"Like what?"

"Like not warning Lucky that a Benandanti might be after her." She closed her eyes, waiting for the storm to hit her.

"Meena! But you said . . ."

"I know what I said. How am I supposed to know how many damn hunters there are left skulking around? But I couldn't very well tell them that." She began to pace. "I just—I have to think of the bigger picture right now."

"So you're choosing the spoon over Lucky and Stella?" Wendy threw the towel down and stood in Meena's path so she had to stop moving.

"Wendy, dear." Meena finally stood still and made eye contact. "I have no idea what I'm supposed to do here, other than keep this team safe and focused, and right now that means staying on mission.

If things change, if he shows up near them, then I'll change tactics. But for now, for just right now, please." She reached out and placed her hands on Wendy's hips. Her wife rarely got mad, and she hadn't even told her that she hadn't been able to reach Lucille since they left Buzzards Bay. "Please, just let me do this my way."

Wendy didn't answer. She just turned and walked out of the kitchen, clicking off the light as she left, leaving Meena alone in the dark.

JAY DROVE 130 MPH MOST of the way to Pennsylvania, slowing down only where the curves were sharp or the traffic got congested. He didn't know this Rattler Ricky that Lucille had spoken of, but he knew the Tender had been telling the truth. He could smell a lie. Most people could, though they chose to ignore it most of the time. A lie smelled like caramel and butter with an after-scent of shit. "Bullshit," people would say when someone lied, or, "What a load of shit." But they refused to acknowledge that falsehoods had an actual scent. Such a stunted species, humans. He was glad he was no longer one.

No, Lucille had been telling the truth. The good thing about torture is that the pain lives on as a blood memory in the generations who come after. It had been fairly easy to push Annie's descendant into giving up the whereabouts of a sneaky little bitch named Lucky, who was on her way to find the seventh spoon. Apparently, that mission led straight into the ass-end of Pennsylvania. All he'd had to do was take Lucille into the bar's back room to relive her ancestor's pain—the pins, the broken fingers, the rope around her neck . . .

"Goddamn wilderness," he muttered to himself, navigating the car over a chopped-up section of asphalt on a neglected road. He hated this part of the country. Too many trees. Too cold. Too many holes to hide in.

Being the apex predator that he was, Jay had no use for hiding places. They only made his work more difficult. And it was hard enough as it was, being the last of his kind. There was no one to share the work, no one to celebrate with at the end of a successful hunt. It was just him now, which was unfortunate, since the witches were once again on the rise. He really could have used an extra pair of capable Good Walker hands, like the old days when they hunted in packs.

He wasn't nervous; he was never nervous. But he had never before dealt with a brauche, a powwow person. As he understood it, they were backwoods preachers—if preachers also did parlor tricks and believed in some feminine spirit of wisdom. And he didn't like how far ahead of him Lucky had gotten. He did not like being out of control. He liked his hunts to be like his sex—he decided when and where. He made the moves. He ended it when he wanted it ended. This was something different, something wild. And it was precisely why femmes were so dangerous. Even when you had spent centuries measuring their responses and timing their emotions, there was always some unknown. They were dangerous because they were always moving, always half in shadow.

He arrived in Schuylkill County after one in the morning but there was no slumber in his body; his muscles held no ache; his head permitted no blur. He was ready to hunt. Now, if he only knew where tonight's prey was holed up, he could get to work.

He pulled over onto the side of the road, took a piss in the ditch, and paused to listen. Low rumblings from several locations. There were people with some knowing around here, but they seemed to be on a unique frequency. He got back in the rental and drove some more. After an hour, he shut down that part of his brain that made decisions, the part that was specific and careful. He probably shouldn't have been driving in that state, but he was pretty much on his own out here on these roads, so he let his instincts guide him. Soon, he was pulling into a little motel parking lot with a shitty bar next door. He was wondering where to park when she appeared in his headlights—a short figure in an oversized blazer carrying a mostly empty bottle of wine.

He smiled. "Ahhh, there you are, Ms. Rattler. Pleased to make your acquaintance."

She squinted at the car, holding her hand over her eyes to block the light. For fun, he revved the engine, and she scurried out of the way. From the way she moved, he guessed she had finished that bottle herself.

He cut the engine and opened his door. "Hello, Ricky. So glad we ran into each other." He got out, gave her a short bow, and closed the door behind him.

She considered his face, looked at the SUV, then back at him. Though they had never met before, her body recognized what he was, and she stood a little straighter. She raised the bottle to her lips, drank it to the bottom, and tossed it behind her. He liked the courage that hung on her. He lowered a cupped hand in front of his hips and moved it up and down, the universal symbol of big balls, then laughed a bit. "You and I need to talk."

He took a step towards her, and she took one back. He took another, and she responded in kind—a predator's waltz. He saw her lips moving before he heard the low whisper of some kind of prayer or spell.

"Now, now, enough of that." But she continued, and he grew angry, like zero-to-a-hundred angry, the way he was apt to do. "I said enough!"

Her lips closed tight, without her permission. She struggled a bit, then resigned herself to silence, throwing her shoulders back and tilting her chin up.

He said, "I have a question about a girl. Have you seen one lately? A strange girl, I'd imagine, travelling with a spoon and an old lady." He took another step forward. This time she didn't move back. Instead, she raised one hand and placed it on top of her hat, pushing the brim down over her eyebrows.

"She would have been sent by a witch from an old family—Good, Meena Good. Ring any bells for you?"

In response, she winked at him from under the shadow of her smushed-down brim and then, quick as a fox, took off running, still holding her hat on her head.

"Oh, for fuck's sake . . ." He spun on a heel and jumped back in the Rover. "Fucking hillbillies."

He caught her in his lights as she jumped over a curb and into the trees beside the road.

He squealed out of the lot and took off in the same direction.

"I'm getting really tired of these games, ladies," he seethed, leaning over his steering wheel, eyes on the trees. He saw her there, a soft smudge in the dark woods, taking nimble leaps over logs and bushes, turning to avoid trunks, and ducking under low branches. This was very obviously her land, a place where she could move with ease. He'd lose her soon; the denser forest was just up ahead, and that was where she was headed, moving like a skinny doe in men's clothing.

Jay bared his teeth, grabbed the wheel tight, and clenched, flexing so that his whole upper body rocked back and forth quickly. Then he blew out a breath, relaxed his grip, and changed tactics. He flipped his headlights off and caught up to her pace and kept it. Once again, he numbed the part of him that was reactive and decisive, and listened. And soon he found what he was looking for.

Bom-bom. Bom-bom. Bom-bom. The sound of her heart as she raced through the trees, a siren pulse of fear and speed.

"There you are," he whispered. "You should come closer. I want to hear you better."

Bom—bom-bom. Bom-bom. Bom-bom.

The heart skipped a beat and then found its rhythm. In the bush, Ricky made a turn that brought her out of the thicker trees, still running well but angling ever so slightly towards the road. She probably didn't even notice.

Bom-bom. Bom-bom. Bom-bom.

She was quick and knew this land, but she was still wine drunk and sixty, if she was a day. Soon enough, her feet were hitting gravel, and she was out of the trees, gasping for air, one arm pumping, the other still holding on to that ridiculous hat.

Jay brought the large vehicle right up beside her. She didn't see him until the last second, when she realized she'd been fished out of the trees, that she was out in the open, and then it was too late. A slight jerk of the wheel and metal met flesh and bones snapped like dry pine. The hat she'd been guarding flew up off her head and landed in the dirt.

RICKY LAY CRUMPLED AND SHOCKED, watching it cartwheel into an oily puddle. "My hat," she wheezed.

She heard a car door. She heard the crunch of good shoes on the shoulder. She heard the whistle in her breathing as the air leaked out of a punctured lung. And she heard her own traitorous heart— *bom-bom—bom-bom—bom . . . bom—*

The man crouched by her head.

He sought her eyes. "Look at me, Ricky. Ricky, look at me."

Her vision blurring around the edges, she did as she was told.

"There's a good girl. Now I'm going to ask you a question and you are going to answer me. The one with the spoon—where did you send her?"

He leaned in closer. She could smell his breath, sweet, like caramel and butter with something rotten underneath. He searched her eyes, his own flicking back and forth and then narrowing, and then he smiled and nodded. "Good girl. Very good."

He straightened up, smoothing the pleat in his slacks, and walked away. She tried to focus on her hat but couldn't see it. Everything was shadows over there. And there was some kind of music, a drum.

Bom-bom. Bom-bom . . .

She tried to focus on it. The trees were getting taller, the moon farther away. She heard a car engine start, headlights illuminated the branches above her, and tires hissed over pavement. But she didn't care anymore. She wanted to hear the music. She had to listen carefully. She closed her eyes to concentrate.

Bom-bom.

Bom-bom.

Bom . . . . . .

. . . .

23

CONFUSION AND

CLARITY

Morticia stood on the front porch sniffing the air. It was ocean and new leaves and loose soil. No hint of sadness. No depression. No Benandanti. "Did they leave?"

"Must have." Meena joined her on the porch. "Let's not let our guard down just yet—we have a witch to find."

Once again, they set the dining room table for their work. This time they filled a copper bowl with rainwater from the barrel out back. The books said a wooden bowl worked best, then glass, but Wendy insisted on copper. "Back home, we use copper. That's what we need to use now." No one argued. She smudged the room with sweetgrass.

"What should we put inside the bowl to help us focus?" Lettie asked. "A crystal?"

"We could." Meena looked over the objects on the table, touching a quartz, then a slice of agate. "But I think we can be more specific than that." She picked up a smooth blob of silver sitting on top of a square of black velvet and held it up.

"Whenever we've found a Salem Witch Spoon that isn't one of the seven, we've melted it down. Since they all started from the same basic ingredients, maybe we can use this to call the other?" She put her hand just above the surface of the water and opened her fingers. The silver thunked onto the bottom curve of the bowl, making a solid sound with an echoey tail that matched the shape of the ripples it caused.

Wendy packed up everything else from the table. They needed to remove all distractions. As Freya lit candles, Meena closed the drapes over the mural. There should only be darkness and the water by candlelight. When they were done, the walls had disappeared, and the shape of the table and chairs had become shadows. There was only the bowl, the water, the candles, and the blob of silver pulling focus.

"Okay, then, let's give it a try." Meena shook out her hands and rolled her shoulders. "I'll go first."

AFTER HOURS OF STARING INTO water, waiting for something to happen, Meena took a break. She retired to the living room. Her back hurt from the hard dining room chair, and the soft couch was a relief. Her eyes were dry and strained, and she meant to close them for just a minute, to give them a rest . . .

She was on her father's front porch, the street out front empty and dark. She wasn't surprised when she turned to see the Crone sitting on the porch swing, smoking, like last time.

"Ah, ma chère, you've made it."

"Made it here? I'm asleep, aren't I?" Meena looked around for some kind of proof that she was dreaming, but the street looked normal.

"You are indeed. I have been waiting."

"You never called back," Meena began.

"We are returning the call now." The Crone looked a bit faded, like she was really a ghost this time.

"This is not a coincidence—this is magic. I can see the strain on you."

"It is magic, as much of this kind of magic as the Oracle has, being as we are not coven witches like you. We are strategists, builders, knowledge keepers. That is where our true talents lie." She held up a hand in front of her eye, and Meena swore she saw her blink through the flesh. "But we are together at this moment, and focusing all our energy to you, to your witches. Expect to have some vivid dreams with our extra push."

Meena had so many questions it was hard to choose just one at a time. She began with "Where is Lucille?"

The Crone looked off to the street and sighed. "I am afraid our darling Lucille has met the same fate as so many of us. She is no longer with us."

Meena felt like she had been punched in the gut, and doubled over. "Oh Christ. Benandanti?"

"Certainement," the Crone answered.

Meena switched tactics, straightening back up. "How many hunters are there?"

"There is but one left, that we know of. We have been keeping an eye on him—"

"Well, you did a shit job of it," she interrupted, suddenly angry. "Why didn't you tell me? All I knew were rumours, old stories . . ."

"And you, Meena Good?" the Crone countered. "Have you told your sixth witch about his visit to Salem? Did you notify her the moment you smelled him?"

Meena didn't have an answer, so the Crone continued. "We all steer as best as we can when it is our time at the helm. He has been staying out in the desert, quiet for some time now. He is only one man, but he is immortal." She raised a finger and waved it like a scolding teacher. "He is not to be underestimated, this one."

As she moved it, her finger began to turn translucent. They both took notice. "I don't have much time left now. We will do what we can to give you all our focus. And we will watch as best we can."

Meena leaned in. She made to grab the Crone by the shoulders, to be as close as she could be to hear her, since her voice was losing volume, but her hands slid right through her.

"What do I do now?"

The Crone shouted, but it came out as a whisper: "We will give you all we have."

"Don't go. Not yet. Tell me what to do!"

"Meena. No one can read what hasn't been done."

"What does that mean?"

"Meena."

"What?"

"Meena." The voice was coming from the street. Both women turned towards it and . . .

MEENA WAS LOOKING INTO WENDY'S face. She was leaning over the couch. "Don't sleep here, love. You'll hurt your neck."

Meena immediately burst into tears.

"Oh, honey, what is it? What's wrong?" Wendy pushed in to sit beside her, pulling her into an embrace.

"It's Lucille."

LUCKY AND STELLA WERE IN Missouri by dinnertime, so they got barbecue from a restaurant that looked like a Western saloon on the outside and not much different on the inside. Next to the front door, there was a wooden sign with an illustration of a blond man in a plaid shirt chewing on a piece of long grass beside the words TODAY'S FIXINS. Underneath was a list of sides written in neat chalk letters: *okra, maple beans, coleslaw*. They ordered heaping metal plates that held a little bit of everything, with big slabs of cornbread and little packages of soda crackers to sop it all up. Neither of them escaped with a clean shirt.

Afterwards, they sat in the Pathfinder, too full and too tired to do anything but digest their food.

"I just want to sleep." Lucky could barely get the words out.

"You can't. You have to keep driving."

"I know."

"We only have six days left, including today."

"Already . . . Hold on." Stella was keeping track of the time? "You sure? When did we leave?"

"When did we leave Toronto? Or Buzzards Bay?" Stella asked.

"The bay."

Stella counted on her fingers. "We left Buzzards Bay Monday. Stayed overnight in Pennsylvania on day eight and left there yesterday. Last night, day seven, we were at the cabin, so we're on day six."

Lucky was astonished. She tried to stay still, as if Stella's lucidity was a bird she was trying not to spook into flight.

Stella turned to her granddaughter, who was watching her from the driver's seat with wide eyes. "Your mother will be waiting for us, so we shouldn't be late."

Fuck. "You're right. We should be on the way." Lucky pulled her seatbelt over her distended stomach and started the engine. They had another few hours to go, and it was already getting dark.

Stella dozed beside her, and the only radio stations Lucky could find were playing country or bluegrass. She chose bluegrass. There was something cheerful about banjos that was also melancholy at the same time. For some reason the word *alligator* popped into her head, and then stuck there.

"Hey, Siri," she called out, over the plucked notes and picked strings. Her phone beeped to tell her it was listening.

"Are there alligators in Missouri?"

"Here's what I found on the web," came the pleasant response. *"Alligators are not native to Missouri; however, rare sightings have been reported."*

"Well, if anyone was going to have a rare sighting, it would be us," she responded.

"I'm sorry, I didn't catch that," her phone trilled back.

"Never mind."

She propped her elbow on the edge of her window and leaned her head into her hand. They'd have to stop soon. She just wanted to get as close as she could to this Yarb witch before they did. That encounter was going to be crazy—she could feel it in her bones—and she'd much rather deal with it in the morning sun.

The reports from Salem continued to be disappointing. Wendy was still recovering from Buzzards Bay—lightweight—and they all missed Stella and sometimes even Lucky. They were still looking in the water for any sign of the missing piece of their coven puzzle, but so far, there'd been nothing but vague impressions of random spoons in places like cutlery drawers and on tabletops. Lucky was starting to think that their best chance of finding the spoon-wielding witch really was out here, with her and Stella, and a woman whose name made her sound like a cartoon character—May Moon Montgomery.

All day, Lucky had been thinking about a cheesy horror movie she'd watched on TV with her mom. Not the movie, really, but the title—*Something Wicked This Way Comes*. She thought it might be from an even older story or maybe it was a poem . . . That line had struck a chord with Arnya, who started saying it to her reflection like an affirmation before she left for the night.

She'd stand in the mirror and give herself the once over, then nod. "Lookin' good, Arn. Watch out, world, something wicked this way comes."

Lucky had never been sure what the saying meant, but today, as storm clouds gathered in the darkening sky around them, she thought of it with a deep sense of terror.

The storm never broke. Not over their Pathfinder as she drove hard down the highway towards the Ozarks. Not when they pulled into a neon-lit motel with a sleepy old clerk who asked for cash and slipped it into his pocket instead of the till. Not when she fell asleep, her spoon tucked safely under her thin pillow. But it was coming. Of that she was sure.

JAY CHRISTOS WAS IN A fine mood. For him, violence and sex came from the same pit of want and power, so stealing Ricky's last moments was satisfying down into his groin. He felt full. He felt whole. And he was closer than he had ever been to Lucky. He could feel her on this very road, like she was dropping breadcrumbs from her exhaust pipe. He knew the moment he passed her, in the small town of Blowsy Creek. He had been speeding, breath shallow and small, and then suddenly, it was like breaking out of a bubble—he was no longer behind her, chasing. He took a great heaving gulp of air and then started to laugh. He'd done it. And now he could move from defence into his favourite position—offence.

He drove another hour, taking the turns his gut told him to. Eventually, he had to ditch the luxury car, pulling off into the bush and covering it with messy vines, of which there were far too many for his liking. He kept going on foot, using his phone as a flashlight. Of all the things Jay Christos was capable of after so many long years of learning and honing, by far his best superpower was self-confidence. He never doubted himself. So, sure enough, after half an hour at a steady pace, he emerged in a small clearing.

The trees at the perimeter of the yard were mismatched—scrubby and sharp, then tall and luxurious, blending together to form almost a solid wall, like a natural fence. A slice of moon leaked silver onto the reedy grass, revealing an old camper leaning to one side, an abandoned shed with an impressive hornet's nest hanging from the eaves like a paper chandelier, and a modest cabin.

Prudence had also lived modestly, though she could have had anything she wanted. He knew that because he, high-born and with a keen eye towards his growing estate, had been first in line to provide it.

Her collarbones were the first thing he noticed, what had hooked him, as if they were lures just under her beautiful face. This was what he thought men meant by witchcraft—the way some women could completely mesmerize a man with a slight curve of bone, a quiet hint of skin. It did seem supernatural, the way a twist of hair against the nape of a neck could make it difficult to walk. It also seemed unfair. To be at the mercy of something so feral, so . . . emotional. It would make a weaker man angry. And for a while, this was what he thought of the Inquisitors, that they were those weaker men, exacting revenge over being made into marionettes. But then Prudence told him the truth.

"YOU THINK I WOULDN'T FIND out? Your father leads the raids. He himself murdered my sisters. Do you know what it is like to collect the ashes of your loved ones?" She had him pinned to the mattress, both of them still naked from their lovemaking, his hands and legs trapped in the sheets as she sat on him, holding a long knife, but what he was most scared of was that she would leave him. "That is what I want for him. To have to sift through the dirt like the animal he is, trying to find the remains of his family."

"Prue, I . . . I am my own man. I am not one of them," he countered, fear making his voice shake. "I am not going to follow in his footsteps. I renounce the Benandanti and all they stand for. I want you. Only you. I swear it." At the time, he'd meant it. He had no plans of taking on the family business. In fact, he had quarreled with his brothers just that morning about it.

She was wild with rage and holding a knife to his throat. Then she spoke the words of a spell, and his limbs seemed to change to rock—heavy, immovable. He was as scared as he'd ever been in his life, a prisoner in his own flesh.

She leaned in to his face, eyes narrowed. "You are them, not blindly, but with eyes wide open. I have seen it. I know what is to come, unless I stop you now."

"I'm sorry I didn't tell you! But I am not him, not them. I am yours!"

Now that he was held by her magic, she moved off him, pacing around the edge of the bed, still holding the knife. "At this moment, they are on the way. I can hear their horses, smell their breath." She looked around her cabin, then began grabbing up her clothes and getting dressed. "And you led them here."

"I did not! I would never." He was spitting with fear and the effort of trying to pull himself loose. Dressed now, she ran about grabbing jars and fabric, jamming them into a sack. "Take me with you," he pleaded.

Ready to leave, she turned back to the bed, standing over him.

"And here I have taken my very own Judas into my bed—one who would haunt generations of my own blood. Well, Iscariot, here's your silver!" She drove the knife down into his chest. Then she knocked over every candle, and as the flames caught, she opened the door. "May your ashes never be found. I wish for your father not to even have that."

And then she was gone.

But she had been right. The men did arrive, and just in time to kick into the room and grab him before the fire devoured him whole.

He survived. And he refused to condemn his assailant, though it wouldn't have mattered, because Prudence had disappeared. Even now, every time his fingers touched the scar above his heart, the raised keloid of her murderous intent, he thought of that night.

He had searched for her, using the knowledge and powers she'd fostered in him. And slowly his love crystalized into hate, interest in her power changing to a jealous hoarding of knowledge. So when the time came for him to join the Benandanti, to bring down witches like Prudence who thought they could break a man and then run off into the night, he took his oath with bravado and pride—not blindly but with eyes wide open.

HE CROSSED THE GRASS, WHISTLING. At the front door, he inhaled— the witch who lived here hadn't been home for a while. He hoped she wouldn't return for at least another day. And if she did, well, he would deal with it. There was a stained-glass moon hanging off the door, a spot of bright in the blight. Why were these women always so poor? One would think they could do better for themselves, what with their insight and all. But that was why men had always been at the forefront of commerce and development, he thought, never satisfied, always striving.

In the growing dark, he stepped back to the edge of the porch and surveyed the untamed field and the dark smudge of trees beyond it. When she got there, he would get inside Lucky's head, see what she knew. If she didn't know anything, he would stop her from moving forward and let the clock run out. Holding her back from helping complete the circle would be the easiest course. For now, all he had to do was climb in the window, coil up like a snake, and wait. Sooner or later, Lucky would come right to him.

24

THE FIRST STRIKE

They both woke up at seven o'clock, almost at the same moment. Even Stella could feel the tension of the day. They were farther from home than Lucky had ever been, which made her feel light and heavy at the same time. She could either float away or sink into the ground. Maybe she would split in two and do both.

Before saying good morning, Stella asked, "Who are we seeing today?"

Obviously, they were thinking the same thoughts.

"Miss May Moon."

"Sounds like an old song."

"Yeah, one where your dog gets run over and your wife leaves in your truck."

"Jeez, who's picking on hicks now?"

They both laughed.

"Listen, Grandma, I think you should stay here."

Lucky could rent the room for another day and slip the guy at the front desk some more money to keep an eye on her. This part of the trip was feeling dangerous.

Her dream hadn't helped either. It had been so clear, so much fuller than other dreams. In it, she could use each one of her senses, and when she woke up, the transition back into consciousness had been confusing. In it, she was walking along an empty road, watching, waiting for her ride to pick her up. Then she heard a rattlesnake somewhere close, that unmistakable hollow, staccato rhythm. She checked by her feet, the ditch, even the hot asphalt—nothing. Then she saw a hat on the other side of the road. As she crossed over to it, the rattle got louder. Having no common sense in the dream, she kept a steady pace until she was close enough to see that this was the hat that belonged to Rattler Ricky. Even worse, she bent down and picked it up.

Underneath the hat was a rattlesnake, of course—it had been warning her for a while that it was there. Except this snake was dead, its eyes wide and covered with a grey film. Instead of relief, she felt overwhelming terror. She stumbled backward into the road. She turned her head just in time to see a large black car barreling down on her. She lifted her arms reflexively and covered her face. That had been when she'd woken up.

Stella sat up in bed. "I don't want to stay in this stinky room all day."

"I just . . . I'm not sure it's safe for you to come."

"I wanna see this Miss Moon. And besides"—she paused, examining her swollen knuckles all of a sudden—"what if I forget?"

"Forget what?"

"I don't know—where I am . . . what we're doing?" Her voice got smaller and smaller.

Lucky felt a sudden and profound heartbreak. She'd never considered for one moment that Stella was conscious of her lapses. It had always been about what those lapses caused for Lucky—the potential for loss, the potential for danger, the potential to screw up plans. And even when she had compassion, she certainly didn't think that once a lapse had passed that Stella would feel it, like a tangle in thread.

She was about to speak, but Stella was throwing the blanket off and getting out of bed. "I'm gonna take a shower. And then we can hit the road." She limped a bit, in that way older people do when their feet first hit the floor in the morning, straightening up as she walked. She stopped at the bathroom door.

"And find us a pancake place there, on your phone. I want pancakes. A whole stack. Can't go to the moon on an empty belly."

Lucky took a moment to enjoy this version of Stella. Somehow, the farther away they got from home, the more aware her grandmother seemed to become. As she climbed out of bed, she started to think that bringing her grandmother with her to Salem, permanently, might just be the best thing after all.

THEY'D HAD TO BACKTRACK A bit to find a diner, but it served pancakes, so Stella was content. She didn't mention her forgetfulness again, and though Lucky danced around it a bit, Stella had either, ironically, forgotten about it or didn't want to have the conversation. They paid their ridiculously small bill and left. Lucky sent a text to Freya before they hit the road:

> On the way to the Yarb. Probably
> won't have service down in the
> holler. LOL. I'll message after.

Before she climbed into the driver's seat, she looked up at the sky. She still had that feeling, the wicked one. But above them there was only blue and sun and the slightest whispers of white clouds.

Following Ricky's directions, she drove until they couldn't go any farther on a road that had become nothing more than a wide dirt path. She parked and reread the instructions: *Walk in the same direction—up—and you'll come across people. Ask for Ms. Montgomery. They'll get you there.* She got Stella out of the car and locked it.

"Onward!" Lucky said, pointing the way forward, trying to motivate Stella and hide her own apprehension.

"Christ, what are we doing here? We should just head back," Stella said before they'd gotten ten feet from the vehicle.

"We probably should," Lucky said. "But let's do this anyway."

THIS HAD TO BE IT. They'd seen no other houses, and Stella had had it. If this wasn't the Montgomery place, whoever lived here better be ready to give them a ride to it. Or take care of a very cranky elderly woman who had managed to snag about five pounds of burrs on each pant leg.

"Try to shake some of that off," Lucky told her, pointing to Stella's calves. "We look like total city losers."

"Listen, if being more comfortable around sidewalks and indoor plumbing makes you a loser, I don't want to be a winner." She took a few feeble swipes at her legs that did nothing to dislodge the burrs.

"Quit stereotyping. You don't know that they don't have plumbing."

"Oh no? Then what is that?" Stella pointed to a wooden outhouse with a quarter moon carved into the door.

"Christ . . . Well, do you have to pee, or what?"

Stella wrinkled her nose in response.

They picked their way through the high grass, over car parts and around boulders as old as the mountain looming over them.

"Think anyone is home?"

"I don't see anyone." Lucky felt nerves popping in her guts like carbonation. She didn't feel powerful or special or even necessarily capable. She felt out of her depth. So far, this whole witch thing seemed to be a bust.

They climbed up to the porch carefully, the stairs sagging, the railing having rotted away, and stepped gingerly over holes and soft patches. A sickle moon hung in the glass on the door, throwing rainbows over the old wood. Lucky took a deep breath and looked to her grandmother, who gave her a long look back; then she knocked twice, adding a third knock for good measure. Everything in threes, Ricky had said.

"Just a minute," a man's voice replied.

"I thought we were going to see a woman?" Stella asked.

Lucky shrugged. "Maybe she lives with family?"

The door swung open to the sound of jingle bells, releasing the smell of dried herbs. A tall man in a pair of worn denim overalls and a grey work shirt stood there, his black hair pulled into a single braid. He smiled, showing admirable dentistry for someone living so far out, and Lucky's pupils dilated.

"Ahh, you must be the one from Salem, come to see May." His accent was strange, a mix of several quilted into one. His voice was low and pleasant but echoed in Lucky's head like a soundtrack to nausea, and her stomach hitched up.

"You alright?"

More echoes. Lucky reached out for the doorframe to steady herself.

"Lucky, you okay?" Stella seemed so far away, it was like Lucky was looking at her down a tube.

"Let's get her inside," the man said. "Sometimes the long walk'll do that to ya. Don't even realize how tuckered out you are until it's right there sitting on your chest."

A hand on her shoulder, one on her waist, and she was being pulled inside the cabin. She wanted to resist, to sit right down on the rotting porch, but she couldn't.

"She eat, this one?" His voice was too close.

"Yup. But she's been under a lot of stress lately. Maybe that's it?"

"Related to why you're up here?" He spoke lightly, but the words fell heavily.

"Moving stress. We have to leave our place soon."

Wait, what? How? How the fuck did Stella know about the eviction? This was the slap in the face Lucky needed to pull herself together. She turned to Stella, whose attention had been grabbed by something else. She let go of Lucky and wandered over to examine some framed portraits nailed to the wall, humming to herself.

"I'm fine," Lucky insisted, pulling away from the man. "Just got light-headed. Probably allergies. I feel . . . stuffed up, a bit hard to breathe just now." She looked around. "You have cats?"

"No cats inside." He closed the door. "Mighta been near some wild ones on the way up."

Lucky cleared her throat. "We've come to see May Moon Montgomery." The nausea had passed, but her limbs felt unhinged, and she couldn't seem to catch a full breath. She wanted to get this over with.

Stella was now examining the shelves that separated a modest kitchen from the main room, each one jammed full of jars of weeds, nails, rocks, seeds . . .

"Well, you found her place, but you got me instead of May. I'm Morris, her nephew. She's away and asked me to step in. Pleased to meet you both." He made a shallow bow from the waist, an odd gesture that felt out of place in this rough setting.

Of course, Stella curtsied in return, pulling at the baggy fabric of her burr-heavy pants. Then she started picking up the jars and shaking them.

"Grandma, why don't you have a seat somewhere?"

"Yes, yes." Morris pulled out a high-backed wooden chair at a round table in the middle of the main room. "Here. Y'all want tea?"

"Sure. Only if you have sweetener." Stella squeaked the legs on the floor, pulling her chair in under her.

"We got honey."

"I'm okay. Never mind."

He took a seat and motioned for Lucky to do likewise, which she did. It felt good to sit, truth be told. She put a hand on her chest and reminded her lungs to fill and release, fill and release. Then she asked, "So where is your aunt?"

"Well, she got called away, but I woulda been here anyway, since she needed me for this visit. I'm not sure how much you know about our ways, Miss, uhhh . . ."

"St. James."

"Miss St. James. About how we operate in these matters."

She had looked up as much as she could in between driving and sleeping. She knew Ozarks people were close-knit. That they had relied on water witches and granny women out of necessity for many years. That they were guarded and superstitious, and that there were rules about how to engage.

"Up here, we don't pass on wisdom between like-sexed individuals. It's gotta go from opposites to work." He drew abstract shapes on the tabletop with the tip of a finger as he spoke, the way others doodled when they were on the phone.

"That's pretty binary. Also incorrect. Opposites? There's no such thing."

He gave a small shrug. "Well, we still run on old ideas around here, whether they're right or wrong to others. So I am the person you need, on behalf of Miss May, of course."

"We need a spoon," Stella blurted. "A silver one. With an old witch on it."

Christ, Stella. Lucky had reminded her on the way to the cabin that she was going to keep things close to her chest; if the woman was actually powerful, she would see the details for herself. Otherwise, how was Lucky supposed to know who was the real deal and who was sending them on a goose chase?

"Salem. A man named Low crafted it." Morris spoke in a monotone, his finger once again tracing shapes on the scarred wood. Lucky found herself watching his hands, which were long, slender—delicate for a man up here. She wondered if they were soft . . .

"You are looking for the sixth . . . no, the seventh of a particular set."

"That's right." Lucky was reassured. Maybe Ricky had called May, and May had briefed her nephew on it all, or maybe he was the real thing. Either way, he was a part of all this. "We need to know where it is. Maybe . . . around here?"

"Well now, let's see." He got up and rattled through the shelved jars.

While his back was turned, Lucky leaned over the table, whispering, "Hey . . . hey." Stella glanced over to her. "You know about the move, about the apartment?"

Stella stared at her for a few seconds, then shrugged. She turned around in her chair, putting her back to her granddaughter, and asked Morris, "You got any gold in those jars? Aren't there mines in these hills?"

He chuckled. "No gold. My aunt and I have no use of it. Now, dandelions? That's gold. Sang, even more so."

"Sang?"

"Ginseng, you call it. We hunt it around here. Use it for medicine. Sell it in town when we need the cash."

Lucky watched his mouth as they formed words. His almond eyes narrowed in on her face, and she felt blood rise in her cheeks. She wondered what he sounded like when he whispered, close to your ear. She wondered if he would grab her neck when he kissed her, hard and insistent. God, what the fuck was wrong with her?

There was a sudden flurry of small taps on the outside of the house, like sharp claws clambering up the siding. She felt the sound in her spine as if that was where the ascent were happening. She shivered when it reached the base of her skull. She got to her feet and went to the kitchen window to look out. The trees closest to the cabin were all bending towards the structure, their longest branches tapping on the walls like urgent knuckles. Her breathing was getting tighter and faster now. "Are you sure there's no cat?"

Morris quickly turned back to the shelves. "Let me see if I can find something to ease your troubled breathing there, Miss St. James." He picked up a jar, opened it, and came over to shove it under her nose. She was distracted still—the trees on the far side of the clearing barely moved. How was the air so different in the same space? She wondered if they got tornados up here.

"Wait," she said, jerking her head away from the jar. "What is that?"

"Just an old remedy. Take a big whiff and you'll feel better momentarily." His accent had changed, and he was speaking at a quicker pace. It made her want to slow down in response. She leaned away from him.

He was moving differently now too—more angles, fewer curves. There was something frantic about his cadence. It felt like there was a flock of birds in the cabin. "Is there something wrong? Morris?"

"No, no. I just want to help," he said, though his eyes were on what was happening outside the window.

"I think we're going to head out before the weather gets worse," Lucky said. She could feel herself being pulled towards the door. She wanted to be far away from him. It was as if he suddenly smelled bad.

"I'll try it!" Stella grabbed his wrist and pulled the jar to her face.

"Wait!" Lucky yelled.

But it was too late. Stella leaned in, nose past the glass rim, and inhaled. Her eyes immediately filled with water. "Smells like pepper. Old pepper and maybe . . ." And then she began sneezing. She sneezed so hard she doubled over and farted, then, laughing, sneezed again and blew a fine spray of snot over the counter.

Morris sidestepped in front of Stella just as she let go another massive sneeze. "Now, if I'm going to help you, I'll just need a few more supplies." He bolted across the main room, disappearing through a door on the far wall, slamming it shut behind him.

Stella caught her breath and wiped at her nose with her sleeve. Lucky asked, "Why would he think pepper would help me breathe?" Her skepticism was moving into suspicion. All she could think about now was leaving the cabin and getting outside so she could breathe.

Just then the front door opened, revealing a tiny, skinny old woman in khaki coveralls, her long grey hair piled on top of her head and held with a silver hat pin. "Well, now, who do we have here?" she asked. The tone was amused, but her face wasn't.

"May Moon?"

"Uh, yes. And this is my house." She waved her arms to indicate the space.

"Yes, sorry." Lucky felt like she was being chastised by a teacher. "Your nephew let us in."

"Nephew?" The woman looked around with a little more urgency now.

"Morris?" Lucky said, turning to point to the far door. "He's in the back room. Getting supplies?"

"Supplies? That's my damn bedroom." May Moon dropped her tote bag by the shoe rack and crossed the room. "Is he looking for bras and an ass whooping?" She glanced back at Stella and Lucky, who seemed to be frozen to the floor. "And who in the hell is Morris?" She didn't wait for them to answer, throwing open the door.

"Well, goddammit . . ."

Lucky suddenly realized that this old woman was facing a stranger by herself and sprinted to her side. The room was dim with the floral curtains drawn and the lights off. A large bed was made up with several layers of patchwork quilts and two rows of pillows. A dresser sat against one wall, the top overflowing with costume jewelry and random jars and even a brown taxidermied rabbit. But there was no man.

"Snake shed his skin," May said, pointing to a pool of clothes on the floor—denim overalls and a grey flannel work shirt. Lucky felt the sudden urge to pee. Fear did that to her.

"You hit the outhouse, then join us at the table," May said, without Lucky having said a word out loud. "We gotta figure this out before we figure you out."

25

THE LIAR, THE WITCH,

AND THE WARDROBE

Sitting at the table now, Lucky told May about the spoon, Meena, Lucille, Rattler Ricky, and, finally, the mysterious nephew who'd been waiting for them at the cabin. The woman asked odd questions, ones that didn't feel relevant, but she did her best to answer them.

"You didn't drink nothing he offered?"

"Nope."

"Didn't take any paper, no words?"

"Uh, no."

"Okay. And you didn't give him any chance to get anything off ya, did you?"

"What do you mean?"

"A fingernail or hair maybe?"

Lucky thought for a moment. He hadn't gotten that close. "No, ma'am."

"Well, I gave him some snot." Stella laughed.

"Whatchu mean, Miss Stella?" May wasn't laughing.

"Uh, well, I just mean he asked Lucky to smell some pepper and she didn't but then I did . . ." she babbled. "I took a big whiff and then I sneezed . . . a lot."

"Pepper?" May stroked her chin. Lucky noticed her nails were long, yellow with age and old dirt. She wore one ring, a large rectangular ruby surrounded by delicate diamonds, on her middle finger. It seemed an odd extravagance for an otherwise unextravagant woman—evidence, perhaps, that she had been loved. Or maybe that her services were valued by people who lived beyond these simple hills.

"Why would he do that?" Stella sounded suddenly hurt.

"I think to make you do whatcha did, Miss Stella. Sneeze. When a person sneezes in front of those with unkind intentions, it gives them a window. A way to see what that person sees, like they're looking through their eyes, for a certain amount of time."

What could he possibly get from seeing what Stella saw? "Why? And for how long?" Lucky asked.

"I don't know why. And for how long? Well now, that depends on the power of the one witnessing." She got up and went to the kitchen, searching around on the counter. She found what she was looking for in the sink.

"Here we go now." She lifted a small green glass. "Did one of youse drink from this glass?"

They shook their heads.

"Alrighty. I'm gonna figure out who we're dealing with." She carried it towards the front door and they followed as she mumbled, ". . . come into my house . . . If I was drawn back sooner . . . Damn pests comin' around playing dress-up . . ."

She noticed that they were right behind her and ordered, "You stay inside. Make a pot of coffee. Instant crap's in the pantry. I gotta concentrate." She shut the door behind her. Stella and Lucky looked at each other as if they were kids left with the babysitter, then went to make the coffee.

When May got back, she was pale and her hair was down, tangled with bits of leaves. She no longer had the drinking glass.

She sat at the table, and Lucky pushed a mug of muddy coffee into her hands. "Well?"

She raised it to her lips and took a sip without answering, her grey eyes far away.

"That bad?" Lucky asked.

May snapped out of her reverie and nodded slowly. "Y'all have something old on your tail."

"He wasn't that old, maybe late thirties, early forties—"

"That's only how he appeared," May interrupted her. "Creatures can be wily like that."

"What does it want?" The question came out as barely a whisper.

"Well now, I think you could probably guess if you thought on it." May got up with a soft grunt to retrieve a small bottle of whiskey from among the herb jars. She made generous pours into each of their mugs and put the bottle in the middle of the table.

And then she remembered what Meena had told her. "Could this man, this thing, could he be Benandanti?"

May didn't answer the question directly. "He's not on the back foot anymore. Now is the time when these men get really dangerous."

"When they know where you are?" Lucky asked, wincing at the amount of booze in her coffee.

"No." May reached across the table and grabbed Lucky's hand.

There was genuine concern in her eyes. "When they feel like they are above you."

LUCKY TRIED TO CALL SALEM, but there was no reception. "Come on, come on." She had to let them know. The stories were true, the Benandanti were real, and not only that, they were after her. All her texts came back undelivered. May tried to calm her down.

"He's gone now, so you're safe. Caught wind I was coming back, probably."

Lucky thought of the trees being tossed about outside the house—that was how he must have known May was on the way.

While Lucky and May tried to figure out what to do next, Stella was taken with the mobile made of butterfly corpses spinning in slow circles in front of the living room window.

"Are these magic butterflies?" She blew gently to make them move.

"Aren't all butterflies magic?" May mused.

"Huh, I suppose they are. Ozzy preferred moths. Crazy old bugger." Stella laughed.

"Miss Stella, you need to be a part of this conversation now. You're on this trip too and we don't want him being able to use you to get to your grandbaby here."

"If Oz could come back to visit, maybe he'd come as a moth." Stella felt the wings of a monarch with the tips of her fingers.

"Oh, never you mind, he's never far from you," May said. "Now, come, sit."

"How did Ricky let you know we were coming?" Lucky asked. She hadn't seen a phone in the cabin, or a computer.

"I was visiting my people in the holler, woke up this morning and dropped a dish rag."

Lucky was confused. "You dropped a rag? How did a rag tell you we were coming?"

May collected the empty mugs from the table and brought them to the kitchen sink. "Just did. And it was real specific too. Landed all balled up, so I knew it would be women. Plus, my nose was itchin' like mad. But somehow *his* visit went un-warned."

"Do you think butterflies are dead people?" Stella was back in her chair at the table, but her eyes were still on the mobile.

"Honey, I think lots of things are dead people. I think we're made up of 'em."

Stella looked at her own hands as if there were bits of crematory ash stuck under her nails. Lucky thought of her mom.

May sighed. "Let's pull ourselves together now, so we can look for your spoon."

They sat up straighter, and there was silence for a minute, even from Stella.

"You had any troubling dreams of late?" May asked.

"I dreamed of a snake," Lucky replied.

"Snakes in dreams mean there's a battle comin'. Was the snake on the attack?"

"No." Lucky could see its filmy eyes, blown wide. "It was dead. Under Ricky's hat. On the side of the road."

May brought her hands together, lacing her fingers. "Might be someone should check on Ricky." She cleared her throat.

"I dreamed about a moth," Stella interrupted.

Lucky gave her a tight smile. "Maybe you think you did? Because you were just talking about—"

"I was talking about them because I dreamed about one. I'm not a moron," Stella snapped.

Lucky's eyes opened wide, but her mouth stayed closed. This was a tone she remembered well from childhood.

"Was the moth grey?" May asked.

"Yes." Stella closed her eyes to picture it. "Long and almost narrow, with its wings closed."

"That's a money miller. You are going to come into some riches soon enough." May patted the back of Stella's hand by way of congratulations. "You should visit me after that happens upon you." She cackled a bit. "But for now, take the snake as warnin'. I would guess, after today's visitor, that the battle is about him."

"That's a safe bet," Lucky sneered.

"Which means, if what he wants is the spoon—or, at least, to stop y'all from grabbin' the spoon—then wherever this battle is gonna happen is probably where the spoon can be found," May said, trying to piece it all together.

"So, my dream is of a snake." Lucky had to take it step-by-step. "And snakes mean a fight is coming. And the fight will be over the spoon. Then if we figure out where that fight will happen, then we know where the spoon is?"

May pushed her chair back and rose again, turning to the shelves to collect various jars. She took a pinch from one and a sprinkle from another and finally a stem from a third, placed all the ingredients into a stone mortar, and crushed them together with a heavy metal pestle at the counter.

"You go out behind the cabin now, Lucky. Walk straight from under the bedroom window to those cedars out back. Just past the first trees, you'll come up to a henhouse. Go in and grab an egg. Don't spend too long choosing, just grab the one that you can't help but see. You'll know when you find it. Then carry it back here, careful."

Lucky stood. She did not want to go traipsing through the field.

She sure as hell did not want to be crawling into an old henhouse. And she did not want to get pecked as some kind of egg thief. But she didn't say a word. She just zipped up her hoodie and, with a passing look at her grandmother, who was cleaning her fingernails with the car key, left through the front door.

The grass was taller behind the cabin. "Here's hoping May has something for ticks in one of those jars." She shuddered just thinking it. Ticks weren't something she had experience with. She imagined insects the size of mice clinging to her thighs by sharp yellow teeth and took high steps across the field, heading for the cedars.

Once again, she found herself in an improbable place—sent to retrieve some sort of magical egg from a hillbilly's henhouse in butt-fuck Missouri with the Benandanti on the hunt. She was well into the woods, which were swarming with a whole bomber team of newly hatched mosquitoes, before she saw the henhouse. It was all rotted wood and slanted roof, surrounded by a tall wire fence. It didn't seem predator proof, but maybe that was the job of the small leather pouch hanging over the coop doorway. She fumbled with the latch and opened the gate.

"Here, chickens, nice chickens . . ." she called. There was no reply. She half expected one to come rushing at her from under the narrow walk-up ramp, or fly in her face from the rafters, but there was nothing.

She searched the ground: scrubby grass, a few moldy feathers, old seed, chicken shit, and gravel, but no eggs. She searched under the henhouse. It was stinky under there, with more feces and an empty ginger ale bottle, but no eggs. She tried to peer inside the open door but couldn't make out anything inside.

She took out her phone and switched on the flashlight, extending her arm to illuminate the interior. She could see straw on the floor, more straw on the shelves against the wall, and a small hanging heat lamp that was missing its bulb. No eggs.

She'd have to go in. "Awesome."

The ramp was steep and creaked underfoot. "If you're in there, hens, I come in peace. Well, I've come to rob you of potential children, but I'm unarmed."

She ducked inside and quickly shone her flashlight into the corners. Nothing. No chickens. Just straw and wood and the smell of feed left to sprout. The coop didn't look like it had been used in years. But then she saw a bit of white peeking out from some straw on the lowest shelf.

"Oh, thank god." She pushed aside the strands and found two smallish eggs covered in a thin layer of dried gunk. "Well, that's disgusting." She pulled her sleeve over her hand to grab one, but then she saw more eggs on the second level. Three this time, a little larger and more beige than white. She moved slowly down the line. Here and there were more eggs of different sizes, some oddly shaped, one broken open, its spilled insides dried in a thick crust. How was she supposed to know which one to take?

In the far corner there was the broken hulk of an old wardrobe, with one of the doors missing. She walked over. It was full of straw, and a little warmer than the rest of the coop. She leaned in and, digging her finger into a nest, found a single egg, larger than any of the others and a bit uneven, like it was leaning forward on its rounded base. The colour was white with a bluish undertone. When she turned to survey the whole selection of eggs along the shelves, this last egg shimmered in her vision as if it were superimposed over the others.

She whispered May's words: "Grab the one you can't help but see." She picked it up, forgetting to use her sleeve to keep her fingers clean. And as soon as she had it in her hand, things became different. *The smell of cinnamon and rubber under the kind of heat that emanates from concrete in the sun. A near-constant sun. A sun that requires rain to break its hold.*

She cradled the egg against her stomach and walked carefully back down the ramp. Before her feet were on the dirt, she felt that sun on her skin along with a wet humidity. She pocketed her phone and walked out of the pen and into the trees. *Water rolling in her ears, moving heavy and slow against rock, no . . . against concrete.*

Before she'd reached the cabin and opened the door, handed over the egg, and watched May Moon Montgomery submerge it in herbed water, muttering as it turned, lightly clattering against the sides of the bowl, Lucky knew the spoon was farther south, in a place butting up against a huge body of water, and she knew she was going to drive to Louisiana.

Next, May told her to pick up the egg and, as she held it, to pull into mind the snake from her dream, to ask it directly where that fight was going to happen. Lucky went there, to the side of the road, held up the abandoned hat, and asked the blank-eyed snake her question. In the kitchen, May took her hands, then together they gently rapped the egg three times against the counter's edge, not to break it open but to shatter the shell. The soft tap sent a network of cracks over its smooth surface.

May leaned in, watching the small seams grow wider, and yet the eggshell held.

"Perfect," May said. "Now we read it."

She lifted the small metal magnifying glass that hung around her neck to her eye. "Miss St. James, please go fetch that atlas aside the couch." She pointed in the general direction of the living room without looking up. Lucky went and found a waterlogged, ancient book and carried it back. As she did, she flipped the pages, stopping at a detailed map of Louisiana, or at least how it was back in the eighties when this edition had been printed.

She placed it, spread open, on the counter. May reached over and looked, saw which page Lucky had picked, and glanced up at her. "Might be a seer, eh?"

Then she went back to examining the cracks in the shell against the lines on the map, back and forth, moving a gnarled finger over the page. After a few moments, she tapped the paper and lowered her glass.

"New Orleans." She and Lucky spoke in unison.

Stella clapped. "Oh, I've always wanted to go to New Orleans!" She danced herself across the linoleum singing a song about crawfish and bayous.

JAY MADE IT BACK TO the rental car in good time. He could move fast when he had to, and he had to now. He didn't know much about this Montgomery woman, but, as a rule, he didn't fuck with old witches, especially not granny women in a bloodline of granny women. Who knew what those wily bitches had passed along to one another? He didn't want to find out. To be clear, he did, but not when he was alone on their turf. And not when he was outnumbered.

He slid behind the wheel and locked the doors, then sat for a moment, catching his breath as he pulled his hair out of the ridiculous braid he'd made to disguise the fact that his three-hundred-dollar haircut was a three-hundred-dollar haircut.

The young Miss St. James had proven surprising. He didn't think she'd realized he was lying, but there was a cautiousness about her, borne of an intuition that usually came with age. He wondered who her parents were and made a mental note to dig when he got the chance. Maybe she was hereditary after all. There was something about her that intrigued him, made him almost happy he hadn't had the chance to kill her, not yet anyway.

That sneeze trick wasn't something he was proud of, but it was a superstition from this land. Magic that takes root and grows in a particular place ends up being part of that land. All he had to do was suspend his disbelief in it, and, because it had been planted and nurtured here for so long, it came forth. It was basic physics, really. He was surprised the same people who went about their daily lives not believing in anything could also be the same people who spoke about déjà vu or hunches with a straight face. Why did they think those things happened to them?

The land. The land held magic like a giant sponge. It could hold it for centuries, and in isolation if need be.

26

WRESTLING AN ALLIGATOR

The witches took turns staring into the bowl for hours at time, focusing and refocusing, falling asleep sometimes, minds wandering to TV shows and long-ago love affairs. It was Lettie who found the final spoon . . . sort of.

She'd dragged herself down the stairs, having almost fallen asleep putting Everett down for a nap. A small yellow bird watched from the chandelier, head tilted, eyes focused on Freya, who was sitting on the bottom step stretching wearily. Plunking down beside her, Lettie said, "*The Giving Tree* three times through is two times too many. I am ready for some adult communication."

"Well you're in for some kind of communication, adult or otherwise, because it's your turn at the bowl." Freya dropped her head into her hands. "I'm done."

"Any luck?"

"Well, I'm pretty sure I now know the meaning of life and the exact location of God's summer house. But a little enchanted spoon

VENCO

somewhere in the USA? Nope." She yawned and put her head on Lettie's shoulder. "Maybe you'll figure it out."

"Alright, baby, you head up for a nap. I'll read you to sleep if you want." They both giggled.

"No, thanks. The kind of trash I read? No one should be subjected to that." She whistled. "You would never look at me the same."

"Vampires?"

"Oh yeah." She kissed Lettie on the cheek and stood. "But only super-gay vampires. And lots of them." She climbed the stairs.

Lettie glanced at the yellow bird and hauled herself upright, using the newel-post. "Okay then, let's see what we can see."

The dining room candles had half melted into fragrant puddles of thick beeswax. There were signs of the others' vigils: a cast-off sweater, an empty bottle of wine, an ashtray, since no one was allowed outside yet to smoke lest they be carried away by ancient hunters.

Lettie pulled a dining room chair over and sat, placing her elbows on either side of the copper bowl. She exhaled so deeply her breath rippled the surface. Through a slice in the drawn drapes, she could see that the sky was overcast, like velvet folded over itself, soft enough to fall into. That was where she tried to go, into the dark sky inside the bowl.

She focused and unfocused her eyes, trying to clear her mind. An hour went by before she could let go of the tension in her shoulders. Another hour flew through the room while she thought of where she would go if this coven thing didn't work out. Would she end up back at the house she'd rented when she first fled? Or would she wake up one day in her mama's house? It was only in the third hour, when the darkness was heaviest, settling around her like a sleepy cat, that the alligator arrived.

First she saw the long, scaly tail swooshing along the bottom of the copper vessel. Her impulse was to lean closer. But she caught herself. If her current focus or lack thereof was the one that brought up the image, then she should maintain it, as if she were watching a movie out of the corner of her eye.

That tail slid along the rounded bottom and curved around the silver stone placed there. Twice, a bubble rose to the surface and popped, each time forcing Lettie to blink, making her tired, making her want to keep her eyes shut. After a while, that was what she did—closed her eyes—and immediately she began to dream, chin propped on hands held up by elbows.

In her dream, the alligator was silver, then black, then finally green—a deep jewel green, like jade. It was long and sleek with yellow eyes and bright white teeth peeking out of the sides of its massive snout. One of its eyes was focused on her, and she stayed as motionless as she could, her breath small and circular in her chest. The gator picked up speed, turning in tighter circles so that soon its tail was grazing its mouth. Then, as if a swipe of an eraser had taken them away, it folded its legs and lay on its belly, completely motionless, with one eye still hooked into hers.

Though she had no body in the dream, she moved closer. There was no floor to walk across, no walls around them, only a shadowy void. But then she heard fat, hard-shelled crickets chirping. And there was a smell—still water and a pungent floral rot. A bell ringing somewhere, coming closer and then zooming away. She knew that bell, and the rhythmic clack of wood and metal that accompanied it. A streetcar! An old streetcar like the one on St. Charles Avenue. She took that streetcar with her grand-mère when they went school shopping in New Orleans every year.

She looked down, and the alligator had flattened into a painting of an alligator, making a circle with tail to mouth. His eye had lost its focus and its menace. The creature was harmless now. And she knew it was alone. Something in the look left in that one yellow orb was lonely. Was longing. Was waiting.

A weak light as if from a hanging lamp did its best to illuminate the background. It was resolved into a checkerboard of red-and-white large-checked gingham, like a tablecloth. And around the painted image of the circular gator were forks, spread out with their tines facing outward like a silver halo. Forks, not spoons?

She woke up all at once, confused and still perched over the bowl. Outside, the sky was fully dark. She knew the spoon was in New Orleans. She also knew, from the gator's loneliness, that the witch it belonged to hadn't found it yet.

LETTIE GATHERED THE OTHERS AND explained what she had seen. The gator, the forks, the streetcar bell. "The spoon is in New Orleans."

"So you *heard* the bell? I thought we were supposed to see things?" Morticia was grouchy. It was the middle of the night, and she had just gotten to sleep.

"*Seeing* is different than seeing," Wendy answered.

"That's super helpful, thanks." Morticia got up to refill her coffee mug.

Meena was pacing around the kitchen in a green robe covered in velvet vines. "This is great, Lettie. We now have the specific location, like, down to the building, is my guess."

Meena's certainty spooked Lettie. "But what if I'm wrong? What if it was just a dream?"

"It was pretty clear, even so. I say we call Lucky right away." And she took her phone out and started dialing. She put it on speaker-phone, and the women fell silent, waiting.

"Hello?" Lucky's voice sounded far away, and the line was full of static.

"Lucky? This is Meena. Well, this is everyone. You're on speaker."

"Oh thank god! I've been trying to get you guys for hours. Stella and I had a hell of a time with the Yarb witch . . ."

"Lucky, listen, we have some news."

"We have news too. We just got back on the highway. Finally got service. I was just about to try you again."

"Where are you headed?"

"South—New Orleans. The Yarb witch sent us there. The location was on an egg."

"Oh thank god. Listen, Lettie had a vision of New Orleans too."

"I *think* it was New Orleans!" Lettie yelled.

"She heard a streetcar and remembered being there as a child. But if the Witch sent you, that means Lettie was right. Listen, we don't want to scare you." She paused, looking over at Wendy, who gave her a solemn nod. They had the final location, and Lucille had been killed. It was time. "The Benandanti was here."

There was silence.

"Lucky?"

"I'm here. That's why I was trying to call . . . He was here."

Meena grabbed the phone in both hands and shouted. "What! What do you mean he was there? Are you okay?"

"I'm fine. We're fine. It was weird, but we're okay. May came home and— Wait, how was he just there? How could he be there and then here?"

The Salem witches looked around sheepishly, not wanting to speak. It was Meena who answered. "Lucky, I am sorry. I made a call. I thought if he was here, you were safe. I told the others not to tell you. He was here days ago."

Lucky's voice sounded even more distant now. "Well, we're going to go straight to New Orleans. I have to make sure Stella doesn't look at anything."

Remembering old Yarb tales, Meena sighed. "Stella sneezed, didn't she?"

"She sure did."

"Do you want one of us to jump on a flight down there?" Behind her, Freya and Morticia raised their hands.

"No. We're good on our own, always have been," Lucky said.

Meena picked up on the anger in her words. "Well, when you get there, go to the Olivier House in the Quarter. We'll book you guys a suite. And, Lucky?"

"Yeah?"

"I'm sorry."

"Yeah."

There was a tension across the miles. No one spoke for a minute.

Finally, Wendy stepped in to finish. "Oh, Lucky, one more thing. You're going to be looking for an alligator."

"Oh, for fuck's sakes. Of course there's an alligator."

"I'll send you the name of a Booker in town. They might be able to help if you need it," Wendy added. Meena had walked away from the others, covering her mouth with her hand, eyes far away. She didn't know how to make this right.

"Great," Lucky said. "Also, has anyone else been having some real intense dreams lately?"

Wendy smiled. "Yes, Lucky, we all have. Meena told us that the VenCo Oracle was going to 'lend us some focus,' I believe is how they put it."

"Oh." She sounded confused. "Sweet, I guess." There was a moment when all they heard was the sound of the road and Stella snoring in the background. "Wendy?"

"Yes, Lucky?"

"Is Meena still there?"

Wendy looked over at her wife, who stood by the window. "She is."

"Meena?" Lucky said. "I understand why you waited. And I'm not mad."

Meena's shoulders quivered a bit, and she wiped at her face, her back turned to the group. She raised her voice to reply. "All you have to do is get the spoon and the witch and come back to us."

"Right."

"That's the important part, Lucky. You come back to us. You come home." Her voice broke a bit at the end.

"Got it."

The line went dead, and silence returned to the kitchen.

"What do we do now?" Morticia was hoping the answer would be "Go back to bed."

Back to her old form, Meena said, "Now that Lucky's on the spoon, we get back to looking for this missing witch, but we switch tactics. Wendy, can you prepare some tea to help us sleep?" But Wendy was already digging through a pile of recipe books behind a glass door in the corner of the cabinet.

"Soooo, we are going back to bed, then?" Morticia was still hopeful.

Meena put a hand on her shoulder. "In a way. Except there will be nothing restful about it. This will be work."

27

THE BIG UNEASY

Morticia had paid extra to make sure their room at the Olivier House was available as soon as they arrived, bright and early the next morning. "We put y'all in the Garden Suite, just over past the pool here," the clerk explained while Lucky filled out the registry. He wore a bright purple golf shirt that cradled his ample weight, with a green belt holding up rumpled shorts. His face was clean-shaven and had impressively unlined tanned skin for a man in his fifties. "It's through the courtyard and at the very back. There's an upstairs loft with a queen bed and a pull-out double on the main floor. Two bathrooms too."

"Can we go in the pool?" Stella had slept all the way here and was ready to party.

"Surely," he answered, already enchanted by her. Gay men loved Stella, maybe, Lucky thought, because she had some serious Carol Channing vibes.

"I have to sleep, Grandma, and you can't go swimming alone."

"That sucks. What am I going to do?" She literally pouted.

The clerk stepped in. "Well now, I have to trade off with Myrtle on the desk and am about to go clean the pool area. I can accompany you if you would allow it." He was looking at Lucky now.

She glanced at her sulky grandmother and then back at the pleasant clerk. She read his name tag. "Listen, Theodore, I don't want to put you out, and besides, no offence, I don't really know you and she needs . . . minding."

"I would like the company too," a small voice said from the side parlor.

A small woman came into the lobby, leaning lightly on an ornate silver cane. "I'm Aggie Duveaux."

"Aggie, these are"—the clerk leaned over to look at the registry—"the St. James women."

"I'm not a St. James," Stella corrected. "I'm a Sampson. Stella Sampson. This is my granddaughter, Lucky. She's the St. James."

"Well now, Stella, I'm glad to know you. And Miss Lucky. And you know my name. You've met my grandnephew Teddy here."

Theodore gave a quick bow. "Aunt Aggie owns this hotel. She also lives in the coach house in the back."

"So we aren't exactly strangers." She smiled. "You even know my home address. So can Stella come out to play?"

What else could Lucky do but relent. Besides, she was cautiously optimistic. Stella had been more lucid lately. "Okay, Grandma, let's go to the room, settle in, and you can dig out something to swim in that isn't track pants."

Stella smiled at her. "Not that I need your consent, but I'll take it. I'll see you poolside, Miss Aggie."

Twenty minutes later, Lucky was pushing Stella out the door in a sports bra and shorts. As soon as she was gone, Lucky lay down. She started thinking about the Benandanti, and the fact that the coven hadn't told her. She really had been angry, but the truth was, if they had told her, she probably wouldn't have gone on. She'd been a witch for all of what—a week? It was a tough call, but probably the right one. She was used to it. Life with Arnya had been full of tough calls. Soon enough, Lucky fell asleep. When she woke up, Stella was back and watching TV with the volume down and the closed captioning on, and it was after two in the afternoon.

"Shit! Why'd you let me sleep so long?" She jumped out of bed and grabbed her phone. It was dead. Her bedroom was on a second floor, up a metal staircase, so she made her way down, carefully. She dug through their bags, still by the door, for her charger.

"What, I'm your butler now? You should have set an alarm."

Lucky waved her dead phone in the air. "Hello? I did!"

"And I'm the one that 'needs minding'?" Stella turned back to her show, arms crossed across her chest. "I know I'm forgetful, but I'm still here."

Lucky plugged her phone in and sat down on the couch beside Stella. For a few minutes, they watched a fishing show in silence as the air-conditioner whirred. Outside, some kids screamed and splashed in the pool. A car drove by on the street playing bounce music at window-vibrating volume.

"I'm sorry," Lucky said. "I forget too. I forget that you're the one who took care of me pretty much my whole childhood. All I remember is the burning popcorn and the weird hats . . ."

"Hey!" Stella chucked her lightly on the arm. "My hats are not weird!"

Lucky leaned her head on her grandmother's shoulder. "They are when you wear more than one at a time." They watched the show to the end, muted, until the credits were rolling. Lucky's phone turned back on and began dinging from the kitchenette counter.

"Right, shit!" She sprang up and checked the screen.

One was an image, a cartoon drawing of a rather stern-looking alligator with its tail touching the tip of its snout. Surrounding it were pencil-shaded forks of various sizes. The second message was from Wendy, with a name and location of the Booker: Claudia Welan, the Moon Over Marigny Gallery & Bookstore. She put the name of the store into Google Maps and got directions. It was not too far from here.

Stella burst out laughing. She was now watching a sitcom on mute.

"You can turn that up now. I'm not sleeping anymore." Lucky raised the volume on the remote herself. Then she softened her voice. "Uh, listen, Grandma, I'm just gonna go grab some towels from housekeeping."

"We just got here. Why do we need towels already?"

Lucky pointed to random towels, wet and strewn around the floor. "Well, you blew through most of those. I'll be right back. Stay here."

She found Theodore near the front door replenishing the brochures for haunted walking tours and the Voodoo Museum. "Hey there, Lucky, how you doing? Oh, your Stella, she's a hoot. Aunt Aggie has invited her for dinner. She's sent my co-worker Myrtle out for beignets. She's real glad to have someone like her to pass the time with. If that's okay?"

It was more than okay, and Lucky said so. She had been about to ask him to watch Stella for a bit while she ran errands, so this worked out just great. She returned to the room and told Stella that Theodore would be by later to pick her up for a dinner date.

"Jesus, you're so bad at reading people," Stella mumbled. "That man is not interested in vaginas, Lucky. Not even mine."

"Well, obviously not an actual date . . . Wait, it was the gay thing that threw you, not the fact that he's, like, thirty years younger than you?

Stella scoffed. "You think I don't got game? I didn't even breast-feed your dad. These ladies are still pointing the right way." She hefted her boobs with her forearm.

On that note, Lucky left.

OUT ON TOULOUSE STREET, RIGHT near the corner of Bourbon, music was already pouring out of doorways and patios and windows, some of it recorded, other strands live. Lucky paused to listen, sheltering under the baskets of flowers hanging from a hotel balcony.

The sun was high over the Quarter. The buildings here were narrow and low. Where they did have second or third floors, each one was wrapped in iron filigree balconies like cursive writing. Across the street, between two slim buildings, a wooden gate had been left open, and she saw a path there that led into a small, lush garden, with green ferns and a crooked palm tree and a small stone fountain. She wondered if every place in New Orleans had a secret garden, if every place was so witchy and beautiful. And for the first time, she was filled with an enormous pride for who she was—*what* she was, all of it. That pride filled the spaces between her bones so that it was impossible not to stand tall.

Anxiety makes everything feel very big or very small, depending on which is more hurtful in the moment. Being suddenly relieved of anxiety in this moment gave her a clear understanding that this was the life she had been running towards. Not necessarily New Orleans, not a distant dot on a map, not a brand-new career, but a life full of secret gardens.

Her Uber glided up the street, and she got in with a smile on her face.

THE MARIGNY WAS OFF-KILTER, LEANING, somehow, in all directions at the same time. The houses were shades of every colour, with contrasting wooden shutters. The roads lay like wrinkled sheets, being knuckled from underneath by old roots and new growth, and the sidewalks were cracked right through.

The Moon Over Marigny was in a yellow shotgun house with massive front windows rammed with lively paintings of Mardi Gras Indians and tunnels of oak trees over old roads. Over the door was a hand-painted sign: BE NICE OR LEAVE. A small speaker on the porch played zydeco music. Lucky took a deep breath, climbed the three steps, and walked inside.

The place was one large room—not a standard stuffy gallery, but an eclectic space with paintings of all sizes from floor to ceiling. Running down the middle of the room were three velvet couches, each more dilapidated than the last, each charming in its own way. One wall was covered in bookshelves, with a library ladder attached to a railing so that you could reach the highest shelves. And at the back of the room, through an archway, she could see a whole studio, riotous and paint-splattered, dropcloths on the floor and works-in-progress propped up every which way. Early grunge, Soundgarden maybe, was coming from a small speaker on a wooden chair.

"Afternoon," a woman's voice called out.

Lucky spun, looking for the body the voice belonged to.

From a corner of the studio, a short woman with pink hair in black coveralls emerged. She fiddled with her phone and the rock music stopped. She wiped her hands on her pants legs and walked into the gallery space.

"How you doin' today?"

"Uh, I'm good."

"Can I help you find something?" Up close, she was older than Lucky first thought, maybe close to sixty. Her cheeks were round and her glasses moved when she spoke.

"I hope so. I'm looking for Claudia?"

The woman beamed at her. "Is that a question?"

"No, I know I'm looking for Claudia." Lucky was not used to this level of joy coming from a person. Mania and no-holds-barred energy, because she was Arnya's daughter. But happiness at that same intensity? That was foreign. It made her a bit shy.

"Well, you're having a good day, then, because I am a Claudia." The woman chuckled.

"Uh, yes. So, Meena—well, Wendy, really—sent me your name. I'm looking for something and I think it's here. Well, not right here, but in New Orleans."

"Everything anyone needs is in New Orleans," Claudia answered, opening her arms wide. "Unless what you need is peace and quiet. Gotta head past city limits for those."

She walked back into the studio, waving for Lucky to follow her. They stepped carefully over uncapped paint tubes and wet palettes and went out a small door in the back that creaked when it was pushed. They walked through a small courtyard of tall grass and drowsy wildflowers beaded with fat bees, with a wrought-iron bistro set in the middle. They followed a narrow path to a small shed, the green paint peeling into curls like gift ribbon. Claudia reached into her coveralls and pulled out a key that dangled on a thin gold chain and used it to unlock the door.

"Mind your feet. I gotta get some lights on in here."

Lucky was expecting must and dirt, since from the outside it looked like a mostly unused garden shed. But instead she smelled incense and old paper. Claudia fumbled with a plug for a moment, and then the space was filled with light.

There was a long trestle table in the middle, reaching from one wall almost to the next, every inch of it covered in books—piled, opened, and sealed. Here and there were scraps of paper with notes in the most beautiful calligraphy. Pens and pencils were scattered in the mess. At first glance, it appeared the back wall was covered in bland, cream wallpaper, but on closer inspection, Lucky saw it was stacked with scrolls, held straight by thin wires fastened to the wall. A striped rug was laid out under the table, and what she could see of the bare floor was swept clean. There was only one round stool in here, the right height for the tall table. It was chaos and order at the same time, and Lucky imagined this was what the inside of Claudia's head must look like.

"Here we are. You want a drink before we get started?" Claudia moved carefully around to the other side of the table, only knocking two pens off the edge with her backside.

"No, I'm good."

"Okay then, Wendy says you are looking for an alligator."

Lucky was confused for a moment. "No, I'm looking for a spoon."

"One thing at a time. You're looking for a round alligator, tail all up in his face, aren't you?"

"Oh, right. Yes. I am looking for an alligator."

"Alright then." Claudia clapped her hands together. "Let's find your gator!"

She searched the tabletop, moving piles of pages and notebooks this way and that. "Now, where did I put it . . . ?"

"Which book are you looking for?" Lucky leaned over to examine the piles.

"Ah! Here is it!" Claudia pulled a laptop from a pile of loose pages and plopped it on top of a botanical encyclopedia. "Now, let's just make sure we're connected to the internet."

"Wait, you're just going to look online?" How was this secret knowledge? Lucky could have Googled an alligator herself. And she had—she'd found swamp tours, a clothing store, three separate high schools with alligator mascots, but no circular gator surrounded by spokes.

"Have some patience and belief there, baby. Let me see the image they drew? Wendy said you'd bring me one." She held her hand out, and Lucky pulled up the picture she'd been sent and handed her phone over.

"Huh. I seen this one before. Long time before . . ." Her voice trailed off, and she tapped her chin with a forefinger. Lucky waited in the silence, shifting from one foot to the other.

The pause went on for so long, Lucky had zoned out watching two small birds fight over a beetle near the open door and jumped when Claudia yelled out, "I got it now!"

She pushed her laptop aside and dug around on the table again, pulling out a hardcover as long as her arm. Across the navy front was gold lettering: *Culinary Establishments in New Orleans, 1900 to 1950.*

"A Booker is more than just books—it's about memory and local knowledge too," Claudia said, flipping the large pages.

"Does each place have a Booker?"

"Every good place does." She turned more pages, running her finger down each one as she searched. "People get it wrong. The magic's not in the person. The magic is in the place. It just takes the right kind of person to pull it up."

Lucky leaned over and scanned the pages as Claudia turned them. Black-and-white photos of men with impressive mustaches, standing in front of glass windows displaying their names; Creole women in aprons, smiling under striped awnings; quaint patios rammed with people in stiff shirtsleeves and giant straw hats. Towards the middle was a section on signs. A magnolia tree with curlicue lettering for roots. The outline of a busty woman in a bustle skirt. A crawfish holding a bowler hat up in one claw by way of greeting. Then a small photo of a brick shop front with a wooden sign by the entrance. They both leaned in to get a closer look, and painted on the sign they saw an alligator with one flat eye, his tail curled up to his snout.

"There!" Claudia jabbed it with a finger. "Ha-ha! I knew it!" She did a little dance, one hand on her waist, the other in the air, wiggling her hips. "We got him!"

Lucky whooped. Then she looked again. "Wait, where are the forks?"

"Oh, baby, visions aren't literal. Sometimes they get crossed on the way. Sometimes they get all jumbled up into one thing when they're supposed to be several. My guess? That spoon of yours is near forks." Claudia sat on the little stool and pulled her laptop close again. "Read me what it says on that page."

"'Croc Monsieur opened in 1937 as the first Louisiana-based project of up-and-coming chef Marco Mayfaire. Though originally intended to be located in the French Quarter, the restaurant eventually broke ground in the Garden District, near Lafayette Cemetery, where diners could take advantage of the St. Charles streetcar line for easy access.'"

"Is there an exact address?"

Lucky skimmed the page again and read the small print under the photo. "Three six nine Prytania Street."

"Three . . . six . . . nine . . . Prytania . . . Okay, here. It's now called the Burial Grounds Café—oh, cute. The tourists gotta love that." She laughed. "I would wager your spoon is in that café and being used as regular flatware. That would explain the forks in the vision. Probably in a drawer with teaspoons and butter knives."

"I need to get there now!" Lucky's hands got itchy. She grabbed her phone and sent a quick text to Meena:

Gator led us to a café—Burial
Grounds—Garden District!

"Says here it's only open for breakfast and lunch. You gotta go tomorrow." Claudia scrolled down. "Oh, they got shrimp and grits. I might have to go myself."

"What time does it open?"

"Eight o'clock. Second thought, maybe I'll go for lunch instead." She closed the laptop and stood up, stretching out her arms. "Well, I'mma finish up for the day, I think."

"Thank you so much. You don't know what this means." Lucky was genuinely grateful and more excited than she'd been this whole crazy trip. So close. She was soooo close. She sent a text update:

closed now, will go tomorrow
when it opens at 8

"Oh, I think I do know what this could mean. I'm rooting for you. In fact, why don't you come out and grab a drink with me, to celebrate?"

Lucky's phone dinged.

GREAT!! Just looked it up. Be
there right at 8 sharp, order the
whole menu. Ask for new cutlery
with every dish, bribe a waiter,
throw a chair through the front
window if you have to!

Lucky texted back a thumbs-up and put her phone in her back pocket. "I would love to, but I have to get back to my grandma. She's waiting for me at the Olivier House."

"Ooo, I love that place. Except for all the ghosts . . ." She shuddered. They walked back into the courtyard, and Claudia locked the shed behind her. Evening was coming, and a slight breeze moved the grass like a breath blown out. "Well, Miss Lucky, guess you better get to it."

WALKING INTO THE SUITE, LUCKY called out, "Hello?" There was no sign of Stella. She should have been back from her dinner with Miss Aggie by now.

She walked up the spiral stairs to the second floor. The bed was made and a note was propped against the pillows. It was from Theodore.

Shift ended. Took Miss Stella and Auntie Aggie out for an after-dinner stroll. Maybe we'll stop to hear some music. Will have them back before midnight. Here's my number in case you are worried or want to make sure we're not kidnappers.

She threw herself on the bed, facedown, arms by her sides. She felt relief, first that Stella was safe, and second that she was being taken care of, so Lucky had time and space. Then, of course, she immediately felt guilty. Stella was with strangers. What if Theo and Aggie *were* kidnappers?

In the last week Stella really seemed to be more like her old self. She hadn't had one out-loud conversation with her dead husband; hell, she was even using the past tense when talking about him. There had been no more late-night wanderings.

She was just tired. Tired of all the driving. Tired of worrying for two. Tired of cataloguing stress so that she knew which thing to be more concerned about at any given moment. She just wanted to be still. To lie here and just breathe. To exist. Without looking over her shoulder. Without trying to parse out a convoluted future. She just wanted to breathe.

In and out.

In and out.

Beyond the walls, the sounds of the bars and bands of Bourbon Street mixed together into a smooth white noise.

In and out.

In and out.

She fell asleep in her clothes on top of the comforter.

IN THE DREAM, ARNYA WAS writing a note on the flattened cardboard of her empty cigarette pack. "Look, just give this to the guy behind the cash. The note says you're buying the smokes for me, and this is the brand I want."

Lucky stood at the front door in red rubber boots and a romper that was getting too small. Her legs had grown so fast that summer, her knees ached. This was the first time her mother was letting her go to the store by herself but—cigarettes?

"I can't buy cig'rettes, even I know that." She was exasperated but was walking the fine line between being allowed to go to the corner store by herself and pissing off her mother by correcting her mistaken idea that this was 1975 and children could pick up smokes for their parents.

"Just take the damn note." Arnya flapped the cardboard towards Lucky, who took it along with the folded twenty. "Tell Tommy they're for me and that he goddamn well knows it. Spent enough money over the years on his expired milk and used lighters."

Arnya had very particular ideas about how the world should work, that there were rules the neighbourhood should follow. Everything was a series of debts and payments, asides and handshakes, all in delicate balance. "Plus tell him I could just as easily get smokes from the rez."

"But we don't have a rez, you said half-breeds don't even get leftovers," Lucky started.

"*I* know that and *you* know that, but you think Tommy knows that? Just say that if you have to. Start with it being no big deal. People are less likely to fight if they don't think you have skin in the game. Then just be kid sweet—not too sweet—don't let him think he's better than you. Then bust out the threats if you have to." She was having a bad day. She was hot and cold at the same time, her polyester nightie stained with yellow sick-sweat, her teeth chattering. Lucky watched her lower herself onto the couch as if she were made of small folds in thin paper.

"Maybe you shouldn't smoke anyway."

"Okay, then, Surgeon General Luck. You wanna stay home and

I'll go? How you gonna get your buck's worth of candy, then? 'Cause if I go, there's no payment owing."

Lucky slipped out the door with her instructions and the money before another word was spoken.

THEY WERE LIVING ABOVE AN electronics store on Queen Street East. It was a great score, since they could hop on the streetcar right outside their door and get anywhere they needed. Also because, being above TVs and computers instead of a restaurant, like their last place, meant way fewer cockroaches. Instead, they had mice, who liked the cardboard boxes in the basement storage rooms. But mice were better than roaches. That was the hierarchy of rentals: mice—tolerable; roaches—terrible; bed bugs—*run!*

Lucky felt different walking down the hall by herself. She had no one to chase after. No impossible pace to keep up with. So she slowed right down, running a hand along the water-stained walls as she went.

She jumped from one grey-carpeted stair to the next, holding the rail for balance, liking the way her shiny red boots broke the monotony. The front door was heavier when it was only her pulling it open, and she muttered her mother's usual words to herself: "Come on, flex those noodles!"

She waited for a break in the foot traffic and then joined the current, clomping down the sidewalk towards the store. The block and a half felt like miles. She stopped to admire store displays and to pet a dog, then heard her mother's voice in her head. *Don't be walking without purpose. That's when the assholes think they can approach you.* She picked up her pace.

Tommy's store was long and narrow. Two lines of shelves ran its length from front to back. If you had to pass someone in one of the aisles, you both had to turn and suck in your gut. Lucky had never gone all the way to the back, where the frozen pizzas and ice-cream cartons collected freezer burn, so that was where she decided she would go, because she was a grown-ass lady and she could do what she wanted.

She hurried past Tommy, who was behind the counter arguing with a short woman pulling a buggy full of groceries from the dollar store.

"I don't care what you think you heard on the news, this lottery ticket is not a winner. Take it. Go ahead. Go check at some other store. It's a dud!"

The woman snatched the ticket back from him, grabbed her buggy, and pushed it out the door in a huff.

She heard Tommy muttering, "Crazy old bat. Tries that every week. With the same ticket, even."

She ran a hand along the kitchen sponges, the garbage bags, and then the envelopes. When she let it rest on a package of unsharpened pencils, she felt eyes on her and looked up. Tommy was standing at the top of the aisle, arms crossed above his paunch, watching her. He ran both his hands through his greasy grey hair and flipped it over his shoulder. With his arms raised, patches of black hair stuck out the sleeves of his Motocross T-shirt. It made Lucky think of fuzzy black spiders. She picked up the pencils, took the time to study them, put them back, and then moved around the end of the aisle and into the next one. She looked up. Tommy had moved too. She could feel her heart beating in her throat, like that time she accidently swallowed a Life Saver whole.

She pretended to browse the cheap shampoo and the stack of hamburger buns as he slowly came towards her. By the time she was at the chips, he was directly in front of her. So, as per the unwritten rule, she turned to face the centre of the aisle and started to sidestep. He turned too.

"You need any help?" He loomed over her.

"Nope." Her voice was small around the lump in her throat.

"You by yourself today?"

Suddenly she didn't want to declare her independence. But he was an adult and Stella said never to lie to adults. "Yup."

"You live around here?" There was maybe two inches between his belly and her. She felt the tightness of that space like a threat.

"Yup."

"Huh, I don't remember seeing you around. You sure you're all alone?" He reached out and put a hand on her shoulder. The heat from his meaty palm, half on the collar of her romper, half on her bare skin, made all her muscles tense at once. It made her stomach flip. She didn't have words for it, just the image of something rotten seeping through her pores. She couldn't move her feet.

Remember who the fuck you are. You're mine and you're yours. No one else's. Ever. Arnya's real voice popped into her head—not the voice of the fragile woman she'd left on the couch, but of the one who talked to her reflection before she went out for the night, red-lipstick-and-big-swagger Arnya.

Lucky let her shoulder drop out from underneath the hand. Stepping past him, she reached into her pocket and pulled out the piece of cardboard. "My mom says to give these to me."

He hesitated, his eyebrows pinched together, then took the note and read it. "Your ma is Arnya?" The way he said her name gave Lucky confidence. He definitely knew who Arnya was.

"Yeah, that's right." She walked with purpose (so the assholes didn't approach) to the counter, right by the front door.

Tommy moved back to his spot behind the register. He scrounged under the counter and threw a pack of Du Mauriers on the plastic scratch-ticket case. Lucky grabbed it and shoved it into her pocket. Just then two teenage boys opened the front door, and she bolted without paying. And even though no one gave chase, she ran up the street and all the way home. Holding the image of shitkicker Arnya in her head like a talisman, she ran back to her as fast as she could.

A few days later, Tommy's Corner Convenience burned to the ground.

"Jesus," Arnya said around a cigarette, as they stood on the other side of the yellow tape that surrounded the rubble. "I heard it was arson. Guess he pissed off the wrong people."

Lucky was quiet. She wondered if all that rot from Tommy's hand had lit a flame he couldn't blow out.

"There's no rebuilding from this." Arnyna flicked her cigarette butt into the ruins. She seemed amused. "Sometimes you need fire to make sure the bad shit can't come back."

AFTER THEY'D DROPPED AGGIE AT her coach house, Theodore let Stella into the suite and quietly hugged her good night. They had stopped in at a bar at the top of Bourbon Street after dinner and shared a drink. They stayed longer than expected after finding out they could sit around the piano in back and sing along. It was the most fun Stella'd had in years. She hummed a tune while changing into her pj's and brushing her teeth. She liked this place, and she liked these people. She wondered if New Orleans felt the same for them, living here year-round, like a treat, like a place running out of time with nothing but time left.

She braided her hair, clucking her tongue at how thin it was getting, how the silver was bleaching white. She was a woman running out of time with nothing but time left. It wasn't a sad thought. She was fine with it. Especially now. She felt clear these days. Once in a while, she fell into the lapses. But she kind of welcomed the confusion that made Oswald alive and well, sitting at the kitchen table doing his crossword before bed. Welcomed the satisfaction of knowing that her son was alive and well and working at the newspaper-printing plant.

She could hear Lucky snoring softly on the upstairs bed, and she went there now, singing "Moon River" under her breath as she climbed the stairs.

The girl was facedown, head turned to the side, and still fully dressed. Her purse was on the bed beside her, and her shoes were still on. She looked just like her father, when he used to stumble home as a teenager, sneak up to his attic room, and pass out. Stella did what she'd done for him: she carefully pulled off Lucky's shoes, put her bag on the nearby chair, and found a blanket to throw over her. As she was tucking her in, she felt the phone in Lucky's back pocket.

She'll want that plugged in, she thought, remembering this afternoon's panic when her alarm hadn't gone off. She carried it back downstairs with her. Tonight, she'd be the one to sleep on the couch. She wasn't tired anyway. She turned on the TV, pleased to find her favourite show playing, and carried the phone to the kitchen, where Lucky had left the charger.

It dinged in her hand, and she glanced at it. A text from Meena:

Don't forget to go alone and stay
alone until you have the spoon.
He'll be watching everything
through her eyes. Message as
soon as you can. Good luck!

There were other messages between them that Stella read through. She was going to text back, but then remembered this was not her phone, it was Lucky's. So she plugged it in to charge, set it down on the counter, and settled on the couch to watch *The Golden Girls*.

JAY CHRISTOS HAD SNARED THE wrong woman with a sneeze and was finding it near impossible to follow them. The old one slept too much, and when she was awake, she focused on all the wrong things. He had managed to follow them from the Yarb witch's cabin and, using the few road signs the woman read, had arrived in New Orleans at almost the same time.

Now he was holed up in a grand antebellum-style house in the Garden District that belonged to an old friend of his—so old, in fact, that the man was in a hospital bed and hooked up to oxygen in the downstairs parlor.

"Oh, Gerard, how nice to see you once again," he'd cooed when he first leaned over the man's bed. Gerard's dim blue eyes had teared up with recognition. He held up a hand made repulsive with knotted veins and age spots, and Jay grasped it, even brought it to his lips to kiss. "I've come back to visit you, my love."

"Christos," Gerard croaked, the plastic mask on his face fogging up.

"Shhhh, now, my oldest, dearest companion. It's okay." He gave the hand a pat and gently placed it back on the white duvet. "I'll leave you be. Your nurse was kind enough to let me pop in to say a quick greeting." He nodded towards the door where a tall Creole woman in pink scrubs stood watch. "But I had to promise I wouldn't get you all riled up. I trust you won't mind if I set up camp here? Shouldn't be for more than a day or two. Three at the most?"

The skeletal patient on the bed nodded as enthusiastically as he could.

"Thank you, Gerard. I am in your debt, and you know I like to pay off my debts, especially when they are owed to such a handsome man," he replied with a wink. He stood up from the bedside and walked towards the door. "I'll stay out of your way," he called over a shoulder. "And yours too," he said to the nurse. "I expect the same in return."

She hardened her lips and looked pointedly away as he moved past her.

After he'd secured the spoon or made sure the witch wouldn't find it, he'd budget an hour for one last visit with his friend. He'd spend it reading Gerard love poems. Then he'd put him out of his ancient misery with a pillow.

Since he'd seen nothing through the old woman's eyes but TV and small talk, he'd spent some time enjoying the house, the pool out back, and the pool boy cleaning it. Now he lay flat on his back in the sweeping master bedroom, unused since Hurricane Katrina, staring up at the massive chandelier he'd convinced Gerard to import from France when they had travelled abroad that one summer so long ago. That was the year they'd installed some extra play features in the room. He wondered if they were still there, after all this time. He reached behind the headboard, and his hand touched a leather strap.

"Oh, Gerard, you dog." He laughed.

He closed his eyes, concentrating, listening with his whole body. He wanted to meet Lucky St. James again. He had a feeling she was more than she seemed, more than maybe she even understood. Playing with her might be an interesting project. But for right now, he needed to find her. Stella was likely asleep, but it was worth checking, since he'd already learned she kept odd hours. He would have only a few more hours before the connection was lost.

Orthopedic sandals walking down . . . Bourbon Street? If she was walking about in the French Quarter so late, she and Lucky had to be staying close by.

A pleasant-faced man with a shiny forehead saying good night.

An old set of rooms and the smell of chlorine and cleaner.

The girl! Asleep in her clothes on top of the bed.

Curving stairs. The TV turned on. *The Golden Girls*?

He was about to call it quits and go grab a shower when he saw a phone. She was holding a phone.

A message notification popped up. Stella opened it. Meena herself. Stella read it. And so did Jay Christos.

He smiled so big that his eyes popped open. He had it now: 369 Prytania Street, Burial Grounds Café.

28

BURIALS

"Oh, fuck me."

Lucky stood on the sidewalk in front of Burial Grounds Café at seven forty-five in the morning. A man with his panting bulldog and a little girl eating a pickle stood beside her, watching the scene with quiet curiosity. The police were keeping people from getting too close to the glass on the sidewalk from the smashed-in window while a couple of workers hammered a sheet of plywood in its place.

A neighbour padded over from next door in furry slippers and a silk bathrobe. He had a folded magazine tucked under his arm, as if he'd been interrupted on his way to the bathroom. "Sweet Saint Joseph, what happened here?"

A ponytailed jogger answered. "They're saying robbery. The cash register was broken open and all the silverware's gone."

"Of course!" Lucky yelled. "Of course it's gone." Distraught, she threw her hands up and paced in small circles, not caring that the jogger and Slipper Man took a step back from her.

A police officer, thumbs hooked on his wide belt, wandered over to talk to Slipper Man. "You live next door there?"

The man nodded.

"And you didn't hear a crash?"

"Not a thing." He shook his head for emphasis.

"Not the most elegant way to break in," the jogger added.

"Well, actually, they broke in through the back," the cop said. "Just lifted an old window and shimmied in. All this damage? Vandalism. There was no need to smash the front in like that."

"All the silverware was taken?" Lucky asked.

"Who wants to know?" The cop walked over to her. "You the owner?"

Uniforms always made her nervous. Arnya had taught her that a uniform was just an easy way to spot a bully. Lucky shook her head. "I came because I heard they . . . they had antiques that I should check out."

"You're an antiques person, then?" He unhooked a thumb and patted his hair into place.

"Uh, yup. From Canada." She wasn't sure how being Canadian was protection, but threw it out there anyway.

"Well, now, I also have an interest in old stuff," he said.

Right—now she recognized the look on his face. The softening around the eyes, the hardening around the mouth. He was checking her out.

"What's your name?"

"Freya," she responded. "So all this damage came after they got in?"

"Yup. Hard to understand why someone would throw a chair right through the front window like that."

She couldn't hear him anymore. All she could think of was Meena's text:

> . . . throw a chair through the
> front window if you have to!

"I . . . I gotta go. My grandmother is waiting for me." She turned and bolted for the cab she saw parked in front of a brick church.

"STELLA! WHERE ARE YOU?"

A toilet flushed in the downstairs bathroom, and the door opened. "Cripes, can't a woman pee in private?" Stella pulled her head back in and turned on the faucet.

"Did you read my text messages?"

"What? No!" Stella regarded Lucky in the mirror as she washed her hands. "Didn't you take your phone with you?"

"Yes, but what about last night?" Lucky was frantic. "I fell asleep in my clothes. I didn't plug it in . . ."

"No, I did. Didn't want you freaking out again about it being dead." She turned the taps off. "You're welcome, by the way."

Lucky followed her out of the bathroom and into the kitchen area. "But did you read my texts?"

Stella poured hot water from the kettle into a mug. "What? No. I mean, maybe." She was getting annoyed. "You're not that interesting, you know."

"Grandma, I don't have time for you to have your feelings. I need to know. Did you read my texts from Meena?"

Stella shook a package of Sweet'N Low, thinking. She shook it for so long, Lucky finally reached out and snatched it from her.

"Hey!"

"Stella, focus. Did you read my texts?"

"Maybe," she said. "Not on purpose, though. I wasn't snooping."

"No, no, no, no!" Lucky turned in a complete circle, hands in her hair.

"What? It's not like there were any secrets there. I'm on this trip too!"

"Yeah, Stella, you are. And you were there at the cabin. You sneezed, remember?"

"What?" She was confused, and then she wasn't. "Oh Lord . . ."

"Exactly." Lucky threw her hands up. "'Oh Lord,'" she mimicked back. "Oh Lord, Stella. I just went to the café to find the spoon. And guess what? All the silverware had been stolen."

"No . . ."

"Yes. It's gone." She sat down hard on a kitchen stool. "I don't even know what to do."

"Maybe you should call Meena?"

"And maybe you should learn to listen. Everything is ruined now. I should have left you in Toronto." She was cutting, but she meant it.

"Lucky . . ."

"But no, couldn't do that, could I? I'm stuck with you."

"Lucky!"

But she was already up and heading out the door. She pulled it open and paused. "The day after tomorrow, Grandma. That's the deadline, that's when this ends. And where will we be then? Huh?"

"You know what?" Stella huffed in return. "I'm meeting Aggie for lunch and then we're going sightseeing and I don't have time for this. So . . . so maybe I don't have time for you either!"

They had a stare off that ended with Lucky slamming the front door behind her and stomping across the courtyard, into the main building, and out onto the street.

She was so angry at Stella she couldn't breathe right. What the hell were they supposed to do now? She followed Toulouse across Bourbon, Royal, and Chartres and turned onto Decatur. She made a left, passing through the French Market, ignoring the stalls of fresh spices and T-shirts, and out the other side, heading for the bank of the Mississippi, where she found a bench and sat. Then she sighed and pulled out her phone. It was time to call Meena.

AFTER SHE HUNG UP, MEENA gathered the women in the garden. They were all exhausted. They'd spent the night in pairs, rousing each other from REM sleep to write down notes about whatever images or sequences they'd dreamed.

"I'm afraid I have some bad news."

"Is the bad news that we're now a morning coven?" Morticia yawned dramatically.

Meena, sitting on the edge of an urn stuffed with ferns, ignored her. "The Benandanti got to New Orleans. Probably using Stella's vision."

"Jesus!" Lettie exclaimed. "Are they okay?"

"They're fine. But he got the address of the café. The spoon is gone."

No one spoke. Even the birds held their breath.

Finally, Freya broke the silence. "What do we do now?"

A soft rain began to fall, and Wendy started gathering up the newspapers and books and pages from the table.

"We stay the course," Meena answered. "Wendy, we need to think of how to keep Lucky and Stella safe. The rest of you, keep on the witch search."

"What's the point?" Freya sulked.

"We don't give up until the clock runs out. We have to keep going."

They all rose slowly, despite the rain, and walked back inside, everyone except for Meena, who sat there for a while, letting the water fall on her face. Then she gathered herself up and went into the kitchen. She still had a group to lead, even if they might never become a real coven now.

JAY CHRISTOS TOSSED THE BAG of cutlery into a bush outside Lafayette Cemetery. He'd found what he needed, and the rest could be retrieved by children or thieves—not much difference between the two.

These witch spoons were small, delicate, and decidedly plain. He wondered how Low had even managed to sell them in the numbers he had, being so far from the Victorian aesthetic. Perhaps it was his Puritan roots that stopped him from going too fancy. That and the fact that the witch figure was so hideous . . . keeping the rest of the design simple meant emphasis was placed where it should be. He tucked the spoon into the inside pocket of his linen jacket and whistled down the street, tipping his hat at a widow toddling to the graveyard with a bouquet of plastic yellow roses. She scowled and looked away.

Well, that was it, the circle was broken. He would bring the enchanted spoon back to the compound and bury it in the desert, in a lockbox, without a marker or another thought. He would put it so far out of mind that it would practically cease to exist in the world at all. It certainly would never be found again.

And while this should have been the end, it didn't feel so, because he couldn't stop thinking about her—not Prudence this time, but the new one, Lucky. He wondered if she had been to the café yet. If she knew it was he who took it. What she said, how she felt, what she would do next. He wondered what her fear smelled like, or her disappointment. Was she despairing now? Or was she scheming on what to do next?

"My money's on a scheme," he said aloud. "My girl wouldn't give up that easily. No, she would not go so gently."

And he smiled. Because thinking of Lucky planning her next move excited him. He felt that excitement as a quickening in his step and the pitch of his whistle. He wanted her to make the next move. He wished for her to show up at Gerard's, to find him on the street, to jump from an alley and stamp her foot at him. In fact, it was all he wanted in the wide world right now, and Jay was not a man who abstained from want.

He doubled back, and when he got to the bush where he'd thrown the café cutlery, he leaned in and retrieved it. Then he carried it over his shoulder like a mustache-twirling thief, back down the fragrant streets and out onto St. Charles Avenue.

MEENA AND WENDY SAT CLOSE together so both of them could be on the screen while they FaceTimed with Lucky. Wendy said, "Find a shop that sells crystals. You need amethyst and tourmaline. Keep them in your pockets at all times. And make sure they're real, not the fabricated ones."

"And they do what?" Lucky was alone in the room. Stella had apparently gone out for lunch with her new best friend. But that was okay. She was still mad at her.

"They keep thieves away. He's stolen something now, something that you were destined to have, so he's a thief. The crystals will keep him away from you."

"But I don't want to keep him away. I want to know where he is. How else can I get the spoon back?"

"Lucky, Wendy and I don't think it's a good idea to seek him out. It's not safe."

"Safe? What about the spoon? The coven? We're just going to let him win?"

"We're trying to keep you alive."

"What's the point if I can't find the seventh?"

"Should I be worried?" Meena leaned in, as if she could touch Lucky through the phone.

"I just mean, what the hell do I have to live for if not this?" Lucky was almost in tears. "This *is* my life now, you guys, Salem, the spoons . . . magic. We're losing our apartment. I quit my job. Stella and I don't have any reason to go home except for a stupid cat."

"You can stay with us, both of you," Wendy interjected. "And the publishing house is expecting you next week. But right now, we have to keep you safe."

Meena nodded. "No one should face that man alone, and we can't get down there and do the work needed before the deadline passes. Plus, we don't know the location of the final witch. We don't even know if she's in New Orleans."

"I appreciate what you're saying. But I want to do this. Me. It's my decision, and I'm going on, with or without your help."

The Salem witches looked at each other. Then Meena said, "You're sure?"

"There is no way I am walking away. I'll search every street and every house in the city if I have to." She didn't even blink. She needed them to see how serious she was.

Meena sighed. "Okay, we'll call Claudia. See if she has any contacts who can help."

"Thank you." Lucky was relieved. They signed off, and she

tossed her phone onto the couch beside her. It was one o'clock. She wondered if it was too early to start drinking.

There was a knock at the door. "Coming." She hauled herself to her feet. She felt older, much older than she had this morning. Stella's key was on the coffee table. "You lock yourself out?"

She opened the door, but there was no one there. No one in the courtyard. No kids splashing in the pool or adults drinking cans of beer at the metal table set under the biggest palm. She looked down. There, on the welcome mat, was a muslin bag, the loops tied in a knot, with a paper tag hanging from a string. She checked left and right of the doorway before bending down to read the tag:

For Lucky, the unluckiest witch in Louisiana

Something about the words, about the precise and fanciful letters, made her feel like someone was laughing at her. She pulled at the closure and opened the top, the contents clattering as she did.

Inside was a pile of silver.

She carried it inside and dumped out the bag on the easy chair. Out poured mismatched forks, heavy butter knives, and different-sized spoons in a riotous jumble. This had to be the cutlery from Burial Grounds. She sifted through the pile with frantic hands, picking up each spoon and examining it, then tossing it onto the floor when it wasn't what she was looking for.

She knelt and checked them all again, then shoved her hands down the sides of the chair cushion in case one got stuck there.

"Fuck!" She kicked the empty bag. It fluttered for a moment and landed by the TV stand. "What is this? Some kind of game?"

She threw herself back onto the couch, her heart beating hard.

Wait—if the hunter was the one who dropped this on her doorstep, that meant he must still be close by! She sprang up, grabbed her phone, and took off.

On the street, she searched in both directions. She spotted a man a few blocks ahead on Toulouse: hard to miss, as he was twirling a walking stick and wearing a cream hat at a rather jaunty angle on his dark head. She ran without thinking, without a plan, and almost got run over by a bike courier on Bourbon.

"Watch it, lady," the cyclist cried out, swerving at the last second.

"Sorry," she shouted, slowing a little to look back at him. When she turned, the man in the hat was gone.

"Shit!" She stopped at Royal and looked up and down the street. There! Two blocks ahead of her. She took off, weaving through tourists window-shopping at antique stores and buskers hoping for spare dollars. She was just half a block away from him when a policeman on horseback cut in front of her and stopped. She tried to get around him, but the horse reared.

"Whoa, whoa there," the officer soothed, as his mount danced. "What's gotten into you?" Blocked by the big animal, Lucky had to cut behind him.

She was starting to realize that the bike, the horse: neither of them was an accident. When her way was clear again, she searched the crowd. Nothing. "Dammit!"

On Canal Street now, she caught sight of him far ahead. This street was wider and louder than in the Quarter. It almost could have been a main street in any city, except for the tall palm trees and the zydeco music blaring from open storefronts. How did he move so fast? He was crossing the street a few blocks up. She tried to cross over to be on the same side, but the traffic was heavy and erratic, so she kept to her side and ran. She muscled her way through walking groups and lost stragglers and made it to the lights. She was stuck waiting for them to turn green while keeping an eye on the cream hat, a foot above the other pedestrians.

Then the St. Charles streetcar showed up, and the hat climbed on board.

"No!" She broke into a full sprint. Just then, he paused on the stairs and, looking right at her, touched his brim in a salute.

"Motherfucker!"

The streetcar moved on, headed towards Midtown, the Garden District, Audubon Park . . . a thousand places out of her reach. She stopped, bent over, put her hands on her knees, and caught her breath. She'd lost him. She was sure it was him, and she had lost him. Her phone buzzed in her pocket, and she pulled it out.

The text was from Meena:

Plan's off. Rattler Ricky's body
was found on the side of the road
near where you met her. It's too
dangerous. Come home.

She stumbled back from the corner and leaned against the brick wall of a shoe store. It smelled like piss and beer. The news about Ricky, it felt familiar, as if she were remembering instead of reading it for the first time.

Ricky was really gone, cut down on the side of the road, nothing left but her strange hat. That was it . . . her dream. She closed her eyes and pictured it, the hat in the gravel, the snake curled up dead inside of it. The car lights coming straight for her.

She opened her eyes and breathed in the urine-soaked air. Things felt different now. She was calm inside this new anger. She stood straight, felt the concrete under her feet, and squared her shoulders. She knew what she had to do. She knew where she was going. But first, she sent a text back to Meena:

> Keep looking for the witch. I am
> going to get the spoon.

She opened her web browser and looked up the number for the Moon Over Marigny.

29

MAPPING OUT THE GAME

For the second time that day, Lucky stood in front of the Burial Grounds Café. She kept a low profile, observing from the opposite side of the street so that she wouldn't attract undue attention. Someone had spray-painted *Sorry, y'all. We reopen Friday!* on the sheet of plywood covering the window.

She pulled out her phone and switched it off; she didn't want to deal with Meena yelling at her to get back to Salem. Then she checked up and down the street—no one was coming—and crossed over. She went right up to the front door and pretended to study the menu posted there, as she checked to see if anyone was inside. The lights were off, and the room was empty. The tables and chairs had been pushed against the wall, and the floor was swept. She pulled a pair of newly purchased toenail clippers from her pocket and set to work prying slivers of wood from the doorframe. She gathered three long slivers and then quickly walked away. No use in getting caught further vandalizing the café. No doubt Slippers was now in full patrol mode.

Along the wall that separated the cemetery from the quiet street, she found a dark nook between two flowering trees that were throwing lacy shadows down the whitewashed concrete onto the cracked sidewalk.

"Okay, Ricky," she whispered, "remind me how to do this . . ."

She held the slivers in her right hand and breathed in deep, focusing so hard she could make out the texture and weight of the wood with her palm, until soon they became all she was aware of. And then she turned her mind to the spoon, sitting in a drawer with other cutlery—to its texture and weight. She thought about it as hers, because it was intended to be hers—it was intended to sit in her hand the way this wood was. It was hers, and it had been taken from her. Then she imagined the man in the cream hat slipping into the darkened café and sliding the drawer open, emptying its contents into the muslin bag he'd left on her doorstep. She pictured the thief's face, remembering the details of Morris, from the Yarb Witch's cabin, sleek and pale, with black eyebrows and an angular jaw, delicate and pronounced at the same time. The Benandanti.

She couldn't recall the exact prayer Ricky had said, so she used the one she knew from going to church with Stella as a child. "Our Father, who art in heaven, hallowed be thy name . . ."

Three times she whispered it, forgetting she was standing in the shadow of a cemetery, forgetting even that she was in New Orleans, just focusing on the wood in her palm and the spoon that should be in her pocket and the dangerous man who had stolen it away. And then the words came.

"O Sophia, Wisdom herself, come forth. O Sophia, Wisdom herself, come forth. O Sophia, Wisdom herself, come forth." She heard them in Ricky's voice but spoke them in her own. "Thief, allow us passage to gather the stolen goods. Thief. Thief. Thief. Guide us to the property taken against the commandments. Thou art not above consequences. This consequence is me."

She opened her eyes. The sun had waned, and the street looked softer, as if outlined in chalk, the air heavy with pollen and dusk. She opened her hand. The wood slivers were damp from her perspiration. She bent down and put one sliver under her right shoe, another in its laces, and the last in the top of her right sock.

"By the wood taken from the building you stole from, we shall find your path. We will come. We will recover. God the Father. God the Son. God the Spirit. Sophia and her daughters, all the gods of heaven will see. Lead us to the taken goods. Thief. Thief. Thief. Guide us to the goods."

Then she clapped her hands together. Ricky hadn't done that, but she needed some kind of ending to the opening ritual so she could get to the next part, the interior work of becoming the vehicle that would carry her where she needed to go.

MEENA TRIED LUCKY AGAIN.

Wendy was pacing in the dining room. "Maybe her phone is dead? Maybe she's already on the road home and can't answer?"

"Maybe she defied orders, went on the hunt, and is lying dead in a ditch somewhere just like Ricky." Meena was angry. Really, she was worried, but anger was easier for her.

She slammed the phone down on the table and sighed. "What are the others doing?"

"Still dreaming," Wendy said. "Should we tell them to stop? Or do you think there's still hope?"

"I have no idea anymore." She tapped her fingernails on the back of the chair she was leaning against. "In either case, I guess it's a good distraction. I'd love to be sleeping the day away too."

Lettie ran into the room, with Freya right on her heels. "Freya has something!" she shouted.

"Jesus, Lettie," Freya said. "It could be nothing." She examined the piece of paper in her hand. "I mean, it looks like nothing. Or a snake maybe? Or a river?"

Morticia came in holding Everett's hand and guided him to a chair, placing his colouring book in front of him. The rest of the witches gathered round as Freya smoothed out the sheet of paper on the table.

"I have no idea which way this goes, but this is how it looked in my head."

Meena squinted at the squiggly lines drawn in black ink. "Tell us a little more about the dream."

Freya looked up at the ceiling, trying to recall exactly. "I was walking, but I didn't know where. It was hot and there were . . . birds—no, bugs, loud bugs. And then I was looking for something, like checking bushes and peeking over fences."

"What kind of bushes?" Wendy asked. "Might give us a clue as to where you were."

"Ummmm, they were thick. Low, like residential. And they had flowers. Yeah, I could smell them. They were pink and some yellow, and more on the fences like vines."

"Somewhere lush. It could have been New Orleans," Meena said. "Go on."

"And then I looked up and there were wooden poles in the sky . . . no, crosses . . ."

"Churches?" Morticia suggested.

"Smaller. Graves maybe. Like headstones. And then all of a sudden I was moving fast, except I wasn't moving. Hard to explain. It was like being in a 3-D theatre when you're supposed to be moving through space real fast and the stars are whipping past you." She moved her hands past her face to demonstrate.

"And the whole time I was like, 'Keep track, Freya. You need to remember.' And then I woke up so fast I literally sat up straight in bed."

Lettie nodded. "It's true, she did. Scared the shit outta me."

"And then there was just like this pattern." Freya leaned forward and tapped the page. "This pattern was kind of burned into the backs of my eyes. When I closed them, I could see it, like I'd stared too long at a neon light. I drew it like that, with my eyes closed."

They all studied the page.

"Okay, so you had a starting point. It sounds like New Orleans. And since that's where Lucky and the spoon were—"

Lettie interrupted. "Were? Are they on the way back? Did she get it?"

"Just . . . We don't know. Let's not get distracted right now." Meena had to figure this out. "Since it's safe to assume you started off in New Orleans and moved here, let's see if this matches anything we know about the surrounding areas."

Wendy went to the sideboard and grabbed her laptop. She opened it and called up a map. "Okay, the café is in the Garden District, right near Lafayette Cemetery—that would explain the graves." She zoomed outward. "Here's the city, all the way to Metairie. Anything look familiar? Or similar?"

They all studied the drawing and the map.

Morticia leaned on her elbow, staring at the drawing. "It's not exactly a masterpiece, if you know what I mean."

"Hey now, at least I saw something," Freya returned.

"True."

Then Meena slapped her palms on the table, and they all jumped, including Everett, who was in the middle of a yawn. He'd missed his own nap, what with all the witches dreaming.

"Lettie, why don't you get this young man to bed? I'm gonna order in a few pizzas and open some wine so we can eat while we work. Wendy, start looking close to that cemetery, then go neighbourhood by neighbourhood. See if anything matches up." She pointed to a blob on Freya's drawing. "That could be a park or a forest or a pond."

"Let's go, little big man." Lettie picked up her son, who was now rubbing his eyes with fists still balled up around oversized crayons.

"G'night, Miss Ladies," he said with a tired sigh.

"Good night, Mr. Everett," they chimed in unison. He smiled, then dropped his head onto his mom's shoulder as she carried him out of the room.

Freya said, "This is a wild goose chase."

"And which part of this whole thing has not been a wild goose chase?" Meena said, and she headed to the wine cellar for some much-needed encouragement.

LUCKY WAS UNSURE OF TIME. Not of what hour of the day it was or how long she'd been standing by the cemetery wall. She just kept focusing, on the spoon, the wood, and the man. It took a lot to keep everything else out, but she did it.

The spoon: the spoon holds hot and cold and lets each warm or cool the metal along its stem by careful degrees. The embossing is unsubtle, holds tarnish in the crevices, throws small shadows into itself. It is small enough to fit between fingers, small enough to feel insignificant. On this spoon, there were seven witch pins, like spokes on a wheel, like a calcified dandelion fluff stuck in a silver field.

The man is tall, thin to lanky but squared off with solid shoulders. He has the kind of build that makes muscle into fingerholds.

He has blood and stories from other places, forests with different insect symphonies, mountains with different potential deaths, but the design of his final architecture is decidedly Western.

The wood was jagged to fray, moist in the centre, porous, and compact. It fit in the biggest line on her palm, end to end, from the meatier heel to the bottom of her pointer finger. Small flecks of white paint clung to the outer edges. It belonged to a door, a door to a place, a place where the spoon sat in a drawer for years.

The spoon: the spoon holds hot and cold and lets each warm or cool the metal along its stem by careful degrees. The embossing is unsubtle, holds tarnish in the crevices, throws small shadows . . .

Her lungs opened wide, wider than she ever imagined they could, and her mouth pushed out to the limits of a symmetrical O as she gasped. Oh god, everything on her body was open, everything was itself to its furthest ability to be. Suddenly, there were new colours in the universe, new smells in the air. And when her feet began to move, her mind was seconds behind them. Even then, she tried not to think about the movement, only the intent. She left the narrow alley-like street and was back out on Prytania.

IN GERARD'S MASTER BEDROOM, JAY Christos sat in a French chair under a Spanish painting by the balcony door. He watched the street, the way the gas streetlamp pushed back the dark with imprecise effort. He was in the shadows. He preferred the shadows. He was the kind of beautiful that demanded light and adoration, but at his core, he was the kind of beautiful that could be truly appreciated only in shadow. From downstairs, the sound of the old man's medical equipment hummed and cycled. He'd made his promised visit earlier in the evening, after dismissing the nurse for the night. He had laid his weight beside Gerard and passed a hand up and down his chest, so that the old man wept from the contact. Then he'd pressed down hard enough for the fragile ribs to bend but not break, hard enough that breathing became impossible. Shushing him in the French they once used to speak to each other, back before age was an impediment, Jay crushed the life from him.

"Au revoir, mon cher," he whispered, marveling once more at how the light in a person's eyes was really only noticeable when it was spiralling over itself and pulling backward. He really should go down and turn off the equipment.

From up the street, a child practiced the piano with tired fingers and wandering thoughts. Jay wondered if Lucky would take up his challenge. He wondered if there would be a next move. He prayed the game wasn't done, because he was bored. Profoundly bored. In hundreds of years, nothing had moved him more than the night Prudence had stabbed him in the chest, missing his betrayed heart by not even an inch. Everything since had been shades of boredom and want.

And then all of his muscles seized. He managed to uncross his legs with a jerk, grasping the arms of the chair so hard the wood creaked. He gasped. He wanted to move, but he couldn't. Wanted to stand, but remained seated. He was stuck near an open balcony door under a hideous painting of a god eating his own children, a painting he had fallen in love with in Spain and that Gerard had purchased for their bedroom, back when it was still *their* bedroom. And then he understood. She was coming. And all he could do was smile, small and brimming with anticipation. Finally, a witch worthy of all his skills.

LUCKY BARELY SAW THE HOUSES she walked by, getting grander now as she went farther into the Garden District. She was a passenger on this walk, her mind looking ahead to the destination. She tried to remember to breathe, but there were stronger urges ruling her body and they came first, so much so that she could barely spare a thought for her lungs, grabbing just enough breath so she didn't fall dead in the street.

Statues watched her pass from behind cast-iron gates. An old woman in a wheelchair by a window waved, but Lucky didn't notice. The woman, witchy enough she could sense the potential of a new coven surfacing, chuckled and muttered, "The game is on . . ." And her old heart swelled with gratitude that she might just live to see them rise.

A flock of small birds, all shades of yellow and green, swooped across the sky, then curved up into a crescent formation that flew past Lucky's head. She felt the beat of their wings as goose bumps up the back of her neck.

She cut through a parkette where a man in a straw fedora waited while his dachshund sniffed the grass. He lifted his hat to her and wished her a good evening. She couldn't respond, so many new truths were running across her brain like ticker tape.

The man with the dog—his name is Marvin. He comes from money but wishes he could work at the market stacking melons and apples. He pays a man to strike the backs of his thighs once a month. His dog's name is Faulkner, but sometimes he calls him Fucker and pretends he hasn't.

She didn't know how she knew, but there it was—knowledge, uninvited and insignificant. Was this what it meant to be connected to whatever reservoir lay under the ground of a place? The more she thought about it, the slower she walked. She had a mission, she had to put everything she had there, so she blocked out Marvin and the fact that she very suddenly understood that the woman who lived in the pink house on the corner had murdered her uncle. Shutting it all out but the spoon, her pace quickened and she continued on.

She turned onto a wide street, bordered by wide sidewalks over-hung with trees. Beside a well-lit colonial with manicured gardens sat a grey mansion with white columns and climbing pink roses, sedate and still. The porch light's gas flame jumped and gestured like a candle on a wooden birthday cake. At the front gate she stopped and turned towards it. The tension let go of her spine so fast, she almost fell.

"The spoon is here," she whispered, scanning the lush gardens, the wide porch, and then the tall windows. "And so is he."

She felt a bit nauseous. It was nerves and fear but also excitement. She had found him.

AFTER HEARING ABOUT RICKY, LUCKY had called Claudia from the air-conditioned aisles of a Walgreens.

The Booker picked up with her same happy energy. "Well, good afternoon! You got Claudia over at the Moon. How can I help you today?"

"Hi, Claudia. It's Lucky. I'm the—"

"Lucky, I know who you are. Did you get to the gator? Get your spoon?"

"Someone got there before me, and the spoon is gone."

"What can I do to help?"

She'd explained about Rattler Ricky's recovery spell. "I'm headed for the café to collect the wood I need. But do you think I can pull it off by myself?"

"Hells yeah, you can!" Claudia was actually excited for her. "But whatcha gonna do with the bugger that stole it?"

This was the problem. "I'm not sure yet. You mentioned how the magic is in the land, not the person," she began.

"Well now, that was a bit simple on my part. It's both. See, belief is something that makes change. It's why prayer benefits people, as long as the people doing all that praying believe. It's why people who get placebos can still get better, because they believe in the medicine they *thought* they got. And when something is constant on the land, like rain or song or even footsteps, the land soaks that in and changes. So there's that. That's true enough. But then you need the people who understand the ways to pull that soak right back up out of the land. That's where study comes in, where the witchiness needs to be. And not all people can get to some kinds of magic. Around here the magic is Vodou Louisian, and it belongs to a very specific people. I'm not sure a lil Métis from all the way up in Canada could tap it, no offence." Claudia chuckled to soften the blow.

"So, then, what do I tap?" Lucky was now in line at the self-checkout, having found nail clippers.

"Well now, this is where you need to be a witch of a certain power. You need to bring your own stuff."

"I don't have my own stuff. I've been a"—she looked around to see if anyone was eavesdropping, but no one was—"been . . . what I am for, like, twenty minutes, with a ten-minute recess."

Claudia gave a big laugh. "If Meena sent your ass down here, twenty minutes is all you need, baby. You just finished telling me you're about to try doing a powwow man's work. You gotta believe you can. Now think about what else you might have picked up along the way, maybe from the land and maybe from other powerful women."

Lucky was silent.

"You there?"

"I'm here," Lucky finally answered. "Can you do me a favour?"

"That's what I'm here for, darlin'!"

"I need to know everything you know about the Benandanti."

Lucky ducked out of the line, stuck her earbuds in so she could listen to the Booker, and headed back down the aisles. She needed Claudia's knowledge, but if anyone had known how to deal with bad men it had been her mother. So she set out to collect the items Arnya had told her were "absolute fucking necessities."

"Man is the most dangerous thing in the world," Arnya had explained while packing her purse for a night out—matches, a pocket-knife, and pepper spray. "Even if you think you know the fucker, hell, even if he's smaller than you, you gotta be ready. No one is going to take care of you the way *you* would take care of you." Arnya had showed her how to put a set of house keys between her fingers to make a punch more dangerous and the right way to deal with an unwanted penis showing up. "The trick is to get the balls—that's the literal soft spot." Most of Arnya's techniques were more street fight than anything, but one night, she'd popped an unlit cigarette between her frosty pink lips and led Lucky out the door. "C'mon. I'll show you one more deterrent, but we got to go to the park to do it. This one was handed down to me from my ma. It's real old, so you know it's a good one."

"I BELONG TO ARNYA AND to myself. No one else," she whispered at the gate, reminding herself of the childhood mantra.

Movement behind a set of French doors on the second floor caught her eye. A man came out onto the narrow balcony. This time he was dressed in grey dress pants and a vest, the top buttons of his shirt undone and his long black hair down. But it was still the man who'd pretended to be Morris, the man who'd stolen the spoon. He leaned on the railing and smiled down at her.

"You did it," he called. His tone was casual enough, but there was a hint of caution in it. "You made it this far, might as well come in for a drink. Door's open."

With his eyes on her, it took her a moment to get her feet to move and another minute to get her shit together enough to push open the front gate. As she started up the walk, he turned and went back inside.

Lucky was expecting a pull or a push back, some kind of change in the atmosphere inside the gate, but by all accounts, this was just a regular house, a regular old generationally-wealthy-for-the-wrong-reasons rich person's house. On either side of the cobblestone path to the porch were small ponds with white marble statues of robe-draped women pouring water from slim vessels. And on each statue's right shoulder sat a small yellow bird, watching her pass.

She nodded to them, then stopped to introduce herself. "I am the daughter of Arnya St. James, defender of women, drinker of gin, fighter of assholes, a fierce half-breed from a long line of fierce half-breeds who took no shit and gave no fucks. I am a witch and I am here." She supposed this was her version of making the sign of the cross before going into battle—reminding herself what she believed in.

She climbed the front steps and crossed the porch. Grabbing the handle, she took a deep breath and pushed the door open, entering the house as if she were going underwater.

THE MOTHER BROKE THE CIRCLE when she abruptly stood up and walked away from the table. Her breathing was irregular, and she pulled at her blouse, pacing in front of the covered windows.

"Come on, we've got to push through." The Maiden was tired but needed to see this to the end. They'd been in this room for days now, as evidenced by the takeout containers and empty bottles. They spent most of the time sitting, heads bowed, hands joined, focusing with everything they had. They were drained and frustrated. The Maiden had even snapped at her favourite receptionist when she had popped in to see if they wanted coffee. The witches were spending long hours searching their dreams for any sign of the seventh witch. It was the Oracle's job to help the dreamers move in the right direction while asleep.

But now the Mother was wigging out.

"I can't breathe," she gasped. "My heart . . . my heart is too loud."

"Now, now, chère." The Crone went to her, rubbing her back in slow circles. "You can breathe just fine. And your heart? She is good. Strong. You are just exhausted. We are all just exhausted."

"No, this is different." The Mother sat on the narrow window ledge. "It's Lucky."

"What about her?" The Maiden was holding her head in her hands, elbows on the table. "Is she dreaming? Did you see her?"

"No." The Mother opened the top button of her blouse and pulled the fabric out to get some air on her skin. "I . . . I think I felt her?"

"We don't usually feel others. Not like that." The Crone spoke softly, trying to calm her colleague down so they could get back to work. "Perhaps intuition?"

"Maybe." The Mother was breathing more regularly now, trying to focus in on the specifics of her anxiety. "It feels like she's falling. Like she's falling and I can't grab her." She put her hands out, fingers splayed as if trying to catch something fragile. "Oh, I don't know. It feels fucking terrible, that's all."

"I can make you a drink?" A Tender at heart, the Maiden prescribed cocktails for many ailments. "Something to help you forget? Or maybe to see the path to get to her?"

"Maybe later." The Mother rubbed her hands up and down her thighs, focusing on her breath—in through the nose, out through the mouth. Her dog came over and licked her right hand every time it reached her knee. "Just give me a minute, then let's form the circle again."

The Crone had never seen the Mother this upset. "It seems you have a special connection to this girl."

"No, I've never met her."

"You don't always have to meet someone to have a connection. Sometimes it's deeper than that."

The Mother knew that was true. She did have a special connection with someone she had never met, but it wasn't Lucky. It was the man Lucky was after, and she also knew that the girl, with every minute that passed, was getting closer.

30

IT WAS ALL A DREAM

The entry hall was ornate—framed tapestries, baroque console tables, veined marble floor tiles. The only spot of chaos was on the round table in the centre, where a vase of rotting flowers littered the teak surface with castaway petals. At the back was a grand staircase that split on either side into long hallways going deeper into the second floor of the house.

Lucky heard noise coming from the first room on the left, so that was where she went, slowly pushing aside the pocket door. The room, once a parlor, was dimly lit by two small Tiffany table lamps in opposite corners. It smelled of dust and uncirculated air . . . and something else, something organic and hollow, like an empty beehive or burnt timber.

In the centre of the room was a hospital bed covered by a mound of white bed linens. The sounds were coming from a collection of machines, beeping and whooshing, lights blinking, one a constant red that seemed to blare in silent alarm.

"Hello?" she whispered, creeping quietly to the side of the bed. Was someone there? Remembering her mother's hospital room, her mother's body, she reached out and touched the shape on the bed, then pulled her hand back. It was definitely a person, and they were definitely not breathing. She backed away, then turned and fled to the foyer.

"Gerard has gone to meet his maker, I'm afraid."

Lucky jumped at the voice. The Benandanti was standing at the bottom of the stairs, hands in his pockets, head tipped to the side.

Lucky jumped. "Oh, fuck . . ." She caught her breath. "Why are you keeping a dead man in the parlor?"

"Why not?" He shrugged.

She tried to compose herself. She needed to be composed. No thread could be dropped now, no boundary unguarded. Not even for a corpse.

"So what is your name, then? It sure as hell isn't Morris Montgomery from Missouri."

He chuckled. "No, it sure as hell isn't. I am Jay Christos."

She put her hands on her hips, attempting to project nothing but strength, even if her bladder felt suddenly very full. "And you are Benandanti."

"Yes, very good. It's an old name, but I find it still fits."

"Everything about you is old, I think."

He walked towards her, nodding. "Ancient, in fact. All the very best things are. Only the strongest things can stand in the midst of all this time swirling about."

She paced slowly in the opposite direction, so that they circled each other around the centre table. She smiled, mocking him. "Strongest? Is that why you ran from a little old Yarb witch?"

Some colour rose in his cheeks. "Strength is measured in intelligence, too, and I am no fool. I was out of my element. She belongs to that place, and I don't, clearly, since I have all my teeth."

He stopped, bending slightly at the waist, a hand in front of him, like a small bow. "Shall we go and get ourselves that drink now?"

His hand was large but shapely, his fingers slender but strong. And his wrist—she had never taken note of a man's wrist before, but his seemed a model for the *David*.

What the fuck? she thought. *The* David, *Lucky? Really?*

He was distracting at an almost elemental level, and something about his invitation was appealing. Still, no way she was taking the chance. "If you need a drink, I'll keep you company, but I'm good."

"Very well," he said, and started back up the stairs.

"Whoa. Why upstairs?"

"That's where I keep the good stuff," he called over his shoulder. "And considering the nature of this visit, I thought only the good stuff would do. Unless you'd rather stay down here with Gerard?"

She sighed. Keeping a safe distance, she followed him up one flight, and then a second, where they turned into a broad hall. She watched him carefully as they made their way past several closed doors. His movements were so smooth, he almost glided, except that there was also something muscular about the motion.

The room he led her to was huge, running the whole length of the house, from the back to the front, where French doors opened onto an iron balcony overlooking the street. Two chandeliers, dark metal arms dripping in crystals, hung low above mirrored side tables, with a larger, older model swagged above a massive bed. Lit pillar candles of different heights flickered from narrow tables in between the windows and along the fireplace mantel. She didn't like the way the room was putting her at ease. "Can we turn on a light in here?"

"This is fine," he answered, and he sounded so certain she couldn't help but agree that it *was* fine.

What the hell, Lucky?

She felt as if her mind and her body were somehow sliding apart. So while her mind was growing complacent, her body was growing more responsive, and to Jay Christos of all things. She closed her eyes for a moment, forcing herself back together.

"Strange," she heard him say from very close. "I can't seem to touch you."

When she opened her eyes, he was right in front of her. Close enough that she could see that his eyes were so dark he didn't appear to have irises, that his skin was unblemished, that he was, in fact, perfect. He walked around her, trying to lay his hands on her, even just to run a finger along her jawline or touch her hair where it curled on her neck. "I can't reach you."

She felt his confusion as her triumph. It worked! She had even picked the cedar from a park, the way she did with Arnya all those years ago as part of her "defence training." *Cedar in your shoes keeps you walking right*, Arnya'd explained to her. *And it's free.*

She raised one foot. "Cedar in the shoes, Christos. Something passed down to my mom from her mother."

"They were witches?"

"Better, they were Indigenous women."

"I am unfamiliar with those practices."

"Maybe you shouldn't be so Western in your education. That's a weakness."

He raised an eyebrow. That hurt him, she could see it. "My, you really are a fascinating quilt of methods and belief. But, you know, even the most beautiful quilt is crafted out of rags after all."

She took that on the chin. "The good thing about rags is, they never stop being useful. They might change along the way—clothes to fabric, fabric to scraps—but they keep on going. They're never trash."

"One could argue that they started off as trash." He threw it out there without much force. Petty insults were beneath him.

"Fuck you," she retorted, and he laughed.

"Trash indeed." He poured a glass of red wine from an open bottle on the fireplace mantel and sipped. "At any rate, how are you going to do this?" He seemed genuinely curious but also smug. She hated smug assholes.

She walked around the room, pretending to examine the paintings, running her fingers along the furniture, all the while watching him out of the corner of her eye. "How am I going to do what?" When she reached the bed, she threw herself on it, shoes and all. Laying on her stomach, legs bent and ankles crossed, she hoped she seemed relaxed, casual. She also hoped he didn't notice her slip the small blade out of her pocket and under a pillow.

"Get your spoon, of course. You know it's here. Otherwise you wouldn't be. And I know you need it. Meena needs it."

Lucky said, "Oh, you're just going to give it to me." She tried to sound confident. The fact that he couldn't touch her had emboldened her.

He studied her face, then feigned shock, placing a hand on his chest. "You're serious?" He threw his head back and laughed. She watched the veins under the skin of his long throat move like small snakes. She suddenly wondered what it would be like to put her mouth on them, to feel the heat and flow of him.

She looked away. She couldn't let him fascinate her this much. "So how does it feel to be nothing more than a cop?"

He stopped laughing. "A cop?"

"Yeah, I mean, isn't the Benandanti thing just being a foot soldier for the dudes pulling your strings?" She moved her hands as if she were making a marionette dance off the side of the bed.

"I answer to no one." His voice was low, almost a growl. "I am in and of myself."

She needed him angry, so she pushed some more.

"It's weird that you all built a whole system to keep women disempowered. That's a lot of work to waste on the 'weaker sex,' don't you think?"

"We didn't create the system. You did." He pointed at her with his glass before drinking deeply. Then he poured himself more wine from the bottle.

"Women created the patriarchy? That's your argument?" It was her turn to laugh.

He glared at her, then switched gears, leaning in. "Lucky, it's too hot in here," he said. "We need to take some clothes off."

Eyes locked on hers, he unbuttoned and pulled off his vest. Without another thought, Lucky slipped off the bed and yanked her black T-shirt over her head. She had heard his words as her own thoughts—that *of course* she had to take her clothes off.

He was undoing his shirt, keeping up a melodious flow of words. "The very earliest witches were the ones who organized a group of men to go forth and do their work, as they sat back and plotted and commanded and spoke with the gods. Pretending they were too precious to get their hands dirty, to be in harm's way. Like we were the disposable ones. And we were just supposed to do it, mindlessly." He yanked his shirttails free.

She sat down to unlace her boots, and her eyes caught on the revelation of his skin, the front of his shirt falling wide open as he undid his cufflinks. Holy fuck, he was smooth. "But you liked it too much, right? Liked playing Big Man too much to just be mindless helpers, right?"

"Why go back?" He shrugged, then pulled his arms out of his sleeves. "If we're pretending to be leaders, why not just lead?"

When her first boot dropped to the floor, he noticed but kept talking. Prudence had taught him the art of commanding without force but with influence. Lucky was under his influence. "Then it was just a matter of making sure the women couldn't snatch it back. A carefully executed plan of bad PR and serious consequences did the trick. The witches were outnumbered, hidden, small . . . disposable."

Lucky's second boot hit the floor, and he pounced.

But still he couldn't touch her, remaining suspended, inches from her face, both of them breathing hard. "I . . . I don't understand . . ."

"The cedar is in my socks." She wanted to sound more sure of herself, but she was panting. When he broke eye contact, she was shocked to find herself sitting there in her bra and jeans.

He scanned her body so slowly she had time to wonder what she would do if he did break through her protection. Would she stop him? Could she at this point? He knelt in front of her, bent so that she saw the curve of his spine, the flex and pull of muscle along his back. He examined her black ankle socks. She wiggled her toes, releasing the scent of cedar.

He looked up at her through dark lashes. "We need to finish getting comfortable."

This time she moved of her own volition. Standing up in the small space between him and the bed, she undid her zipper and pushed her tight jeans down over the curve of her ass and hips. She stepped out of them, kicking them away.

Standing in front of him in her bra, panties, and socks, she whispered, "Now you." She fought to keep her arms at her sides. She wanted to cover herself and she wanted to touch him, and both urges gave her a deep shame that was thrilling.

She watched his Adam's apple move as he swallowed hard. He unbuckled his belt, the clang of the metal clasp loud. He stepped out of his pants and removed his socks, looking at her body the entire time. Then he stood. Jesus, he was beautiful in his tight boxer briefs, made tighter in his excitement.

He was a foot taller than her, and Lucky had to tip her head way back to smile at him. She nodded, then poured all her shame and anticipation into her voice so that each vowel was filled like a teacup. "Good boy."

His black eyes flickered and narrowed with sudden realization. *She* had commanded *him* and he had listened.

She sat down on the edge of the bed. "Now, let's talk terms, shall we?"

He turned away from her and stared out the window, biting his lip. When he looked back, his face was closed. "You think you know what you're doing. But I've been playing this game for a lot longer than you have."

"I don't disagree. And I think we should honor that. Let's do this old-school."

"Old-school?"

She shimmied back on the bed and lay her head on the pillow. "Weren't you guys called Good Walkers because you used to leave your bodies at night? Isn't that how you supposedly found the witches who were out wandering around without their skins?"

"Yes," he said, looking for the trick in her words.

"So let's meet there, in that place—the original place."

"You understand that you're not walking around without your

body exactly? It's more like we would be dreaming the same dream." He wondered if she really thought she could take him on in a dream. Her little sock charm wouldn't work without her physical body. He didn't think she'd thought that far ahead. She was young, impulsive, so new to this she was telling him her secrets without his even having to ask. He would allow her to think she was, once again, leading him in her direction. He paced a small circle, frowning in fake concentration. "How can either of us be sure the other won't just wake up and kill us while we sleep?"

Here she paused. She was a bit embarrassed by this part, but it was key, and she had to pull it off. "Because we're going to be tied up."

She had managed to surprise him yet again. He surveyed her sleek body laid out on the bed. "Well now," he said. "This is getting more and more interesting."

Gerard's bedroom closet was home to all sorts of bondage gear, and his bed was fitted with a restraint system. They lay side by side and got strapped in. They tested their ropes by struggling against them, then adjusted the zip knots and tension until each was satisfied the other was truly secured.

"Wait." The anxiety in Lucky's voice wasn't faked. "How do we untie ourselves after?"

Smiling at her across the foot of space in between their nearly naked bodies, Jay said, "We'll cross that bridge when we're at the water's edge." There were teeth in that smile. Of course, he knew how to get out of these particular restraints, and, of course, he was not going to tell her that.

"So now we just wait to fall asleep?" She was wide-awake. Adrenaline was not a relaxing chemical, and she had it in abundance.

"Yes," he said, and caught her eyes.

Lucky knew that if, at that moment, he had suggested she somehow slip out of her knots and take off the last bits of lace she wore, she would have done it. She watched his lips as he spoke.

"Lucky St. James . . . now we go to sleep."

And then, together and apart, they did just that.

SHE WAS WEARING A VOLUMINOUS dress, all tulle and ruffles in ox-blood red. The collar was high and sheer, and so were the sleeves, ballooning out and caught at the wrist by tiny fabric buttons. Her hair was pulled up into a braid and tied off with a thin blue ribbon that fell to her waist. She was in a forest, but not the one she knew, the one she went to in her own dreams. No, she was somewhere else completely. This forest smelled like rot and wet and was full of low and twisty trees hung with heavy vines. Fear settled in her stomach.

She lifted the hem of her gown and walked across a carpet of neon moss, so soft that her bare feet sank with each step. Wait—bare feet. Her cedar was gone.

"Lady Luck, to what do I owe this pleasure?" a familiar voice called from behind. She spun around, all her skirts twirling out in the movement.

There he was, in a short-sleeve shirt and low-hanging jeans, his exposed skin covered in colourful designs and pictures.

"Malcolm?" She could barely breathe. "What are you doing here?"

"Just thought I'd stop by. I missed you." He smiled, that sweet smile that let you know the kind of boy he had been when he was young, all mischief and the right amount of charm to get out of it.

"Oh my god. How did you get here? Wait, are you really here, or am I imagining you here?" She stopped moving towards him.

"Does it matter?" He laughed. "I don't even know. But who cares?"

She had something she was supposed to be doing, but god, Malcolm. She hadn't thought she missed him this much, that she could even think about anything from her old life, but seeing him made her feel safe and untethered at the same time. And he was right, who cared how he had gotten there?

He held out his arms, and she lifted her skirts and began to run towards him. He was normal, he was away from . . . Where was she now . . . ? Well, he was home, was what he was. She threw herself against him, and he squeezed her, lifting her off the ground.

"Oh god, it's so good to see you. You wouldn't believe . . ." She tried to speak her relief into his chest.

"I know, I know. And look, I'm sorry for being an ass. I just—I just don't want to lose you. And look what happened anyway? I lost you." He sighed and held her tighter.

"I'm not lost. I just had to . . ." She tried to remember. She fought the fog and tried to find the memory of now. "I had to go get something. I'm looking for something . . ."

"You don't need to keep looking. I'm right here." He pulled her back just enough to kiss her. She was shocked by it. They had made out before when they were drunk enough and single enough, but this was not that. This was different.

She pulled away. "Oh! I'm in New Orleans!"

"Shhhh, you're with me now." He moved his hand to the back of her head and brought her face back to his, opening her lips with his.

A small voice inside the fog—*Remember the spoon, Lucky. And the wood.*

She broke the kiss again. "I am looking for a spoon. And I need to . . ."

But he had pulled her back again. This time the kiss was more insistent. And his hands were reaching down, were just under her ass, moving up the backs of her thighs, pulling the soft layers of her dress with them.

This is important! Get the spoon. Remember the wood. She recognized the small voice now—it was her's.

"Malcolm, I need to go. I have to find the spoon." But he dropped to his knees in front of her.

"Just stay, just for a little bit." He had lifted her hem so that her legs were bare. He kissed each thigh, grazing his face along her skin so that she felt a rush of blood to those exact spots. "Just a little while longer."

He lifted the fabric to her waist. She wasn't wearing underwear and his breath from each word fell directly on her skin. Her eyes rolled back. Oh god. Her toes clenched the thick ground.

He leaned in closer; now his mouth was almost on her, so close even his breath felt like a touch. "Just . . . one . . . more . . . minute."

It's not Malcolm!

"Wait!" she called out suddenly, and he looked up. His eyes, they were the right shape, but the colour—so dark he didn't seem to have irises. She jumped back, and her skirts tumbled down to her feet. She took a step away.

"You."

"What's wrong, Miss St. James?" It was still Malcolm's voice, but his words, the way he enunciated them was . . . off. "I was led to believe this was what you wanted. This boy. This body." He stood up, unfolding to Malcolm's full height. "Is this not your preferred lover?"

"I don't want a fucking boy. I want more, and I'm almost there." She was angry. She felt violated. She turned on the slippery ground and ran.

"Where are you going?" he called after her.

She put distance between them while she collected her thoughts.

She was in New Orleans. She was after the spoon. Somewhere in the Garden District, she was tied to a bed beside the Benandanti, and this was their final battle.

Remember the wood.

"I will," she answered, and she ran into the gnarled trees. She just needed to find a spot, somewhere to stop, and then she would get ready. She needed to cross out of his landscape and back into her own, even if he followed—especially if he followed.

IT WAS NEARLY FOUR IN the morning, which meant it was three A.M. in New Orleans. Meena was struggling to stay awake at the table. Wendy was making a new pot of coffee, and Lettie was passed out on the floor pillows they kept stacked by the back window. Morticia and Freya were still at it, comparing Freya's dream scribbles to the online map. They had eliminated every neighbourhood in the city of New Orleans and had moved outward to the surrounding parishes.

Meena sighed. Was she being a fool? It felt like mapping was the way to go, and what else could the image be? She picked up the piece of paper for the hundredth time and examined it, though she could have drawn it from memory at that point.

"Christ." She slapped it facedown on the table. She didn't want to look at it anymore. "What if we're wrong?"

Freya and Morticia stared at her without a word, like children up past their bedtime. They weren't used to hearing her vent.

"And why isn't Lucky answering her phone?" She checked her phone, also for the hundredth time. Nothing. No missed calls, no texts, not a peep. She slammed it down on top of the page. And then something caught her eye.

"Freya, what's this?"

Freya stood and walked over to Meena's end of the table. "What's what?"

Meena pointed to a small scribble on the back of the page.

"That's something I started to draw, but then I lost it."

"What do you mean, you lost it?"

"After I drew the map, I remembered this other image, so I flipped the page and started to draw, but it faded on me before I was done." She leaned in to look at the curved lines. "I think it's just bullshit."

"Okay," Meena said, her hand on Freya's back. "That's okay."

Freya went back to the laptop to work, and Meena picked up the page and carried it into the kitchen. Wendy was pouring strong coffee from their French press into four mismatched teacups lined up on the counter. She looked up and frowned when she saw Meena's face.

"What's wrong?"

"We're properly fucked."

"Why? Did you hear from Lucky?"

"No. It's this." She slid the page across the counter. "Does it look familiar to you at all?"

Meena waited while Wendy put her reading glasses on.

"Think back. Think about how we ended up at Buzzards Bay," Meena coached, as Wendy studied the lines under the bright stove light.

"I can't . . . Oh, wait, I see it! It's the brooch."

Meena went over to her and used a finger to trace a distinct line. "The brooch that led us to the Tender, the one that belonged to Lucky's dead mother."

Wendy wrapped an arm around Meena's waist. "Oh, baby, we've been over this. How could her mother be the final witch?"

"But we asked the women to dream about the location of the final witch and this is what we get—Arnya St. James's brooch. If it's her, we can't complete the coven."

"But the brooch belongs to Lucky now. What if Lucky is the final witch?"

Meena leaned against the counter, gathering the will to even continue to have this conversation, it was so bleak. "Lucky is already one of us. She can't take up two spots."

"Why not?"

"Because that's not how it works."

"Says who?"

They heard a shout; then Freya rushed into the kitchen. "You'd better get in here. We found something!"

Wendy and Meena looked at each other for a long few seconds, then followed Freya as she ran back out.

They found her pacing behind her chair. Morticia held out her hand. "Can we get that paper back quickly?" she said.

They handed it over and joined them at the laptop.

Morticia held the paper up beside the screen, comparing the lines and landmarks. "Yes, this is it!"

Meena leaned in to read the name of the town that sat on top of the *X* on Freya's dream image. "Okay. We have a place."

"And that means we have the witch!" Freya grabbed up Morticia from her seat and danced her around the dining room, spinning her wildly.

THE TREES CHANGED FROM TWISTY to tall, and the air became a cool inhale instead of a damp exhale. There was the familiar scent of mushrooms and bark replacing the insistent, slow rot. She'd made it home—this was her own landscape. She turned a quick circle, smiling through exhaustion. This was now *her* dream.

She closed her eyes. First things first—she needed to protect herself the way Arnya had taught her.

Make it impossible for the monsters to move. Just like real life, you can't get caught if the fuckers can't catch up.

She pushed her feet into the ground, and purple violets began to erupt through the soil, unfurling like fragrant land mines all around her. Everything in place, she turned to Ricky's spell.

She held her right hand in front of her chest, palm up and fingers curled so she could visualize every detail of the fragment of wood she'd cut from the Burial Grounds Café, details she'd memorized for this exact purpose, so that she could recall them with her eyes closed, even outside of her body.

The wood was jagged to fray, moist in the centre, porous, and compact. It fit in the biggest line on her palm, end to end, from the meatier heel to the bottom of her pointer finger. Small flecks of white paint clung to the outer edges. It belonged to a door, a door to a place, a place where the spoon sat in a drawer for years.

"Lucky . . ." The voice was somewhere between Malcolm's and Jay Christos's and full of condescension. "Lady Luuuuck. Where are you?"

The wood was jagged to fray, moist in the centre, porous . . .

"See, this is why you need to hold your cards close, my dear. Once you told me the repelling charm was a physical talisman, all I had to do was remove you from the physical world. You offered me the solution yourself." He laughed, and it echoed through the forest until the leaves rattled on their branches, falling around her like sudden rain.

"Foolish girl. So many foolish girls."

Small flecks of white paint clung to the outer edges . . .

"I love a good game of hide-and-seek." His voice was all Christos's now. "Boo!"

He yelled it from somewhere close, making her jump.

Ow! A sharp pain in her hand.

She opened her palm and saw the slivers of wood. One of them had pierced her palm, drawing blood. She'd done it—she had brought Ricky's spell into the dream. Now all she had to do was let it pull her to the spoon, the same way it had pulled her through the Garden District to this house. She bent down, slid one piece under her bare foot, another in between her toes, and placed the third on the top of her foot. Then she closed her eyes and waited.

"I can smell you now. All that good wet. All that want. Come out now so I can touch you again."

A branch snapped close by. She opened her eyes, and there he was, even more beautiful in the murky light, black hair against pale skin, a red tunic and pants, bare feet and a big smile.

"Mmmm," he said, sniffing her deeply. "I am going to devour you." He moved towards her, but it was as if he were walking underwater. The effort caused his veins to stand out in his temple, in his throat, at his wrists. She closed her eyes and focused.

The spoon holds hot and cold and lets each warm or cool the metal along its stem by careful degrees. The embossing is unsubtle, holds tarnish in the crevices, throws small shadows.

"No!"

She opened her eyes. He was so close she could bridge the distance between them by extending one finger. He was perfectly still, a statue—a *David* even, except for the eyes. His eyes were anxious.

She took a step back from him and then walked around him slowly.

"Foolish boy," she cooed, leaning close to his ear. "All I had to do was let you think you were smarter, and you would follow my *misguided suggestion*." She grabbed a handful of his hair and pulled until his head was bent back. His eyes darted frantically, seeking hers. "See, in my dreams, time is slow. It's almost impossible for anyone to move if I don't want them to. My mother taught me that when I used to have nightmares."

He hissed, "You don't know nightmares, Lucky St. James. Not yet."

"And this is why we are taking it back, the magic, the control, all of it. Because you were never capable of handling it in the first place." She slid her other hand around his waist, down his stomach, over his cock.

"Too vain, too self-important. Even trying to mansplain the apocalypse." She planted a soft, wet kiss on the side of his neck and then released him, backing away into the trees. "Maybe the end your kind has brought is not the end of the whole world. Maybe it's just the end of *your* world."

"I'll bring you nightmares, little witch!" He was spitting now, his face flushed and his hands balled up into shaking fists. "Nightmares you can't begin to imagine."

She willed time to move for her alone, the spoon imprinted on her thoughts. She closed her eyes—she no longer needed them. Her body was being pulled, and she trusted the spell to take her where she needed to go. The forest grew quieter, the chirping and peeps fading to silence. When she opened her eyes again, she was walking up the front steps of the mansion where her body lay sleeping beside the most dangerous creature on earth.

In the foyer, she was pulled into the parlor, where the medical machines still blinked and hummed, and to the hospital bed and the body under its white sheet. And then she was released.

She steadied herself, no longer puppeted by the spell, then reached out and pulled back the sheet. An old man, a smile on his thin lips, most definitely dead, cold when she touched his cheek. And there, in the top pocket of his paisley pyjamas, was the seventh spoon.

She'd found it. Her heart raced: as soon as she woke herself up, Jay Christos would be released from her protective paralysis. He would be pissed, and he would be looking for her. She wouldn't have much time.

"Okay, here we go. Time to wake the fuck up." She took a deep breath and dialed up all her courage. She ran into the foyer and up the stairs to the second floor, dashing into the first room she found unlocked. Picking up speed, she threw herself against the tall front window as hard as she could, and then she was falling . . .

She jolted awake in the bed. The sensation of falling always woke her up right away. She went to wipe away phantom glass shards from her face, but her hands were stuck. She was tied up. And beside her, so was the Benandanti, twitching in his sleep now. She wondered how long it would take him to figure out she was gone from the dream. Once he was awake and free, she was as good as dead.

Nudging the pillow out from under her head, she uncovered the small blade she'd hidden there. Awkwardly, carefully, she managed to pick it up with her teeth and put it in her fingers, then bent them down to saw away at the restraints on the same wrist.

It only took a few minutes with the sharp, new blade, but it felt like forever. With one hand free, she made short work of the second strap, then used them to tie Christo's legs spread-eagle to the bottom posts. Next, she reinforced the bonds holding his arms. She was tying the final knot when he began to speak, not quite conscious but moving towards it.

"Back to the house, eh? I'm on the way . . ."

She jumped away from him, even though she knew the double restraints would hold him, at least until she was out of there. She gathered her clothes and slipped her T-shirt on, then carried her boots and jeans out into the hallway. She shut the door behind her. She checked the knob and—thank god for old houses—it could be locked from the outside. She clicked it and finished dressing. Then she ran down the hall.

"*LUCKY,*" he roared from the bedroom as she reached the top of the stairs. "I'm going to kill you!"

Gone was all the seduction, the charm, the soothing lilt.

"I will fucking kill you!"

She ran down the stairs, her heavy footsteps competing with the thumping of the bed shaking. She ran so fast she crashed into the round table in the foyer, and the vase tipped, spilling fetid water and decaying flowers across the rug. She jumped over the mess and ran into the parlor where Gerard lay. She pulled back the sheet in one quick motion.

A scream shot through the ceiling from the bedroom above. "I'm gonna kill your grandmother! I'll find that old bitch and peel her muscles from her bones like orange slices!"

Lucky reached into Gerard's chest pocket. Her fingers hit metal. "Oh thank god!" She pulled it out, the seventh spoon. She found it! She had it! She slipped it into her bra, next to her skin, and dug from her pocket the last item she had bought at Walgreens—a box of matches.

She looked around the room, the windows shuddering from the movement above, the whoosh and suck of the monitors and the oxygen machine. Christos was still screaming about what he was going to do to her and how he was going to do it, but all she heard instead was her mother's voice.

Sometimes you need fire to make sure the bad shit can't come back.

31

LUCKY NUMBER SEVEN

Lucky was a block away when the oxygen canister blew.

In classic New Orleans style, the neighbours arrived with breakfast cocktails before the fire trucks did. Some would swear they heard screaming, but the coroner ruled that Gerard Dumont had already been dead for at least a day at the time of the explosion. Some said they saw someone leave through the flames, maybe the old man's spirit itself. Soon, an out-of-town architect would buy the land, clear the rubble, and rebuild with a modern eye, much to the chagrin of the traditionalists in the neighbourhood.

Lucky walked through the bright heat of the morning back to the hotel. She didn't check her phone or flag a cab, she just walked. Even though the clock was still ticking on finding the last witch, she needed some time to reconcile everything that had just happened. She, Lucky St. James, had secured the spoon, used magic, and committed arson, not to mention murder. All the way back to the Quarter, she carried the seventh spoon in her hand, checking every few blocks that it was real. She didn't even realize that she had been crying until she stopped crying, somewhere around Canal Street.

Walking into the air-conditioned reception area of the Olivier House was such a reprieve, she stopped to appreciate the cool air and quiet. Passing the front desk, she saw her name on a piece of paper.

Message for Lucky St. James, Room 107. Call Meena
Good asap

Why was Meena leaving messages at the front desk? She took her phone out of her back pocket and realized she hadn't turned it on since the cemetery. She did that now, as she crossed the courtyard.

Seven voicemails. Six missed text messages, two of them from Theodore, the rest from Meena. She hit call on the last notification.

"Lucky? Hello?" Meena sounded out of breath.

"Yes, I just got back to the hotel."

"Oh Jesus, you're alive." She started to laugh.

"I'm alive. And I got the spoon."

"You got the spoon! Oh for fuck's sakes—that's great news!"

Lucky heard the sound of screams and clapping in the background.

"Yup, it's right here in my hand."

"Okay, listen, we found where the witch is, maybe . . . probably. It's not far."

"She's here in New Orleans?"

"Freya's dream-map says the witch is in Lafitte, just south of the city, about a forty-five-minute drive. If you leave now, you'll be there before lunch. You'll have a few hours to search before you'd have to hop on a plane and bring her back here."

"Okay, okay, got it. Do we have an address? Even a name, maybe?" She put her key in the lock, then realized that the door was open. Classic Stella move.

"No, we don't. But we do know one thing—you need to wear the brooch."

"What brooch?" Lucky turned into the first-floor bathroom.

"The one you wore in your hair the first night you were here, the crazy one. You have it with you, right?"

Lucky rummaged around in the mess of their stuff on the sink. A hair dryer, toothpaste with the cap left off, toothbrushes, a washcloth, and, yes, her small bag with a few cosmetics and jewelry. She unzipped it and dug around. "Got it."

"Okay, thank you, Goddess. I want you to pin it on your shirt right now, so you don't forget."

Lucky did as she was told, her T-shirt sagging under the weight of it. "Umm, I've got it on, but what for?"

"I'm not really sure. All I know is that it has something to do with this."

"Okay, look, I gotta go. I need to wake Stella first, and get her ready, and then we'll hit the road." There was always just one more step . . .

"Lucky, we're going to go ahead and reserve three seats on a flight back. Let us know as soon as you find her."

"Right. I'll text you when we get to Lafitte." And Lucky hung up.

She had just tucked the spoon back into her bra when there was a knock on the door.

She opened it, and there was Theo on the doorstep, smiling. "Oh, good, you're up. Aunt Aggie wants to know if Stella would be so kind as to join her in the parlor for some breakfast coffee and Kahlúa."

"Morning, Theo." Lucky returned the smile. "Sorry, but we gotta head out today. I was just about to start packing up."

"Oh no!"

"I'm sure we'll be back—Stella loves this place." She turned and yelled up the stairs, "Stella, you decent? We gotta hit the road. Theo's here, so you can go say your goodbyes to Aggie first."

Silence.

"Stella, you awake?" Lucky started up the stairs. "You're not still mad at me, are you?"

The bed was empty.

"No!" Lucky yelled, and Theo came pounding up the stairs. "What's wrong?"

"She's gone. You didn't see her this morning?"

"No, not since last night." He rubbed his head, thinking. "We sat around the courtyard after I got off work telling old ghost stories, and she was in fine form, talking about this maniac who tunnelled into her building. I walked her to her door at about midnight, I think? Weren't you already in bed?"

Lucky didn't know what to say, so she just shook her head.

"Okay," she said, finally, reaching for both of Theo's hands, trying to hold it together. "I'm gonna go out and walk around to see if I can find her. If you think of anywhere she might have gone, you call me. If she comes back here, you call me. If you hear anything that could help in any way, you call me. I'm giving this an hour, and if I can't find her, I'm calling the police."

He nodded.

"Theo, say it all back to me," she insisted. "I need to know you understand."

"I'm to stay here. If she comes back, I hug her and call you. If I remember anything, I get real excited and call you. If anyone comes in here and says there's a fabulous old bitch wandering the Quarter, I scream at them until they tell me where, and I call you."

"That is exactly right." She let his hands go and ran for the door. Just outside the hotel entrance her phone rang.

"Stella?"

"Lucky. It's Meena."

"Meena, I can't talk now."

"Lucky, just wanted you to know we got seats on the ten P.M. flight."

"Stella is missing."

"Wait, what? Where are you?"

"Still at the hotel in New Orleans."

"Lucky, you need to get to Lafitte! Where is Stella?"

"I just told you, she's missing!"

There was a pause, and Lucky was on the brink of hanging up when Meena said, "We're running out of time. You need to make a decision, but it's one I don't think I can ask you to make."

Lucky closed her eyes and leaned against the brick wall of the hotel. She was the one who had walked out on her grandmother after a fight. She was the one who'd left her with strangers in a city neither of them knew. And she hadn't thought of her at all—not when she was searching, not when she found the Benandanti, not until the very moment she found her gone. She could be at the bottom of the Mississippi. She could have been mugged or hit by a car. She remembered what Jay Christos had screamed—he was going to kill Stella, he was going to tear her apart.

"Meena?"

"Yes?"

"I need to find Stella," she said, and hung up.

She chose Stella. She would always choose Stella.

LUCKY WALKED THE STREETS, UP and down each one, from Canal to the Esplanade. She searched every alley, too, and walked into each bar, every open restaurant, most still empty at this hour. She showed the staff the photo of Stella she'd taken on her phone the day before they left Toronto—Stella trying to feed cereal off a spoon to Jinx, who was busy staring down Lucky with the particular menace he saved just for her. No one could remember seeing her.

By eleven A.M. she had crisscrossed Bourbon from Decatur to Rampart, and the first drunks were starting to appear, with their plastic to-go cups and disapproving wives, not yet throwing up in the garbage bins but heading there. At the door to a vintage store that might have caught Stella's eye, her phone rang again. It was the hotel.

"Theo? Is she back?"

"No. She's not. But I know where she is."

"Thank god! Where?"

"Aggie found her. They're at the Blacksmith's Shop. It's a bar at the far end of Bourbon. You'll think you've missed it 'cause there's houses in between it and the main drag, but you haven't."

She put him on speaker and opened her map app. "What's the cross street?"

"St. Philip, just past Dumaine."

She shouted into the phone before she hung up, "I'm on the way." Then got her bearings and ran. All she could think of was Jay Christos standing over her little grandma and her even smaller, older friend.

Theo was right—she thought she had missed it at first, catching the sound of glassware and raised voices at the last minute. She hustled through the open door and then paused. It was so dark inside, she needed to let her eyes adjust.

"Watchu having?" the bartender asked.

"I'm looking for someone." She fumbled with her phone as he

stood with one hand on his hip, bar rag thrown over his shoulder. "Hold on, I have a picture of her . . ."

"Hey there, Lucky."

She almost dropped her phone. She turned, and there was Aggie, sitting at a two-seater by a small window, casually drinking a beer.

"Where's Stella?"

"Powder room." She took another sip.

Lucky fairly collapsed into the open chair. "I don't know how to thank you. How did you find her?"

"I watched." Aggie wiped the corners of her mouth with a napkin. "That's what I do. I'm a Watcher."

"Wait . . . I've heard about Watchers."

"I've sent word back to VenCo, to the Oracle, that you are here. They seemed very invested in your little adventure." Something caught Aggie's eye over Lucky's shoulder, and she smiled.

"Hey, can we get another round over here?" Stella called out.

Lucky rushed to her grandma and hugged her. "Oh, shit, Grandma, Jesus Christ. Where have you been?"

A little shocked, Stella returned the embrace. "I was out walking and then I stopped in here. Then Aggie joined me."

Lucky hugged her again, even harder. "Oh man, am I glad to see you."

"So I guess you've forgiven me, then?"

Lucky mashed her face into the old woman's neck and hung on. "For what?"

"For ruining the plan?" Stella laughed. "Or maybe you forgot, so I better not remind you."

Lucky let go, wiping her eyes. "The plan worked out. I found the spoon. But we have to go."

"Hold on just a minute. I paid for another beer, and I'm drinking another beer with my friend. Then we can head out." She sat and looked her granddaughter up and down. "You look terrible."

"Thanks." Lucky sighed, already past her relief. "Seriously, we have to get out of here and hit the road to Lafitte. Grab a to-go cup and take your beer with you. Aggie, we'll walk you back to the hotel."

Instead, Stella reached up to touch the brooch pinned to Lucky's T-shirt. "Oh, I haven't seen that in years."

"Stella, look, we need to go now. We still have time to get to the final witch . . ."

Stella ran a finger over the beaded surface. "I just assumed your mother stole it. She tended to forget to give things back when she liked them."

"Yeah, she probably did. She was a shoplifter for sure. But that's not—"

"Oh, she didn't shoplift it. Unless you count my bedroom dresser as a shop."

"Wait, what?"

"That's my brooch. Oswald gave it to me on our third wedding anniversary. We didn't have much money, but he thought the blue would go well with my eyes. He bought it off an old lady who used to sell junk off a blanket near the subway." She smiled. "I actually hated it, but he was so proud to give it to me."

Lucky crouched beside the table. "This is your brooch?"

"Yes, it is. I thought maybe she'd lost it or pawned it or whatever. I'm glad to see you have it." She looked at Aggie, who was watching them with a small smile on her face. "Oh, Aggie, I so do love this place. When's Mardi Gras? I think I should come back for that."

Lucky stood, slowly, feeling like the wind had been knocked out of her. If this was Stella's brooch, if it had been hers all along, then . . .

She spun around, looking at all the walls, the shelves behind the bar, the lights, the signage. She pulled the napkin out from under Stella's pint.

"Hey, careful now."

"What is the name of this bar?"

Stella smiled. "It's great, isn't it? Theodore brought us here first."

Aggie was the one who answered. "It's named after an old pirate. The story is it was once his hideout."

Lucky reached across the wooden table and grabbed the woman's hand in desperation. "Aggie, what's it called?"

"The Blacksmith Shop. Jean Lafitte's Blacksmith Shop."

Lafitte. Everything folded in and then blew back out at twice the size. Lucky reached into her bra and pulled out the spoon, warm from her body, and handed it over to her grandmother.

Stella watched her granddaughter, concerned—why were there tears in her eyes, why was she breathing so hard, why was she fumbling around in her shirt? And then she saw the spoon being held out in front of her, and nothing felt right until she could hold it for herself. Her hand was shaking when she reached out and stopped shaking when she grasped it.

Nothing made any sense—that didn't change. But what did change was the understanding that nothing had to make sense. That everything was okay. That she was okay, that they would be okay. Stella pulled the spoon in to her own heart, closed her eyes, and felt its exact shape and weight there, against her fragile ribs, held by her own hand, a hand that had felt empty until now.

"It's you," Lucky whispered, her voice shaking. Stella Sampson, her beloved, infuriating grandmother Stella was the seventh witch.

"It was always you."

Stella opened her eyes and smiled. "It's us, Lucky. And it's always been us."

32

SEEDS

They had walked back to the hotel together. Then they'd packed their bags, said a tearful goodbye to Aggie and to an overwhelmed Theodore, and driven to the airport. They left the Pathfinder in long-term parking and checked in for their flight. When they each put a spoon into the bin as they went through security, they smiled at the confusion on the screener's face.

They were too overwhelmed by events to talk much, but just as they were joining the boarding line, Stella grabbed Lucky's forearm.

"Is he gone?"

"I think so, but I don't know for sure."

Stella patted her arm, nodding, then handed her boarding pass to the woman at the podium.

Lettie brought Everett to meet them at the airport early on the morning of the ninth day. He ran to them when they walked out of Arrivals, and Lucky wondered what she had done to deserve this kind of love. She wondered if one even had to do anything to be deserving. Both Stella and Everett fell asleep in the back seat on the way back.

Lettie whispered to Lucky, "The rest wanted to come to meet you, but we have to bring the spoons together and Meena wanted everything prepared."

When they turned onto the now-familiar street and Lettie declared, "We're home," Lucky teared up. It felt as if she really was home, and maybe for the first time. That terrified her the way the very best things did.

They walked into an empty house.

"They'll be out back," Lettie said.

They set their bags down by the front door, and Everett took Lucky's hand, pulling her through the house to the kitchen and out into the yard.

"Kids look good on you," Stella baited Lucky as she followed along.

"And sanity looks good on you," Lucky teased back, "but some things are just borrowed."

Everett let go and ran down the narrow path into the backyard greenery, chasing the little birds that swooped low. Though the sun was up, it was so early that the long lines of fairy lights were still twinkling in the branches.

Walking towards the witches, towards the completed circle—her circle—was the only thing in the world Lucky could have done at that moment. It felt like the drunken part of falling in love, the erratic and uncompromising compulsion that made you do dumb shit and your best shit at the same time. She had to stop herself from running. She had to stop herself from crying or screaming or both. It felt as if she were underwater and at the end of her oxygen, with the surface, where she could finally take a deep breath and live, just above. She wanted to live. She wanted to live full-on, to the hilt, with every cell.

Lucky felt a weight in the air that made her slow down. That was how she knew Meena was coming up behind her even before she felt a hand slip into hers.

"Hello, Lucky."

"Meena."

They walked like that for a few steps, with no words, with intimacy. In gratitude.

"I thought the seventh was your mother for the longest time."

"That would have made more sense. Arnya would have been a great witch."

"She was, in a way. She made you who you are. Gave you magic. Gave you guts. Mothers are the witches we know best but never acknowledge."

"She also made me anxious and broke my heart."

Meena squeezed her fingers lightly. "A cunning woman if I ever heard of one."

"What's next?" Lucky asked, finally looking over at Meena, who wore her hair out, her curls a loose crown. She was still in her pyjamas, under a silk robe patterned with little yellow birds.

"I'm not sure," she admitted.

"Shouldn't you be?" Lucky was only half joking.

"None of us should be. Nothing is predetermined. Everything is in play." Meena swung their joined arms as she said, "We put the spoons together and then . . . we wait."

"Wait for what?"

Meena smiled, looking up at the sky above them, long clouds like a bundle of ribbons, unspooled on top of one another, waiting to be stitched, to be braided, to be pulled down to the ground. "For everything to change."

When they stepped into the clearing, the rest of the coven

jumped up and ran to them, grabbing Lucky, kissing Stella, laughing and cheering and welcoming them home.

NOW THAT THEY WERE TOGETHER and safe, they took their time. Lucky told them about Ricky and her battle with the Benandanti. Stella told them about swimming naked and sneezing in the Ozarks. Freya and Lettie described their work with the bowl and the dreaming. And, sitting on pillows they'd brought to the clearing, they feasted on strawberries and drank coffee to celebrate the return of the retrievers and the completion of their circle.

When the laughter and the stories had died down, Meena led them in the invocation to create and hold a formal circle. They cleansed themselves with smoke and called in the four directions. Then, once more, and as a complete set, they brought out the spoons.

Acting on instinct, Lucky got up and carried hers into the very centre of their circle and laid it down. "One," she whispered, and returned to her spot.

After a moment, Morticia crawled to the centre and placed her spoon down beside Lucky's, as if it were the next spoke on a wheel. "Two."

Meena was next, but she felt putting her spoon down might mean not picking it back up, not as an individual piece anyway. It would be something else entirely. Eventually, she got up and placed it beside Morticia's. "Th-three," she faltered.

Wendy lay a hand on Meena's shoulder, making sure her love was steady, before she walked her spoon into the circle. "Four," she said, and set it down.

Lettie stared at her spoon, then at her son, who was collecting buttercups from the grass around them, and she gave a little groan.

Like the others, she was attached to her piece of silver. Her spoon hadn't given her freedom, but it was a symbol of the freedom she had claimed for herself. She closed her eyes and counted to three, then dragged herself forward. "Five."

Freya took the longest. Usually always ready with a joke or a barb, Freya held hers like a baby and wept, rocking quietly. Then she stood, swiping at her face as if the tears were bugs and she wanted them off her skin immediately. She walked slowly into the middle, placing her precious spoon on the ground as gently as if it were a newborn. "Six." Then, recovered, she threw her hands up, fingers in the classic rocker devil's horn.

Stella looked around the circle, taking in each beautiful face, stopping last and longest on Lucky's. "I am seven," she declared, and she crawled in and slotted the elusive seventh spoon into position as the last spoke. The wheel was complete. Now they just needed to know where it was going to take them.

There was no flash of lightning. No cosmic shift that they could see or hear. They sat quietly as the minutes passed, enough minutes for them to get concerned and to eventually speak their doubt.

"Maybe one of the spoons is a fake?"

"Did we miss the deadline, maybe? Are you sure it was today?"

"How do we know this is what we're supposed to do?"

"Is this how it all ends?"

All the questions were asked of Meena, who sat quiet. She didn't look away from the spoons they'd gathered from webs and boxes, tunnels and forests, the one they'd wrestled from the hands of the Benandanti. She thought about every step they'd taken—the dreams, the spells, the Tenders, and the Bookers. What was it the Crone had said when they first met? *Everything changes. That's how it begins.* For once she was certain.

Just then Everett began to giggle, jumping up and snatching at the sky. "The stars!" he shouted. "The stars are falling!"

The women watched him, distracted by his glee. Then they saw them, landing all around them like weightless snow. Falling from the sky were hundreds of dandelion fluffs, outsized and iridescent in the morning sun.

Freya picked up one from where it landed on her lap and spun it in her fingers. "They look like the spoons," she said, wonder in her voice. And she was right: each bundle of seeds was arranged like delicate spokes of a wheel, just as they'd laid the spoons down.

Lettie joined her son, catching fluffs out of the air. Stella closed her eyes and let them fall all around her like memories sliding in on the notes of an old song. Lucky let one fall into her hand and felt every cell in her body cry out with the connection.

Meena stepped into the circle, head thrown back, eyes wide open, while the fluff tumbled out of the clouds, from nowhere . . . from everywhere. She turned once, clockwise, watching the ground fill up with gossamer stars, and she knew exactly where they were in this story. This was not even close to the end. Everything changes. That's how it begins.

She raised her arms, taking in the spoons, the magic, and her coven, because now that was just what they were, a coven of extraordinary witches, and she smiled. Now the real work could commence. Now they were ready.

Epilogue

HOW IT REALLY BEGAN

FRANCE

Sophie kissed the sweaty arm before she lifted it carefully off her stomach, where it had been thrown in sleep. Marie-Elise wasn't supposed to spend the night, but, to be fair, they had only fallen asleep at dawn, so it wasn't technically a full night. She took a second to admire the curve of her lover's bottom before covering her with the sheet.

She pulled on a pair of boxers and a T-shirt from the floor and padded silently across the hardwood in her bare feet. She closed the bedroom door behind her and yawned her way across the open expanse of the apartment, sparsely furnished, with more paintings than seating, and over to the kitchen area, where she flicked the kettle on.

She'd wake Marie-Elise soon, but for now, she would have some tea in solitude. Yawning, running both hands over her cropped blond hair, she went to the double doors at the other end of the living space and pulled them open, stepping onto the small Juliette balcony. Spring had arrived with sudden heat and a burst of colour.

Below her, Montmartre was laid out along narrow streets and winding paths, all the way to the Sacré-Coeur. Church bells in the near distance announced the lunch hour. Doves shot her uninterested glances from the rooftops.

She leaned on the railing, taking it in. She loved Paris. She travelled a lot, from Palm Springs to Phuket, but she had only ever lived here. This was her home, ancestral and chosen. The food was delicate, the art exquisite, and the women remarkable. Her coven was here and had always been. She would never live anywhere else.

A tiny bird the colour of fresh butter hopped from the flowers cascading from the boxes under her windows and landed on the railing beside her arm.

"Bonjour, Armand." She called every bird Armand. "Quesque tu fais?"

He hopped closer and chirped.

"What? What is it you are telling me?" she asked him in English, as if they could understand each other.

The bird turned his head, fixing an eye on the space above her. She turned to look. Falling very slowly in the afternoon breeze, back and forth like a lost feather, was a dandelion fluff. It was the wrong time of year. And, even so, there were no lawns around here.

She held out her hand, and it parachuted directly onto her palm. And then she understood. It was a message. A declaration. The North American witches were finally gathered.

She turned to regard the little bird, which was quietly watching her.

"Ça a commencé," she told him. "Armand, it has begun."

He chirped once and flew away, leaving the French witch with the fallen star she had caught from the bright Paris sky.

Mexico

Octavia loved the open water. It sang a song that could not be scored, could not be manipulated with air or strings. She turned off the boat engine and let the silence rush in so she could better appreciate the water's chorus. She was in the middle of the Sea of Cortez, somewhere between Mazatlán and Cabo. Because of the tourists, out here was the only place she could truly hear it anymore.

It was just before dawn, but already hot. Still, the sea made that heat gorgeous. She left the driver's seat and climbed around to recline on the prow, the metal still cool on her bare skin where her shorts ended. She folded her arms under her head and crossed her ankles, looking up at the sky. There was an excitement under her ribs, one she didn't have an exact name for. Anticipation?

As the boat rocked her gently, Octavia whispered a prayer of gratitude for this territory, for her breath, for whatever was coming that had her marrow buzzing. Her grandmother liked to remind her that gratitude was the strongest spell, one that attracts, that transforms, that makes clear. She had even prayed gratitude the day her grandma had passed, weeping her thanks for the years she had been given.

A small crack appeared above her, a rip in the near darkness that sewed itself back together so quickly, she thought it might have been lightning, so quiet she might not have seen it at all. And then there was a small light, a glimmer, really, right above her.

She tried to focus her eyes in the dark. Under her, the boat settled as if she had hit dry land. There were no more waves, and even the gentle sway had calmed to stillness. What was it? She sat up on her knees and reached out. And still, it took its time to come to her, tumbling into her cupped hands.

She brought it close to her face. She knew this thing—this ball of translucent spokes. A dandelion fluff. Dandelions were called weeds and grew as such, undaunted, in spite of every effort to control their spread. But they also made tea, wine, and medicine. People didn't want them, but only because they didn't understand what they really were.

Octavia held her breath, watching the small bundle spin and settle against her skin. She tipped her face up and spoke to the sky that had dropped this gift to her, in the middle of the sea, no land that could host a dandelion in sight.

She called to her grandmother, her sisters, her coven. She called to the witches who sent the announcement, perhaps even without knowing that was what they had done. She spoke the excitement in her bones and the gratitude in her blood, the blood already rife with old magic passed down to her. At last, the northern coven had found one another.

"It's time."

UNITED STATES OF AMERICA

Jay Christos limped into the park around lunch hour, just as the office workers and schoolchildren came out to stretch and breathe. He had broken bones wrenching free of the restraints and held his right arm against his chest, his hand a bag of mush held together by purple, marbling skin. The fire had burned his torso and some of his hair, the skin of his skull showing, red and pitted. For the first time in his life, he was not beautiful.

This witch had left more than a scar over his heart. *This* witch had stripped his skin right off. It was the most romantic thing he had ever experienced. He had to get back to his compound to heal and get ready, so he could find her again.

"Excuse me, ma'am," he croaked, approaching a woman sitting on a bench eating a tuna sandwich. "I have been gravely hurt and am in need of some assistance."

The woman glanced up then, a look of horror on her face, dropped her sandwich on the ground. She got up and walked away as fast as she could, looking back to make sure he wasn't following her. This was not the reaction Jay was used to getting from people.

He sighed, coughing at the end of it, and tried to rearrange his remaining hair to cover the burn, smoothing the sweater he had pulled from a clothesline tight over his chest. Then he limped towards some teenagers playing frisbee in the grass.

"Excuse me," a woman's voice called out from behind him. "Do you need some help?"

He stopped, trying to ready his best smile, pulling himself up straight. Maybe he hadn't completely lost his touch. "Why, yes, thank you. I should have known that a damsel would come in my distress." He turned.

The Mother stood in the path. She gave him a small wave, a distraction, as the Maiden stepped from the hedges with a jerry can and sloshed gasoline across his back. He screamed when the chemicals soaked through to his broken skin. From a nearby bench, the Crone stood, lit her cigarette, and tossed her Zippo to the Mother.

Jay turned in circles. All around him was quiet. The teenagers were gone, the paths cleared. Even the birds had stopped singing. Instead, they sat and watched. Now there was only the Maiden, the Mother, and the Crone. He tore at his wet sweater. "What is this? Who are you?"

"Damsels. Who have come to you in your distress," the Maiden answered with false sweetness.

The Mother stepped towards him. "Do you know what happens when a witch has children who don't inherit her power?"

"You are making a grave mistake." He swung around wildly, trying to keep them all in focus.

"They become Watchers, like me," the Mother continued, pointing to herself. Then she indicated the Crone. "Or Bookers." Then, finally, the Maiden. "Or Tenders, like the one you killed in Massachusetts."

"Stay away," he growled, trying to hold his wounded arm against his chest. "Just stay back!"

"That means we are all descended from witches." The Mother rubbed the Zippo against the side of her skirt as she walked so that the cap clicked open and shut. He couldn't take his eyes from it. It was like the ticking of a clock, counting down. "My mother, and my grandmother—who you murdered, by the way—and all the way back, were witches. In fact, you've managed to kill four witches in my line alone."

Jay took a step to the side, getting ready to bolt, and the Maiden moved to cut him off. He recoiled.

The Mother was calm, moving closer as she spoke. "But probably the most interesting witch in my family was one who lived many, many years ago. Her name was Prudence Worthy."

"Prudence?" Jay twisted up his mangled face, trying to understand. "*My* Prudence?"

"No," the Mother shouted. "*My* Prudence." She took a breath and lowered her voice. "She was chased out of her village, but not before becoming with child. That child, as it turns out, was the product of an affair with a Benandanti. And that Benandanti, responsible for so much carnage, stands now in front of his own blood, a sad creature. My own pathetic ancestor. The father of witches."

"No." He shook his head. "No, no, no . . ." The image of a painting came to mind—a god eating his own children. "It can't be."

"It can," the Crone said. "It is."

"Ironic that, since the only way to truly be immortal is to have descendants. And to be the one who devours them, when one craves immortality above all else?" The Mother took two steps and was now right in front of him, her eyes blazing, her breath on his raw skin. "And I am here to end it."

Jay Christos turned. He was encircled by the Oracle, with no chance of escape. The Mother lifted the Zippo, flipped it open, and flicked it into flame.

"Seriously?" he cried. "Oh, fuck me."

"Yes." The Mother smiled. There were teeth in that smile. "Seriously . . . fuck you."

Acknowledgments

Enormous thanks to my work coven: Dean Cooke, Rachel Letofsky, Rachel Kahan at William Morrow, Anne Collins at Random House, Paige Sisley, Joe Veltre, Olivia Johnson, and everyone at CookeMcDermid who keep the trains running on time.

So much love to Ben Haigh and the AMC team for believing in these witches (and this witch). A special shout-out to Gina Mingacci, who listened to me talk about this FOREVER, and then, as soon as the baby book was born, swaddled it and ran across the field to bring it home.

As always, I owe everything to my family—my kids, Jaycob, Wenzdae, and Lydea; my love, Shaun; my parents, Hugh and Joanie; and my brother, Jason. Thanks for taking care of me so I could take care of this story. Thank you to my extended family, the Georgian Bay Métis community, for your support and love and for working to keep these lands magic.

Throughout history, witches have been the stand-ins for all people who have felt "outside" or "different." I say, fuck it—go outside, be different, be so different they have to loosen their grip on the world because you are proof there is so much beyond them. Live fully, feel it all without apology, be weird and powerful and amazing. Because ultimately, that is who this book was written for—the wild witches that no man (and no system) could ever begin to contain.

In closing, I would like to remind you that it's always a good day to hex the patriarchy.

About the Author

Cherie Dimaline is a member of the Georgian Bay Historic Métis Community in Ontario. Her 2017 book, *The Marrow Thieves*, won the Governor General's Award and the prestigious Kirkus Prize for Young Readers' Literature, and was the fan favourite for the CBC's *Canada Reads* in 2018. It was also named a book of the year on numerous lists, including that of National Public Radio, the *School Library Journal*, the New York Public Library, the *Globe and Mail*, *Quill & Quire*, and the CBC, and was selected as one of *Time* magazine's 100 best YA books of all time. It has been translated into several languages and continues to be a national bestseller five years later. Cherie's novel *Empire of Wild* became an instant Canadian bestseller and was named Indigo's #1 Best Book of 2019. It was featured in the *New York Times*, *The New Yorker*, Goop, and the Chicago Review of Books, among other outlets. Her most recent YA novel, *Hunting by Stars*, was selected as a 2022 American Indian Library Association Young Adult Honor Book. She is currently writing for television, working on a new novel, and adapting some of her works for the stage and screen.